# Awakening

The Ydron Saga

A Novel by Raymond Bolton

Awakening
published by arrangement with the author


ISBN-10: 0991347102
ISBN-13: 978-0991347100

Fiction
Otherworld Fantasy

How does a world equipped with bows, arrows and catapults, where steam power is just beginning to replace horses and sailing ships, avert a conquest from beyond the stars?

Prince Regilius has been engineered to combat the Dalthin, a predatory alien species that enslaves worlds telepathically, and to do so he must unite his people. But when his mother murders his father, the land descends into chaos and his task may prove impossible. Faced with slaying the one who gave him life in order to protect his world, he seeks a better way. Set in a vast and varied land where telepaths and those with unusual metal abilities tip the course of events, AWAKENING goes to the heart of family, friendship and betrayal.

For information about more of Raymond's books, go to:
**www.RaymondBolton.com**
Or e-mail him at **author@raymondbolton.com**.

Bolton, Raymond (2014-01-01). Awakening. Regilius Publishing

# ACKNOWLEDGEMENTS

First and foremost, I would like to thank my wife, Toni, who has patiently and supportively endured the countless hours I have spent writing, with no promise my efforts would ever amount to anything beyond a time-consuming hobby. She has served as my first reader and editor, spotting typographical errors and inconsistencies I missed over numerous reads and revisions and has never hesitated to let me know when part of the story or a particular ending "sucks." Because of her honesty and her uncanny intuition for what makes a good story, if you have enjoyed reading *Awakening*, it is in part because of her.

I would also like to thank my Facebook friend, New York Times best-selling author, Melissa Foster, without whose websites, Fostering Success, http://www.fostering-success.com/, and World Literary Café, http://www.worldliterarycafe.com/, this book might never have made it into your hands. If you, or anyone you know hopes to self publish, the knowledge and tools these online resources provide will be invaluable aids.

While you really cannot tell a book by its cover, an outstanding one helps persuade a reader to pick the fruit of an author's labors from among the thousands of titles lining the shelves of the world's bookstores, real and virtual. *Awakening*'s cover was created by Natasha Brown, whom I found through World Literary Café. Her unerring taste and obvious talent brought this remarkable illustration from concept to reality in less time than I would have thought possible.

I also must thank feminist artist, graphic novelist and cartoonist, Maureen Burdock, for turning my sketches into the map of Ydron.

Culture photographer, Jennifer Esperanza, was the eye behind the lens of the author's headshot on the last page of this book.

I was privileged to have author and iconic former Redbook Magazine editor, Audreen Buffalo, lend an early version of my manuscript her critical eye and set my feet on the path to proper writing.

Lastly, I give a grateful nod to my childhood friend, George "Pooge" Pryor. He was an early reader of my book, and his encouraging comments kept me working to get *Awakening* published, even through discouraging times.

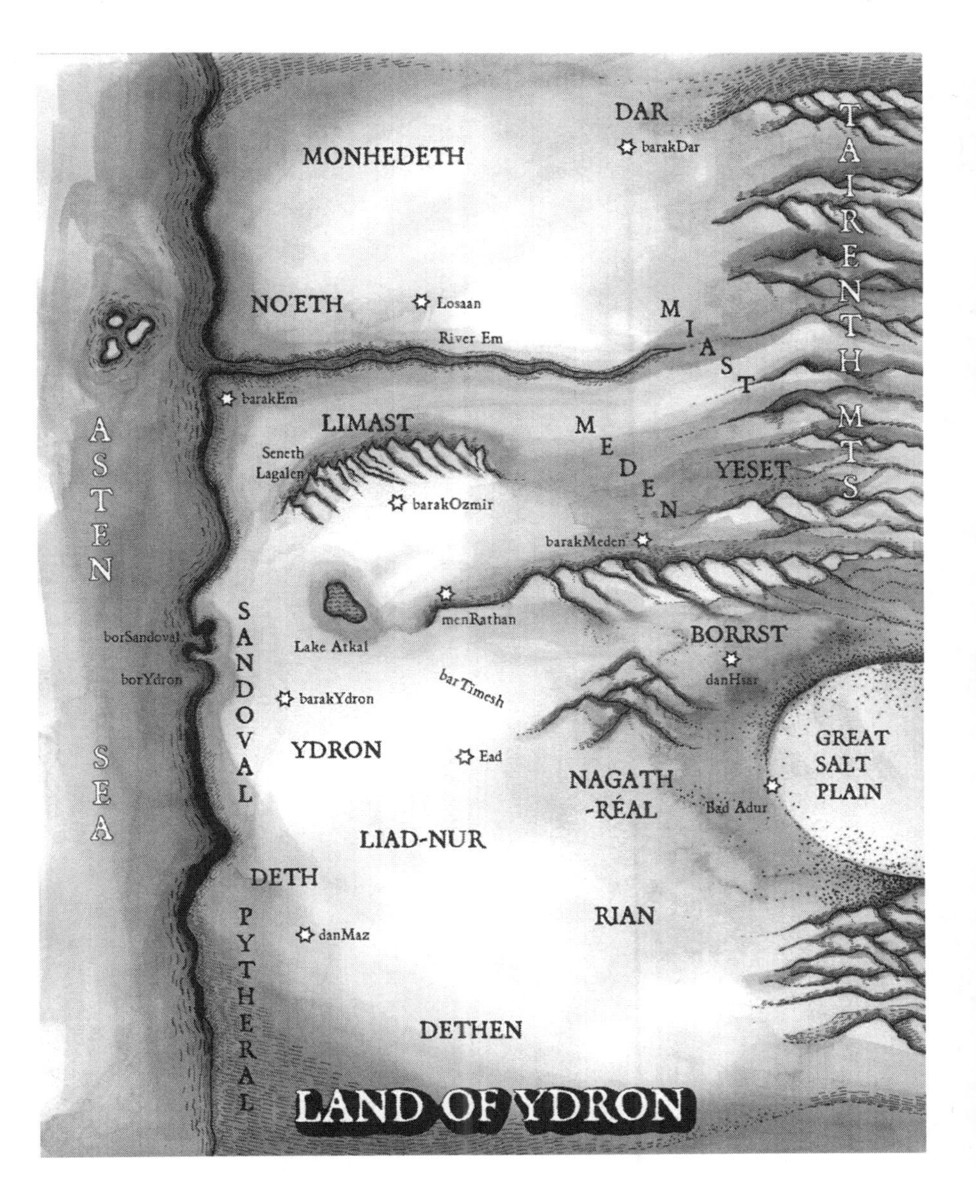
DAR
barakDar
MONHEDETH
TAIRENTH MTS
NO'ETH
Losaan
River Em
MIAST
barakEm
LIMAST
MEDEN
Seneth Lagalen
YESET
barakOzmir
barakMeden
ASTEN SEA
menRathan
SANDOVAL
BORRST
borSandoval
Lake Atkal
borYdron
danHsar
barTimesh
barakYdron
GREAT SALT PLAIN
YDRON
Ead
NAGATH -RÉAL
Bad Adur
LIAD-NUR
DETH
RIAN
PYTHERAL
danMaz
DETHEN
LAND OF YDRON

# CAST OF CHARACTERS

Royal Family:

| | |
|---|---|
| Regilius Tonopath (Reg) | prince of Ydron |
| Lith-An Tonopath (Ria) | Regilius' little sister |
| Manhathus Tonopath | Regilius' father |
| Duile Morged Tonopath | Regilius' mother |

Reg's friends & their families:

| | |
|---|---|
| Ered | the boatkeeper's son |
| Pedreth | Ered's father, the king's the boat keeper |
| Danth Kanagh | one of Reg's childhood friends |
| Leovar Hol | one of Reg's childhood friends |
| Lord Emeil | apparent conspirator, eventual ally |

Palace Personnel:

| | |
|---|---|
| Satsah | palace cook |
| Marm | Reg's nursemaid |
| Ai'Lorc | Reg's teacher |

Royal Advisors:

| | |
|---|---|
| Meneth Lydon | Manhathus' chief advisor, conspirator |
| Badar Endreth | minister of foreign affairs, conspirator, executed |

Peers of the Realm:

| | |
|---|---|
| Lord Asch | a conspirator, ruler of Pytheral; eventual ally |
| Lord Kareth | a conspirator, ruler of Rian |
| Lord Danai | a conspirator, ruler of Dethen |
| Lord Ened | a conspirator, ruler of Liad-nur |
| Lord Hau | a conspirator, ruler of Miast |
| Lord Mon | a conspirator, ruler of Deth |
| Lord Bogen | ruler of Limast; Regilius' ally |
| Lord Dural Miasoth | ruler of Meden; eventual ally |

Rebels:

| | |
|---|---|
| Pithien Dur | rebel leader |
| Jenethra | dancer at the meshedRuhan pub |
| Benjin | Jenethra's husband & pub owner |
| Bedya | brought Marm to Pithien Dur's table |
| Roman | the redhead |
| Loral | one of the outlaws at Dur's table |
| Justan | "number four", driver of the get-away coach |

Losan monastery:

| | |
|---|---|
| Hazis | high priest. |
| Osman | on watch at the gate |
| Jez'ir | killed by Dargath |
| Mordat | killed by Dargath |
| Bort | a monk |

Dalthin:

| | |
|---|---|
| Husted Yar | poses as Duile's advisor |
| Pudath | captures Danth |
| Dargath | tracks down Regilius |

Miscellaneous characters:

| | |
|---|---|
| Barnath | tailor & former beau of Marm |
| Ganeth | another tailor & friend of Barnath |
| Samel | the wayfarer Pedreth encounters at Hassa's Pass |
| Ohaz | runs the hotel in Bad Adur |
| Orim | runs Lord Bogen's kitchen |
| Ghanfor | agent of Lord Dural |
| Boudra | Lith-An's foster father |
| Sa'ar | Lith-An's foster mother |
| Bakka Oduweh | Regilius' Haroun guide back home |

# PART ONE

## Flight

# 1

*Father!*

Regilius awoke with a gasp. He attempted to sit, but the damp prickling bedding entangled him. Drenched with perspiration, he tore off the covers, propped onto his elbows and peered into the darkness. On a table to his right, dimly silhouetted against a blinded window, stood a light globe. Rocking onto one arm, he stretched toward the sphere and tore off its cover, bathing the space in soft blue light. The room was plain, sterile, and while he could not say where he was, he was certain this was not the palace.

He was trembling as he tried to remember where he might be and how he had arrived. The hand he ran through his hair came away dripping, while his mouth was parched and his tongue, thick and leathery, stuck to the roof of it. He reached for a glass of water, but as he tilted it to his lips, the room began to spin. Confused, he managed to empty it into a vase of morrasa blossoms before the world turned black.

He awoke again, this time his mind awash with images of murderers entering his home, of carnage and things that should not be. Yet, unlike childhood nightmares that become ethereal and fade, these coalesced into semblances of truth, of substance. Struggling to clear his head, he pushed them aside and searched for the tumbler. Miraculously, it lay unbroken on the nightstand. He was looking for a pitcher when his eyes fastened onto the vase. The blossoms, once white and fragrant, were now black, twisted, grotesque.

The door opened and he jumped. Light poured in and a woman wearing a nurse's cap peered into the room.

*Ah!*

The utterance was not spoken. It filled his head and settled among his thoughts.

*Still alive, young prince?*

She stepped inside and closed the door.

*You are truly remarkable. I have never sensed one such as you. You perceive my thoughts. Such a predicament for me and mine.*

The nurse—no, the thing, for it felt as wrong as the flowers—approached his bed and the hairs on his arms, neck and scalp stood erect. His instinct was to bolt.

*Stay where you are.*

He had not moved, yet it had anticipated him. As the creature neared, it started to shimmer. Its shape and color began to change and the abdomen of its now soft, gray, wormlike body rippled. Something like a mouth opened where its belly should have been, then closed, followed by another mouth and another until there were several opening and closing.

An appendage sprouted from its torso and snaked toward him. He had once seen something similar under his tutor's microscope when a tiny cellular predator reached out to snatch a meal. Eyes wide, unable to move, he was following this manifestation when, faster than he could react, it wrapped around his ankle and began pulling him toward it. As he opened his mouth to scream, light flooded the room.

He tore his eyes from the thing around his leg and turned to see a doctor and two orderlies entering. The physician paused, regarded his patient closely and asked, "Your Highness? What in the world have you been doing?"

Prince Regilius found himself at the foot of the bed, clenching a handful of sheet. The covers, seemingly frozen as they streamed from the pillow, marked how he had been dragged. Yet, except for his odd location, all else appeared normal. His eyes went from the physician to the nurse and saw she appeared quite ordinary, her face betraying nothing.

"I want to get you into something dry and change your bedding," the doctor was saying, but as he followed the prince's gaze, he started when he noticed the woman in the corner. "Nurse, why are you here?"

"I was on my way upstairs and saw the light. I thought I would look in," she replied.

"Well," said the doctor, releasing his breath, "since you're here, perhaps you can assist us."

She and the orderlies set to work, and after several minutes the prince was clean and dry, wearing a new gown on a freshly made bed. The doctor ordered them out, and after a brief examination said to Regilius, "You have improved some, Your Highness. That is encouraging. I will check back again in a few hours. Meanwhile, please try to sleep." He covered the light globe and left, closing the door behind him.

Were it not for the flowers, Reg might have done as the physician had ordered, but their misshapen forms insisted he was not safe. Instead, he padded barefoot to the closet where he located his clothing. As he shed his gown and with trembling hands struggled to dress, an odd awareness overtook him: a cold certainty the nurse, sensing he was leaving, was returning. Assuring himself he had forgotten nothing, he went to the window, struggled briefly with the latch, and as the blackness of night gave way to the deep green sky of morning, he slipped out and down to the street below.

Glancing over his shoulder, still sensing the presence behind him, he hurried along the cobblestone streets between the granite and marble edifices of the upper city. Eventually, however, his weakened state returned him to a walk. Feverish and thirsty, he spotted a fountain. He approached it and plunged his face into its waters. Stunned by the cold, he tossed back his head and gasped, sending a shower skyward. Then, leaning against the wet stone lip, he brought hand after handful of crisp refreshment to his lips. Satisfied, he wiped his mouth with his sleeve, breathed deeply and pressed on.

There was no question now he would walk. After drinking so heartily, he knew he would cramp if he pushed too hard too soon and the pace gave him time to consider the event that had brought him here.

Just yesterday, he had been engaged in a brisk game of platter with his friends, Danth, Leovar and Ered. He recalled how Leovar had made a brilliant backhand catch. Without pausing, he had whirled and hurled the disk toward Regilius. It was an errant toss and Reg had leapt to grab it. Then… nothing. No memory of a catch, or a miss, or of landing—nothing until he awoke in the hospital. And now he was fleeing from apparitions and a voice in his head with only instinct to guide him. He shook his head.

By the time the road had begun to slope up toward the palace, morning had arrived and the city was awake. Mahaz, the giant orange sun, had risen two hours above the horizon and second light would follow shortly when its smaller but hotter and brighter companion, the white dwarf, Jadon, appeared. More than enough time had elapsed for anyone looking to have discovered his absence and mounted a search, so he left the road, favoring footpaths to pavement. Ordinarily, he would have made directly for the security of home and family, but the visions that persisted warned him away, even from his own battalion. Despite everything within arguing to the contrary, he decided to leave the city. Although he would pass near the citadel, he did not need to enter its ramparts to reach his goal. Yesterday, before the game, he had dropped off his roadster at the club. Too small to carry four, he had left it, and with his friends had taken Leovar's coach. The club lay between him and home, but he reasoned if he could make it that far he could escape undetected.

As he climbed the ever-increasing grade, fatigue overtook him. He had abandoned the more commonly used paths for those he had known as a child and the soil here was not always compacted. His legs grew rubbery and his feet slipped on loose earth in some of the steeper stretches. Climbing eventually reduced him from walking to scrambling, using hands for support until breaths became gasps and exhaustion forced him to halt.

He dropped to the ground behind a small shrub at the ridge top. Rolling onto his back, he could see how far he had climbed above the city. He shifted and spotted a brown and white speck overhead, a messenger pigeon winging toward the palace. Most likely it had been delivered to the hospital so word could be sent to Manhathus, his father, should his condition change. His eyes traveled from the bird to barakYdron, the fortification toward which it flew. Bright specks of color were proceeding up its causeway. They were banners, and the change in coloration from one van to the next indicated that guards from several houses made up the procession. Since their number, pace and direction suggested their activity was unrelated to his, he decided he could move on.

He was beginning to rise when movement caught his eye. As he peered from behind the bush, a vehicle rounded a bend in the road, passed beneath his vantage point and slowed. Its top was down and the trio within craned their heads in his direction. He tried to flatten into the ground while their eyes probed the undergrowth. It braked to a halt, the passengers shimmered and to his amazement changed form. Three great gray slugs like the nurse emerged.

He had made no sound and was certain they could not have seen him, yet they seemed aware of his presence. At first, they cast about uncertainly. Time and again, however, they returned to his location until their eyes fastened on the spot where he lay. When they began to scale the hill, he could feel their minds reach out and he started to panic. As they neared his hiding place, he grew sick and began to perspire. He wanted to run but was too weak. His breathing quickened and his heart began to pound. Could he somehow throw them off, he wondered? Oddly, as the thought emerged, he sensed something small and warm nearby. At that awareness, his body shuddered and he felt his mind cast something in the direction of that tiny presence. Simultaneously, the small furry animal burst from the brush below. It was a marmath. The creatures had apparently startled the rodent and it dashed from its burrow past the trio and across the road. Their bodies jerked erect and they turned to stare after it. They looked again to Reg's hiding place, then back toward the marmath. They swept the brush with their gaze and appeared to be debating among themselves. Minutes passed and Reg feared they would decide to resume their search. Then slowly, hesitantly, they returned to their vehicle and departed.

He did not know what to make of it. Had they actually been attracted to the rodent rather than to him? Somehow, he doubted it. If not that, what had happened? It was as if, upon the animal's escape, he had been left without… what?… scent?

The carriage disappeared around the bend and Reg slowly rose from cover. He paused to insure they had driven from sight, then he crested the ridge and warily descended.

# 2

Half an hour's trudge through underbrush put Reg on a plateau overlooking the club. Despite the early hour, it was bustling with activity. Smoke from its kitchen wafted into the still morning air. Several members had arrived and a few were gathered near the place his roadster and other steam powered vehicles were parked. Although his hope of leaving unnoticed had vanished, he considered it unlikely any here would yet be aware of his predicament. Since waiting and wondering would accomplish nothing, he gathered himself and strode into the compound. He knew he looked awful, but he put on a smile and hoped for the best.

"Lord Emeil, good morning," he hailed as he walked toward the group.

Emeil was the seniormost of the peers assembled near his car. Curiously, as the prince approached, those standing with the lord bowed and backed away.

"Your Highness," Emeil blurted when he saw Reg approaching. Visibly startled by the intrusion, he still had presence enough to bow appropriately. "What is Your Highness's pleasure?" he asked, eyeing Reg's rumpled clothing.

"Would you please help me fuel and fire up my roadster?" Reg asked. Then, noticing Emeil's stare, he gave a twisted smile. "I overslept."

"So this is not some affair of state?" Emeil asked, suppressing a smile.

"I have adequate attire awaiting. I need to get to Lake Atkal before midday," Reg lied, hiding his annoyance at the need to explain himself. "We are supposed to be shaking down the sloop deArdano for next week's regatta. If I don't hurry, my crew will think I have deserted them."

"We certainly don't want you left stranded. The staff has already fueled and watered those vehicles left here overnight, but it will be my pleasure to fire it up for you." The lord turned to a couple of servants laboring nearby. "Boys, lend a hand."

The youths immediately left their work to attend to the car.

"Since you have some assistance," said Reg, "I'll run to the kitchen. If I'm not to starve, I will need provisions."

"With your permission, I will send for some."

"No, thank you. I need to use the facilities," he said, gesturing vaguely at himself.

"Very well, Your Highness. Your car will be ready when you return."

As the servants set to work, Reg trotted off to obtain what he needed. Not only was he hungry, he also wanted to advise his friends of his plan. The club kept messenger pigeons, and with luck, they would have one that would home to either the house of Hol or the house of Kanagh to get word to either Leovar or Danth.

He was nearing the clubhouse, preoccupied with the morning's events, when an unexpected event caused him to stumble. His mind seemed to open, to reach out, and Lord Emeil's thoughts were laid before him for an instant. Like a window to another world, the momentary glimpse revealed that while Emeil bore him no immediate danger, he was nonetheless a threat. Not to Regilius. He meant instead to unseat Manhathus. Nor was he alone. A conspiracy was unfolding and smacked of the visions Reg had been having. Unsure if this were some fantasy or a genuine premonition, he decided to continue with his plan, then send his father a warning as soon as he reached safety.

Minutes later, as he was leaving the clubhouse, shouldering a satchel of goods and contemplating the virtues of a nap, sounds of trumpets carried down from the palace. He snapped awake and hurried to his roadster, pleased it was already generating healthy amounts of steam. Even without consulting the gauges, Reg could tell the boiler's pressure was up. One of the servants took his bag and placed it on the passenger's seat. Fearing his face would reflect his newfound distrust, he forced a smile as he slipped behind the wheel.

"All is ready, Highness," Emeil assured. "The day grows older by the minute."

"Thank you. Once I leave the outer city, I can make up for lost time," said Reg as he patted the dash. "This baby really steams. I will be there in plenty of time."

"Please be careful. I would be very distressed to learn something happened to you."

"What could possibly happen?" asked Reg, eyeing him squarely.

"Country roads can be treacherous. No doubt you are a fine driver, but a loose patch on the roadway can cause the tires to slip, especially at speed. I care about your well-being."

"Thank you," Reg replied, detecting no threat. The advice seemed driven by genuine concern, nothing sinister.

He glanced around and saw more peers assembling. It was time to depart. He managed another smile and a wave, then opened the throttle, spewing gravel behind him.

He cleared the gates of the inner city without raising alarm. Once beyond the wall, he accelerated hard and the roadster bounded around a corner showering dust in its wake. Fortunately the car's suspension was good, because the roads here were poor.

The outer city contrasted sharply with the inner one. Here barrows and carts lining the streets were the centers of commerce, not the stone edifices above. Ragged banners of blue, green, red, black and other hues, a color for each trade, marked every stall or cart, telling the buyer each business's nature. Beasts of burden, rather than machines, brought the goods sold here. Women with dirty, naked babies on their hips quarreled over the price of cheese, bread or deleth fruit, while men idling in the shade of awnings or barrel stave trees sat gambling or gossiping.

The road descended steeply, and as the roadster plunged deeper into the throng, conditions worsened. On an earlier occasion, Reg might have thought of these souls as peaceful simple folk blessed with basic needs and lives. Not today. The fleeing royal saw things as never before as their stories invaded the sanctum of his thoughts.

There was no happiness here. His perception of a tranquil populace gave way to a vision of ones who had long since abandoned their hopes. Some wandered aimlessly or leaned idly against the sides of shanties. They walked with the staggering saunter of the drunk. They limped shoeless, unshaven and dusty. Derelicts abounded. Children sat in puddles, their faces and ragged clothing muddy, destitution's hallmarks in full view.

From the battlements above, where the fortunate of Ydron were nurtured and protected, the outer city would appear as a colorful patchwork fading into the muted tones of a distant countryside. It intruded neither on the lives nor the senses of the fortunate few who inhabited those heights, but existed as the source of labor and revenue. It was simpler to think of it in impersonal terms than imbue it with a face. This way consciences were never strained and the pleasant tenor of the day was never impinged upon. For Reg, however, it had more than a face. Today it had hundreds and they impressed themselves firmly onto his thoughts.

A woman carrying her washing glanced his way and he saw the abuse she had always endured. In her childhood, her father, reduced to bestiality by alcohol and the hopelessness of his circumstances, lashed out at the easiest of available targets, at the one least able to fight back. In later years, palace guards, so-called protectors of the realm, found the young woman desirable, then showed her the lashes of their whips and the bluntness of their staves when she defended her dignity and rebuffed their advances. Those for whom she labored in her maturity as likely as not rewarded her work with a cuff of their hand to accompany the one or two bronze coins they paid.

A young boy watering a broken-down horse at a trough, glanced at the blue blur hurtling past his father's cart, and Reg knew deprivation through the lad. For the child, the prince's shiny toy-on-wheels was beyond a lifetime's expectations. Last night he had eaten the first real meal in days: a soup of vegetables and grain. His father had gotten lucky in the market, and soup was the best way to put the few simple victuals into the most mouths when there was also wood for a fire. Usually, though, he ate scraps foraged from the bins behind the market stalls, then cried himself to sleep, with hunger his bedtime companion and food the stuff of dreams.

The roadster careened around a corner, just as one with younger reflexes pulled back an ancient man about to step into its path. This old soul still labored daily. He could dimly recall his childhood if he tried. Even then he had worked. Now, arthritis bound him with sharp, biting manacles. Fatigue pulled and tugged until thoughts of mortality became sweet fantasies of liberation. And every morning, his thoughts dulled, ambition long dead, he arose, an automaton stepping through paces endlessly rehearsed…

The wife of another unfortunate had long ago abandoned the hopes that marriage offers a young girl. The expansive possibilities that bond opens to the imaginations of the young were truncated now into a long, dark, narrow tunnel of servitude…

By his barrow, a merchant, his face lined with worry, his voice hoarse, hawked his dirty wares. They had interested only an occasional buyer for more days than he could recall. Few who were interested had money to buy, so he could never afford better…

On a stoop, a young man, once bright with potential, gathered with his friends to plan a robbery…

Reg was awash with faces. Their stories came upon him like a flood. Wave followed wave and inundated him to the point of drowning. These were not simply imaginings. They were beyond any concepts he had ever known and many were contrary to his way of thinking. As he fought to retain stable footing in what was rapidly becoming a maelstrom of misery and despair, he grew uncomfortably aware of the vividness and intensely personal feeling each experience brought. These were not other lives. Each seemed to be his own. It was he, Regilius Tonopath, who had been beaten, who drank, who failed and despaired. It was he, the heir to the throne of Ydron, who was the robber, the washerwoman, the child. On one hand, he knew this could not be, and contrarily he recalled each life with the clarity and certitude with which he knew each step and turning of the palace corridors.

Beneath this misery, simmering steadily to the surface, arose ever new and alien thoughts. Immersed as he was in these lives, his perceptions of things familiar were changing. Soldiers, his lifelong protectors, were not to be trusted, but rather, feared. No longer guardians and enforcers of the law, they were the source of brutality and kidnappers of husbands and children. Women hid themselves from the helmet and shield of the throne.

It did not pay to be successful outside the palace walls. Any surpluses or gains were sure to be confiscated. One could never quite pay one's tax. The collector made sure of it. When one had managed to acquire a little more than one's customary lot, a visit from the taxman was inevitable. Since none ever knew how the news got out, each suspected his neighbor. It probably was true spies were everywhere. A word in the right ear would likely put food in an empty belly, so distrust abounded.

Reg's head hurt and he trembled as he drove through the horror. He could not believe any of this could be true in the land his family ruled, but the images were relentless. This flight from danger had become a plunge into reality. He was unprepared for and unable to come to terms with what each moment drove home. Had he been so sheltered he could not see his world as it was?

Somehow—he knew not by what providence—the roadster hurtled on without incident. Even when he tried, he could barely focus on his surroundings. Carts, streets, banners, men, women and children all blurred into a stream, while the dreams or revelations—he could not say which—bombarded him until he was lost in the confusion. He no longer knew where he was, yet the car careened onward.

Eventually he passed through the city's outermost wall. He did not remember the gate or the guards, but the density of outer danYdron thinned into scattered farms and villages and his head began to clear. He breathed deeply, with only dim recollection of his purpose as the cacophony of sights and sounds receded. Like a badly beaten fighter trying to see through senses numbed by countless blows, staggering toward his corner and his seconds for relief, Reg drove westward. Familiarity kept him on his path, though his mind was still dazed, unaware of the road spinning under the wheels and away behind him.

… … … … …

Scores of brill winging across the meadow sent up waves of crisp, clear cries like wind chimes. The West Wind blew steadily from the sea, bringing the scythe grass blanketing the coastal plains to resonant song. Caverns in the face of the palisades boomed hollow and long in lower octaves and the ocean waves crashed against the wall's rocky feet, punctuating the endless symphony of Sandoval.

Alone beside the songful yellow sea of waving blades, beneath the deep green vault of heaven, the shiny blue skin of the roadster reflected the glare of two suns. Some distance away, perched at the palisade's edge, oblivious to the surrounding splendor, a tiny figure sobbed discordantly.

Reg squatted, rocking to and fro', demanding but getting no answers to the countless questions the events of the day had raised. Tears coursed down his cheeks. He lifted his hands in a despairing gesture, then stared in numb surprise at the dark blood welling from his knuckles and the edges of his palms. He had been beating them in anger and frustration against the stone, and though they should have hurt, he felt nothing.

Never in his life had he been so confused. He had been taught to take control, to master every situation, yet nothing, not the teachings of Ai'Lorc, and certainly not the pleasant tales Marm wove in the shade of the old falo'an tree, had prepared him for such a series of events. Unable to distinguish what was real from what was delusion, terrified at the prospect of losing his mind, he began to tremble. Everything he believed in had grown twisted. His family, his kingdom and the people around him were no longer to be trusted. He could think of nothing upon which he could rely and it was all he could do to keep from tumbling headlong into despair. So here he sat, at the edge of a cliff overlooking the sea, welcoming the cold blast of the West Wind. He relished it, found strength in it and embraced it.

"Is it as hard as all that, Your Highness?"

Reg jumped at the intrusion. Turning, he found the face of an old friend.

"Ai'Lorc!"

# 3

Released at last from his teacher's embrace, Reg felt calmer and stepped back to examine the countenance that had appeared so suddenly. Ai'Lorc's clear gray eyes conveyed an intensity that usually startled others, though the prince saw in them rare purpose and clarity. His dark complexion marked Ai'Lorc as from the eastern provinces, and in fact, he claimed Nagath-réal as his home. To say his prominent nose was beaklike would have been insulting. It was finely sculpted and perhaps its size left more to admire. In fact, the same might have been said of his high cheekbones and expansive brow. Exaggerated features on some yield an ungainly appearance, but in this case their perfection of form made for a memorable combination. His dark prominent brows and beard accented the image. He was well-groomed without foppery, well-dressed without affectation. As Reg's teacher, he had proven himself adept in all matters academic and social. He was as comfortable in the abstract worlds of pure mathematics and philosophy as he was in the more concrete realms of engineering and chemistry. It seemed there was no language he could not speak, and it was through this foreigner the prince had developed his understanding of the responsibilities and duties of a sovereign, of daily protocol within and without the palace walls. Ai'Lorc was in all regards remarkable.

As Reg beheld him, he became alarmed.

"How did you know I would be here?"

If Ai'Lorc saw suspicion in his pupil's eyes, he nonetheless smiled gently, placed a reassuring hand on Reg's shoulder, and in a quiet voice filled with affection replied, "I am not one you need to fear, Your Highness. The guards at the city gates indicated the direction. I have always known this is your secret haunt. Didn't you once confide this is where you come when you are troubled?"

"What made you think I was troubled?" Reg persisted.

"A friend told me. Come. Let us walk and I will explain

everything."

Reg responded automatically. He was unable to make decisions of his own now, and he sorely needed a friend's guidance. They strolled along, two figures casting four long shadows beneath binary suns across the expansive plain above the sea. Their leggings of oreth hide warded off the cutting edges of the knife–sharp grass. Scythe grass blades could be deadly, but with protection it was possible to take a careful stroll out here where none dared disturb. It was one reason Reg had chosen this place as his sanctuary.

"It is impossible," said Ai'Lorc, "to answer your question without addressing the events of these last two days."

Reg looked sharply at his teacher.

"Oh, yes! I know momentous things are happening to you, and I suspect much more than I can say. But before we discuss these matters, I need to teach a bit of history."

"If you mean to expand on how my father governs his kingdom," Reg offered, still sensitive to what he had learned, "I am already aware."

"I am glad you have discovered some of that already. That is a good sign. But no, I mean something much more significant. I intend to impart a far greater understanding of your country, your people and the world at large than what you have already learned. Certain matters I will not be able to substantiate directly, however from your recent experiences you will be able to test much of what I say. You also know me and what kind of man I am. From all of this, you must judge how much I tell you is true.

"The first fact you need to know is that I am a stranger to your world."

"I know. You are from Nagath-réal."

"You are not listening. I did not say I am a stranger to your land. I said I am a stranger to your world."

Reg paused, not comprehending.

"I come from another world a great distance from here." He gestured expansively upwards. "Beyond the stars. My people and I first arrived in your distant past. There were many of us. We came to a marvelously pristine world where possibilities abounded. In those days there were no cities, no civilization."

"Impossible," the prince protested.

"Very little in this universe is impossible. The cosmos is unimaginably vast. The realities it contains even more so. We travel between stars as your people sail the seas."

"I'm sorry, but I do not believe you."

"Before today, I scarcely would have expected you to, but I think the recent changes within you will bear me out when I say all is not as you have suspected it to be. I think you can see, when I speak of these changes, I possess special information you would have thought no one had but you."

"You've spoken with the doctors," Reg countered.

"They have no idea what has happened to you. If they did, do you really think they would have allowed your escape?"

Reg could not respond.

"Of course not. They would have guarded you closely. They would have wanted to study you, that is, had they believed you. On the other hand, the possibility is far greater they would have considered you unbalanced and would have placed you under special care, convincing your parents it was for your own good. Do you really believe doctors provided me with this information? For argument's sake, believe me when I say my people and I are not of this world and we have been among you since those days you refer to as the beginning of time. Believe me until you have heard me out, then decide."

Reg stopped to consider, then nodded.

"When we first arrived, we found your distant forebears quite primitive, barely more than the beasts with which they shared this place. At that time their future could have been anything or nothing. We wanted to see how a race might evolve, but as we observed your world over successive expeditions, we looked in vain for signs of advancement. Perhaps, given greater amounts of time, progress would have occurred. But we were new to exploration. We grew impatient. And we were consumed with our new ability to travel great distances. Full of self-importance, unable to keep ourselves from tipping the scales, we conceived a grand experiment. To see how well we could craft a world, we altered you."

"What do you mean, altered us?" Reg found the thought comical and it made him laugh. "Do you mean you removed our tails or some such?"

"More subtly than that. You will recall from our studies in biology that within each of us are tiny units of life."

"You mean the cells we have examined under a glass."

"Exactly. Within each of those lies all the information about the organism at large: how tall, what color, life span, intelligence and so on.

In a word, Your Highness, we altered some of that information within your ancestors in order to hasten and direct their development."

"I find that incredible, but nonetheless, see where we are today. We have accomplished so much. If what you say is really so, I see no harm in it." He chuckled.

"And just where are you today? There is much wrong in your world and the many social ills are but symptoms."

"Mightn't these have happened in any case?"

"And again, they might not have. It is all moot at this point. The deed has been done. At any rate, some of us felt responsible. We felt compelled to insure nothing disastrous resulted, and admittedly, some of us were curious how our experiment would develop. We left a few of our people here to watch, to learn and to report. That is why I am here."

"Are you not a little concerned what action I might take after you have revealed your identity?"

Ai'Lorc laughed. "You?" He stifled his amusement. "I'm sorry. I mean no offense, but I know you too well and I am not the least concerned."

Reg cocked an eyebrow, uncertain what the remark implied.

Ai'Lorc stopped, faced the prince and said, "You are not that kind. It is not your nature."

Reg paused, rolled the thought around as one might savor a fine wine, then smiled in recognition of the truth. Yes, he was not that kind.

They proceeded again and Reg noticed they were making for a cluster of damass trees. A good idea, he thought. As evening approached, the wind was growing colder and the trees would provide some shelter. He drew his cloak closer and Ai'Lorc continued.

"In some respects you are correct. Ordinarily, I would not have revealed who I am, and my reason would have been for safety's sake. However, your people would not have been my first cause for concern." To Reg's questioning eye he replied, "I suspect you have already met a few of those I fear most. They will have been most curious about your transformation."

Not understanding at first, Reg's puzzlement slowly changed to comprehension.

"Ah! You have met them. We call them Dalthin. They are at once your greatest danger… " He paused. "… and your very reason for being."

"My… ? What do you mean? Who are they?"

"My people are not the only ones who visit other worlds. While the motives of my race are sometimes questionable, there are others whose intent is purely evil. I do not like the word. It is too absolute. Then again, so are they. The Dalthin are evil.

"When they discovered your world many years ago, they happened upon a place ripe for their purposes, a place they could exploit, though not without some difficulty. Fortunately for you, their home lies a great distance away, and as a result, there can be no easy communication. In fact, any transmission from here would require over forty of your years to be received. A vessel, in turn, would need more than four times that to arrive here in response.

"To a certain extent, the passage of time is helping them. In order for them to succeed, they must infiltrate your society as pervasively as possible. The vessel that brought them, like as not, could have carried only fifty to a hundred individuals. Knowing what they need to do, they have been fitting into your world."

"To what end?"

"They wish to subjugate you. Your people will harvest the globe's resources for them, and worse, the Dalthin will harvest you."

"Harvest? You make it sound as though… "

"They will raise you as you raise your herds of cattle and sheep."

Failing to comprehend, Reg could only stare.

"I will be plain. They will harness you for labor and… ," he hesitated a moment, clearly finding the words distasteful, "they will breed you for food."

"What?" cried Reg.

They had reached the damass trees and he slumped against a great gray trunk. The wind was growing, and as his cloak beat about his arms and legs, the leaves of the trees magnified the West Wind's roar. The feeling that everything was enjoined in an assault against him returned.

"But why would they resort to subterfuge? It would seem a race so mighty would merely bring a great ship, crush us under their heel, and the world would surrender."

"So one would think, but it does not work so simply in fact. People such as yours possess a certain nobility. They would not surrender easily. Many would be killed trying to resist. From their viewpoint, it would be a great loss of resources. The decimation of your species does not suit their purposes. Moreover, with the world as your hiding place, the conflict would continue for generations. Many of them would perish as well. While they possess technologies taken from the civilizations they have conquered, they are not invulnerable. Further, any empire that has spread itself as far and as thin as they have will have problems maintaining supply lines. Instead, it will be easier to control and persuade from within.

"Their first move will be subtle and disguised. When their great ship arrives, they will come as friends. Those already living among you will work to persuade and to change opinion. If all goes well, some of you will begin to labor on their behalf, either in response to the marvelous gifts they bring, or more likely because they will have entered your minds. It will be some time before they show any hint of their true intent. By then, it will be too late."

"I don't understand."

"Much of their strength comes from their ability to influence thought."

"Like the mentalists from Nagath-réal who entertain in my father's court," Reg volunteered.

"The Dalthin do not put one into a hypnotic trance," said Ai'Lorc. "Instead, they reach out and touch a thought as you reach to pluck a flower. They make you see what is not there and feel what you otherwise would not."

"And so, they will herd us aboard their ships and haul us away to their world. Who among us could survive such a journey?"

"They do not intend for you to make that voyage. While they have the means to insure you would survive, they have learned most species fare best on their native world. So, very simply, in the end they will colonize this world and you will supply the colony's needs."

Reg, who had fixed his gaze upon the horizon, turned to face his teacher.

"And tell me, please," he said, "how these loathsome creatures are—how did you phrase it?—my very reason for being."

"My people did not tamper with your race only once. When we detected the Dalthin, many of us became alarmed. Some wanted to avert their plan. Others felt we should leave you to arrive at your own solution. In the end, we decided to take the former course by helping you to help yourselves. While your people and the Dalthin share certain basic perceptions—specifically those of sight, hearing, touch, smell and taste—your foes possess senses you lack. They use these to communicate beyond the detection of your society. We decided it would be immensely helpful if some of you could perceive the world as they do. But it is one thing to snatch a primitive to perform some alterations. It is substantially more difficult to do the same among a people as advanced as yours. Kidnappings draw considerably more attention." He smiled wryly.

"In addition, there are very few of us here—slightly more than a dozen on this continent, only two in this kingdom. Our resources are as thinly spread as theirs are and over comparable distances. It was incumbent to have easy access to our chosen citizens and for them, in turn, to be in a position both to influence those around them and to move about freely."

Reg gave an inquiring look and cocked his head, so Ai'Lorc explained. "We were fortunate to have two of our team within barakYdron, as well as a doctor—now gone from this world—in attendance to the royal family. So it was that we chose and altered you, Your Highness, and one other."

"You *what*?"

"We gave you the ability to deal with the Dalthin."

"When? How?"

"When you were an infant. I haven't the expertise to tell you the how of it. I am not a surgeon."

"I cannot believe your arrogance."

"Who, then, would save your world?"

"You know the Dalthin. Your people are more advanced than ours. You deal with them," Reg shouted. "How dare you sit back and idly observe us like mites under the glass, then dispassionately stick us, cut us open and manipulate us to suit your whims?"

"We can't help you nearly as well as you can help yourselves," Ai'Lorc countered.

"And why is that, do you suppose? I'll wager there is more than a hint of cowardice in your veins."

Ai'Lorc refused to rise to the bait. "We can only detect the presence of the Dalthin, and not very well at that. Your nervous system is much better suited to the task. We are very different from you, despite the outer similarity."

"Which I suppose you also engineered."

"Correct."

Reg was at a loss for words, unprepared for the implications of that response. Until now, he had no reason to accept Ai'Lorc as anything other than what he appeared to be. He was not prepared for such a simple, candid, yet astonishing admission. He had expected a denial or an excuse. He could have taken either in stride and they would have provided other grounds for attack. Faced with neither, he had to regroup.

"Do you think I am now prepared to take on another world?" he asked.

"Not at all. Your senses have only begun to awaken. You must allow them time to develop. When they have, you should be more than equipped to defend against this enemy."

"Until their ship arrives," said Reg, "at which point they will simply destroy us."

"As I said, they need your people far too much to destroy you outright, which may increase your chances. We are counting on it."

"Counting on it? What if you are wrong?"

"Had we sent for one or more of our ships at the very moment we learned of their presence, they would arrive here years after the Dalthin's vessel and you would have had no chance at all."

Ai'Lorc paused. Reg could not respond.

"None at all. Your race would have been enslaved and nothing we had done prior to that point would have meant a thing. Nothing we might have done afterwards would have mattered either. We are not prepared to engage in war. There is nothing much left of my people—that is to say, those who are still free—for the Dalthin have conquered my world as well. As for those of us who have escaped, our resources are meager and the only factor allowing us to attempt this strategy is that our lives are enormously long compared with yours. I have been able to live here and to work and observe for a very long time. Now, at least your people have a chance. You were born to lead and now you have a cause to give purpose to that leadership. There is but one thing left for you to do in order to improve that chance."

"And what might that be?"

"You must leave Ydron."

Reg looked at him.

"It is the only way to give your abilities time to develop. Right now, while your senses are raging, you are like a beacon to the Dalthin. It is as if you are standing in a great darkened hall, shouting as loud as you can, wondering how long it will take others in the hall to find you. In time, it should not be so, but for now it is only a matter of days or hours until they locate you."

Reg was immobilized by the immensity of what he had been told, so Ai'Lorc, ignoring the impropriety of the act, gently took the prince's elbow.

"Come, Regilius Tonopath. Your friends await you at pelPedreth in Sandoval. We will go to them tonight. In the morning, you will sail away. When you return, you will enjoin your father's kingdom to hunt out and destroy the invaders."

"That is not very likely."

Ai'Lorc halted abruptly.

"And why not? Are you afraid?"

"My cowardice or bravery has nothing to do with it. Dear Ai'Lorc, should I return a demigod, it will not matter one bit without a kingdom."

"I am afraid I don't understand."

"Do you not know what is transpiring? Even as we speak, certain nobles are banding together to destroy my father. They will serve him no longer. By the time I return, there may be no kingdom to lead."

"How certain are you?"

"You gave me the ability to see."

"And when might this overthrow begin?"

"It is already underway."

"Then all may be lost despite our efforts." Ai'Lorc paused to consider his next revelation. "In light of what you say, I must tell you I fear for Marm's safety."

"For my nursemaid? She can be of no great concern to the traitors."

"She is the other one stationed within the palace; the one who told me of your condition, I might add. If what you say is true, then I fear all who dwell there are at risk."

# 4

Mahaz was setting and Jadon paced steadily toward the horizon. The blades of scythe grass sang as they were beaten about by the gusts and breezes coming in from the sea. In the cove below, protected from nature's severity, boats bobbed and tugged at their moorings. Masts swayed and danced to the rhythms of the waves and the varying breaths of air. Smokestacks of the handful of steamships berthed in the harbor were more sedate in their gyrations.

Danth broke the silence. "This is ridiculous."

He was leaning against a pillar on the verandah, arms crossed, gazing out toward the sunset. As he turned to his friends, the wind blew his long blonde hair into his eyes and he swiped it from his face. Leovar jerked upright. He had been lost in thought and the sudden comment startled him.

"Why do you say that?" he asked.

"We are here at the request of someone I no longer know, idly watching the day come to an end and waiting for Siemas-knows-what, and you have to ask?

"Furthermore, I'm not used to being treated as scum. You may abide hospital hirelings rudely shoving you aside, but I did not find yesterday's proceedings at all satisfactory. In fact, when today's fiasco is over I intend to return and set things straight."

"We weren't shoved aside. We were sent away because there was nothing more for us to do," Leovar reminded. "Would you rather they take us into their council, seek our opinion, perhaps entertain us as well?"

"Not at all. It's just that their kind… "

"Their kind?" Ered interrupted. "That sounds a little elitist, coming from you."

Danth, like Leovar, while the son of a lord, was outspoken about treating everyone as equals, even though peers outside of this group would have considered that position dangerous. Further, Ered's reprimand was not the sort of comment permitted to one of common birth, such as he. A stranger would have gasped at this breach, but here he was not treading on thin ice. Despite their different social stations, in all else they were equals. They had grown up together and had associated as no others of similar circumstances had done. The races they had won or lost on Lake Atkal or at sea, they had won or lost as teammates and were equals in each other's eyes.

"You know they were only following standard procedure," he reminded.

"And what kind of procedure are we following?" asked Danth.

"What do you mean?"

"Our lunatic friend sends us a note to meet him here. How could he possibly believe they would release him so soon? Are we to spend all week waiting for him to show up?"

Danth was referring to the note they had received a few hours earlier. It was in Reg's hand, bore his insignia and read, "Wait for me at pelPedreth. I will join you soon to explain."

In response, Ered had gathered a few things they might need and prepared to visit pelPedreth, his father, Pedreth's, house on the coast, never dreaming to question Reg's wishes. Even Leovar required little persuasion. Nevertheless, Danth, then as ever, was suspicious and almost did not come. It was only after he had left his father a note explaining where he would be that he agreed to join them. Even then, he insisted he would stay only one day.

"Did you see how his mouth foamed?" Danth continued, referring to Reg's collapse on the playing field. "Things like this don't just happen. Your friends do not fall to the ground quaking. They took him away in an ambulance, bound like a mad dog."

"You exaggerate," countered Ered. "He is not mad. He became ill. That's all. Perhaps it was a *grand mal.* He was strapped and gagged so he wouldn't hurt himself."

Danth pressed his point. "How long have we known him? All our lives. If he ever had seizures, we would have known by now. But he has not. Ever. I don't know who that was."

"Whatever the reason for this seizure, it was due to an illness, perhaps a sudden fever. If he feels it has passed, he will be here."

Leovar got to his feet and joined in. "And if he does not, we will go home and nothing will be the worse for it."

"And so we wait?"

"One short day," Ered replied, "most of which is already gone. Let us see what transpires. We will leave in the morning if there is no news. If we were home, what more could we do?"

Danth shrugged. As he often did, he deferred to Ered's judgment.

Ered was a year older than his companions. When, as boys, they had come to Lake Atkal to learn to sail, his father was the one who cared for, mended and cleaned their boats. But while Pedreth—boatkeeper for king Manhathus—tended their vessels, he had left their training to his son. Even in those days, Ered was an extremely capable hand at the tiller. He had been sailing almost since he could walk and handled the crafts with such elegant facility his noble students looked up to him from the outset. He, on the other hand, never mocked their first, erratic attempts at steering, but taught them to focus on a distant point and to keep part of the rigging fixed upon it until their hands moved rhythmically in response to the vagaries of wind and wave. When they had become completely frustrated, cursing the sheets and halyards, red-faced and sweating, enmeshed in the knotted tangles, his calm voice guided them to sort out and coil the lines and set the cockpit in order. Ered made a game out of discipline, and when it came to racing, brought discipline to the game. He taught them the authority of the captain and the obedience of the crew. If things were to happen quickly and they were to act as one, there was no other way. They had sailed together and grown together. Always a team, Ered, Leovar, Danth and Reg never put one above the other.

"I'm hungry," said Leovar. He entered the cottage and began uncovering the light globes. "Come inside," he called. "Help me put a meal on the table or I'll eat alone."

The chill would have driven them in soon anyway, so they followed.

... ... ... ... ...

The wind had grown in volume. It rattled the windows and resonated down the chimney, occasionally drafting smoke back into the room. Amid the racket came a pounding on the door. Leovar and Danth were slow to rise, so Ered made directly for it. He threw the bolt and turned the handle, grasping it to prevent the door from flying open as the wind rushed in, momentarily damping the fire. Ered's eyes were slow to adjust to the darkness outside. As he peered into the night, a solitary figure forced its way past him. He was torn between shutting the door and seizing the intruder when the man straightened and turned.

"Father!" he exclaimed.

The door banged hard against the wall as the wind tore it from his hand. Loose objects skittered across tabletops and papers took to the air before Danth gained enough presence to rush past Ered and shut out the elements.

"Thank you, Danth," gasped Pedreth.

Ered's ineptitude was atypical and his father could not stifle his smile, shaking his head as he dropped his burden. He doffed his cap and searched the room.

"Well, where is he?" Pedreth demanded.

"Where is who?" Ered asked as he regarded the bundle.

The wind suddenly boomed, rattling the windows and shaking the door against its lock and hinges.

"Goodness, it's a real blower tonight," Pedreth said, as he drew back a curtain and peered outside. He tossed his cap onto a chair, loosened his cloak and hung it on a hook by the door, then began unfastening the closures on his coat. "I need some hot tea and a chance to catch my breath before I go down to check the moorings."

"We were down there earlier, Father. Everything is secure."

"Oh? Well, good. I shouldn't have given it a thought but, well, you understand. Old habit."

Danth took his coat.

"Thank you again." Pedreth shook and ruffled his hair with both hands to loosen what the cap had matted.

Leovar stepped forward with a cup of steaming tea. "Please, sir, I made a stew earlier and there is still plenty left. Would you care for any?"

"Yes, I would." Pedreth smacked his lips at the offer. "Yes, I would. I have quite an appetite."

"Father, excuse me."

Pedreth paused and turned slowly. "Yes, Ered?"

"Who were you expecting?"

"Didn't he tell you?"

Danth stepped forward. "Do you mean you spoke with Reg?"

"Reg?" Pedreth seemed puzzled. He looked around again. "Isn't prince Regilius here with you?" Then, seeing that he was not, he continued, "No, I'm sorry, I wasn't referring to His Highness."

"Who, then?" Ered persisted.

"Why, Ai'Lorc, of course," he replied.

"I'm sorry, I don't understand."

"Ered, I'm hungry and not a little tired. Please allow me to eat something and then I will explain. Obviously, you have not spoken with the Easterner, so then I am also a little unsure of events. But, please, a little patience is in order," he said as he sat at the table.

… … … … …

Pedreth wiped the plate with his bread. As he took a generous bite, it crumbled onto the dish and stuck to the stubble of his beard. He wiped his mouth with the back of his hand, then washed down the coarse, grainy bread with a swallow of tea. At last, after downing two large bowls of Leovar's stew, he was feeling content.

"So, Ai'Lorc never spoke to you?" Pedreth pressed.

"Not one word," Danth replied.

"Odd. Yet I am positive he told me you had mutually arranged to meet here."

"No, father," Ered injected. "The reason we are here is this note." He produced the piece of paper from his pocket and handed it across the table.

Pedreth examined it. "The prince gave you this?"

"No. It arrived by pigeon."

"Curious. I'm sure an explanation is forthcoming. Ai'Lorc said he would be here, and your note promises the same from Reg."

A knocking interrupted and Leovar arose to answer it.

"I suspect we do not have long to wait on that account," Leovar observed. "I wouldn't be surprised if this were one or the other."

He was doubly right.

Ai'Lorc and Reg were visibly troubled as they warmed themselves by the fire. It was apparent enough their friends kept conversation away from the obvious until the two had thoroughly rested. Once the dishes were cleared and they all had settled down, Pedreth, Danth and Leovar began to question them, incredulous as Ai'Lorc and Reg related events and offered difficult explanations.

"So, what you are saying is that everything familiar is gone, disaster is upon us and we are to run for the hills, tails between our legs," said Danth. "Well I, for one, am not afraid of shadows."

"You will pardon me then, if I remind you bravado in the face of superior numbers is usually unwise," replied Ai'Lorc. "This is neither the time for heroics nor emotional reaction. If you survey the room, my Lord, you will see we are only six. We certainly lack the numbers to turn a coup and I assure you we are far short of the force required to put down the Dalthin."

"With all due respect," said Leovar, "why can't your people protect us?"

"My ship left this world many years ago. All there is to represent my people in this part of the world are Marm and myself. We couldn't help you against any threat."

"So you sit and patiently await the outcome," said Danth.

"We have no choice."

"You have nerve to sit here and talk about this so dispassionately. I say we throw you out and send you back to your own kind."

"You are right," Ai'Lorc admitted. "My people are not very admirable. I wish I could do something to change that, but I cannot. Still, for as much or as little as it is worth, I will not abandon yours. Although my ship has departed, I have cast my lot in with you and would not desert you if I could.

"Furthermore, please consider this." He studied their faces. "We did not bring the Dalthin to you. Had we never come, had we never played god with your world, they still would have come."

"Why did your people leave you here?" asked Danth.

"Their fuel was running low and could not be replenished here. In addition, these ships, as well as other resources necessary for the survival of our race, are not within our present ability to replace. We need to keep them out of harm's way, by which I mean out of the Dalthin's way. If the few of us who have chosen to remain here survive and all goes well, and if we still are able to communicate with them by then, they hope to return. If they do not or cannot for any one of a dozen reasons, then at least they will survive. We will carry on here as best we can."

"Tell us more about these people, the Dalthin," said Pedreth.

Ai'Lorc turned to him and replied emphatically, "These are not people we are talking about. True, they are intelligent, but they possess no emotions, no caring. They are unlike anything you have ever encountered. They are parasites, unfeeling devourers of entire races. They create nothing, but only use and take, stripping and enslaving entire worlds. Other races created the ships that carry them between the stars. The crew that man those crafts are poor souls who have either been given promises of better lives that will never be fulfilled or, worse still, whose minds are under the Dalthins' control. The slaves in your mines have it better."

Reg, who was still trying to come to terms with Ai'Lorc's tale, pressed his teacher. "Earlier you admitted you are not like us and your people have acted to exploit us. By your own admission, your appearance was altered so you will look like us. Why should we take the word of one alien over another?"

"Your Highness, while I am different from you, I am not so different as you might think. My people have not as much bodily hair as yours. In addition, our facial features are more exaggerated. You will probably note some remnants of this in my own countenance. In addition, our hands and feet each possess an extra digit. On the other hand, like you we are warm-blooded." Ai'Lorc grasped Reg's hand, and looked him in the eye. "But more important, we are very much like you within. We are sympathetic to other living beings. It pains us to watch another suffer. We laugh, cry, and are moved by beauty. We create and we strive to improve ourselves and the world in which we live."

He sat back, now addressing the rest of the company.

"The Dalthin are of a radically different nature. To call them cold-blooded would liken them to you much more than they deserve. Their entire make-up is unlike yours. Oddly, it is only with regard to the manner in which your neural synapses operate that there is any resemblance at all. In that regard, you are almost identical. The chemical basis is radically different, but the activity of theirs mimics the process of yours entirely. You must also be aware that, on this world, tales of people with psychic abilities abound. These tales are not unfounded and mark the inherent nature of these abilities to your people. Further, Highness, you have met the Dalthin. Perhaps, you even touched their minds and perceived a little about them. Have you sensed any similarity between them and me? I think not."

"You are right," agreed Reg, shuddering as he reflected. "I have not."

"Then, you believe me." This was more of a question than a statement of fact. He paused inquiringly. When there was no immediate response he offered, "I think you would like to, but are still unconvinced. I have one small way remaining to prove what I say is true."

Ai'Lorc produced a small, metallic box from one of his pockets. He opened it, revealing an interior filled with numerous colored lights. While his audience tried to guess at its nature, he began to manipulate it. All at once, to a chorus of gasps, a luminous scene appeared in the air between them. Gradually, the story of an entire world unfolded—

scenes of mountains and rivers, marvelous cities unlike any they knew, a world filled with beautiful people. Suddenly, there were images of ghastly creatures, and wordlessly the box revealed the enslavement of a world. Each one in the room became so engrossed, that when at last the story concluded and the apparitions disappeared, each remained silent, amazed at what he had seen.

Ered broke the silence. "It's magical."

"Did a sorcerer from Mitheron or Glaudion give it to you?" asked Danth.

"No, Lord Kanagh, it is neither magic nor a product of the Lost Arts."

The fire had begun to die, so Leovar arose and began to stoke it back to life.

"Now, now! That is hardly becoming, my Lord—working like one of us poor folk," Pedreth chided.

Leovar, squatting upon the hearth, poker in hand, turned to his old sailing master and attempted to smile. "You never seem to mind when I fold the canvas or wash the decks."

Instead of responding, Pedreth simply returned his smile, then turned to Reg. "So, Your Highness, do you subscribe to your teacher's advice? Do we pack and run?"

Reg paused a minute, obviously weighing his reply. "I do. I have seen the Dalthin and they frighten me. And the kingdom… " He paused and looked helplessly at his friends. "… is falling as we speak. As Ai'Lorc intimated earlier, there has indeed been a coup."

Pedreth could not hide his incredulity and laughed aloud. "You are making a joke. The kingdom has stood for generations. Even the attack on barakYdron, after the battle at menRathan, was not enough… "

"No, Pedreth. I only wish I were joking. Lord Emeil, certain of my father's ministers and many peers of the realm have conspired together. Even as we speak, they are within the palace walls."

"You are certain?"

Reg nodded.

Danth had stopped pacing. "Reg, should we return to rally the guard?"

"I am afraid there would be few to rally. I suspect they are mostly dead or have gone over to the other side."

"Does this include your own?"

Reg nodded.

"Such treachery is unheard of," Danth said.

"Was unheard of," Reg corrected.

"How fares your family?" asked Leovar.

Reg's composure began to crumble. Tears welled in his eyes and he clenched his fists.

Ai'Lorc volunteered to complete the account. "Even as we spoke upon the palisades, he became aware the assault was underway and his father had been slain."

They looked alarmed.

"Thus far, his mother is alive and both the princess Lith-An and Marm are safe. Due to those events we discussed earlier, Reg has begun to acquire certain perceptions enabling him to see things unfolding elsewhere, as if he were there. Unfortunately, these new perceptions are not always timely or complete. He knew of the plot when he fled, but not of its imminence. He felt he would have had time to send a warning. Now he knows it is too late."

"But he could be mistaken," Pedreth suggested.

Reg wiped his eyes and replied, "Before you came here tonight, but after you had packed your van, you stopped by the cottage of the widow Miened. Even though you had visited two days earlier and ordinarily would not have stopped in again until Fifthday evening next, you chose to revisit because you felt something was amiss."

"Who told you this?"

"No one. Who could have? I am not asking you if this occurred. It happened just as I said. You know it did. It is with the same certainty I tell you the kingdom is lost. And now… " He struggled against more tears. "I also know it was my mother who murdered my father."

"No!" cried Ered. "That can't be true."

"Oh, but it is, dear Ered. It is." He wrapped his arms around his chest and sobbed.

"How could that be?" asked Danth. "Why would she do such a thing?"

For a moment, Reg did not answer. Then he looked at his friend and said, "I cannot say, but I am certain it was she who brought the traitors into barakYdron and I am also certain it was she who drove the dagger into my father's heart. I see it as clearly as I see you now."

His friends looked stunned and did not speak. Finally, Leovar broke the silence.

"What of the houses of Hol and Kanagh? Our ancestors fought beside yours when this land was founded. Our fathers would not let this happen, Reg."

"Your father, Leovar, along with Danth's, has sided with Emeil. I cannot say why."

"And they willingly joined in the murder?" asked Danth in disbelief.

"I cannot tell you why but, yes, they did."

Pedreth sat stunned and silent. All of his arguments had left him.

"Reg," said Ered. "The pictures from Ai'Lorc's box are not the first visions I've seen."

Reg looked at him quizzically. "No?"

"When you fell on the playing field, sights and sounds filled my head. I had forgotten about them until now."

Danth, usually the skeptic, agreed. "I did as well, now that you mention it."

Leovar nodded. "I must say I did, too. Did we all?"

All but Pedreth nodded. "Why didn't I, do you suppose?" he asked.

"All except you were near Reg at that moment," Ai'Lorc replied. "I was certainly much farther away than the boys, but I experienced much the same. When Marm met me in her room and announced something marvelous was happening, I was not at all surprised. I suspect, somehow, most within the city walls had the same experience but, like you, did not know what to make of it."

"What do you make of it?" Pedreth pressed.

"It was certainly the moment marking Reg's transformation. Somehow, everyone within a certain radius must have been touched. I cannot explain it any better than that. What disturbs me is, just as we were aware, the Dalthin must have been as well."

The group digested Ai'Lorc's remark.

"I can't believe we are helpless," Danth said and began to pace.

Reg motioned him back to the table. Then, in the quiet voice of one recovering from a blow, he spoke. "While there is much we can do, and much we must do if ever we are to right this, confrontation is not among our options."

"Reg," asked Ered, "Can you now see all things?"

"No. Some things come to me without my bidding. If I concentrate on someone, I become aware of certain events that have either recently happened or are of great importance—things at the forefront of their minds or events happening around them. When I think of my family, I see fear and flight, chaos and blood." Tears came to his eyes and he struggled to maintain his composure. "What I see is not always clear and focused. Sometimes it is more like scenes from a dream, but with far greater clarity. I will tell you this: I am certain disaster is upon us."

"What do we do?" asked Ered.

"Ai'Lorc says I must flee."

"Do you agree?"

"I must. It is the only thing that makes sense, and I can detect nothing about Ai'Lorc to indicate he is other than whom he claims to be."

"Thank you," responded Ai'Lorc, obviously relieved. "I have never needed your trust and belief more than I do now."

Pedreth leaned back in his chair, rocking and balancing on the back legs. He whistled long and softly. "Such a night I have never known."

Ered turned back to his friend. "When do we go, Reg?"

"Ai'Lorc has told me I need to give my senses time to develop. I believe he is right. I must leave before the Dalthin find me. Until I gain control, they will come to me like homing pigeons. In all honesty, I think it would be best for everyone if I were to go alone."

"No," Ai'Lorc insisted. "You will need your friends if you are to survive, and they need you. We must all go together."

"But where?" asked Pedreth.

"The only thing of which I'm certain," said Ai'Lorc, "is we must leave Ydron's boundaries, as well as the neighboring lands."

"Then, I would like to make a suggestion."

"Please, Pedreth, we have brought you in with us for good reason. We value your opinion."

"The lands to the south are warm and hospitable—just the direction I would suspect someone to flee. However, when I was younger, some of us who were testing the seaworthiness of a new vessel sailed up the coast, northwards of Limast, and happened upon a group of islands. They seemed uninhabited and there was good water, stands of timber and some game."

"Your choice sounds good. If we can stay there long enough, perhaps we can return through Limast when the time is right," suggested Ai'Lorc. "I only wish the storm would pass so we can depart at once. Any delay could be disastrous."

Ered laughed, then smiled broadly. For once, his experience as a seasoned sailor put him above this scholar. "This is no storm, teacher. Storms come out of the North. The strong wind upon us is from the West and it is our friend. It is strong tonight, but if you stop and listen, you will hear it has already abated a little. It will continue to calm throughout the night, then build again in the late morning, reaching its greatest strength after noon and into the evening. If a storm is coming, these winds are not it."

"He's right," Leovar joined in. "And, moreover, it is to our advantage. I will bet the Dalthin are no sailors. Heavy airs will certainly intimidate the novice, but to us they only mean swift passage. When we race, air like this provides the greatest speed."

"And the most excitement," added Danth.

"With the right boat," continued Lord Hol, "we can suit these conditions to our needs."

The growing enthusiasm infected Reg. "We have five good hands and, Master, you will learn quickly. I move for two masts, a cutter-rigged ketch. With a good, long waterline and enough displacement, we can balance her fore and aft against the beat to the North."

Ai'Lorc looked lost, so Pedreth explained, "We need a boat fast enough and heavy enough to drive through the strong chop, in other words, the large waves that will be driven against us. We will find a two-master, like the ketch, easier to control and faster under most circumstances, than a single-masted vessel."

"I'll take your word for it, Pedreth, and I will place myself under your tutelage. But tell me, did you bring what I asked for?"

"For the most part. You asked for a great deal, and it was all I could do to find room in my van. Fortunately, I have some provisions here as well. We should make out alright."

"What have you brought?" asked Leovar.

"Food and clothing. You young gentlemen don't have much of either do you?"

"Not unless you would prefer bread and cheese for a while," Reg quipped. "But we should get moving. It will take all night to stock the boat, and we will need to fill casks with fresh water for drinking. Which boat do you suggest, Pedreth?"

"I agree with your choice. Such a boat will serve us well. The denaJadiz is moored here. Her bottom is newly cleaned and she has a full complement of new sails.

"One thing more," Pedreth said. "Ered, if you will come with me, I have something else we will need in my van."

"What's that, father?"

"Weapons."

# 5

The floating dock creaked on its pontoons as it reacted to the motions of the water and the tromping of feet. Pedreth walked rhythmically, knees bent, so he could respond to the rise and fall. When he reached the denaJadiz, he allowed the bundle to slip from his shoulders, caught it before it touched the planking, then grasped it and handed it up to Ered. His hands now freed, he climbed the railing, stepped aboard and sat on the low cabin roof. He was perspiring profusely, both from the exertion and the coat he was wearing against the morning chill.

"The years are catching up with me, Ered." Pedreth tore off his cap and wiped his brow with it. The morning was cold and his breath blew in streamers from the corners of his mouth. "It's too early in the day to be this tired," he said.

"Since you didn't get any sleep, technically this is still yesterday and you deserve to be tired."

"You're not tired and you didn't get any sleep."

Ered handed the bundle down the hatch to Leovar, then replied, "True, but over the years you've had a few more sleepless nights than I."

Pedreth smiled and winked at the jab. "Ered, it's the years, not the nights, that are telling. I am supposed to feel this way. I just don't like it."

"Why don't you rest? We will be underway soon."

"I will rest once that happens. When I can hear the rigging creak under the strain of the sails and the wind whistling through the shrouds, then can I rest."

"You know, father, you don't have to come along. Stay here. This journey doesn't have to be yours."

"Doesn't it? Please tell me how I can remain after a boat from the royal fleet has been pirated. It would be bad enough were it merely scuttled and sunk. Were it merely scuttled and sunk, I would probably only be flogged. I could live with flogged. Wounds heal. Pain subsides. But do you have any idea what would happen should His Majesty discover one of his finest and swiftest new ketches had been stolen? Do you think it would assuage his wrath even a little were he subsequently to learn that his son, my son and their friends had also disappeared without a trace? Hah! I would venture he would be somewhat less than pleased. No thank you. I will come along. Besides, what kind of hand do you think that Easterner will make? You will need more than four experienced hands to comfortably man this boat."

"And you will be welcome, Pedreth," said Leovar as he climbed from the hatchway. "Although, if Reg is right, it will not be Manhathus you need to worry about."

Pedreth cocked an eye. "I had forgotten. Nonetheless, I am certain how he would have reacted. His successor might be no better, and with my luck, probably worse."

Leovar gestured down the quay. "Here comes that Easterner."

They watched Ai'Lorc make his way toward them. His usually dignified figure was almost comical. The stiffening breeze whipped at the corners of his collar and his cloak beat madly about him, making him look like some great fowl trying to take flight. Amid this flurry, his hands were trying alternately to constrain his garment and retain their grasp on an awkwardly large burden. When he reached the ketch, Ered and Leovar reached over the railing to take the load and Ai'Lorc climbed aboard.

"I've brought your sack, Pedreth."

"Thank you, Ai'Lorc. Ered, open it please."

Ered released the drawstring and peered inside. "Borlon's eyes! You could not have done better." He upended the sack and Leovar helped him dump the contents onto the deck. Surveying the yellow garments and their velvety surface, he said, "Sandiath skin clothing and sandiath boots! I was wondering how these shoes of ours were going to manage upon these decks."

"We will be dry!" Leovar laughed. "Sandiath skin is wonderfully waterproof," he remarked to Ai'Lorc.

"Have you enough to go around?" asked Ai'Lorc.

"I followed your directions, although I cannot be absolutely certain about the fit. I tried to err on the large side since we wear them baggy, so I think they will do. Why don't you all put them on? I have marked them with your names."

Ered and Leovar were already locating their gear and setting the others' aside.

… … … … …

"It's awfully quiet." Danth said, shifting the bundle on his shoulder. He and Reg had removed the last of their things from the house and were carrying them to the boat.

Reg looked around, listening. "What do you mean?" he asked.

"There is no one here but us. This is a shipyard. Where are the workers?"

"Today is Secondday and it is only the seventh hour. The workers won't arrive for another hour or more."

"Funny, I have this image of a shipyard being busy around the clock."

"If this were the yard at borYdron, where ships are built, you would likely be right. However, these are just the docks for my father's pleasure boats. It is larger than the harbor at Lake Atkal, but nonetheless, it is the same."

The two made their way down the sloping meadow toward the piers. After they had covered about a quarter of the distance, Danth noticed movement near the cabin.

"It appears the workers here are more industrious than you think." He gestured behind them. "The first have arrived. We had better go before they realize we are taking the boat."

Reg glanced back and nodded, but after only a few steps he froze and jerked as if something had struck him. He stood staring, eyes wide and nostrils flared like a predator tasting the wind.

It only took a glance for Danth to realize something was wrong. "Reg, what is it?"

Reg struggled with the word, licked his lips, finally uttering, "Dalthin."

Danth looked up the hill and saw six peasants in work clothes climb from their run-down sedan. They were carrying toolboxes and had the customary lunch sacks tied to their belts. They seemed to be sharing a joke or amusing tale, because they were laughing. One spotted Danth, waved and he returned the gesture.

"They're just workers, Reg. Look at them. It's alright."

But Reg, frozen in place and trembling, seemed in a trance. Danth looked toward the boat, but his friends were too far away. He grasped Reg's shoulders and tried to rouse him to no avail. Once again, Reg was behaving oddly and it frightened him. He had to get help. Like it or not, the workers were his only hope, so he put down the sack and headed toward them.

… … … … …

When the sedan appeared beside the cottage, Reg didn't have to see its occupants to know who had arrived. All of his senses had come alive and his entire body tingled. This was the same fear he had felt on the hill above the club, the same terror he had felt in the hospital. While he was dimly aware of his friend, he focused on the approaching sentience.

As the sedan's doors opened, he felt hatred and vicious intent wash over him. Its presence was so strong, so real, he found it difficult to remember these feelings originated outside himself. For the first time, he was not merely sensing another consciousness. He *was* the other consciousness. It was exciting and it galvanized his entire being. His breathing deepened and his heartbeat quickened.

He knew this was wrong, but it enveloped him so completely he could not think what to do. He needed a new perspective, so he removed himself from the world of emotion and saw once again with his eyes. Six gray slugs, like nothing of this world, had emerged from the vehicle. Their eyes were orange, like Mahaz, and below them, where a mouth should have been, dozens of tendrils writhed and twisted. They seemed to fester with some vile fluid dripping from the cluster. His eye traveled down to what should have been the underbelly. The entire area continually opened and closed like squirming wounds that fell apart, healed, then reopened in a new location. Ai'Lorc's remark about the similarity between his nervous system and theirs was at once incredible and repulsive.

They reached out to him and this time the sensation was soothing. He began to feel warm and comforted. Reg wondered how he could have been so mistaken. Familiar sensations filled him with pleasure: Satsah's baking, warm, fresh and sweet in his nostrils; Marm's soft lullabies and her fingers running gently through his hair.

*No!*

He tore himself free from the lies. The cool breeze was upon his face, perspiration trickled from his brow and he vaguely heard Danth asking what was wrong. As he treaded the boundary between two worlds, he mustered the one word that described the danger.

"Dalthin."

As he spoke, his perceptions opened a bit and he became aware of other waves of thought wafting across the meadow. Soft, warm, sleepy caresses descending upon his friends on the boat as the Dalthin soothed them into a passive stupor. Reg watched, as from a great distance, as Danth dropped his burden and headed up the slope toward the aliens. The Dalthin were molding and directing his thoughts too.

Reg felt he might be able to do something if only these new perceptions were not so overwhelming. He struggled against them, but it was like trying to run in waist-deep water. Danth was striding toward the creatures. The crew had been lulled almost to sleep. Reg wanted to reach out, to shout or to stand in Danth's way, yet he remained immobile and helpless.

Two of the invertebrates were descending the slope toward Danth. The young lord, oblivious to their true appearance, greeted them as friends and attempted to enlist their aid.

Ever more thought bore down upon Reg. It was faint but persistent, coming from a new direction. He looked past the cottage, toward the main road, as a glimpse of color caught his eye. Another sedan was arriving. Within were several passengers and he realized two of them were Dalthin as well.

He was beginning to grow nauseous, and like a drowning swimmer, was struggling to breathe. His legs were growing weak and were threatening to abandon him. If only he could build a wall to shut it all out…

With that thought, the clamor subsided and he realized what he had done. He gasped, filling his lungs with the air he had been craving. He rubbed his face with his hands and ran his fingers through his hair, struggling to regain his grasp on the real world. Though he could not say how he had accomplished it, he had built a mental wall. He had shut out the Dalthin and was himself again.

A familiar voice caught his attention and he glanced about to locate its source. With a shock, he realized how disoriented he had become.

"Danth!" he shouted.

His friend, now far up the slope, was oblivious to his cry with only a few steps separating him from the aliens. Reg began to call out again, but just when his mouth opened and his throat tensed to form the words, he knew it was not the action to take. Instead, he extended his mind to surround his friend with another mental wall.

Danth halted mid-stride, then recoiled. The obscuring veils lifted and Reg knew he could see the creatures. Danth screamed.

"Danth!" Reg shouted. "Danth!"

Slowly his friend turned.

"Come on. Run!" he urged, gesturing frantically with his arms.

Danth hesitated.

"Please, Danth! Hurry!"

Reg felt helpless. He could not possibly cover enough ground to reach him in time.

"Mas'tad take me," he swore.

He had to do something. He began to run, though he knew he could not get there soon enough. Simultaneously, Danth seemed to comprehend his plight. He turned and bolted down the hill. The two did not need to consult. With legs and arms flailing, they headed past their discarded baggage straight for the boat.

It was quite a distance from Pedreth's cabin to the water, but Reg and Danth were covering ground quickly. If they ignored the path and headed directly across the meadow, they could have made even better time. Their leggings would have protected them, but at this speed a fall into scythe grass could have been fatal. Their feet pounded the hard soil and their breath came hot and fast. As they neared the harbor, their lungs began to burn.

The harbor seemed a clutter of masts, all moving and swaying. All the spars looked alike and Reg panicked. He knew the ketch was moored at the far end, near its mouth, so he looked for two tall masts moving in unison.

After a moment, he cried, "I see her!"

With their goal in sight, they ran harder. Almost immediately, Reg knew he had another problem. He had to alert the crew. The vessel they had chosen was swift indeed, but that was only when fully under way. With her heavy displacement and laden as she was, she would be slow leaving the dock. He hoped the crew were readying her. He reached out to sense them, and what he sensed dismayed him, slowing him almost to a walk. Conversation and preparation aboard the denaJadiz had ceased.

Danth looked back and slowed as well. "Come on, Reg. What's keeping you?"

Reg picked up the pace and they were running again. The lethargy that shackled the crew had nearly bound him as well. It felt as if the entire meadow and boatyard were enmeshed in a tangle of intent.

As their feet struck cadence on the boardwalk, Reg estimated the distance to the denaJadiz. Unsure how physical distance affected his new abilities, he reached out to them. Somehow, he had to rouse all four. As he erected a wall of thought around them and began to wake each one in turn, like a juggler with too many balls in the air, he dropped one.

"Reg!" Danth cried.

Reg sensed terror envelope his friend as Danth felt he was about to die. Suddenly, Danth's legs collapsed and he fell face first onto the planking.

# 6

Dancing blobs of orange and white shimmering on liquid green resolved into two suns reflected on water. Ered looked up and away with a start. How long had he been staring? He shook his head like a drunk trying to regain sobriety. He clung tightly to the ketch's shrouds as he struggled to regain his bearings and recognize the figure standing beside him. It was Ai'Lorc staring off toward the horizon, jaw slack, eyes blank.

"Ai'Lorc! Ai'Lorc! Are you alright?"

At the sound of Ered's voice, Ai'Lorc's body tensed. "Darmaht protect me! What was that? It felt as though someone called."

"I did. I called you. You were staring and… "

"No, Ered. I heard you. That is not what I meant. It was as if Reg… " He paused, trying to clear his head. "That's it! It was Reg. He was calling out to me. He is in trouble and he is coming."

Pedreth and Leovar were beginning to stir and were moving tentatively, testing their limbs.

"Pedreth, we must ready the boat," Ai'Lorc urged, "Reg is coming."

The others were not rousing themselves fast enough, so Ered leapt over the railing and began to unfasten the spring lines that secured the middle of the hull to the dock.

"Father," he shouted, "Raise the mainsail. Ai'Lorc, help him. He will show you how. Leovar, put up a jib."

He looked down the length of the slip and could see someone approaching. He seemed to be staggering under a heavy weight. Glancing back at the crew, Ered realized Ai'Lorc was confused. Releasing the last of the lines, he climbed aboard.

"I'll take over. Go help Reg," he said to the tutor.

Ai'Lorc looked relieved. "I will," he said. He leapt over the railing and sprinted down the dock.

… … … … …

Reg felt the wall go up. He was not certain he had roused the sleepers, but he knew he had shut out the enemy. Then it struck him. Danth had fallen. He stopped, slipped and nearly lost his footing. Whirling about, he saw his friend crumpled on the walk, his chest heaving with sobs. The Dalthin had unleashed Danth's darkest fears, filling him with horror and despair, unleashing monsters from depths of his soul. Reg returned and knelt beside him. He lifted Danth's head. Twin freshets of tears traced the contours of his cheeks from the hollows of his eyes past the quivering gash of his mouth, swollen and bloodied by the fall.

"Oh, Danth. What have they done to you?"

There was a crashing sound and Reg looked up. Two sedans were bouncing down the path through the meadow toward them. They had covered most of the distance and had nearly reached the quay. Farther up, near the cabin, two new arrivals had appeared.

There was no time. Reg grabbed Danth's arms and lifted his torso off the ground. Then, turning and stooping, he pulled the arms over his head and hoisted his friend onto his back. Drawing Danth's wrists across his chest, he struggled to his feet, then tried to run with his friend draped over his shoulders. When he stepped onto the floating dock, however, his footing grew less certain. The West Wind was stirring the water, and the dock, built on pontoons, moved with it. Suddenly, it fell away and Reg almost collapsed. He halted and braced himself to keep from pitching over the side. Steadying himself, he breathed deeply and tried to boost Danth's body higher, but in doing so, nearly dropped him. It was no use. His strength was gone.

"I have him, Your Highness."

The weight lifted from his shoulders and Reg looked into the smiling countenance from beyond the stars.

"Ai'Lorc!" Never had he welcomed this face more.

"We must hurry. Follow me."

Ai'Lorc gathered Danth into his arms and ran toward the ketch. Marveling at the ease with which his teacher handled the weight, Reg hurried to keep up. Unencumbered, his breathing came easier, his legs cooperated and he could reinforce the crumbling mental wall around the boat.

Behind them, the sounds of pursuit resonated on the boards.

… … … … …

Pedreth was worried. Launching the boat safely with so few hands in this strengthening air would not be easy. Earlier that morning, he had anticipated this possibility and moved the denaJadiz her to her present location at the end of the pier. He would have preferred that she were anchored in deeper water, clear of the docks and other vessels. There, they could fill her sails and depart with ease. However, readying her had taken all night and morning and kept her close in.

The denaJadiz was tied alongside the quay and parallel to it—not headed into and between two slips, as were the other boats. This would help the crew sail her out more directly. Now, however, with the Dalthin in hot pursuit, Pedreth faced his worst fears. They would have to depart quickly. Worse yet, with Reg, Danth and Ai'Lorc still ashore, there were only three aboard to man her. If she struck anything near the waterline while trying to depart, it could scuttle and sink her before she ever saw open water.

He appraised her readiness. Danth had released the spring lines, leaving only the bumpers—thick padded pieces dropped from her sides—to keep her from jostling the dock. Only the bow and stern lines held her now. The mainsail and one of the twin jibs, or headsails, had been raised and Leovar stood ready on the foredeck. Pedreth, stationed amidships, would trim the main once all were aboard. Ered, whose hand was unequaled, was at the helm. He would release the stern line, call the orders and guide the ketch out of the harbor.

Pedreth looked down the jetty and saw the three returning. "They're coming, son, and they've got pursuit."

"Ready on the bow line," Ered called to Leovar.

When the trio arrived, they would have to depart without hesitation.

"Ready," Leovar answered.

Once under sail, all would have to function as one. They began to fall into the call and response of a racing team's protocol—not quite naval, but efficient.

"Father, go to the railing to help them aboard. Once that is done, go straight to the main."

The urgent pounding of footsteps announced their arrival. Ered took a breath and shook out his arms and hands. He needed to stay loose to maintain his reflexes.

"Let me help," Pedreth called to Ai'Lorc.

He leaned over the railing and grabbed Danth's forearms. With Reg and Ai'Lorc helping, the injured lord was soon up, over the rail and on board. With no time to take him below, Pedreth laid him on the deck.

"Back the heads'l to port," called Ered.

As Leovar pulled the trailing edge of the headsail toward the port, or left side of the boat, the wind caught it and the bow reacted by slowly swinging to starboard, the opposite side, and away from the dock.

"Grab the railing and climb aboard," Reg shouted to Ai'Lorc.

"Ease heads'l," ordered Ered.

The bow was moving steadily. If it swung out too quickly, they could lose control. As Leovar released tension on the bow line, the pressure of the wind on the headsail eased and the bow swung more slowly. Ai'Lorc climbed from the dock and Reg began to hoist himself aboard.

"Trim sails," called Ered, ordering the crew to align the sails to the airflow.

Leovar hauled on the starboard line to present the sail to the wind, but in doing so, he could no longer manage the line tethering the boat to the dock and the bow began to swing wide.

"Ease sails. Ease! Ease!" shouted Ered.

Reg vaulted the railing as the man-things approached, only a few strides from the stern.

"Reg! Look out!" Pedreth cried.

The prince whirled as two hands reached for the stern rail. The boat, driven by the momentum of the swinging bow, began to back into the dock. The denaJadiz voiced her protest with a loud, wooden groan, as tons of ballast shoved bumpers aside and tested the strength of her timbers.

"Father, watch your trim!" cried Ered.

Pedreth returned to his task and winched in the main sheet to fill the mainsail and regain power. His eyes turned aloft to see the wing of cloth align with the air and he smiled. Reg grabbed a winch handle, and wielding it like a club, advanced on the Dalthin.

"Leovar, the sail's backwinded. Trim! Trim!"

Leovar had allowed himself to become distracted. He winched the headsail in, filling it with power as a second Dalthin fixed Reg with its stare. Reg's body quaked as he met its gaze and they struggled against one another while the foremost Dalthin attempted to board.

"Ease!" demanded Ered, ignoring the distraction, insisting the sails be adjusted to meet the changing conditions.

The ketch's sails filled but the boat lacked momentum. Under the wind's pressure, her bow again pivoted out. At the stern, the first creature toppled onto its companion and Reg saw a wooden shaft protruding from its chest. He turned and saw Ai'Lorc holding a crossbow.

"Ease sails!"

It sounded as though the ketch's hull was about to burst and the crew let out the sails to fill them with air.

"Ease!" cried Ered.

Then, blessed silence as the wind across the sails created sufficient force to pull her from the dock. As she began to move, Ered released the stern line and felt the rudder take hold as the boat gained momentum. The air was coming directly across the ketch's side and Ered nosed her higher to windward, more parallel to the dock.

"Alright, gentlemen, sheet them in."

As they aligned the sails to the wind, hull speed combined with wind speed and the boat began to accelerate.

"Reg, man the port jib sheet. I will need you to take over from Leovar when we tack."

Tacking, or turning into and through the wind, would require a coordinated effort and Ered began to place his crew where he needed them.

Ai'Lorc fitted his weapon with another bolt. He raised it to aim and fired. The second Dalthin, crawling out from under his companion, collapsed as the shaft imbedded in its head. It fixed its eyes upon the archer, and Ai'Lorc's legs trembled for a moment before the eyes dimmed and the creature shuddered.

"Hard over! Helm's a'lee."

Ered had given the order to tack and he put the rudder over. As the bow slowly swung through the wind, the sails beat like storm-battered flags and the sound of these tremendous panels resonating was almost deafening. Pivoting on her rudder, the denaJadiz continued through her arc, then her sails filled again, snapping into shape with a thunderous boom and she was under power, silent once more. The ketch cleared the dock, heeled to port under the wind's driving pressure and the deck shifted. Ai'Lorc lost his footing and fell. He did not see those creatures remaining on the dock shimmer and change form.

# 7

The boat's performance pleased Ered. He looked aloft to examine the shape of the sails and they were full from top to bottom. The gurgle of water streaming past the rudder gradually amplified as the hull surged forward. His breathing had quickened and deepened and it came to him as he stood at the helm he was not afraid, but rather, exhilarated. Years of competition had taught him to love the chase.

As the denaJadiz slipped past the docks toward the end of the breakwater, the widening channel eased his concern over her increasing speed. Even with only two sails set and the hold fully laden, this boat knifed through the water and responded to the wind coming over the jetty as if she were on open seas with unimpeded air.

They had escaped cleanly, or nearly so, and from here their course should be unobstructed. Even so, something seemed amiss. His glance shifted to the breakwater as the mass of gray riprap panned past, a wall of stone keeping the ocean's moods at bay. He turned and looked to port, down the liquid aisles between the rows of boats and saw only dark, smooth, undulating green reflecting bobbing masts and hulls. The harbor seemed devoid of life.

Recognition struck.

His eyes shifted from the stretches of water to the swaying spars. When he could not find what he was looking for, he checked the boat's course, then quickly and urgently looked aloft like a hunter scouring the heavens for elusive prey. It did not take long to recognize the truth. The prey was not elusive at all; it simply was not there. The shore birds had completely vanished. This place was quiet because danger was present. The Dalthin were near and even the birds could sense it. Unshielded from Dalthin minds, they had fled.

He returned his attention to their own escape. Reg was still forward, trimming the heads'l. Pedreth was on the main. Leovar, without anyone asking, was readying the stays'l that would improve the airflow between the two sails already aloft. Ered searched for Ai'Lorc. *Voreth's horns! Where is that Easterner?*

"Leovar," Ered called, suppressing his irritation. "Secure that halyard and come aft. I need you to raise the mizzen when we tack. We can raise the stays'l after.

"Father," he called to Pedreth, "we're going to tack as soon as we hit open water. Be ready on my command."

*By Siemas!* he thought, *Even if I could find him, he would be useless.*

"Ered. I've taken care of him and I think he will be alright now."

Ered's head snapped around at the sound of Ai'Lorc's voice. He was climbing from the hatchway, smiling as he emerged.

"What did you say?" asked Ered.

"I've taken Danth below. He is still unconscious. I would like to examine him closer when there is more time, but he is sleeping peacefully and his breathing is calm and even. I've tied him to his bunk, so he doesn't fall out if we need to maneuver abruptly."

Ered was chagrined. It was not like him to prejudge anyone and he realized stress had gotten the better of him. Moments before, this man had saved them with the crossbow, and now he had looked after their comrade while the rest tended the boat.

"Is there anything else I can do?" Ai'Lorc asked.

"Keep your crossbow ready, friend. We will need it. If you will go forward and position yourself just behind Reg, he will tell you how to help when we tack."

Ai'Lorc nodded and went to Reg's side.

Ered barely had time to chide himself over his rashness, because ahead, beyond the opening in the rock wall, another craft had pulled into this channel and was making directly for them. It was a power launch, small, steam-driven and swift. In these protected waters, it would be far more capable than anything under sail. Several figures were aboard her. He could not be sure, but from their size, at least three, perhaps four on board were Dalthin. The others were probably his father's workmen.

Turbulence and lighter colored water ahead marked the passage to open sea. The ketch was nearly there. The Dalthin's boat was perhaps thrice that distance away, but she was throwing quite a bow wave and closing rapidly. The denaJadiz should beat her to the opening, but the ocean's chop would slow the ketch on first contact, allowing the power launch to narrow the gap even more. However, once both boats were at sea, he reckoned the ketch would prevail. Her design and displacement would make her completely at home on the ocean's rough waters, while the lighter craft would flounder.

On the foredeck, Reg was instructing his tutor and Ai'Lorc

responded with great animation, imitating Reg's gestures.

It was a shame, Ered thought, that Danth had been hurt. They needed him. If only he were capable, the five of them could handle the sailing and Ai'Lorc would be free to serve as marksman. As it were, every hand would have to work the sails. Short even one pair, the crew would have difficulty maneuvering the vessel quickly enough to gain an advantage.

Whatever happened, Ered knew, the only thing that mattered was the safety of his friend and lord. Whatever happened… He began to sob uncontrollably. For the first time in his life, he was uncertain of his abilities. Whatever… A deep, gnawing fear was overtaking him. *What…* The blood drained from his face and a chill ran through him. His hands on the wheel began to ache… *ever…* The wind seemed to blow right through him and fear overcame him. *What is happening?* he wondered and started to tremble. As he watched, the flesh of one hand fell away, leaving only bone and sinew clinging to the wheel. His throat opened and an involuntary scream escaped.

… … … … …

"Then, as soon as you release the headsail, I am to pull on this rope…," Ai'Lorc' offered.

"Sheet." Reg corrected his terminology. "We call the controlling lines sheets."

"I am to pull on this sheet as hard and as fast as I can."

"Exactly."

"I think I have it."

"You will do fine. When we tack, there will be a lot of commotion from the wind in the sails, but if you focus on me and follow my lead, all will go well."

"Very good… "

Ai'Lorc's voice trailed away and he stared vacantly, then collapsed and fell to the deck. In that instant, the prince felt his own body sag as if he had been struck.

Ever since the boat had slipped the first attack, the press of Dalthin malice had become manageable. Quite naturally, Reg had assumed he had mastered the assault. Now, it became painfully clear these creatures had lulled him until they could strike this concerted blow. Wave upon sickening wave of vicious intent washed over him. He reached out to shield his friends, but once again, he felt like a juggler out of control.

One by one, they collapsed all around and the deck resembled a ward for the hopelessly insane. Leovar, Ai'Lorc and Pedreth lay crumpled, their faces distorted by inner horrors. Reg clung to the headsail's sheet. It seemed his last handhold on reality. All hope was ebbing, past failures revisited him and each of his private fears became all-consuming terrors. The violence of the sea and every painful form of death that it or the Dalthin might inflict overwhelmed him. His insignificance against the immensity of his task dwarfed him. He could never succeed. It was useless.

All at once, a voice cut through the morass of despair. It was Ered. He was screaming. Unable to understand what his friend was saying, Reg struggled to clear his head. With a sudden effort, he erected a wall and the world rushed in around him.

They were in danger. The bow was swinging toward the breakwater. The power launch had halved the distance between them and Ered was howling in terror at his hand. Reg did the only thing he knew to do and imagined a wall around the helm.

"Ered!" he cried. "Ered. Hard to port!"

Shielded from the Dalthin's assault, sighing with relief as his hand became whole, Ered nonetheless remained frozen in place.

"Ered, please! Put the rudder to port."

Ered reacted instinctively and spun the wheel. As the rudder bit, the sails filled and snapped into shape. The boat swung away from the wall, wandering a bit. Then, as Ered's mind cleared, he looked up and further adjusted the ketch's course, bringing the boat into the channel's center.

While Ered regained his presence of mind, Reg surveyed his companions. The onslaught was stretching him to his limits, but he knew he and Ered could not manage the boat alone. If he could only shield one more mind, the three might manage the turn into open water. He focused on Pedreth and tried to shield him as well. The man stirred, shook his head and looked around.

"Pedreth."

"Yes, Reg," he gasped.

"We need to come up to weather quickly. Can you help on the main?"

Breathing deeply, Pedreth replied, "I can do that."

To Reg's relief, Pedreth gathered up the controlling line and positioned himself for the maneuver.

"Ered, we have to head up now," Reg prompted.

The ketch was clearing the end of the jetty. As the full force of the West Wind struck, she heeled gently in response and Reg smiled. The boat, fast as she was, was built for heavy seas and heavy air and she had reacted to this gust as to a kiss.

Ered raised his head and met Reg's eyes. He acknowledged with a nod, and in a weakened voice gave the alert. "Coming up."

He slowly turned the boat upwind, glancing tentatively at his hand. As the ketch left the harbor, Reg and Pedreth struggled to winch in the sails to match to their new course. As the denaJadiz began to heel, tilting her deck to the press of air, she met the first swell and rose to let it pass.

At that same moment, Reg felt something hiss past his head and heard a cry from behind. The power launch was nearly upon them. An archer holding a bow was standing at the forepeak with his legs braced against the pulpit railing. He shouted something, then reached toward his hip quiver for another shaft. As he did, the power launch struck the swell with such force it became air-borne for an instant. It crashed back into the sea with a shower of spray. Catapulted by the impact, the archer arced through the air, arms flailing futilely for balance or purchase. Finding neither, he plunged into the water and disappeared.

The Dalthin sent another man forward. Reg assumed he was sent to rescue his comrade until he, too, brandished a bow. Suddenly, ahead of the steamer, a head and arms broke the surface. Whether their helmsman saw him, Reg did not know, but the vessel never swerved. The swimmer disappeared beneath the hull as the power launch rode over him.

Despite the launch's lighter weight and shallow draft, the sea was doing little to slow it and it continued to close the intervening distance. However, while the ketch rose and fell with the sea's undulations, the steamer, built for the harbor's calm waters, bounced madly as it came.

The replacement archer had dropped his weapon and was clinging to the railing. He would have little luck maintaining his footing or shooting from the bouncing deck. The Dalthin sent a third man forward. Over one arm, he carried coiled lines and grappling hooks. Clearly, they intended to board. Reg knew with only himself, Pedreth and Ered as able hands, a tack or other complex maneuver would be impossible, nor could they mount a defense against a boarding party. Consequently, the best they could manage would be to hold their course until they were far enough from shore to be certain of deep water. Then, they could fall off the wind and run for it. With their pursuers closing in, however, Reg doubted their ability to hold out.

The mental press of the Dalthin left him weak with nausea. In order to protect Ered and Pedreth, he had to allow a certain amount of this concerted malice to touch him—a precarious balance of forces at best. If he kept himself entirely protected, his crew would suffer too much to function. If he allowed too much through to himself, he might lose control completely and all would be lost. Reg hung on and prayed the ocean would tip matters in their favor.

Somehow the steamer was maintaining its reckless progress. As it crashed through a wave, it drew within a boat's length. The two souls huddling at its bow were thoroughly drenched and looked forlorn and miserable. Reg wondered what private torments kept them so committed to this pursuit. No rational man, and certainly no seasoned sailor, would dare venture across these waters in such a craft. He doubted they knew whom they served, let alone the purpose of the chase.

He surveyed his own crew. Ered seemed in shock, holding on with grim resolve. Pedreth, while apparently not so shaken, brushed some imagined thing from his arm. Poor Leovar! His arms were about his knees and he had drawn them close to his chest. He sat at the foot of the mizzenmast, rocking and sobbing softly to himself. As for Ai'Lorc… Reg looked about for his tutor. He was not where he had been moments earlier. Reg cast about before spotting him. Recognition dawned and through all this, brought another smile to his lips. Somehow, without Reg's aid, his erstwhile teacher had galvanized himself into action and was making his way along the railing, crossbow in hand, toward the stern.

… … … … …

Fear struck Ai'Lorc like a blow to his middle, leaving him on his knees, shaking and crying. Yet, while his flesh seemed to come apart one moment, then swell and bloat, ready to explode in the next, he knew it was all a lie. Though sickened to the depths of his being by the sea of vile fluids and stench through which the boat seemed to sail, he knew this nightmare was only a contrivance. That the Dalthin were manipulating him so caused a far stronger emotion to well through the revulsion and horror. Ai'Lorc was furious these creatures would so dispassionately inflict such pain and terror. As he sat, immobilized and overwhelmed by it all, indignity and frustration began to override the other feelings. He located the crossbow and took it, ignoring the swarm of wriggling, biting creatures upon it. Then, after making sure he carried enough bolts, he grabbed the rail and pulled himself erect. Though trembling and weak, he made his way aft and the tears that coursed down his cheeks angered him all the more.

*I am not a toy!* he protested.

As he made his way toward the stern, the intensity of the illusion grew and his vision tunneled. With great effort, he focused on his goal and strained to hold all other thoughts at bay. Although he stumbled unseeing past Pedreth, he paused and knelt over Leovar's rocking, trembling form and placed a hand on his arm. He tried to reassure him, but his emotions welled in his throat and it was all he could do to stifle a sob. Rising again, he made his way past the helm and braced himself against the railing, freeing his hands. Placing a foot in the crossbow's stirrup, he drew back the bowstring and fitted a bolt into the groove. His knees threatened to buckle and the world began to spin. He leaned against a backstay, bracing his knees against the railing and lifted the weapon to take sight on his target. Drawing a breath, he faced his pursuers.

The small boat had nearly overtaken the ketch. As he focused on its bow, Ai'Lorc found himself looking into the eyes of two madmen. One of the pair was whirling something over head. Suddenly he threw the object and Ai'Lorc saw, almost too late, the hook. He ducked as the claw flew past and fell clattering onto the deck. As its talons dug in, Ai'Lorc returned to his task.

He might have considered either man on the forepeak his target, but he was loath to shoot anyone the Dalthin controlled. While these poor souls were probably his most immediate threat, his eyes sought only Dalthin hides. One was visible over the cabin, so he fixed his sight upon it. Slowing his breath to steady his hand, he tried to calculate what he must do. Following his target with the bow would send the bolt to where the creature had been at the time he fired. He would have to anticipate the craft's rise and fall and allow not only for its progress, but for the force of the wind. Thankfully, the wind blew steadily. Were it not for the two vessels' proximity, he would have considered his task futile, especially in view of his condition. The small, writhing creatures that hung from his hair and reached for his eyes had become minor distractions.

A second grappling hook snagged the rail to his left, yet Ai'Lorc tried to relax and get in synch with the rhythm of the sea. Almost as if to assist him, the gray slug behind the cabin drew itself upright. Ai'Lorc's finger closed on the trigger and began to flex. Then, while he watched, the creature shimmered and changed form, turning into a large bird of prey, but with such claws as he had never seen. The bird rose from the boat, took to the air and flew straight toward him. He was about to raise his bow to follow it, when intuition struck. He fixed his sights on the spot where the Dalthin had been. As the boat wallowed in a trough and wings beat the air and delirium seemed the only reality, Ai'Lorc fired.

... ... ... ... ...

Nausea fell away and clarity returned. Reg took a deep breath of clean ocean air. Then, as suddenly as it had departed, the oppression returned, but without its prior intensity. It was during that momentary respite, Reg knew Ai'Lorc's dart had met its mark. The bird had been a distraction, but because Ai'Lorc had remained focused, the bolt struck its intended target. For an instant the Dalthin reappeared, trying to assume another form, then collapsed. One mind had left the chorus and Reg found he could distinguish each of the remaining three, as one can distinguish the alto from the tenor from the bass. Of that trio, one mind stood out and its intent was clear. For the first time, Reg was able to follow that one Dalthin's thoughts as it gathered itself and prepared to act. It accumulated its energy, built upon its intensity and shaped it into a form it could use. When it was satisfied it could strike with the desired effect, the Dalthin focused on its target. As that focus narrowed, Reg understood thought could kill. The Dalthin intended to strike down Reg's tutor like a hand swatting an insect. Before it could act, Reg reacted in kind and lashed out at the thing, startled he possessed such power. The strike was clean, forceful and accurate. His remaining strength evaporated and he fell to the deck. Darkness closed in. Before he blacked out, however, he saw the launch swerve. Then, as a wave washed over the pursuers' port beam, Reg saw no more.

# 8

Grainy aromas from stacks of bread arrayed throughout the bakers' stalls filled the nose and caused the mouth to water, reminding the belly one had not yet broken fast. At other stalls, dew-flecked piles of red, yellow and green deleth fruit, chobollahs and tesberries beckoned. Still farther along, large glossy urns steamed and sang while old men brewed fragrant teas. Finally, came the butchers. Carcasses of cattle and sheep hung in shop windows and fresh cuts were displayed at the stands the herders set up each morning. It was Secondday, the upper market and the morning crowds had been shopping for nearly three hours.

Suddenly, a convoy of royal troops bore through the marketplace. Their reckless pace forced shoppers and merchants alike to duck from their path, and strewed chobollahs and deleth fruit across the cobbles. Many scrambled after the rolling spillage while others clutched horses' halters to keep the beasts from bolting.

In their wake, a cloaked and hooded figure made its way through the scrabbling crowd. The hood was drawn low and the cloak was clutched close to the breast. Had there been less confusion, such a mysterious shape might have drawn curious looks, but the crowd's attention was on restoring order, so none so much as glanced. The figure ducked into an alley between two shops and disappeared down a narrow passage, the opposite end of which opened onto meshedOstar, or tailor's street.

The figure paused as it entered the lane, looking first one way, then the other. After a pause, it turned up the street, examining the emblems emblazoned on the faded banners above the shops. Stopping at one door, it raised a hand and rapped. When no one responded, it raised it again, but before it could knock a second time, the door opened.

"Yes?" The man who peered out attempted to see beneath the cowl. "May I help you?"

"Barnath?" asked a muffled voice.

"What did you say?"

"Are you Barnath, the tailor?" the stranger demanded.

"Who wants to know?"

The figure pulled back the hood just enough to reveal the face and the man squinted to see.

"Marm? Is that you?" he asked.

She tossed back the hood.

"Ydron's walls! Marm, what has happened to you?" he asked, staring aghast at her face.

"I didn't recognize you with your beard," she said.

"You didn't recognize me? I almost don't recognize you."

Deducing from her furtive glances she did not wish to be seen, he glanced left and right, then gathered her with his arm and drew her inside.

"Please, come in," he said and closed the door behind her, bolting it shut.

Once inside, Barnath drew some thin, tattered drapes across the window.

"You'd think, as a tailor, I'd have better than these old rags," he apologized. Then, regarding her face, he asked, "Are you alright? What has happened?"

"May I sit?" she asked. "I am very tired."

"Of course," he said.

He removed several bolts of cloth from an old wooden chair, put them on a counter and set the chair beside her. Marm untied the cloak and Barnath hung it on a hook by the door. When he turned, she was struggling with some straps securing a bundle to her torso. He hurried to help and discovered this was no mere bundle, but a child.

"Borlon's eyes! What have we here? Are there no end to surprises this morning?"

Marm wobbled, weak and unsteady, so he took the child, cradling the sleeping girl in one arm. With the other, he helped Marm sit. He looked at the peaceful face of the youngster he was holding and placed her on a pile of cloth in a nearby basket, then returned to his friend.

"You rest and I will bring some water," he said.

In the next room, as he removed the lid from a large ceramic urn, all sorts of thoughts raced through his head. When a bloody woman arrives at one's doorstep with a sleeping child strapped to her back, one does not expect to embark upon a nostalgic discourse into the events of the last fifteen years. It was only his distrust of the agents of law-

and-order that kept him from running out the back door to get the authorities. Despite his misgivings, he replaced the lid, hung the ladle on its hook and returned to the front of the shop with the cup. He knelt at Marm's feet and put it to her lips.

"There, that's a good girl. Drink up. Slowly, now. Not too greedy. That's right."

She drank as he directed, and it was only when she had finished and he had set the cup aside that he asked, "Right. Now, what happened?"

Marm described how, in the early hours of morning before first light, sounds of fighting within the palace corridors had awakened her. She had quickly risen and bolted the door against intruders. Then, feeling there was no time to gather any of her possessions, save one small bag, she made her way through a passage to the princess's chamber. When she reached it, the room had already been invaded and the child had been slain.

"Then this is not Her Highness, Lith-An?"

"No." She covered her eyes. "This is Ria, the daughter of Satsah, the baker."

She explained how, in room after room, she had found only carnage. Sometimes, she hid in closets, or worse, had lain on the floor among the corpses, in their blood until the troops had passed. Finally, when she had made her way to the lower levels, she stumbled upon a room like the others—death everywhere. However, here she had heard a low rhythmic guttural sound coming from one corner. She felt her way through the bodies until the noise brought her to the little girl. Ria was sobbing and clutching the still body of her mother.

Barnath's eyes went to the sleeping form. That she came from the palace was undeniable. She was dressed in fine cloth, though not the exquisite fabric a princess might wear. Even here he had occasion to work with such material whenever a special order might be sent his way.

"Why does she still sleep?" he asked.

"I could not be sure she would remain silent if I took her with me and I could not leave her behind. So I reached into my bag, took a small pinch of the sedative I keep and placed it under her tongue. Then, when she was asleep, I strapped her to me and made my way out."

The tale would have been incredible had Barnath not known the teller. True, it had been years since he had last seen her. In those days she would sometimes make her way from the palace, and in the company of friends, visit the upper market. He had been drawn to her then and found an excuse to place himself in her path at every opportunity. Eventually, she noticed him and a romance was kindled. She found many excuses to shop outside the walls until the queen, Her Highness Duile Morged Tonopath, learned of her nursemaid's excursions. They came to an abrupt halt. Later, Marm found an opportunity to inform Barnath of the queen's decision. She had risked a great deal to tell him and he had admired her for it, though he never again saw her until today. She had changed, but he still recognized her and the memories brought a smile.

"I'm glad you managed to escape," he said.

"Barnath, I have lived within those walls for more than twenty years. There are numerous ways in and out of which even Manhathus was unaware. The troops could not have prevented my escape once I had descended far enough into the bowels of the palace. How do you think I managed to see you the last time?"

"Then, why did you never return?"

"I could not risk having my absence noticed. I cared for you very much. Please do not doubt it, but I dared not arouse Her Highness's wrath."

Barnath nodded. "One thing puzzles me. You say you awoke to the sound of fighting within the corridors, not to an assault from without. It would seem as though these invaders were already within barakYdron."

She paused. "Until now, that did not occur to me. Things transpired so quickly. But, yes, I believe you may be right. It is rumored that yesterday, at morning audience, king Manhathus was angry because several of his advisors were absent. He let it be known, and by afternoon each had arrived and His Majesty was placated. However, word also has it each advisor arrived in the company of his personal guard, as had several visiting nobles."

"Why did they admit the guard?"

"It is not unheard of for a noble to arrive so accompanied. Certainly, if one arrives directly from business abroad, he will be accompanied by a troop. Naturally, his men are given hospitality. I must say, though, I have never known so many to arrive so accompanied at one time. In fact, the commotion their arrivals caused calls it to my attention. We all thought they had hastened to respond to the king's summons in order to avoid his wrath, so they brought their men with them. Now, I am not so certain these apparently coincidental visits were not planned."

"What do you think has happened to the royal family?"

Marm stared at the ceiling in despair. "I do not think anyone was spared. Save for this girl, I know of none in the palace who survived."

"There is you, my dear." He grasped her hand tenderly. "Be grateful you are here and safe."

"I cannot stay for long. If I am found, you will not be safe either."

"Am I to lose you again after just finding you?"

"We will all be lost if you do not help me. I must leave while there is confusion."

"First, you and the child must bathe. You cannot go out again looking like this."

Marm looked down at her bloody garments.

"I have a cistern outside," said Barnath. "I think there is enough water for both of you to bathe. Then, you will need new things to wear. I have some cloaks already made I can alter. I will have to make new dresses, but I can work through the night if I must. In addition, I will see you both have something to eat. By morning you will be rested and ready. Then, you can go."

"Thank you, Barnath. I cannot begin to thank you enough. However, there is one favor more I must ask."

He gave an inquiring look.

"You must help me find someone."

"And who might that be?"

"I need to find Pithien Dur."

"Pi...," Barnath could not bring himself to utter the name.

# 9

Barnath sometimes referred to himself as a man of the cloth. This, of course, he intended as a joke. A tailor, as much as anyone, needs a sense of humor. After all, one would think work that would cramp the hands and rob the eyes of vision should pay well when all was said and done. "But, when all is done, there isn't much left to say," he would quip. Of course he had grand visions of the work he would like to create, but he needed to afford the fabric. More important, he needed someone to buy those creations. In this part of the city, such a patron was rare. Oh, there might be the occasional order "from On High," but not much more. Very little of a glamorous nature ever happened to him, except once, when he thought he had found love some fifteen years earlier.

He broke off the thought. *Here she is, and once again she is leaving.* He was angry and wanted to show it. The problem was he was a good man. The problem was, after so many years he still loved her. The problem was, he could never hurt the ones he loved. So there was no problem really. In the end, he would do whatever he must to help her.

As he examined a bunch of tesberries in a market stall, he asked himself, *Whom do I know who can take her to Pithien Dur?* That was the crazy part.

... ... ... ... ...

"Hold still, please."

Marm grabbed a slick, bare arm and tried to pour water over the wriggling girl. A short while ago, the child had awakened from the drugged slumber. Now she was irrepressible, splashing the tub's contents all over the floor.

"Oh!" Marm exclaimed, receiving a lapful. "Enough! You must do as I say."

"No, no, no!" the child protested.

"You can play as you wish when you've finished your bath. Right now, we have to play a different game."

"Q'estions game?"

"Yes. The questions game."

Marm had lied to Barnath. She could not afford for anyone to learn this child was indeed the princess. They had murdered everyone at the palace and Lith-An's life, like her brother's and Marm's, was in peril. Marm had devised a ploy to disguise the girl's identity and now all she had to do was secure the cooperation of a toddler.

*Mas'tad! I must be mad.*

"A'wight, Ma'm."

"Good. Now, what is your name?"

"Lith-An."

"No. What is your name?"

"I fo'get."

Marm rolled her eyes to the ceiling. It seemed hopeless. "Your name is Ria."

"Oh, yes. Wia." Lith-An said the name deliberately.

"What is your name?"

"My name is Wia."

"Very good. Who is your father, Ria?"

"Ma'hasus."

"No, dear one."

Marm was verging on panic. It would never work. She should have left the child. This would be her undoing. One mistake and she would be dead. She could never go to see Pithien Dur with the princess. That would be a prize he could not resist. *Calm*, she told herself. *The girl will never respond if you panic.* She gathered herself.

"Ria. Would you like a raggedy doll?"

"Yes."

"If you can remember all of the answers, I will make you a raggedy doll."

The girl's eyes lit up and she nodded emphatically.

"Very good. Now you must be Ria."

"A'wight, Ma'm."

"Who is your father?"

"Sah-sah."

"Yes. Satsah is your father. What does your father do, Ria?"

"Cook."

"And what is your name?" She held her breath.

"Wia."

Marm sighed a small sigh of relief. "Very good, Ria. Very good."

The girl smiled coyly and clasped her hands. Marm applied soap to a cloth.

"If you play so well this afternoon, you will surely have your doll. Now let us try, again."

… … … … …

"My dear, I've brought a fr…,"

Barnath stopped mid-sentence, stunned by what he saw. Perhaps upon entering, another would have noticed nothing more than a woman brushing a child's hair. The tailor, however, beheld a vision. Mahaz' golden light penetrated the shop's closed curtains enough to flood the room with a soft, warm radiance. It washed over the woman, the child and all the room's contents, imparting a surreal, almost magical coloration. Marm, after finishing her own bath, had changed into the robe Barnath had provided. Her hair fell about her shoulders in a cascade of copper curls that framed a face he would have sworn belonged to a goddess.

"Yes, Barnath?" she prompted.

"I've…" He struggled to regain presence of mind. "I have brought a friend who may be able to help."

Marm's eyes widened. "Yes?"

"Marm, this is Ganeth. He has helped me for many years. He is young and knows his way around the back alleys. He promises he knows a place where one might meet Pithien Dur."

Ganeth removed his cap. Marm nodded in his direction.

"I am honored," she said.

"The privilege is mine, my lady," he returned, keeping his eyes averted downward and his cap clasped nervously to his chest.

"I am not of noble blood, Ganeth. You need not call me your lady. Marm will do nicely, thank you."

"Thank you," he replied, a bit more at ease. "Marm. If you please…," he hesitated. "One thing bothers me."

"Yes?"

"When Barnath told me there was someone who wanted to meet Pithien Dur, I expected the worst sort of woman. Please forgive me, but you do not appear to be that kind."

"Certainly, I forgive you." Marm smiled. "In fact, I thank you for the compliment."

"Then why would someone like you… ?" He could not finish.

"Why would I wish to find someone like him?" she finished for him.

Ganeth nodded.

"I am sorry, but I cannot tell you. As incredible as this may sound, something very good may come from this meeting." To his raised eyebrows, she replied, "If helping me find him is distasteful, I will understand if you decline to do so."

"No, Marm. I never said that. If you are a friend to Barnath, then you are mine as well, and I always help my friends."

"And what have you brought with you, dear Barnath?" she asked, eyeing his bundle.

The tailor looked at the sack he was carrying and smiled. "Dinner," he said triumphantly, and held up the sack. He began to remove its contents. Stepping to the counter, he placed each item upon it for all to see. "Tesberries, bread, parm—I remembered you liked this cheese in particular—wine and," with a flourish, "a beef shank!"

"Wonderful!" she exclaimed, clapping her palms together. "We shall have a feast."

"Oh, yes," Barnath continued. "One more thing," he said, removing a small jar. "Milk for the child." He approached the girl and said, "I have fresh milk for you. Do you like milk?"

The girl nodded.

"Tell me, little one, what is your name?"

Marm almost dropped the brush when the child opened her mouth to speak.

"Wia," the girl replied.

Barnath looked up at Marm to confirm the pronunciation. "Wia?"

"Yes." She beamed. "Her name is Ria."

"And what is your dolly's name, Ria?" he asked.

"Lith-An," the princess replied, matter-of-factly.

"I hope you don't mind if I borrowed some materials to make her doll," said Marm. "It's just that she's been through so much and I promised her one."

Barnath examined the figurine. "That's quite alright, but it's just a raggedy doll. Would you like a fancy one?"

Ria shook her head and her tresses swung with each shake.

"Alright," replied Barnath. "Would Lith-An like some milk as well?"

"Yes," the girl said.

"Very well, if everyone is hungry, I shall prepare our meal." He turned to his former love. "Dearest Marm, the clothes I have made are hanging in the closet. While I busy myself, will you try them on to see how they fit?"

Marm could barely disguise her excitement and went to see what Barnath had made, feeling much better. Now, Lith-An might accompany her, but in a different persona. A slip on Ria's part would be less deadly. People might consider it a reference to the doll. She might just get away with this audacity. Maybe.

# 10

"My, Barnath! That was wonderful."

Marm dabbed at her mouth with a napkin and glanced at the child. Ria had managed to smear as much of her meal across her chin and cheeks as she had over the tabletop. She was pleased how easily Lith-An had adopted her new name.

"I'm glad," he replied. "But do you not like your clothes? Perhaps they are too loose or too tight?"

"Could you not see how she fairly twirled to show off her dress?" Ganeth said. "Of course she is pleased."

"Oh, Barnath. How careless of me. Have I not made myself clear? Of course, I love the dress. And Ria is so beautiful in hers."

"But the cloth is rougher than you're used to."

"It should be. We should not stand out."

He looked troubled.

"What is wrong, Barnath?"

"Nothing. Really."

"Your look says otherwise."

"I just wish you would tell me the real reason you are seeking Pithien Dur. He is a dangerous..."

A pounding at the front of the shop interrupted him.

"I wonder who that could be," he said.

The pounding grew louder and he rose from the table.

"I'd better see who that is." As he entered the storefront, Barnath called, "Who is it?"

"Palace guard. Open up."

"I've done nothing," he called.

"Open up."

Barnath returned to his friends.

"Marm, I am afraid. Could they have come for you?"

"It is possible," she replied, though she knew in her heart they were looking for the princess. "We must leave."

"Why would they want you?" asked Ganeth. "Does it have anything to do with why you wish to see the outlaw?"

"I'm afraid I can't say," said Marm.

"Is it not possible they are here on other business?" suggested Ganeth.

"Yes, but not very likely," Marm said. She lifted Lith-An from her chair and placed the cloak about her shoulders. "Barnath, Ganeth, hurry! We must go."

"How did they know you were here?" asked Ganeth.

"It may only be a house-to-house search," said Marm. "On the other hand, someone may have seen us. Let us go!" To Marm's consternation, the tailor made no move to follow. "Barnath! You must hurry. We are taking too long."

As in reply, the pounding grew louder. "Open at once," came the order.

"I can't leave. If I do, they will surely follow."

"If you do not, it may be your life."

"No. I belong here. If I answer the door, I can stall them, maybe send them away."

"They will not be put off easily. With this delay, they will surely suspect something."

"I am coming," Barnath shouted. Then, with a soft voice that somehow conveyed all the emotion he had yet to express, "You must listen to me. For the sake of the child you must leave at once. There is no hope for any of you if I go too. If I stay, there is just a little." He turned to Ganeth. "Please take this woman and protect her until I can join you. Take care of her and the child. Now go!"

Marm drew the cloak around herself and Ganeth moved to take her arm. She hesitated, then accepted his hand and looked to Barnath. *Please*, her eyes implored.

"Go," Barnath said, tenderly.

Ganeth ushered his charges out the back door. The pounding on the front door had now changed. No longer knocking, the soldiers were battering it open. As the three escaped into the soft light of dusk, they heard Barnath call, "I'm coming." Then, it sounded as if the door burst open.

Ganeth gathered the girl into his arms and told Marm, "Hurry. Follow me."

He dashed down the alley as fast as he could. Marm hoisted her skirts and followed. She thought she heard Barnath cry out and her heart skipped.

Ganeth did not run very far. He stopped at the rear of another shop where there were two large, clay cisterns and peered inside.

"Get in," he ordered. "It's a place to hide."

She hesitated. What would he do with the child if she complied?

"Get in," he insisted. "We can't keep running. The alley is too long. We will be seen."

She had to trust him. She hoisted herself over the edge and tumbled in after confirming it was empty. Recovering quickly, she stood, half expecting to see the two disappearing down the alley.

"Here. Take her." Ganeth handed her the girl and ordered, "Now sit."

Marm complied and barely had time to see Lith-An's face when objects showered around her. When she looked at Ganeth, he said, "Stay down. Cover yourselves with your cape." He threw more refuse into the cistern. "If they look, but are in a hurry, perhaps they won't recognize there are people inside."

Understanding, but still suspicious, Marm sat in the bottom of the cylinder. She placed the girl in her lap and covered her with scraps Ganeth had thrown in.

As he placed a lid on the jar, he whispered, "Trust me. I'll be back."

She sat with the girl in the darkness because she had no other choice. She thought she heard commotion outside and listened as the sounds faded into the distance. She sat that way for a long while, unable to see, once more alone. Even were Ganeth with them, she had only his word he could help. She had no choice but to trust—both in him and in fate. She calmed herself while the sounds of the search came and went, marveling how Lith-An, now Ria, seemed oblivious to the clamor.

# 11

Companionship and solace, these were the reasons people came to the public house on meshedRuhan. Tonight, as on most nights, its great room was packed with the workers of the city of danYdron. Joviality abounded and the laughing faces and boisterous manner of the crowd belied the hardship of their days. Almost every hand held a glass of wine or beer and the servers hurried to keep up with demand.

In one way, this night was unlike any other. Something different was in the air. The increasing numbers of soldiers in the streets gave credence to the rumor that had begun to circulate: the House of Tonopath had fallen. Word had it something undetermined, yet swift and decisive had occurred within the palace, barakYdron, in the early hours of morning. Yet, something had gone wrong and some had escaped. If this were true, the soldiers were not talking. Certainly, if there were survivors, any pretender's claim to power would be called into question. The royal house had stood for nearly two hundred fifty years, ever since the Great Conflict and The Joining in which all the neighboring lands had been brought together under one hand. The validity of the Tonopath line would outweigh all other claims. The news was almost as difficult to accept as were the rumors Lord Emeil and certain advisors were involved.

Stories came and went like zephyrs across a meadow. Newcomers to the house would bring something else and interest would mount for a while. Yet, these folk lived in a world wherein stability and predictability were hallmarks and change was the stuff of dreams. The reality was tomorrow would be the same as yesterday, and today connected the two. So it was, while these tales sparked momentary interest, curiosity was short-lived.

Above the commotion, music played. In the corner farthest from the door, a small stage had been built. Light globes hung above and around it imparting a festive look. At its foot, five musicians hunkered over their instruments, while on the platform, Jenethra, the dancer and wife of Benjin the owner, the bartender, the bouncer, moved to the frenetic beat. Her pulse throbbed in her temples and her breathing was deep and rhythmic. She had danced thus for as far back as memory could take her and she could continue till the last customer left. The press of bodies kept the room hot, so rivulets of perspiration, glistening blue in the glow of the light globes, ran down her face, arms and legs.

To the astute, it would have been evident she was not as engrossed in her dancing as might first appear, for occasionally her eyes moved from the audience to the door. Those who chose to leave their conversations long enough to watch her, however, would have been hard-pressed to catch her distraction through their drink.

It was late in the evening when she recognized the objects of her vigil and moved to the side of the platform nearest the band. As she ran her fingers through the wet strands of her hair, apparently to shake it loose, she removed an earring and dropped it over the side of the stage onto the floor near one of the musicians. Its fall did not escape his attention and he glanced up to meet her eye. When her eyes went from his to the door, he followed her lead to the trio who had entered. They were the only ones in the doorway and were casting about as if looking for someone. The musician gave Jenethra a nod, and as she continued her dance, he set aside his flute and made his way across the room to a large table in the farthest corner.

... ... ... ... ...

"Do you see him, Ganeth?"

"I'm not sure," he said. He rose onto his toes, trying to see across the crowd.

"Are you sure you even know what he looks like?"

"No, Marm, I am not," he replied impatiently. "I'm not even sure why I've brought you here. This is not the kind of place I'd choose to bring a lady, or especially a child."

Earlier, Ganeth had returned to the alley to retrieve the two from their hiding place. He had surprised himself nearly as much as he had surprised Marm, not only for being brave enough to return, but also because he had waited until the back door of Barnath's shop had opened before taking off. Fortunately, his youth also gave him speed, and the soldiers, encumbered by their armor, failed to overtake him. He had returned after darkness had fallen, hoping Marm and the girl had remained where he had left them. They had and the soldiers had abandoned the scene as well. Unfortunately, by the time they peeked into Barnath's shop, the tailor was gone and the place was in ruins. Fearing the worst, they had no choice but to continue their quest.

Now, having arrived where Ganeth had assured Marm she would find Pithien Dur, she glanced at Ria and thought, *This is not the kind of place I would have chosen, either.* Instead, she replied aloud, "Thank you, Ganeth, but I can't very well see him coming to find us, even if we knew how to tell him we are looking."

"Oh, he knows, Marm. He knows."

"What makes you so sure?"

Before he could answer, a hulk of a man pushed past them and Marm managed to pull Ria out of his way before he could step on her. As Ganeth responded to her question, she drew the child into her arms.

"My friends will have told him. It is not necessary I know him. Only that I know the right people. Whether or not he will meet with us is another thing altogether."

"It will be a shame if he doesn't. I have something very useful for him."

"But what does such a man have for you?"

She was about to reply when a rough-looking, bearded fellow halted before them. He looked each of them up and down, barely containing his laughter, and turned to Ganeth.

"Come with me," he said, then turned abruptly and started across the room.

Ganeth, visibly startled by the man, stood his ground. Marm grabbed his arm and tugged.

"Come on. I think we should follow."

"You don't even know who he is."

"Well, he seems to know who we are. Are you really expecting polite introductions? He's our man."

"And if he is not?"

"Then we will find out soon enough. Come on."

Marm's pleading came a little late. The man returned, looking irritated.

"Problem?" he asked Ganeth.

"Tell us who you are," Ganeth commanded, trying to stand a bit taller. His attempt at bravado was unconvincing, however, as he could not return the man's stare.

"I've come to fetch you," the man replied.

"That does not tell us who… "

"We will come," said Marm, stepping forward.

"Good."

Satisfied, he turned again and picked his way through the crowd. Ganeth started to protest, but Marm, with child in arms, strode after the stranger leaving him no choice but to follow. She crossed the room, shifting Ria higher onto her hip. The girl was too big to carry easily, but this was no place to let one so young walk freely. Marm had planned to leave her with Barnath, but the soldiers had put an end to that idea. This was a dangerous time and lives were at stake. To accomplish her goal, she needed to keep the welfare of both herself and the child foremost. Ultimately, however, her mission was beyond mere survival. Unless she could find Pithien Dur and persuade him to help, doubtless a great deal more than these few lives would be lost.

As for the outlaw, who was this man, she asked herself? If one were to listen to rumors, he was a rogue, a thief, and leader of a band of criminals. He had terrorized danYdron and its upper class with impunity for years and had become a hero to its poor. She reflected upon her own world's mythologies. Despite the land, despite the culture, there always seemed to be such a hero who could stand up for the helpless. She would not have been at all surprised to find it were so all over this world. In a score of other lands there might be as many such characters, all based to some extent upon a historic figure. Yet here in Ydron, he was very much alive. The question was: could he live up to the tales? If he could, it would likely be to a limited extent and Marm doubted he was a hero at all. Still, there were hints in the tales that led her to suspect something special. So, while she knew him to be dangerous, the danger he posed was nothing compared to the one this world faced. She had no choice but to meet with him.

Marm arrived where the bearded one led, to a large, round table in a corner. Two men, one with bright red hair, and a young woman sat around it. Glasses and plates littered its top and the table glowed faintly blue, suggesting someone had broken a light globe. Once exposed to the air, the microorganisms that had provided the globe's illumination would deteriorate and their light-emitting properties would disappear in four to five days. None of the three seemed concerned with this luminous piece of furniture.

"This is her," the large man said.

"She," Marm automatically corrected.

He turned an unappreciative eye and she apologized.

"Sorry." *That's two missteps*, she thought realizing the second—the apology—might be taken for a sign of weakness. *Not an auspicious beginning.*

The redhead perused her thoughtfully, examining her dress and demeanor. Slowly he smiled, and Marm began to relax.

"So this is the reason we're wasting our time?" His smile shifted to a sneer. "This small baby-sitter? Which kethna-sipping sot bribed you to bring this crown-kissing pile of manure to our table, Bedya?"

Bedya looked dumbfounded.

"Take her away!" ordered the redhead. "We have enough to do without listening to her prissy whining."

"Like filling your over-large belly with brew and smashing light globes?" Marm retorted.

"What! Do you have any idea who I am?"

"I know who you are not. You are not Pithien Dur, and that's whom I came to see."

"And what makes you so sure of that, you little puke?"

"The very fact you are sending me away. Had you not, I might have wasted my time swallowing your insults and telling you my tale. Pithien Dur, however, would have recognized at once he has never met one such as I. It is a very great shame he has chosen not to meet me, but rather sent one so revolting as you. I have endured all your repugnance I can, so I will leave you gladly." She shook her head. "This is a great loss to all."

Marm turned to find Ganeth standing in her path, frozen to the spot and blocking her exit. The girl in her arms encumbered her as well, so she could not readily depart.

"Halt," came a voice from behind.

Marm did not turn or reply, but handed Ria, who clung tightly to the raggedy doll, to Ganeth.

"Take her," she said. As he extended his hands, Marm leaned forward and whispered, "Take her away, but keep your eye on me. At the first sign of trouble, leave. If I have to, I will meet you in the upper market near the fish mongers in the morning."

He took the sleepy child, nodding vague comprehension.

"One thing more." She caught his sleeve as he turned. "Look in on Barnath. See if he returns. I can't stop thinking about him and I am afraid what may have happened."

Ganeth tried to smile, mumbled what Marm thought to be, "I will," then slipped back into the crowd.

"Do you think you can walk away so easily?"

Taking a deep breath, Marm turned and faced them. It was not the redhead who addressed her.

"You appear not to have been paying attention," Marm said to the young woman. "Your foul-mouthed companion is insisting I do just that."

"But he is not Pithien Dur," the woman said.

"You definitely have not been paying attention. I have already told you as much."

The woman smiled at the impasse. "But is not Pithien Dur the reason for your coming?"

Marm put her fists on her hips, screwed up her mouth before responding, and gathered all her patience. "Have you anything new to say?"

"I believe you are the reason Pithien Dur came here tonight," the woman replied.

"But, as you just explained, this one," Marm gestured toward the redhead, "is not…"

"No, he is not." The woman said, then paused for effect. "I am."

Marm's patience was running out. "And next your other friend is going to make the same claim, and soon you will all be Pithien Dur. I grow weary of this. Good night to you."

Responding to a gesture from the woman, Bedya barred her way.

"You were correct when you said I would not let you walk away so easily," continued the woman with a relaxed air. "You are certainly unique. I have never sensed anyone like you. And while I cannot say exactly what it is about you, I know you are not one of us."

"Of course I am not one of you. As your companion already made clear, I am a crown-kissing pile of…"

"Roman does, indeed, have a descriptive gift but, no, that is not what I meant, for I can see you are also unlike anyone in the palace, or the city or, for that matter, this entire land. In fact, I cannot say what you are, my dear, but you have my attention."

Marm paused. Until now, anything this woman said could have been gleaned from the preceding conversation. This last observation, however, struck at the greater truth Marm had only hinted at earlier. She looked into the woman's eyes, probing for what might lie behind them. The outlaw returned her gaze without sign of guile, apparently intent to hear her out. Marm was at once wary and amused. Could this delicately boned, almost beautiful young woman really be the fabled scourge of Ydron? She decided she had to call her bluff, if bluff it were, and stepped closer. Planting both hands upon the table, Marm leaned forward and fixed the woman with her eyes.

"Come close," she said in a voice barely audible above the growing clamor. When the outlaw leaned forward, Marm said, "I will tell you why I've come."

A bottle shattered against the wall behind the table. Marm turned and ducked away from the flying shards of glass. She cautiously shook her hair and then her cloak.

Commotion across the room caught her attention. A fight had broken out near the bar. She could not make out who was involved, but this eruption hardly surprised her. The vein of unease running through the city was certain to spawn more than a few altercations.

She searched for Ganeth, and after a moment spied him. He had backed away from the struggle to a place near the entrance and was holding Ria to his chest. Apparently he felt her eyes upon him, because he turned to meet her gaze. Recognition brought a smile and he gestured to indicate the girl was alright. Marm nodded comprehension.

There was a flurry of color behind him. Guards wearing the blue and orange of Lord Emeil had entered. They had probably heard the disturbance from the street and had decided to investigate. While they would not know Ganeth, the odds that one would recognize the princess were great. Marm felt the blood drain from her face. Although the room was not terribly large, it would still take too long for her to cross it. Further, if she did and a guard identified her, everything would be finished. Marm looked again to the simple stranger who had brought her here, and once more found his ready glance. Ganeth nodded his understanding. He drew his cloak over the child, and while the guards quieted the fray, he slipped behind them and out, into the night.

Her relief over Lith-An's safety rapidly gave way to a feeling of loss, but she had no time to ponder her emotions. From behind her, a hand grasped her elbow and a voice said, "We must get out of here. Come."

Marm looked back and saw the young woman. The outlaws gave her no time to think. They ushered her past the table and through a doorway she would have sworn was not there earlier. Strong hands guided her through an unlit passage and she sightlessly submitted to their lead. Then, as suddenly as she had been plunged into blackness, she found herself outside under starlight and Bedya released his grip.

Dur, Roman and the other from the table approached a canvas-covered object and pulled the tarpaulin aside to reveal a large coach. Bedya ushered Marm forward, as a fifth outlaw opened a door, tossed his jacket inside and donned the coat and hat of a chauffeur. It was then she noticed the coat of arms painted on the door as that of Lord Bogen, the ruler of Limast.

"Get in," said Dur.

Puzzled, Marm turned to her and asked, "Do you work for Bogen?"

"Marmath brain," sneered Roman. "Do you think the lord paints his own coach? Stablemen have other loyalties. They are perfectly capable of painting an emblem on anything they please."

"Last week this was Miasoth's coach," laughed the fifth outlaw, as he hastened to fire up the boiler.

"Get in," repeated Dur.

No sooner had Marm taken a seat than the rest climbed inside. Bedya and Roman drew the curtains. If number five—as she thought of the fifth one—knew his work, he would get a head of steam up and be underway in minutes.

# 12

"In the final analysis, " said Marm, "this remains. If I can escape the palace undetected when all known entrances have been commandeered, I can get you inside any time I choose. In exchange, all I require is sanctuary."

"And why would I want to get inside, my dear?" asked Dur. "I have all I need outside its walls without the risk."

"Don't be coy. If you were simply a thief, you would be content to confine yourself to living off the spoils you take. However, you are not. When you raided Lord Miasoth's mines near danBashad, you set more than forty slaves free, then left his overseers tied to the entrance gates in some rather humiliating poses." Marm smiled. "After you stopped the coach from barakDar and captured princess Vintyara, you returned her immediately after you forced her father, Lord Yued, to negotiate improved conditions for his field workers. You subsequently abducted her again when he went back on his word, and continued to hold her until he fulfilled all the terms of his agreement. You are no robber. With every act, you make political statements."

"My, my! And you think all this was my doing?"

"Who else would it be?"

"There are scores who would lift your wallet should you blink."

"Lift my wallet, yes. I do not doubt it for a minute. Still, how many would insure the diversion of entire shipments of grain or produce to the lower city so the people would not starve? These are not the acts of petty thieves."

"Why pin them on me?"

"You make it sound as though these are shameful acts. The people know their benefactor well and proclaim her name to the world."

"Her name? They think Pithien Dur is a man."

"They name Dur. It is you who claim the name."

The outlaw, cornered, tried another tack. "Suppose I might someday wish to enter barakYdron. Why shouldn't I do it on my own, without your kind assistance?"

"No one has ever penetrated those walls unassisted."

"Not ever?"

"No."

"Not even yesterday, when Manhathus was unseated?"

"He was not unseated. He was murdered."

"Are you sure?"

"On both counts," said Marm. "That he was murdered, and that the coup was aided from within."

Dur paused and clicked her tongue. Suddenly, she drew the coach's curtain aside as if some light would help. Marm was aware again of the others, Bedya, Roman and Loral, who were riding with her.

"Then it really was she who let them in. I thought so."

"Most are convinced Manhathus' ministers were responsible. You sound as though you have information to the contrary," said Marm.

"Of course, they are responsible. They and certain of the peerage commanded the troops necessary to pull him down. Without their combined might, even a bumbler such as Manhathus might still rule. But clearly it required Duile's complicity."

"For someone who has never been inside that sanctum, you seem very well informed."

"Only a little clarity of thought is required. The puzzle is not that complex."

"You could not have gleaned this from rumors. No one knows the mind of the queen. To all eyes, she was a loving wife and strong ally. One might think you are imagining."

"Am I? You tended her children. You answered to her directly. You know her as well as any in this land. You tell me. Without Duile's participation and consent, do you really think so many lords' guards could have gained entrance at once? Certainly, the king would have admitted a few as bodyguard, but bodyguard alone would not have provided sufficient force for such a move."

"You would like me to confirm that," said Marm.

"My questions are purely rhetorical. I do not require your aye or nay. Further, you intimate the queen is dead when you speak of her in the past tense. You should know she still lives."

"How can you say that? You were not there. She may have helped them gain entry, but surely they murdered her once they were inside."

"Really, my dear. You do not possess all of the information about this event," said Dur.

"What information do you possess?"

"Aside from what you have told me, some of which confirms what I only suspected, and a certain knowledge the queen lives, I know hostile forces gained access to the fortress, and before nightfall, held barakYdron as securely as I hold you now."

"Hold *me*?" Suddenly, Marm was indignant. "I have come with a gift, perhaps the greatest ever laid at your feet, and you return this courtesy with a threat?"

Dur evaded the question. "Again I ask you, why do you think I would want to enter those walls? I have all I need without."

"Your adopted name betrays your ambitions. You have taken the mark of nobility. In all this land, none but the peerage has a surname. I almost feel compelled to call you by your title, until I recall you have none."

"You are right, but I am not seeking the mark of nobility." When all she received was a skeptical look, Dur continued. "No one should be robbed of her history, nursemaid. The family name is the tool by which the nobles trace their lineage. Without a surname, common people lack this ability. Without the continuity such a history provides, they can have only a limited sense of self. The peerage possess an immeasurably greater awareness of who they are and where they come from. The commoner is trapped in the present and a limited past, knowing only his parents and grandparents.

"Further, empowerment evolves from purpose. Purpose can never begin to arise without a sense of origin. You have to know who you are before you can develop a sense of self, before you can decide where you are going. A surname provides a personal history."

"Your name provides no history. You created it. It was never given."

"You are right. For me, it is just a name. It will be more for my children and for theirs in turn. This, now, is a great gift I have to give."

"Children? How long do you think you can continue to run? How long must you hide? Is this also what you will bequeath your heirs? Until you can change your circumstance and seize your fate, what kind of life can you give your children? This is why you need what I offer.

"You are no mere thief and you care for more than just yourself, otherwise you would not have found a place in so many hearts. You are a leader of the people, not just those who accompany you each day, but all of Ydron. Until the oppression waged against you and your people ends, you cannot be content. The new forces within the palace will not be kinder to your cause. No name will ever lift their tyranny from your shoulders.

"In this, I am not mistaken. Nothing would please you more than entering barakYdron and taking for the people what is rightfully theirs. The palace will never relinquish power to its subjects, and at present, taking it is beyond your grasp. This is for me alone to provide. All I ask in return is asylum for the girl and myself."

Marm had played her hand. Despite the significance of what she offered, she was still uncertain she had really appealed to Dur. If her offer went unaccepted, she held nothing else of value. Her fate and the girl's hung on just this thread. Ai'Lorc, her only contact with her own people, was gone. Further, while she would never have been placed in so sensitive a position had she not been unusually strong, at this moment Marm was isolated. She, like her compatriot, had chosen to remain and help. However, unlike Ai'Lorc, who was among friends, Marm was utterly alone. Who knew what had become of Barnath? As for Ganeth, whom she hardly knew, he had fled with Lith-An, now Ria, to she-knew-not-where.

*You are mad*, she told herself. *Why does the plight of this backward, out-of-the way little world mean so much? You risk everything—your very life—and why?*

In her heart, she knew. One cannot live for years among people like these without growing to understand and to love them. Lith-An was like her own child. She could never have abandoned her. Even now, separated like this, she was growing increasingly anxious.

The taking of barakYdron had come unexpectedly. In an instant, all of her and Ai'Lorc's carefully laid plans had become meaningless. Still, while the event had caught her off guard, she had a few resources remaining at her disposal. All of the years spent chasing after the children had taught her more about the lesser-known passages of the fortress than even the palace security knew. When the soldiers had turned their killing hands elsewhere and she was able to make her escape, she reacted as would a mother for her child. She had felt certain Duile had been slain, so when she found the child still lived, she took her.

A strategy for survival began to form almost as soon as she had left the palace walls behind. As she made her way through the city streets and discovered her communicator was missing, she realized that with Ai'Lorc gone in search of Regilius, there remained no one who might help her. It was then the plan to find Pithien Dur evolved.

She had always been fascinated by this living legend. And while she knew such people seldom lived up to the mystique built around them, intuition told her that hope rested with this renegade, if with anyone. She needed someone who could hide them and keep them alive and safe, and she did not believe the outlaw to be a murderer.

Beyond the need for protection, her greatest concern centered upon what to do if and when Ai'Lorc returned with the prince. Their original plans postulated a kingdom united against the Dalthin. Now, with power in uncertain hands, everything had changed. In order to defeat these creatures, were that possible at all, it was essential to unite the people. Above anyone she knew, Dur was the only one who might tip the balance of power, as well as the sentiments of the masses, in the right direction, provided she were so inclined. Tonight, Marm had tried to provide some reason for such an inclination. Even so, there was no guarantee events would turn out as she hoped. Reg might return someday, but it was anyone's guess who would occupy the palace, or on what terms. She hoped she knew what she was doing and suspected no one else in her situation could say with greater certainty.

For no apparent reason, Pithien Dur came upright in her seat. Her body tensed and she cocked her head as if listening to something. She gazed into the distance, as if through the confines of the carriage. Her nostrils flared and her chest swelled with every breath. Bedya, Loral and Roman, who had seemed to be dozing, were at once alert and watching her.

After nearly a minute, Dur's face became animated and the look of rapt attention shifted to one of horror, then to panic, then to anger. Then, just as suddenly, she was with them again.

She threw the window open and shouted to driver, "Justan! To pelMusha! As fast as you can!"

Roman's jaw dropped, as the coach lurched forward. "Your mother's house?"

Dur turned, and in a voice that showed how desperately she was struggling to contain her emotions, replied, "They're killing everyone."

# 13

Dur's temples reverberated, refusing to stop. The heart in her chest—a madman pounding his fists to get out—threatened to make her sick. The vision that possessed her enveloped her with sights and sounds she would never have contrived on her own. She could have drawn comfort, she thought, were she going insane, but over the years she had learned these visions were rooted in reality. Bound by the nightmare and shackled by terror, Pithien Dur could only cling to her seat while the coach lurched and hissed through the night. Alone in her hell, the torture enveloped her. Perspiration ran from every pore. But though she wanted to cry, her eyes burned dry in their sockets and no sound emerged from her throat.

The coach hurtled around a corner and threatened to overturn. Miraculously, it held the road and raced onward, its passengers gripping whatever they could to keep their seats. Yet for Dur, the journey was a crawl through the darkness.

The sound of the tires changed and the chug of the engine slowed as the coach parted from the cobbles of the better roads. Now, it pitched and lurched wildly while the wheels bounded over bare earth scarred with ruts and potholes. Despite the reduced speed, it was clear Justan was pushing as fast as he dared and the coach seemed ready to come apart from the shaking.

As they neared their destination, the bombardment of images shook Dur as violently as had the ride. Her world had always been awash with images, seldom with words, more often with emotions, always with pictures. Like street noise, however, these images usually faded into the background, and she could live, move and think, largely unaware of their presence. Whenever she did focus upon a single, alien thought, she found it could be isolated and identified as easily as a puppy's whine. At other times, something particularly loud, something concentrated, might catch her off guard and grab her attention. It was only when someone directed their thoughts at her that she found it impossible to turn off the images. The mental cries of anguish now washing over her pled for her to come, to help and to save them. Her people, who by now thought of Pithien Dur as almost divine, beseeched her. She saw through their eyes the atrocities they were suffering. She did not have to endure the actual pain, or that alone might have killed her, but their indignities and horrors were hers nonetheless. She began to crumble and wondered how long the ordeal would continue. Then, quite abruptly, the visions changed. She looked about and said to her companions, "We're too late. The soldiers are leaving."

"But we're nearly there," Bedya protested.

"They sense our arrival and know they are outnumbered."

"Outnumbered!" blurted Marm. "How can that be? How many are we? I count but six. How many soldiers are there?"

"Twenty," Dur replied, her head still bent.

"I do not understand." Marm was baffled. "How can we pose any kind of threat?"

"I have summoned others," Dur stated matter-of-factly.

Marm looked to the other three and Roman replied, "She has called them," as if that simple statement should suffice.

… … … … …

Suddenly, Marm understood and sat back in her seat. This confirmed her suspicions. Dur was a telepath. It was that simple and it was partially upon this suspicion that Marm had approached her. It was the reason for Dur's success. It was the reason she repeatedly eluded capture. It was the reason she had sized Marm up so quickly in the public house. But while Marm had suspected Dur could read thoughts, it was now clear she could also communicate with them and was clairvoyant as well. Marm and Ai'Lorc had considered the possibility. The nervous system of this race was right enough, but until now the prospect had been nothing more than speculation, a theory with some anecdotal evidence. Nonetheless, suspicion was one thing. Having confirmation dropped right in her lap was quite another. Marm closed her eyes and allowed the ramifications of this revelation to sink in.

The coach braked to a halt and Dur and her companions climbed out. For a moment, Marm remained behind, enmeshed in thought, peering from the cab.

At first, she thought it was dawn, so golden was the sky through the coach's window. Then she realized only minutes had passed since they had left the public house. At the latest, it could only be a little past midnight. Then it struck her. Buildings were aflame. She had grown so accustomed to the soft blue of the ever-present light globes in the upper city that the sharp bright glow of fire, coupled with the ubiquitous torch and lamp light of the lower city, caught her off guard. When she emerged from the cab and stepped into the road, the bracing cold of the night brought her suddenly awake. The West Wind delved beneath her garments, chilling wherever it reached. Marm pulled the hood over her head, drew her cloak closer and tried to constrain its flapping.

She struggled with her emotions. Although she knew she was stepping into a terrible scene, she felt an eerie sense of triumph. She had confirmed her suspicions about the rebel leader. *Dur had known*, she thought. *She had known what was happening here in advance.* As soon as she could, Marm would confront her, but before she could tuck the thought away, she rejoiced. *I was right!*

She made her way across the uneven surface of the road toward the fire. Golden light filled the windows of the houses and shadows danced. Two coaches bounded down the road and narrowly missed her as they braked to a halt. Their doors flew open and several men leapt out, swords drawn. She shook herself from her reverie. If she were not careful, the arriving vehicles would strike her down. Three more bore down upon her and she dashed out of the street to safety. Dur's friends were arriving.

Shouts caught her attention. She could make out figures carrying bundles from the homes into the streets. As she approached, flames erupted from one of the nearer houses, illuminating the scene while the wind carried sparks and embers to adjacent rooftops. Soon, this entire part of the city would be an inferno. It was already beyond control and none were foolish enough to carry buckets. There were more important matters. These folk weren't carrying possessions from their homes, but rather the bodies of friends or family. She thought she spotted Dur just ahead and hurried to catch up. When she arrived, she found a cloaked figure, obviously distraught, crouched and cradling the head of one of the victims.

"Dur!" Marm exclaimed. "I am so sorry. Was… was she your mother?"

The person did not respond and Marm began to ask again, when she felt a hand on her shoulder.

"No. She was Roman's."

Marm whirled at the touch and came eye-to-eye with the rebel leader.

"Many still believe he is Pithien Dur," she said, gesturing toward the redhead.

"I don't understand. How would the soldiers know to come here?"

"They were brought," Dur replied, offering nothing more.
"Bedya!" she cried. "How goes it?"

Bedya, out of breath, arrived at his leader's side. Although he towered over the woman, his bearing was deferential.

"Loral, Mikah and their men are searching above and below here. They told me to tell you they have not found anyone yet. Should I tell them to continue?"

"They won't find anyone, but it is better to be safe. Can you send someone in your place?"

Bedya nodded, indicating a person nearby. "One of Mikah's men."

"Perfect. Have him tell Mikah to order his people to continue until they confirm it is safe, then I want him to gather the families and take them to Limast. That should be far enough away to provide safe haven, and the road there is good enough the journey won't be too hard on the sick or elderly.

"As for Roman, leave him to his grief. He can assist us later. I want him to depart with us in the morning, but give him time to say good-bye."

He turned to go.

"Bedya." She stopped him.

"Yes, Pithien."

"We cannot take the dead and we can't risk smoke from funeral pyres." She gestured toward the burning houses. "Tell everyone these homes must be our pyres in this deadly hour. Offer your prayers here, then care for the living."

The burly fellow paused a moment to consider the extraordinary request, then nodded. "Consider it done."

Marm had been waiting somewhat impatiently for Dur to finish her instructions, but could no longer contain her curiosity.

"Who brought them?"

"What?" Dur turned, caught off-guard.

"You said the soldiers were brought. Who brought them? And who warned them we were coming?"

"You wouldn't understand."

"Have you a traitor in your midst?"

"No."

"Who, then?"

"It would be meaningless to you," Dur insisted.

"I might surprise you."

"Believe me, nursemaid. Neither you, nor anyone in the palace would understand if I said it was the work of shape-shifters." She turned sharply and marched off.

Marm, equally surprised, felt a single word roll off her tongue, no more than a whisper, "Dalthin!"

Too far from Marm to have heard, the outlaw halted abruptly.

… … … … …

Dur turned and appraised the stranger. Here was a mind she could not unravel. While she sensed no threat, its feeling was odd in a way she could not define. This mind held secrets. More important, this woman knew one thing known to no other.

"You know their name!"

# 14

Delicate needlework hung from the walls. The fragrance of morrasa blossoms filled the room and mingled with the soothing muskiness of brewing mure tea. Stoves warmed the kitchen and the fireplace crackled and snapped in the main room of the house. Dur had taken Marm to pelBenjin, the home of Benjin and Jenethra, not the robbers' den Marm had expected. In fact, if there were such a place, this was not it. In the kitchen, the couple were preparing a meal to ready their friends for flight. It would be simple, nourishing and would keep for the journey ahead. In the main room, the outlaw sat motionless, head bowed, fingers buried in her hair. After a while, she looked up and reappraised the woman seated opposite her.

"Nursemaid, you astound me."

Marm had been awake for the entire night and was on the verge of nodding off. The voice startled her and her head snapped upright.

"What…?" she managed.

"I said you astound me. For so many years, I have puzzled over these things, half suspecting the truth. Then, last night you confirmed all my suspicions with a single word as your mind held a picture of their form."

With an effort, Marm pulled herself up from cushions. She looked incredulously at Dur and said, "I astound you? You see the slaughter at pelMusha while half a city away. You, out of all in this world, are aware of the Dalthin. You read my mind and you dare to say I astound you? Darmaht protect me!"

"I cannot read your mind, nursemaid."

"Come now. Do you take me for a complete idiot? These have not been lucky guesses."

"I can make out certain things about you, it is true, but there are parts of you I cannot reach."

"You cannot examine me as we sit here knee-to-knee? Really, Dur, do you expect me to believe that?"

The outlaw paused a moment, then explained. "I see many things with clarity. I can look, as you say, half a city away and I can see much within another's thoughts, but your mind poses a problem. I can make out only… how should I put it? During the feast of Samsted, children float tesberries in mathry punch. Only a small portion of the fruit shows above the surface of the drink. Most is submerged beneath the dark liquid. Your thoughts are like those tesberries. Much is hidden. You are not like any I have ever met."

Marm peered into Dur's eyes, unable to see any sign of deception. If the rebel leader spoke the truth, then it was possible… She caught herself and dropped any thought of her hopes, lest any image of Ria/Lith-An surface.

"What astounds me," Dur continued, "is what you have been saying about worlds beyond our own. I have always known in my heart that the shape-shifters… " She corrected herself. "The Dalthin do not belong here, and I have sensed they are… " She paused, as if struggling to find the word, then shook her head. "Wrong, somehow. I have never been able to say why."

"Wouldn't you have known that when you read their minds?"

"I do not read minds. At least not in the way you think. I do not experience your thoughts as you do. If I saw the world from your perspective, I do not think I could keep my own self separate, and I only speak to a meeting of two minds. In a group or a throng, I would lose myself completely and I would surely go mad. So, perhaps to protect myself, I only see pictures. Even then, they appear as vignettes. Other times I experience emotions. Occasionally there are words, but they must be deliberately directed at me, and that does not happen often. Also, I sense honesty better than most."

Marm recalled what she had seen of this woman only hours ago in the cab. She wondered whether this alleged detachment from the thoughts of others was protection enough. Dur had not appeared to have merely sensed emotions, but clearly had been overwhelmed, perhaps because they came from so many. While Marm could not say what this woman had experienced, it was clear she had been no mere onlooker. She chose not to point out the apparent contradiction and instead replied, "Then you know I am not lying and come to you with honorable intentions."

"I said I sense honesty better than most, but not perfectly. Much of what you are saying is true. I also know there are some things you are deliberately withholding, and that is what bothers me."

"Then, you still hold my offer suspect."

"You bring enticing gifts, but many lives depend upon whether I choose to take you up on it. You already know far more than I would like you to. Therefore, my only real problem is what to do with you should I decide to decline." She smiled an odd smile.

Marm wondered what Dur meant by that, but changed the subject. "Don't the Dalthin pose a threat to you? I don't see how they could let you survive, knowing what you do about them."

The smile disappeared. "Some time ago, several Dalthin made a concerted effort to find me. A number of my followers were hurt or lost. Then we learned they could effectively focus their attention on only a few at a time. One or two Dalthin might control a handful of us. Eventually, however, we found when enough of us come upon them, they are unable to maintain the upper hand. They need to relinquish control over some in order to stop others. With this strategy we are able to overpower and destroy them. Because we are so many and they are so few, the loss of one of theirs means more to them than a similar loss to us. Consequently, they have chosen not to confront us directly.

"Their existence, though, has puzzled me greatly. Until you explained their purpose, I was unable to explain certain happenings."

"Such as?"

"Occasionally a man or woman disappears from the lower city. Some believe they have gone to the mines. I have always believed the Dalthin took them. Before you told me why they are here and what kind of creatures they are, I could only speculate to what end." Dur clenched her fists and her jaw as she held back her anger. "Now, when I think what an awful fate my friends and neighbors must have met..." She brought a fist down upon the table.

"Tell me," said Marm, "what was tonight's raid about? Did twenty Dalthin really come together just for you?"

"Those were twenty of the king's soldiers the Dalthin had manipulated and sent. I think they were trying to bait me."

"So, it was a new development?"

"These days are full of new developments. You are a new development."

Marm nodded. "As you are to me."

Before Dur could respond, a sharp rapping at the door brought the outlaw to attention. She counted the cadence of the knock, then just as suddenly, she relaxed.

"That's Loral's knock. Would you let him in, Benjin?"

The publican left Jenethra's side and went to the doorway. He had barely thrown the bolt and released the latch when Loral pushed through and rushed past. Once inside, he tossed back his hood, located Dur, and strode to where she sat. She rose to greet him. They clasped hands in a flickering display of affection, then she drew him down so they could sit as they talked while the others gathered closer to hear.

"What did you learn in the marketplace?" asked Dur.

"It is not easy to move about there. Soldiers are everywhere, questioning everyone."

"Asking what?"

"They want to know if anyone has seen any aristocrats or royal familiars in the market of late. An odd question, I thought. But then I was told certain of them have inquired about a woman and a child."

Dur raised her brows and glanced at Marm.

"Did you learn whose flag these soldiers are serving?" asked Dur.

"Several colors are flying today. The blue and orange of Emeil and the purple of Lord Asch were most visible, but we also spotted the colors and insignia of Lords Kareth and Danai."

"I understand the involvement of Asch, Kareth and Danai," said Dur. "They have always been at odds with the House of Tonopath. Manhathus had reduced their holdings over the years and a coup would have served them well. What I cannot understand is Emeil's involvement. In all the land, he has the fewest enemies and had no grudge against Manhathus. Of anyone, he is probably the only peer the king respected."

"Emeil is a good man and his greatest concern is the well-being of his charges," Benjin volunteered. "I suspect he feels had Manhathus exerted a stronger hand, much of what is wrong today would be different."

"So you think Emeil is in it merely to right some wrongs?" asked Dur.

"With due respect," Marm said to her hosts, "Manhathus' indifference was only part of the problem. His house has been in power so long he took his rule for granted. The distance he kept from his people prevented him from understanding their plight. The malaise that affects the land is so deep and pervasive only a fundamental change could help. Perhaps Emeil felt this was the only way change could take place. There was almost no room for such a possibility within the law. I am only disappointed it came as it did."

"What do you mean?" Benjin asked.

"I would have hoped the people would have risen up. A coup only opens the door to more of the same."

"And the people still may rise," returned Dur. "But, had they done so at the outset, many lives might have been lost. The palace is a fortress."

"I would remind you it need not remain impenetrable."

Dur did not reply, but looked Marm squarely in the eyes as if to say, "I am considering it."

Loral continued. "The squads are working hard to put the fear of Siemas into the citizenry. They are becoming brutal, dealing harshly with those who don't cooperate. Most times, they simply take them away."

Jenethra came from the kitchen and offered Loral a bowl. "Please take this. You must be hungry."

He accepted the steaming bowl of stew with a smile.

"Did you see Ganeth while you were there?" Jenethra asked.

Startled, Marm sat up. "How do you know Ganeth?"

"Silly girl!" The dancer smiled. "Who do you think helped him arrange this meeting?"

Benjin laughed and added, "Not likely anyone from meshedOstar could call up Pithien Dur just like that!" He snapped his fingers.

Loral paused as he swallowed. "No, I did not see him, but I met one in the upper market who seemed to know him. She had left word with some of the merchants to keep an eye out for his friends. When she learned I was on an errand for Pithien Dur and was making inquiries about a man and a girl, she sought me out. She gave me this as a token by which to trust her."

Loral produced a small, red cord.

"From Ria's dress," gasped Marm.

Loral handed the tiny rope to her. She took it and examined the clever knots Barnath had placed at either end.

"She said Ganeth and the girl have left the city."

"Left the city!" Marm gasped.

"Yes," Loral said. "He was afraid he could not keep the girl safe here for long. He is probably right. We were nearly apprehended ourselves."

"Where have they gone?"

"She could not say," said Loral. "Ganeth only said he would be with friends in the countryside. He told her he would try to send word when it became safe to do so."

Marm felt lost. In three days, her world had changed from a wondrous place to a deep black hole. "Then, that may be never."

Dur placed a hand on hers. "We will help you find them."

Marm looked at Loral. "Did she have any word of one called Barnath?"

"No." When he saw her expression darken, he added, "I am sorry. She spoke of no one else, and I did not know to ask."

"His shop is on meshedOstar and I am afraid he has been killed."

She could no longer control her emotions. The horror of the past few days combined with these new losses were too much to bear. Her composure crumbled and she broke into sobs.

Perhaps Dur finally sensed the woman beside her was no enemy. "Don't worry," she said. "You may stay with us, my puzzling ally. We will help you find your friends."

Although Marm did not show any sign she heard, Dur repeatedly paused to reassure her with a touch or a word while she put together a plan for the days ahead. Anguish eventually yielded to sleep and Marm slipped away, growing quiet and still.

As for Dur, she found it difficult to focus on her task. A bright new source of thoughts had recently come to her attention. She had never touched another mind like it. While most minds intruded gently and the Dalthins' pricked, this new mind fairly sang. When, early the previous day, the ketch slipped away and out to sea, taking with it this new radiance, she did not know whether to be glad or sorry. Although another of the House of Tonopath was gone, he was someone with whom she felt an odd kinship and his departure left her empty.

# 15

Something warm and liquid passed his lips, helping to separate his tongue from the roof of his mouth. The Dalthin, sails and soldiers filling his dreams receded. Another sip and Reg opened his eyes to the smiling countenance of…

"Leovar," he whispered.

"How do you feel?"

Reg considered the question as he struggled to sit. He grabbed his ribs, then his forehead and winced. He felt a bandage.

"You fell," Leovar explained. "I placed a poultice to reduce the swelling. I will remove it in a day or two to see how you are healing."

"I hurt all over," he grimaced.

"You fell hard."

"The Dalthin. Where are the Dalthin?"

"At the bottom of the sea," Leovar answered and fed him another spoonful of soup. "You and Ai'Lorc finished them."

"How is he?"

"The Easterner? He is fine."

"I wish everyone would stop calling him that. He is our friend and without him I do not think we could have survived. He deserves better."

"I am sorry. It is a thoughtless habit. Nevertheless, I shall think before I open my mouth."

"Please ask the others to do the same."

"I will." Leovar smiled again and spooned more soup into Reg's mouth. "You need to finish this."

Reg swung his legs over the edge of the berth and took the bowl and spoon.

"I can manage."

"Good," Leovar replied with a smile. "I am tired of playing nurse."

"How long has it been?"

"Today is Thirdday. You've been unconscious all of yesterday and part of today and caused us no little concern. If you feel up to it, would you come topside once you've eaten? The rest would like to see you."

"How is everyone?"

"As well as can be expected. I am still shaken."

Reg noticed someone in the neighboring berth. "Leovar," he said, gesturing toward the figure.

Leovar turned. The deck shifted and he steadied himself with a hand on an upper berth. Seeing where Reg was looking, he inclined his head toward the motionless form and said, "Danth. He has been like that—no real sign of life, except his breathing. It has even been hard getting nourishment into him."

As Reg's eyes adjusted, he could see Danth was lying on his side, eyes open, knees drawn to his chest and he appeared to be shivering.

"Is he ill?"

"There is no fever, but he trembles uncontrollably. He does not move. And while he does not respond to touch or voice, he never seems to sleep." Leovar shook his head. "No one knows what to do for him."

Reg set the bowl aside and crossed to the other bunk. "I will sit with him. Perhaps I can help."

"I think it would be better if you ate and rested. There is not much you can do before landfall. We have tried everything."

"Has he improved at all?"

"No, but neither has he worsened. Come topsides. Drink your soup and join us. The fresh air will do you good. Until we can find a doctor, Danth will be fine where he is."

"All the same, I want to try something." When Leovar did not move, Reg said, "Don't worry. I will come up soon, but I think I may be able to help him."

"As you wish," said Leovar, and he turned and climbed the companionway stairs.

Reg regarded Danth. His mouth was swollen and his lips were scabbed over, discolored with a yellow powder Reg suspected to be one of Leovar's preparations. By the light from the portholes, Reg could make out stitches holding the gash together. He smiled. Apparently, there was already a doctor aboard.

He placed a hand on Danth's forehead. There was no fever, but his skin was moist, his pupils were dilated and his breathing irregular and shallow. As Reg peered into his eyes, he grew transfixed and his breathing began to mimic his friend's. Perspiration rose upon his brow, scalp and the nape of his neck. His vision tunneled until all he could see were the two glossy doorways to Danth's soul. Then he saw deeper.

The writhing wounds in his belly opened, rehealed, then reopened anew, exposing then concealing orange gashes of exposed gut. No scar remained to show where one wound closed—nothing to indicate where the next would reveal itself. He tried open his mouth, but found in its place a cluster of wriggling tentacles dripping fluid, their wet forms colliding. He tried to walk but could not feel his legs. He looked down to see a gray undulating mass. He could not scream. He could not cry. He could neither escape, nor undo this horror. He could not, he could not, he could not, we could not, we could not, we could not... We?

*Danth.*

*Who is it?*

*It's alright. I am here. Everything will be alright.*

*Reg?*

*Yes.*

*Where are you?*

*I am here.*

*I can't see you.*

*I know, but I am here. You can feel me, can't you?*

*Yes, but I wish I could see you.*

*You will in a while. When these things are gone, you will see me.*

*They won't go away. I have tried to make them disappear, but I can't.*

*We will make them disappear together.*

*Wait! How can I be talking? I have no mouth.*

*You do have a mouth. And arms and legs. You just can't find them. I am going to help you find them, and then this will be over.*

*Where are you, Reg? I'm so scared.*

*I am closer than I ever have been. I am in your thoughts.*

*Reg?*

*Yes*

*I'm sorry.*

*For what? This is not your fault.*

*But I'm not like this. I'm not,* Danth hesitated, *so weak.*

*We are all weak. And we are all strong. You are hurt and frightened and so should you be. You are not equipped to handle this. The ones who did this to you know how to tamper with minds and play upon fears. Although you have no way to deal with this, you have not crumbled. I am going to try to put an end to this nightmare. I want you to help by focusing on my presence. I need you to hold on and not let go. Do not drift. I will not be able to talk to you for some time because I am going to be very busy. I am going to be learning how this was done so I can undo these things.*

*Reg.*

*Yes, Danth.*

*You have never done this before, have you?*

*You know, as each day passes, the abilities I have acquired seem increasingly natural. It is as if this is the way things are supposed be. I don't yet know how I am going to accomplish this, but I am confident I can.*

*I can feel it.*

*Good. You are already growing comfortable with this joining of minds. You don't know, any better than I, how we are doing this, yet you can feel the rightness of it.*

*You're right. I trust you, Reg. Do what you must. I can hold on, now that you are here.*

*I will be here if you need me. Don't think I have gone if you don't hear from me. If you panic, call me. I am going to work now.*

*Alright, Reg. I will be fine.*

With that, the heir to the House of Tonopath set about his new task as healer. At first, he began to explore this new ground, learning what he could about these images and how they came to be. Then, he reached out to grasp one with his mind and found discarding it to be as easy as picking up a piece of paper, crumpling and tossing it away. Once removed, the illusion simply vanished. First a smell, next some tentacles, one by one, he erased each element. He was puzzled by the ease with which he could undo the Dalthin's work. Perhaps it was because they had never dealt with someone who could play their game, he decided. At any rate, this part was easy. When he was done with this, he would have to study Danth to learn whether or not there was any scarring. If so, he would have to tread carefully. Nonetheless, these phantoms were easy enough to handle. Danth's mental health would require much more care.

Lost in his work, he found a satisfaction he had never known and this cerebral laying on of hands seemed appropriate. He did not doubt his ability. One does not question how well one can breathe. The less he tried, the easier the task became.

Ai'Lorc had told him once about a system of beliefs taught in the province No'eth called the Katan. It taught achievement without effort.

One did not progress by struggling to succeed or master the work. One succeeded by becoming the work. The Dalthin had created illusions to frighten Danth, so Reg became Danth. Once he understood the pain, he was able to remove it. While there was much to do, the task was not impossible.

# 16

Reg climbed from the companionway and sat on the coaming near his tutor. He faced into the wind, closed his eyes and filled his nostrils with the sea's clean, briny fragrance. He sat like that for several minutes, savoring its sound and its smell, finding the wind especially refreshing after the closeness below decks.

"I see you have learned a little since we set sail," he finally said to his tutor.

Ai'Lorc adjusted the wheel, his hands moving in rhythm to the rise and fall of the swells. "And I see you have decided to join us," he chided.

"Danth is terribly hurt," said Reg.

"I know."

"What concerns me is how deeply."

Reg reached out with his mind and examined each of his comrades.

"The Dalthin have hurt you all to some extent, but I do not sense the intense scarring Danth has suffered."

"Leovar said you were tending to him," said Ai'Lorc.

"As well as I could. I have been removing the images that bind him, but the real substance of him, the part that makes Danth who he is, has been injured profoundly. He used to have a fundamental courage I once considered bravado. Then, just before the Dalthin struck him down, I got a very good look at him. He had a genuinely admirable quality I can no longer find. It is as if he has known real fear for the first time and cannot rally himself against it. I do not know whether I can restore him."

"It sounds as if you have done a great deal for him already. You have certainly accomplished more than any of us could. You should feel good about yourself."

"I feel I should do more."

"Your Highness, you have been given a profound gift," Ai'Lorc said. "However, the gift is still new. Perhaps in time you will learn to do more. Until then, you should not reprimand yourself for failing to do the impossible. After all," he smiled, "nothing can be considered possible until it has been done successfully at least once."

"How do you feel?" asked Ered.

"I am fine," Reg replied. "I am still weak, but other than that, I am alright."

"We have all been concerned since we put you and Lord Kanagh into your bunks," Pedreth said. "We saw little change in either of you and were not a little frightened. Lord Hol has many remedies at his disposal, but he is hardly a real doctor." He glanced at Leovar and said, "I am sorry, my Lord. I mean no offense."

"There is no offense to give. I am not a doctor. Those few cures I have are only for hunting injuries. Don't feel you need to be delicate. And please, my name is Leovar. I would be honored if you called me by my name. We are all in the same boat now—quite literally—and there should be no grounds for offense among us. Station is meaningless here."

"Leovar is right," agreed Reg. "We will soon be coming to strange lands where we will not know friend from foe. We may need to dispense with our old identities and assume new ones. I think it is the best if we set aside title and station at once. A seagoing vessel requires order of a different nature. I have often served as your crewman with no grudge. Now, we must travel as equals or we may perish."

"It should still be you who leads us," insisted Ered.

"I will lead when we make landfall, but Pedreth is ship's captain. He has far more experience and we will all be safer if we entrust ourselves to his judgment. In any case, I will not lead as prince with you as my subjects."

Leovar stepped in. "I appreciate the need to dispense with titles, Reg. It will undoubtedly help us function better as a team, but you should not be so eager to set aside house and line. The kingdom has its problems, but it is still the focus of our efforts and the reason for our eventual return. You are still our prince."

"We certainly hope to return and restore order," said Reg. "However, I am not so sure I am the one to succeed my father. I have begun to see things differently. Further, my people have lived under unjust conditions so long, I am afraid I may not retake the throne unless I force myself upon them. Power flows from the people. It can be wrested from them, but that kind of power can be toppled. It is why we have any hope of returning."

"Reg," Pedreth interrupted, "I say we should find new lives for ourselves in a safe haven. I do not know if I am suited to play warrior. Certainly, I could don armor and shield and follow you home, but younger eyes and faster hands would cut me down before I get within ten miles of the city. Understand I will follow you if you command me to. I am no coward and would die for you."

"I have already witnessed your courage," Reg assured.

"Still, I have enough wisdom to know my limits," the boatkeeper concluded. "Good intentions alone will not unseat your mother. Have you given any thought to how you will accomplish it?"

"Although I was taught to give orders, no one taught me how to command my people's loyalty. I suspect no one else in the palace knows either."

He turned to the others. "I shall not be staying on those islands to which we're headed. I would only be in hiding. I have a new destination in mind better suited to my purpose. Since we have set our course northwards, once we make landfall I shall make for the province of No'eth. At its heart lies a monastery of the Katan where I hope to learn that lesson."

Pedreth appeared skeptical. "Do you believe monks who hide from the world can teach you how to live in the world?"

"How many times," countered Ered, "have you told us that wisdom can come from the unlikeliest of sources?"

"Perhaps, but I do not trust mystics."

"If I were you, I would look to those who could arm us and provide soldiers," offered Leovar.

"Mercenaries." Reg mouthed the word with distaste. "No better than the ones who helped my mother. I would last as long as she will and my people would be no better off."

Ai'Lorc put his free hand on Reg's shoulder and inquired, "Do you really want to return as your mother's foe? I should think you would find that too painful to bear."

"I appreciate your concern, but I suspect she will be removed long before I come home. My father's ministers have thirsted for power too long to relinquish any portion of it. When they reach for the throne, if they do not kill Mother outright, they will imprison her. Then, over time, they will kill each other until only one remains."

Ered shook his head, "I still don't understand Emeil's roll." He paused, then said, "There is one thing I will say for certain. You will not journey to No'eth alone."

"No?"

"I will go with you. The road will be too dangerous to travel alone."

"I would rather take that risk without endangering you."

"I disagree," said Leovar. "It makes little sense for us to have traveled with you this far, only to remain huddled on some scrap of an island. Ered is right. We departed Ydron as a company of six and we will travel to No'eth the same way."

There were nods all around.

Reg considered it a moment, then relented. "Very well. We go to No'eth together."

As they sailed, Reg fell to the task of examining his friends and removing whatever evils the Dalthin had planted. He would need a strong, courageous company and they could not help him if their judgments were clouded. Tending to his friends also eased the loss of his father and anguish over what his mother had done. It alleviated the guilt he had done nothing to stop her and had fled as his world was collapsing. He missed his mother as well as his father. When she committed that terrible act, any illusions he harbored died as well. The loss was as real and as painful as if she had actually perished. He was twice orphaned and it cut him to his soul.

For now, the only tool he possessed to help him cope was his new vocation as healer, so he worked. The warmth of the suns and the rhythm of the craft soothed them all. They would not have another respite like this any time soon.

# 17

As tiny Diamath trod among the stars, a patient observer could discern the moon's progress. Slowly, the luminous orb would pass between two bright points, then overtake and devour one. Its speed took it from horizon to horizon in less than a night. On some nights it would begin its trek setting in the west, only to rise in the eastern sky two or three hours before dawn's first light. It was the only palpable measure of time once the suns had set.

The lights of a distant city were passing to starboard. Ered suspected it was barakEm, the fortress guarding Limast's northern coast. He checked the compass heading. Its pale blue glow, like that of a tiny light globe, was bright enough to reveal its needle without compromising a helmsman's night vision. If he had measured the ketch's progress accurately, they would soon be off the coast of No'eth and would sight the islands that were their original destination by morning.

As night wore on, he became aware of certain changes. Little by little the hiss of water against the hull grew louder and the deck tilted farther under the force of a growing wind. The wake unrolled pink and luminous, lit by the phosphor of billions of haz, relatives of the blue microorganisms used in the light globes. The rise and fall of the denaJadiz increased until she began to pound through the swells and spray blew across her bow. The shrouds sang and the sailcloth boomed as the wind shifted.

A thin, blue shaft of light appeared at the gangway, then widened as the hatch opened and a figure emerged.

"Need a hand?"

"Storm coming in, father. It will be upon us soon. Can you call the others? We ought to reef the sails."

"How close, do you think?"

Ered looked up. Celestial tongues licked at the moon. As he watched, the clouds devoured Diamath, the stars disappeared and the sky darkened.

"Very close. It is almost upon us. Feel the swell."

"Any chance we can find shelter?"

Ered shook his head. "The coast has been an unbroken wall since yesterday. I have brought her out quite a bit for safety. I hope it will be far enough. Wouldn't want to run aground."

Pedreth nodded. He ducked below deck, returning in short order with the crew. They hastened to reduce the amount of canvas they were flying. With too much sail aloft, the power of the wind would escalate beyond their control. When the first large wave broke over the deck, Ered realized that reefing, or reducing the amount of sail area, would not be enough.

"Storm sails," he cried.

The tempest was gathering quickly. Pedreth turned to Ai'Lorc and together they lifted the forward hatch. Ai'Lorc climbed down and began handing up the tiny storm sails while Reg and Leovar stuffed masses of wet sailcloth into the hold.

The swells were now coming in sets of three. Everything above deck was drenched in brine and its planks were becoming treacherous. With the last sail stowed, Ai'Lorc climbed topside and managed to secure the hatch before another large breaker left the deck awash. The incoming deluge knocked him from his feet and he grabbed the hatch cover to keep from sliding under the railing. He held on through the next two volleys, then stood upright, wiped the water from his face and looked about.

Reg was just forward of where Ai'Lorc was standing. His arms and legs were wrapped around the forestay while he worked. The forward storm sails were in place. Leovar had raised the mizzen but had failed to secure the controlling lines and the cloth flailed madly. Ered struggled to hold the ketch into the wind so Leovar could complete his task and Ai'Lorc hurried to assist. As he ran, the bow lifted sharply as the ketch struck a huge swell. Water exploded in all directions. Ai'Lorc became airborne and hurled aft, into the blackness. A hand reached out and grabbed him. Someone shouted into his ear.

"One hand."

"What?"

"One hand," Pedreth repeated. "Keep one hand on the boat at all times. If you do not, we will lose you overboard."

"Sorry! I didn't think."

Pedreth clapped him on the shoulder and drew him to his feet.

"Now you know," he replied with a wink.

Leovar had secured the sail and trimmed it as the denaJadiz fell back on course. The storm was raging hard as ever, but the ketch now handled steadier and easier as the smaller storm sails reduced the wind's effect.

"It's a real blower, but you are in good hands," Pedreth assured Ai'Lorc, shouting to be heard. "This is a good boat and my boys know their job. If you want to help, go below and see that Danth is secure in his bunk."

Glad to have work he could handle, Ai'Lorc made his way to the cockpit and went below. Belowdecks was drier than topside, but Ai'Lorc knew he did not want to be there long. He was no sailor and his stomach told him so. Out in the fresh air he was alright, but down where the air was close and everything rose and fell, he began to feel sick. He went straight to securing Danth, so he could leave as soon as possible.

After he had obtained some rope from the forecastle, he returned to the main cabin where something caught his eye. Danth had moved. He was no longer curled up and trembling, but instead lay on his back. The terrors that had gripped him seemed to have passed, for his chest moved with the gentle rhythm of a peaceful sleeper. Reg's ministries had quelled the nightmare.

As he fastened the first knot around the young man's legs, the ketch heaved violently and Danth opened his eyes.

"Hello," he said, rubbing his face with his hand. "Have I been asleep very long?"

Feeling an honest reply might be disconcerting, Ai'Lorc answered with a question of his own. "How are you feeling?"

"Very weak."

The ketch pitched again and Danth tried to sit. The light globes swung wildly, shadows shifted and everything seemed to move and stretch.

"Where am I?" he asked. "What's happening?"

"We are at sea and it has grown rough outside. Don't worry. Your friends have everything under control, but I must secure you to your bunk."

"No. Please, let me come topside and help," he protested and struggled to sit.

"If you were stronger, I might allow it," Ai'Lorc said, as Danth sagged under the effort. "But you would be in great danger above. I will release you as soon as the seas have calmed. In the meantime, I will come down to look in on you regularly. Right now, you need to rest."

He brushed Danth's hair from his face and the young lord closed his eyes, exhausted. Then he tugged each of the knots. Satisfied they were secure, he made for the companionway. As he grabbed the ladder's railing, the bow lifted and the sea exploded like a cannonade. The denaJadiz' timbers groaned in protest and she sounded as though she were coming apart. The deck tilted near vertical and anything loose went flying. He grabbed a tread and clung to it, looking to see if Danth would be secure when the sea struck again.

Another explosion and the craft took off like an unbroken horse bolting against its first rider. He held tightly with both hands, pressed his cheek against the handrail and wrapped his legs around the stairs as the next wave struck. It sounded like a bombardment, and for the first time since they had fled Ydron, Ai'Lorc feared for his life. He could feel the craft lift, then drop a great distance. When it struck, it was all he could do to hold on. He could not tell the size of these waves, but he knew they were larger than any he had ever seen. No crew, he thought, could manage against such forces, so when the next monster wave struck, he held on and prayed.

Ai'Lorc felt he could not remain where he was. Besides, his stomach was not going to remain contained very much longer. He looked to Danth's berth, envying his ability to turn everything off, and was starting upwards when the hatch opened.

"Where do you think you're going? You'll only get washed overboard," Pedreth chided with a wink. Amid all this buffeting, he was actually smiling. "Now, get out of the way. It's not a fit night out."

Mouth agape, Ai'Lorc moved aside as Pedreth descended, followed by Reg, Ered and Leovar, who secured the hatch.

"Who is minding the ship?" Ai'Lorc asked.

"She's minding herself," Pedreth replied. Then, noticing Ai'Lorc's bewilderment, he explained, "The helm is tied off and she will do fine for now. It is a bad gale, but no worse than the worst I've seen. Hove-to, she will keep her bow into the wind and ride out the storm. Topside, we risk losing everyone overboard. We will send someone up from time to time to survey her, but for now, we are better off where it is dry. We will take turns tonight, although most of us will stay below unless she decides to break up."

"But won't the storm carry us aground?" Ai'Lorc wanted to know.

"The spin of the storm is bringing the wind up from the south. I do not think we will move much farther toward shore. Unless the storm shifts, we should manage to stay well out to sea."

"What if it does?"

"If it shifts, I will do what I must," Pedreth replied.

Another wave struck and everyone grabbed what he could.

"What do mean?"

"Look, Ai'Lorc," said Ered, "if you are going to worry like that, you are going to have a very rough night. There are certain forces one can control, and others one cannot. When you go to sea, you need to sort out which is which, deal with those you can manage and don't worry too much about the rest. Otherwise, you will drive yourself mad."

"Here." Leovar produced a small flask from a cabin locker. When Ai'Lorc refused it, he insisted. "Drink it. It will take some of the green out of your face."

Ered laughed, "Drink it, man. It is one of Leovar's small miracles. You look like a tesberry's cousin."

"Please," urged Leovar, "It will settle your stomach."

Even though he doubted he could keep anything down, Ai'Lorc accepted the flask. He wrinkled his nose, then took a breath and downed it.

"Good! You will soon feel much better." Leovar smiled.

It was too soon to tell, but if it worked half as well as he hoped, he would be deeply indebted. While he prayerfully held on, he noticed Reg standing over Danth's bunk with a look of satisfaction on his face.

# 18

Reg came wide awake at someone's cry for help. The bunk rose beneath him and the cabin tilted nearly ninety degrees. The denaJadiz seemed to be screaming and everything was in motion. Before he was fully aware, he was thrown forward against the ceiling and took the blow full in the face. Somehow he remained conscious, but his nose, forehead and mouth throbbed. He fought to disentangle himself from the bedding, but it came away with him and he arrived at the foot of the bunk, half suspended in space. Just when he managed to free one hand, everything shifted again and he was hurled onto the deck between the bunks. Grasping wildly for anything secure, he found the leg of the chart table and struggled to pull himself upright. He sat and was puzzling why his seat and legs were wet when he heard someone cry, "We're taking on water!"

It was Ered, descending from the hatchway. He grasped Reg's arm and pulled him to his feet.

"Voreth's horns! Your face is a mess. Are you alright?"

Reg put his hand to his mouth and it came away bloody. "No teeth lost. I don't think I broke anything." Looking at Ered, he asked, "What happened?"

"Nearly buried the bow. She threatened to pitch-pole," he said, referring to an unusually severe roll, stern over bow. "It looks bad out there. In fact, I could say the same of you. No time for chatter, though. The storm is growing worse. Come. We must hurry… "

The crash of wave upon hull and the relentless wind masked the rest of what he said.

"What?" Reg shouted, cupping his free hand to an ear for emphasis.

"She may not weather the storm," Ered repeated.

Reg nodded. He glanced about and realized the rest of the crew had gone topside. He looked for his coat. When he found it, he halted abruptly.

"What is it?" asked Ered.

Reg stared at the next bunk. "I can't leave Danth. You go up. I will follow."

"You go," Ered countered. "You're hurt. I will bring Danth."

"We'll do it together."

He donned his coat, then came to Ered's aid. He was surprised to see Danth was awake. More remarkable, after days of clinging to consciousness, he was smiling and alert.

Another wave struck, so they moved with urgency. Kneeling by his side, they untied the bindings. As they worked, Reg thought he heard Danth speak.

"I guess I came along with the madman after all," he said.

"I never doubted you would," replied Reg. "Where would you rather be?"

"Can't think of a place."

The exchange ended abruptly as seawater exploded through the cabin's hatch. The blast tore Ered from the bunk and sent him hurtling into a bulkhead. Gasping for breath, arms and legs flailing, he struggled for footing. It was all he could do to get to his knees. A hand reached out and he took it. As he climbed to his feet, Danth grasped him and drew him toward the stairs.

There is an old saying among seamen: When Mae'is is vexed, even Voreth hides. Pilots were wont to recite the adage about Mae'is, the sea god, as they tucked their vessels into the shelter of a cove or harbor before an approaching storm. When Reg emerged from the cabin, it took all his strength just to hang on to the handrail. This seemed to be one of the sea god's worst moments. The sea's phosphorescence revealed towering mountains and yawning valleys of water. Waves broke over the deck and washed across the ketch's back in rivers. One moment the denaJadiz climbed toward the heavens. The next, she teetered upon the brink of a precipice, only to hurtle again into the ocean's maw. Mae'is was trying his best to devour her and there was nowhere to hide, not even for Voreth, the devil.

"Who is manning her?" Reg wondered aloud. Leovar and Ai'Lorc, looking like drowned marmaths, had lashed themselves to the railing. No chance of trimming even the storm sails against the incredible force of this storm. All they could do was try to prevent themselves from washing overboard. Reg braced himself and clung to the hatchway as a wave broke over the deck. It passed and he futilely wiped his wet face with a dripping forearm. Peering through the spray he thought he saw

Pedreth, so he worked his way toward the helm.

Pedreth was shouting something, but the wind carried his voice into the darkness. When Reg gestured he could not hear, cupping his hand behind his ear his and shaking his head, Pedreth held up a length of rope and wound it around his waist indicating he wanted Reg to secure himself.

Reg was awash with thoughts, drowning in them. If the storm did not do him in, the flood of voices and images would. He felt punched, beaten and limp as he extended his hand to accept the cord. The spray was fierce, making it hard to see, and the salt stung his eyes. Water was everywhere. It ran in a stream down the length of the cord he was holding, then whipped into droplets, whirling and disappearing into the night. It ran in a hundred small courses down Pedreth's hair and beard and down the wrinkles and folds of Reg's coat. Another wave struck and shattered into torrents. It ran down the rigging and poured down the faces of the sails.

As Reg secured himself, his body sagged and his heart filled with despair. Ever since he had departed Ydron, his mission had buoyed him. The vision of saving the kingdom had given birth to a plan for doing so. He had broken the task into elements, each of which he could control. He could call upon various powers to influence the course of events. He knew he could turn the happenings of the last few days, and he knew he possessed the will to do what he must, but now the storm was swallowing all his plans. He had never seen anything so severe. The denaJadiz would come apart should the storm last much longer.

He felt tiny and hopeless and he wanted to cry. The bruises his body had suffered were insignificant. The loss of his home and family was something he could eventually rise above. But should the ketch go down—and he was certain she could not survive these seas—none aboard would live to see tomorrow. Despite the buoyancy of the sandiath skins, the seas would either drive them beneath the waves too long to return to the surface alive, or they would perish lashed to the railing or adrift like so much flotsam. He found Pedreth's determination admirable, but regrettably foolish. The boatkeeper would hold the ketch on course until she either broke apart or capsized. Although he remained at the helm, squinting through the spray, in the end it would amount to folly.

Other thoughts intruded. Reg turned to see Ered and Danth emerging from the cabin, huddling to duck the full force of the elements.

"Ered! Danth!" he called.

Surprisingly, they heard him.

"We're alright," Ered responded and Reg could hear him as well.

The noise had diminished. It had diminished radically! The buck and shudder of the deck was calming and the rain began to fall, no longer coming at them horizontally.

"Pedreth!" Ai'Lorc shouted, gesturing to the cord around his waist. "Is it over?"

The boatkeeper smiled wryly, wiped his face and shook his head. "The eye, my friend. This is the eye of the storm." As he answered, he kept his gaze upon an unseen point somewhere beyond the bow, squinting hard, as though the added effort would part the mist.

The company of friends looked about. Pedreth was right. The eye was upon them. The sea was beginning to calm and the wind was losing its force far swifter than it had built. The clouds parted, revealing the sparkle of starry skies. They had grown so accustomed to the darkness the starlight seemed brilliant. Then, some distance ahead, as the storm's mist lifted, a strange black shape interrupted the marine glow. Initially, they could not identify it. Then, in an instant, they could see the looming cliff for what it was.

"Land ho!" cried Pedreth. "Hah!" he laughed. He pounded the wheel with his fist and rejoiced. "I had hoped as much."

"Hoped for what? There's no beach here." Ai'Lorc, baffled, was struggling to his feet.

Pedreth could not contain himself. "I have been trying to run her aground all night! Hah! Haven't you noticed we've had the wind to our beam?"

"Aground? I thought you wanted to keep her at sea."

"I did, until it was clear we could not win with that tactic." When Ai'Lorc appeared not to understand, Pedreth said, "Never become married to a strategy. Change with the circumstances."

"But there's no beach!" Ai'Lorc protested.

"Haven't you seen the way the surf has been breaking? That is because the bottom has been shallowing up. I expect we'll run aground and be able to wade ashore any time now. I knew she couldn't hold together much longer, but I also knew if I could run her aground we might have a chance. Slim, but better than none. The direction was no problem; simply head east. I just didn't know if we were making progress. Waves like those can hold you in place all night. Still, I felt this is a good boat and heavy enough to make her way against these seas. She proved me right and now I see it's shallow enough we won't have to wreck her."

Suddenly, the denaJadiz lurched with an accompanying thud. Ered and Danth fell to the deck.

"We're aground," Pedreth rejoiced and grinned. "Hurry! Untie yourselves. Even if we are lucky enough to catch the eye dead center, we will not have much time before it passes and the storm rises again. Hurry below and put together as many provisions as you can."

"I'll get the sails," said Danth.

"Don't bother. Just release the halyards so she doesn't sail away before we're off her."

# 19

"Mas'tad take me! Can't you silence that noise, Lydon?" shouted Duile.

The chief advisor to the late Manhathus was unsure if the question was rhetorical, but he dared not take the chance.

"The men are only trying to extract the information as quickly as possible, Your Majesty."

"I am aware of that," she hissed. "Do you consider me stupid?"

"Never, Majesty! Of course n…"

"Then silence him!"

The cries of pain had grown so shrill and guttural they had begun to sound feral. Meneth Lydon, chief advisor to her late husband, understood what Duile meant by silence. The poor soul had long abandoned rationality and now, infinitely more than the queen, he wished for the same blessed peace with all his being. He would not, or else could not, deliver up the information that would have spared him—not from death, but from extended agony. Even should he respond, his state of mind would cast doubt upon the reliability of any statement, so his usefulness had passed.

Lydon's face contorted into a scowl as he rose. So long as Duile was unhappy, his life would be miserable. Both heirs to the throne had slipped her grasp, and so long as they were free and abroad, they posed a threat. She needed to find them, yet each passing day brought her no closer. Her patience had vanished so that even the death of another unfortunate would yield her no pleasure. Lydon hurled the chobollah he had been eating against a wall and the piece of fruit shattered.

"And clean that up!" she snapped.

"Yes, Majesty."

He was unaccustomed to cringing. Certainly, he had fawned on Manhathus, but he always knew where groveling would leave him. His was servitude with a purpose. As advisor, he had always had Manhathus' ear, so much of what the king had ordained was at Lydon's behest. He was the will behind the will, and in turn, cowered to no one. These days were different. Duile was unpredictable. Heads rolled, lands were given and taken away and power shifted at her whim. With every dawn he questioned anew the wisdom of his treachery. As he reached the door at the end of the room, he motioned to the guardsmen, jerking his thumb toward the scattered fragments. They nodded and ran to clean the mess.

"Lydon!" Duile shouted and jumped to her feet. She had intended to humiliate him by having him clean it up himself, but he had already rounded the corner. Clenching her fists and biting back her anger—for she knew he had understood her—she whirled.

"So, Endreth," she hissed through her teeth. "Is this the best you have been able to do?"

"M-majesty?"

Badar Endreth, minister of foreign affairs under Manhathus, was temporarily stepping aside from those duties to supervise the effort to find the queen's children.

"There are a hundred thousand eyes in Ydron and again as many ears. Has no one seen them or heard of their passing?"

"Your Majesty, the city gates have been secured and we are going from house to house. We will surely find…"

"Bribes!" she cut him off.

"What?"

"There are enough hungry mouths that the promise of food will loosen a tongue or two. Bribe them."

"Majesty, we have offered rewards of every sort imaginable, yet none will break their silence."

"I want Lith-An back. Here! Now! With me! I don't care if there is not a single hovel left intact. I want every house searched, gutted if necessary until you find her."

"She may have already departed the city, Majesty."

"Then search every farm and cottage. Reduce them to kindling. No! Reduce them to ashes if they do not have the sense to cooperate."

"Yes, Majesty."

"What about the ship? I want my son, as well."

"I don't know which fool brought you rumor of a ship, Majesty. We have checked the boatyard and it is abandoned. No one there at all. There is no inventory of which boats should or should not be moored, but I doubt anyone could have escaped by sea. The storm would have destroyed anyone foolish enough to set sail. I sincerely doubt your informant knew what he was talking about."

"Don't dare doubt me," she hissed. "Regilius and his friends left by that port. I am not asking you. I am telling you and you will not question my veracity. There are no finer sailors in Ydron than my son and his friends. Despite the danger, with the right vessel they would have had a better chance than any, even in the face of such a storm. Have you sent for word from Limast?"

"I didn't see the need, Majesty."

"Didn't see the need? Do you think you will continue to enjoy your accustomed comfort without producing results? If you continue to refuse my instructions, if I do not see results within a fortnight, I promise it will be you who will see results." She fingered the tip of the tiny dagger hanging from a chain around her neck.

Endreth blanched. He did not doubt for an instant she would make good her word, yet he knew with each passing hour his chances of success diminished.

"I will not fail you, Majesty. My men will not enjoy a night's sleep until they have returned your children to you."

The corners of her mouth turned upward for an instant before, in a voice barely audible, she intoned, "I think you've gotten into the spirit of the search at last, Minister. Take care the passing of the days."

As he bowed to leave, she turned her back. The sound of his retreating footsteps barely registered upon her consciousness. Angry and preoccupied, she walked to the windows, pushed one open and closed her eyes at the inward rush of cool breeze. Beyond the continual drip of water from the eaves, artifacts of the tempest's passing, low clouds rushed eastward.

*The West Wind has returned to clear the air and restore order*, she thought. She was determined it would be so. She had lived in her husband's shadow too many years and had watched him grow ever more self-serving and less ept with the reins of power. Not since before the Great Conflict had the kingdom been in such disarray. So, when she could tolerate the situation no longer, she had seized upon the greed of a few lords and the ambitions of certain advisors and took the throne. Had not her children disappeared, it would have been perfect. Now, so long as they were gone, there was risk they would fall into the hands of her enemies and her pretext to the throne would crumble. After all, they were heirs by blood. Her claim was by marriage. Marriage, like all other legal institutions, was subject to challenge. Bloodlines could never be severed and were more apt to foster allegiance.

*It would have been perfect. It would have been perfect.* The thought repeated until she thought she was going mad. At the sound of laughter, she whirled.

"Who dares laugh?" she roared.

The room, unlit except by window light and a few scattered light globes, fell into shadow at its farthest recesses and her eyes could not discern what lurked in the gloom.

"I am sorry, Majesty," came the reply amid stifled chuckles.

"Step forward so I can see you," she ordered. "Guard!" she called.

As two guards strode from their post at the door, the figure stepped into the light.

"I am terribly sorry for laughing, Majesty, but I am amused by the incompetence of those fawning clowns."

Duile strained to recognize the face. The shadows across his features did nothing to help. She was exhausted and reluctant to exert the mental effort necessary to identify the stranger. Then, just as her men laid hold of him, recognition crept over her and she raised her right hand.

"Halt," she ordered. "Let him go."

They stared at Duile, as if they had not heard correctly. Then, as they saw anger spread across her face, both released the intruder. In unison they retreated a step and stood at the ready.

"Return to your posts," she ordered.

They exchanged glances, but snapped to attention, saluted and returned to the door. Duile, who had never removed her gaze from this newcomer, was disconcerted.

"I feel I know you, but by Siemas, I cannot say your name."

"I am Husted Yar, Majesty."

"Tell me how I know you. How did you arrive within this chamber unnoticed?" She did not like this uncertainty. "And why should I not have you permanently removed?"

Yar's upper lip curled. "I have been with you all along, Majesty, ever since you decided to take the throne. I have been your closest confidant."

"My closest…?"

"Confidant," he affirmed with a nod, completing the sentence for her.

"Confidant," Duile repeated, sounding less confused.

She turned her back, contemplating this new development, wondering how she could have forgotten her friend. Then, as a soothing wave of comfort washed over her, she released her doubt and never gave it another thought.

Yar's abdomen rippled and its shape flickered briefly. It had not really been with the queen since her decision to take power. In fact, it had only recently decided to take advantage of the chaos within the citadel. Ordinarily, should it have attempted to enter barakYdron, the sheer number of guards would have proved impossible to deal with. These days, however, most were occupied with the search. It had correctly sensed the opportunity and had made its way to this most strategic of places.

"And, of course," Yar assured, "You remember all of our encounters now, don't you, Majesty?"

"Of course, dear Husted," she smiled. "Why would you suggest otherwise?"

"Why, indeed?" it concurred. "Come. Let us talk of Regilius and Lith-An."

Duile smiled. She extended her hand for Yar to take and the pair strolled off to more private quarters.

# 20

"Not Wia! Not Wia! Not Wia!"

"Hush, little one. Please stop crying," Ganeth pleaded.

"Not Wia! Not Wia! Not Wia!"

"Please, Ria. We must be quiet now."

"Not Wia! Not Wia!"

The tantrum continued and he was at a loss what to do. He had never had any contact with children, and now he fervently prayed for someone—anyone—to tell him how to stop the tears. *Borlon, guide me!* he prayed to the deity who was the guardian of the watch, the protector in the darkest hours. He ran a hand through his hair. What had begun as a simple request from a friend had turned into a convoluted odyssey, taking on all the qualities of a nightmare. When Barnath had entered his shop, the matter appeared so simple.

"I have a friend who needs to speak to Pithien Dur," Barnath had declared.

For years Ganeth had hinted, or sometimes stated outright to anyone who would listen, he had friends who knew the outlaw. It was a way of elevating himself in the eyes of his peers and lifting his life above the tedium. In all the years he had made this claim, no one had ever required him to prove the boast. Until now.

At first, he had simply smiled and puffed out his chest. "And so, my friend, you naturally come to me."

He could not hide his smugness and assured his fellow shopkeeper of the simplicity of the task. No sooner had Barnath departed, however, than he began to worry. Years ago he had overheard friends claim to know the outlaw. Although the claim was never repeated—for perhaps it was merely a slip of the tongue—he held onto it because it made him feel important to be one step closer to Dur. Over the years, whenever he needed to feel superior, he would find a way to turn the conversation toward the outlaw so he could boast of his association. This supposed intimacy warmed him and made him feel as though his life were a bit more exciting.

So, when actually pressed to make good on his word, fears began to creep in. He never had proof of his friends' association. What if it were another empty and long-forgotten boast like his? He would be humiliated. Ganeth wanted to run after Barnath to explain why doing this favor might not be possible, but no good excuse came to mind. So despite his fear, he donned his hat and made his way to meshedRuhan to speak with Benjin and Jenethra. He was sick with worry, prepared to hear the worst. To Ganeth's surprise, however, once he had explained the reason for his request, the pair admitted such a meeting might be possible. Naturally, they would take appropriate precautions. They made no guarantees, but they would contact Dur, provided Ganeth promised not to reveal their identities. His heart leapt. Naturally, he agreed.

Everything afterwards unfolded with ease, right up to the moment when Marm put Ria into his arms. Even then, he was so caught up by events he did not pause to consider what must happen when he slipped away with the girl. Palace guards were everywhere. Although Ganeth did not know why, he had the distinct impression this girl should not fall into their hands and it would go badly were she found in his possession.

At first, he had thought to wait outside the public house in the dark of a nearby doorway, but it soon became evident the squads combing the streets were looking everywhere. As one unit approached, Ganeth knew what he must do. Tucking Ria under his cloak, he turned his back and ducked down an alleyway.

His next plan was to go to the outer city, amble around or find a friend with whom to spend the night. Then, at dawn he could return to the upper market to meet Marm. It was not long, however, before he could see remaining anywhere in the city was not an option. He had never seen such activity. Soldiers were searching every house, questioning every citizen. More than once, Ganeth barely escaped their attention.

When at last it became clear he must leave altogether, he no longer knew how to return the girl. For the moment, that was unimportant. Tomorrow would provide the solution, should they make it that far. It helped that Ria had fallen asleep. She was less likely to make unwanted sounds. Before Ganeth disappeared, however, he was possessed by an uncharacteristic presence of mind. While still in the upper market, he knocked on the door of a friend. He explained his plight and told her, should Barnath or any of the citizenry come looking after him by name, to tell them he had left the city with the girl. He handed her a small red cord from Ria's dress as proof, then made his way outside the city walls.

Fleeing danYdron was one matter. Deciding where to go next was quite another and Ganeth's forté had never been anticipating the second step. So it was he found himself staring at signposts.

"Darmaht," he implored the protector of wayfarers, "Tell me where to go. I think I have an uncle in No'eth, but I haven't seen him since I was a child. What if he is no longer there? I think my mother once told me about cousins in Dar, but that is to the north of Limast, if I remember rightly. I cannot carry this child through all the provinces, nor can I sit outside the walls. We will need water and food. How are we to manage on the few coins in my pocket?"

He looked down as Ria stirred in his arms. He would have to find a place to lie down until morning.

"Ma'm?" Ria inquired, as she awakened.

"No, Ria," Ganeth answered. "Marm's not here."

Perhaps because she did not recognize the strange voice in the dark, she began to cry. "Want Ma'm! Want Ma'm!"

"Shhh, Ria," Ganeth tried to soothe her. "We'll find Marm soon."

The girl refused to be consoled. "Want Ma'm! Want Ma'm!"

"Please don't cry, Ria," Ganeth implored, not knowing what to do or say.

"Not Wia," she howled. "I Lith-An!"

Confused by this declaration and believing the girl was still half-asleep, Ganeth replied, "I have your doll in my pocket, Ria. Lith-An is alright."

The princess was indignant. "Not Wia!" she shrieked. "I Lith-An!"

Ganeth kept trying to calm her to no avail. He could not for the life of him understand why she was claiming the name of her doll. Barnath had not told him Marm and the girl had come from the palace, so it would never occur to him the girl might really be the princess.

As he struggled to reason with her, a new problem arose: the sound of approaching horses. Inter-city travel was almost unheard-of after dark. Light globes perched upon a vehicle were much too feeble to illuminate the rough, rutted roads of the countryside. Diamath was too small to produce any usable light and starlight did not reveal the presence of potholes until too late. Without the added light cast by street lamps, travel at night was extremely hazardous. It startled him, then, when he heard horses' hooves. Perhaps the riders considered the hazard posed by palace guards sufficient to justify such travel, but he was also aware that bandits and other unsavory types roamed the byways after dark. He hurried into a ditch and prayed the girl would cooperate and be still.

"Please, Ria," he implored, as the clomping grew louder. "You must not cry."

"Want Ma'm!"

"Please, Ria!"

"Not Wia! Not Wia!"

He began to panic. His breath grew fast and shallow and perspiration ran down his forehead, temples and neck. "Please!" he begged, but the girl continued to protest.

"Not Wia! Not Wia! Not Wia!"

The riders drew to within a short distance and stopped, listening.

# 21

"This is not good, General. Are you sure?"

Ever since Lord Emeil had agreed to join hands with Duile, he had been waiting for a sign of the queen's treachery. He had no idea what form it might take or what her motive might be when it came, but this development reeked of her. Although she needed him, he knew she did not trust him. *And rightly so*, he thought. Given the chance to eliminate the threat he posed, she would do what she must.

"My Lord, our agent has come from an emergency meeting called by Lord Kareth's and Lord Danai's chiefs of staff. Both camps are in disarray and are accusing you and Lord Asch. Kareth and Danai each allegedly received an invitation last night to meet the two of you in private. Shortly after the dinner hour, each of them left his quarters accompanied by a squad of bodyguard, to meet at an undisclosed location. Neither party has been seen since."

"What proof of authenticity was given?" asked Emeil, then added, "I issued no such invitation."

"They were approached by messengers wearing your colors as well as those of Lord Asch, and bearing a scroll sealed by signets with each of your crests," General Meiad explained.

"Who guards my signet, General?"

"Major Saed, and he assures me it has never left his care. He was able to produce it upon request and he is vouched for by three senior officers."

"Have you contacted Asch?"

"I have, my Lord, and his representative insists they had no part in it either. Had your reputation not been what it is, they would be pointing a finger at you, although Lords Ened and Hau have each come close to doing so. As it is, they are baffled. I must confess, so am I."

"It is not so confusing, General. We are within barakYdron and Duile controls these premises. If she is seeking dominance, then seeding the air with fear and suspicion is her handiest weapon. She certainly has craftsmen enough to counterfeit uniforms and crests on short notice. Did you manage to obtain an invitation so we can compare its imprint with my signet?"

"No, my Lord. It seems the documents were lost along with each party."

"Making it impossible to prove whether or not they were forgeries. How unfortunate. I would have hoped the involvement of myself, along with Lords Kanagh and Hol, would have provided sufficient checks and balances to maintain at least tenuous stability. Now, how do we protect our interests and select a new ruler? If my suspicions are correct and Duile is at the heart of it, there may barely be time to flee with our men. If not the queen, then I'm sure Lord Kareth and Lord Danai's chiefs of staff are plotting our end, even as we speak."

"Flee, my Lord? Wouldn't it be better to remain where we can keep an eye on developments? If we leave now, we assure the queen victory."

"Imprisoned within these walls, we are at Duile's mercy. Fleeing, provided we can actually escape, assures us a tomorrow from which to plan our next move."

"My Lord, you know your men will fight to the death to protect you," Meiad argued.

"I have no use for dead men. I am where I am because I pick my battles. Winning the war often depends upon knowing when to retreat. This is such a time.

"Inform the queen I have reason to believe I know the whereabouts of both her daughter and Pithien Dur."

"Dur, my Lord?"

"I need a reason to deploy all my men. An unexpected development like this should catch her off guard and allow us to depart, if we don't give her time to think about it. If it really was she who dealt last night's hand, then she is well aware of my innocence and she will not risk losing this opportunity to apprehend both her daughter and the outlaw. Send word to the queen and assemble the men. Don't give them a hint we intend to do anything other than what we tell her. Order them to bring only enough provisions for a few days' foray, and protection in case the weather grows foul. This way, they will leave our encampment intact and their possessions behind, indicating to any informant in our midst we have every intention of returning."

"Yes, my Lord. At once."

"One last thought."

Meiad paused. "Yes, my Lord?"

"Don't go yourself. Send someone who is not privy to our information. If Duile even remotely suspects deceit, our plan will fail. The queen must not detect any trace of a lie in the eyes or voice of the messenger."

"Yes, my Lord," Meiad replied with a smile. "I understand."

Emeil sighed. The events since the coup had not approached his expectations, and while he knew Manhathus had to fall, he had not foreseen Duile's ambition. Who would have guessed, as she sat quietly in her husband's shadow, she would conduct such wholesale slaughter? She had promised, looking him straight in the eye, that Manhathus would be imprisoned and tried for his crimes, and he had honestly expected a bloodless coup. In retrospect, he was dismayed by his naïveté.

While he had been her dupe, he would not be party to her evil. No one was surprised when he refused to participate in the house burnings. She would have killed him for this alone, had he and his men not worked so hard to conduct their own searches. He had imprisoned far more of Manhathus' guards than there was room to hold, but while he had argued for the construction of a stockade until they could build more permanent cells, the queen simply ordered those men killed.

Fortunately, Emeil was a man of quick resolve. Now that the followers of Kareth and Danai had been turned against him, he knew what he must do. After removing his men from immediate danger, he would begin to expand his force. Asch would be struggling to survive, so would cease to be a threat, and in the wake of Duile's treachery, might even convert into an ally. Lords Kanagh and Hol, whose houses had proven consistently trustworthy over the years since the Great Conflict, had already pledged their allegiance. Since the palace was an island with limited resources, it could be isolated, its supply lines could be cut and Duile could be brought to her knees. If he acted with care, he could accomplish what he had intended from the beginning: the new ruler would be selected by the people.

# PART TWO

## Resolve

# 22

When Obah Sitheh assumed control of the lands now collectively referred to as Ydron and assumed the name Tonopath, or Conqueror, he was a mere warlord, the successful chief of a long and bloody campaign that had taken many lives. He was by no means of royal descent, yet during the Great Conflict, when anarchy ruled the land and family set upon family, brother murdered brother and ruler attacked ruler, his will, like his sword, cut a swath through the chaos. Fifteen years of slaughter, petty rivalry and confusion came to a halt because, in the end, no one was brave enough or foolish enough to challenge him. Fortune had so smiled on him during all his campaigns that he never lost a battle. Certainly he was brilliant, but weather and circumstance had so consistently turned ambiguous outcomes to his advantage he soon became a legend. His troops were feared as no others, and he was revered almost as a god. When finally he claimed dominance in the region, there was none who would contradict him.

Obah Tonopath was more than a great warrior, or he would not have been able to hold sway forever. Eventually, even a fearful enemy will sense when the one he fears has grown old and weak. Obah understood in order to retain power he would have to acquire allies and turn enemies into friends. First, he decreed the sixteen lands to be provinces under his kingship. Although he kept Chadarr for himself, renaming it Ydron like the land, he gave each of the remaining provinces to those generals and warlords he respected most in combat—those who fought hardest and bravest. The cowardly, he reasoned, could never be trusted for they could not trust even themselves. Likewise, the dull of wit could not appreciate the value of the gesture. On the other hand, those with intelligence and courage would understand that, although he had the power to disgrace them outright, this recognition of their worth honored them. By honoring them, he bought their loyalty, thereby surrounding himself with strong, grateful allies.

Next, he married Esmi, the daughter of Hath the Terrible. Not only did he create blood ties with the one most able to unseat him, but he also kept a grip on Sandoval, the province he had given to Hath. While Ydron possessed the largest harbor, Sandoval held the only other suitable for shipping, the coastline from Monhedeth to Sandoval and the coasts of Deth and Pytheral being far too rocky and inhospitable. This reduced his dependence on Nagath-réal and its caravans and insured he could defend the only accessible stretches of coast from invasion. Because Esmi was both beautiful and intelligent, this marriage insured that his offspring were suited to their inheritance.

During his remaining years, he worked to bring prosperity to all the land. He recruited the finest minds, found new and better ways to grow crops and advanced trade relations so food and goods were never in short supply. This period, immediately following the Great Conflict, became known as The Joining. Except for the unsuccessful siege of Ydron after the battle and siege at menRathan, when the kingdom was briefly threatened, Ydron grew and prospered for nearly two hundred fifty years. It was not until the reign of Berin, father of Manhathus, that matters took a turn for the worse.

Berin, more than any of his predecessors, sought to immortalize himself with the construction of monuments and massive additions to barakYdron, his citadel. These required expansion of the quarries and more workers. At first he used prisoners. Then he added debtors, so they might work off their debt, although their debts seemed to grow under this system. Eventually, others kidnapped from regions outside Ydron found their way into the pits. Finally, the poor were taken and a system of slavery was born.

Berin found new ways to exploit his people. Wealth began pouring into the palace as he levied increasingly burdensome taxes and still he could not be satisfied. By the time his only child, Manhathus, was reaching adulthood, Berin had begun to increase the tribute he exacted from the provinces. What had previously been a fair exchange for the protection he gave, began to exceed his subjects' ability to pay. There was no end to his appetite.

When he suddenly died of gluttony, everyone gave thanks and said among themselves—sometimes even openly—it was a fitting end. An air of celebration spread and the coronation of Manhathus was the grandest ever. The exultation did not last, however, because it became apparent the lot of the oppressed was not going to change. While Berin had been active in his exploitation, Manhathus was apathetic, content to allow things to remain as they had been. Although he did nothing to increase his peoples' burden, he did nothing to alleviate it.

Manhathus was the antithesis of Obah. While Obah had been thoughtful and shrewd, Manhathus was insensitive and careless. Whereas Obah had been careful in selecting his queen, Manhathus Tonopath could not have been more foolish when he selected his. Granted, Duile was both beautiful and intelligent, but her late father, Armitage Morged of Rian, was a weakling like Manhathus and she had grown to despise weakness. While she did not relish passing from one such household to another, she cooperated because of Ydron's vast wealth. Although this was a trade of one unhappy circumstance for another, under the law her father's lands would pass to her simpleton brother. And when, upon their father's death, her brother could not assume the throne, everything passed to their father's half-brother, Lord Kareth—not to her. As queen of Ydron, she could have everything. The only thing she needed to do was to find a way to eliminate Manhathus. It never occurred to her it would be difficult. She was right.

In the twenty-first year of her son's life, Duile had the opportunity to visit the province of Borrst. Accompanying her were the minister of trade, his deputy, and Meneth Lydon, Manhathus' chief advisor. The party was ostensibly on a mission to enhance trade relations, but the queen had a different agenda. They met in the capitol city of danHsar with rulers of certain other provinces. Through her companions, Duile made it clear she wished to change the status quo in a manner that could work to their mutual benefit. While they initially met her advances with suspicion, none could afford to ignore the offer. Once they understood this was no deception, it did not take long for the conspirators to become of one mind and the plot to overthrow Manhathus was born.

The cause quickly assumed a life of its own and moved with an alacrity Duile had never anticipated. Even Lord Emeil surprised her when he revealed he wished to join her, and his apparent naïveté amused her. The others, she knew, were in it more out of greed than any other reason. She was glad, however, because Emeil would have been a fierce opponent and his alliance added the face of legitimacy to the endeavor. While this would initially work in her favor, Duile realized she would eventually have to eliminate him. He would never stand for anything less than the coronation of a legitimate successor, and Duile would never stand for anything or anyone to bar her way—

not Emeil, nor for that matter, her children. So long as Regilius lived, he, and not his mother, would be the legitimate heir. And while there was no precedent for a female child ascending to power, because Lith-An was a direct blood link to the throne, were she to marry someone of appropriate stature, the law was worded in such a way to cast doubts on Duile's right. Child brides were not unheard of and she suspected this would not elude any would-be successor.

It was well past midnight. Unable to sleep and angered by recent events, Duile had risen from bed and began pacing in her chamber. There was a knock at her door.

"Yes?" she demanded, making no effort to mask her irritation.

The door cracked open and a head poked inside. "Ma'am. I saw your light and wondered if you were alright." It was Duile's chambermaid.

"Get out!" Duile shrieked. Then, before the terrified servant could withdraw, she thought better and stopped her. "No. Wait."

The girl appeared relieved as if, for once, her mistress might appreciate her efforts.

"Send for Husted Yar," Duile snapped.

The girl nodded.

"And don't bother me again until I summon you," Duile shouted at the top of her lungs.

The girls eyes widened in fright, but she kept her head long enough to reply, "Yes, Ma'am," in a voice barely above a whisper. She closed the door, taking care not to slam it.

If Duile were angry before the intrusion, she was well beyond it now. These days, everyone and everything became targets of her wrath. Rumors of her children's whereabouts were always without substance. Her attempt to discredit Emeil had not gone well, and the straw he had handed her was obviously a ruse to allow his escape. She didn't know if she could take any more.

When, after nearly half an hour's wait, another knock sounded, Duile nearly erupted, but stopped short. A wave of calm washed over her. She smiled, then went to the door and opened it, knowing it was her trusted advisor. She neither knew nor cared how she came to this realization, nor questioned how her mood always changed for the better in his presence, but the quiet reassurance he brought was enough in itself.

"My dear friend," she said to the Dalthin, extending her hand, "Thank you so much for taking time to see me, especially at such an hour."

"Of course, Your Majesty. What are friends for?"

Were others of its kind present in greater numbers, the Dalthin would not have bothered with such niceties, but until sufficient numbers arrived, it would have to play countless games in order to mollify her. The success of its mission meant following the path of least resistance. Having worked its way into this strategic location, nothing remained but to wait. Upon The Arrival, it would have a different role to play. Until then, it would disrupt the queen's affairs as little as possible, taking only such actions to survive. To this end, Husted Yar would soothe her anxieties, meet her wishes and—oh, yes—it would feed discretely.

While the Dalthin did not share any emotional equivalents with these people, they did possess certain physiological needs that could be expressed in common terms. One of these was appetite. It was an overriding concern for Yar, greater in fact than for most of its kind. In order to manage its voracious hunger it needed to accomplish two things. The first was to engage in as few strenuous activities as possible. Fortunately, this was in keeping both with its mission and its disposition. The second was to establish a link with a sector of the population that would not be missed. To this end, Yar had persuaded Duile to put it in charge of the slaves. When one of these came up missing, no one questioned the disappearance. This arrangement proved satisfactory enough it would continue to indulge her.

"So kind of you to say so," she smiled. Then, her smile faded. "I am concerned, dear Husted. I have lost all hope of finding my children."

"Please don't worry. My informants tell me we are close to finding both Regilius and Lith-An. I would say more, but I would rather not until I have them in hand, knowing how you detest disappointments. I will only say there is another you seek who might also turn up. So please, I beg you, be patient."

"Another? Whom do you mean?"

"Please, Majesty. Have I ever disappointed you?

"No, Husted. You have not. I will trust you."

"Thank you."

It knew the general direction Regilius had traveled and periodically a burst of thought helped isolate his whereabouts. Although the prince was gaining control, one Dalthin in the north was patiently tracking him. Unless Regilius acquired complete mastery soon—a suspected unlikelihood—it was only a matter of time until it located him.

Yar's cryptic reference to "another," alluded to a female telepath who had long interested both the Dalthin and the queen. After two Dalthin stationed in Bad Adur had stumbled upon some of her cohorts, capturing one in the process, it had not taken long for her to come looking. She was more experienced than Regilius, however, and had managed to evade them, but not before they had taken the remaining two, as well as an unexpected fourth. It had been a long time since they had tasted the flesh of that race.

The telepath had escaped with the last of her company, but they might catch her yet. They had found a way to surprise her, to trump her, so it was only a matter of time.

One new radiance, however, had surprised Yar. The mind had flared just once, but with such brilliance and power Yar could neither ignore nor help but recognize the source of those angry thoughts.

*Not Ria! Not Ria! Not Ria!*

# 23

The Great Salt Plain was the greatest facilitator of commerce aside from the seas themselves. A near perfect expanse of compacted salt extending many days' travel outward from its center in all directions, its continued existence in this form made possible the rapid transcontinental transport of goods, or surely it would have been mined exhaustively. Certain of its edges had indeed been excavated, but the plain proper remained pristine. As a result, great sail driven vessels rolling on wheels and laden with goods crossed its surface at speeds otherwise unattainable, thanks to the nearly unabated winds.

At every point where the land sailors embarked or arrived, port towns sprouted up. Bad Adur, in the province of Nagath-réal, was one such. Despite the wealth passing through its streets, the absence of adornments belied the fact. Its storefronts were shoddy and its houses' exteriors were dingy. If their interiors were nicely furnished, they provided no indication to the rogues who sometimes accompanied the caravans. Partly because Bad Adur was so remote, and partly because so many faces passed through its streets, Pithien Dur had chosen it as the perfect place to hide and plan.

As she and Marm conversed on a café's veranda, a tiny whirlwind spouted in the roadway and danced through a group of children. Marm watched it dodge, first one way, then another, now halt, and finally careen through the cluster, only to vanish a short distance beyond. All the while, the boys and girls continued playing, oblivious to the micro storm's passing. This street was a far cry from the playing field of danYdron, but the children reminded her of the incredible turn of events a short time before. She, like the dust motes and bits of trash caught in the funnel of wind, felt tossed and helpless.

"Why us, Marm?" asked Dur, interrupting Marm's reverie.

"What do you mean?"

"You know what I mean," she replied. "Of all the people on all of the worlds, why have the Dalthin chosen us?"

"Quite simple. They multiply like marmaths, and there are only so many food sources. There are trillions of stars, billions of planets, millions of worlds with some form of recognizable life. But worlds with a truly advanced life form compatible with their needs? Only a relative handful. Honestly, it was only a matter of time until they discovered you."

"Compatible with their needs?"

"It seems they require life forms with minds of a certain complexity."

"I should think they would prefer a simple mind—something they can mold."

"I would have thought so, too. But time after time they have bypassed simpler species in favor of creatures with higher intelligence. We have invented countless hypotheses and still cannot explain it."

"Perhaps it is… What did you call it earlier? The nervous system? Perhaps a complex nervous system satisfies their… " She grimaced. "Nutritional requirements."

"That's a plausible explanation, and frankly, one we have never considered."

"So meanwhile you run from world to world, trying to stay one step ahead of disaster."

"We have no choice."

"And you think this time you will succeed?"

"Really, I don't know. We hope we will not fail, but despite all our theories, we still do not understand our enemy. We caught and killed one once. Examining its remains gave us many new insights. But like those who constructed the first flying machines and launched them from rooftops and cliffs, only to be injured or killed in the attempt, we have nothing more to go on than the hope we will eventually prevail."

"And you believe my people have what is required to defeat them?" Dur pressed.

"It is only a theory, but we believe our plan may work—so much so, we have devoted many years and all our efforts to it."

"But it may fail."

"It may fail," Marm assented. "It's just a theory."

"Tell me about it."

Marm was fond of the concept. Her hope in its correctness was one of the factors that led her to remain on this world and she was eager to share it.

"The Dalthin control with their minds, and in sufficient numbers entirely dominate the thoughts and perceptions of those they subjugate. It follows, if they are to be defeated, it must be by similar means and with similar numbers. Just as they require victims of a certain complexity, we believe minds of such a complexity might control them.

"You are telepathic," said Marm. "We have already been through my reasoning on this. I'm not only referring to your ability to read minds, but also to influence perceptions."

"Yes, but I possess only a shadow of what you are describing. Clearly, I can't even read the details of what you are telling me."

"Nonetheless, you have some ability. Further, you are not alone." Marm leaned closer. "There are others."

"Naturally," said Dur. "I have been aware of them for most of my life. How could I not? Sometimes their thoughts come like a whisper. At other times they nearly deafen me. But nearly always they are disjointed and garbled, without control, as though they were sent by accident."

"I am not talking about those with rudimentary skills. When you first heard Prince Regilius, how did his thoughts compare with the others?"

Dur paused, holding a piece of bread in front of her mouth as she hunted for the right words. "Crisp. Clear. Focused."

"Not like the rest?" Marm probed.

"Not at all."

Marm smiled a bit. "Then, perhaps we have succeeded."

The tromp of running feet halted the conversation and Dur reached for her dagger. She turned to see Loral approaching. He dropped to one knee beside her and she relaxed.

"They have taken Bedya," he gasped. "He is gone."

"Who's taken him?" Dur asked.

"I don't know."

"What do you mean, you don't know?"

"Roman, Bedya and I were returning to the coach with the provisions you ordered. Roman and I were some distance ahead. You know how Roman walks quickly when he starts talking."

"The point," Dur urged.

He looked apologetic. "We heard Bedya cry out, and I think Roman thought—like me—Bedya was trying to get us to slow down. When we looked back, two men had him by the arms and were leading him around the corner. We dropped everything and ran after them, but when they saw us coming, they just looked at us. Suddenly, we felt sick and scared and couldn't stop shaking. We couldn't move. When we finally were able, they were gone! You know as well as I do, Roman is never scared."

"Neither are you. Where is Roman now?"

"He said he would follow them while I went to find you."

"Dur, do you know what this sounds like?" Marm asked.

"Dalthin."

"What?" asked Loral.

"I'll explain later. How long ago was this?"

"Just now. A few minutes ago. I came straight here."

"Dur," said Marm.

The outlaw turned.

"You didn't sense them, did you?"

"No, and that bothers me." She arose. "Wait here. We are going to find Bedya."

Dur followed Loral into the street, straining to locate her companions. Although she could usually find any of her company without difficulty, she could not sense either Bedya or Roman and that frightened her as well. Had the Dalthin finally managed to gain the upper hand? Had they somehow disabled her senses? This was the second time, including the massacre at pelMusha, she felt beaten.

# 24

It was an hour after Dur and Loral had begun their search, Marm was becoming ever more fearful. She knew the Dalthin, had seen them kill. As a girl, she had hidden while two devoured her parents and infant brother. There had been no remains for her to mourn over because the Dalthin left nothing to indicate their victims ever existed. She struggled to repress her tears as the memories surfaced, to retain the composure that had kept her alive through the years, knowing she would be useless if she crumbled. It did not help that the waiter repeatedly descended, determined to squeeze from her every coin he could, pressing her to order yet another pot of tea, hinting the table was needed. Although she wanted to leave, to run into the street and search for her friend, she remained where she was because Dur was expecting her to be here. It therefore startled her when Dur's voice sounded in her head.

*Marm!*

The cup slipped from her fingers and shattered on the floor. She was unaware of heads turning or the waiter crying out, throwing up his hands in dismay.

"Pithien," she cried, then caught herself, realizing this was not a name to invoke in public. "Where are you?" she asked in a softer voice, looking around.

*The marketplace. Please come.*

Marm put her hands to her mouth as, for an instant, she saw the market all around her. She had tried to imagine what mind-to-mind contact might be like, but the reality was unsettling.

"Of course…," she said, then hushed, realizing speech was unnecessary. *I am coming.*

Hoping Dur had heard her, she rose abruptly, toppling the chair. She fumbled through her purse, threw some coins onto the table and rushed down the stairs into the path of a nomad leading a team of oxen. Barely in time to avoid being trampled, she threw herself out of the way. Climbing to her feet, she took a breath and dusted herself off. Then, gathering her wits, she hurried to find her friend.

It did not take long to reach the market. Once there, however, all she could see were merchants' stalls, donkeys, a few women and scores upon scores of men, robed, turbaned or hooded against the heat and dust, but no sign of the outlaw. She fought back panic and calmed herself.

Glancing about, she realized her perspective was wrong. She had not viewed the scene from this location. Believing she must have seen it from Dur's point of view, she moved around the square's perimeter, trying to duplicate her recollection. She remembered a tall whitewashed building with pigeons perched along the roofline. Craning her neck, she surveyed the surrounding structures and spotted it almost at once. She continued around the plaza until thought she had it right, then turned to see what lay behind her. Between two buildings ran a narrow passage. She approached it slowly, allowing her eyes to adjust from the glare of the suns. A short distance beyond the opening, heaped against one of the walls was a pile of rags, or so it appeared. Marm moved closer, not wanting to believe it was… but, yes! It was Dur. She rushed to her side.

"Pithien," she whispered, listening for a response. When Dur did not reply, she repeated her name. "Pithien," she called, this time louder.

Still no response.

She dropped to her knees and was relieved to see the rise and fall of the outlaw's chest. Her face was unmarked. Although she was unconscious, she appeared uninjured. Marm sat beside her, placed Dur's head in her lap and sobbed.

Eventually, she roused herself. She knew they could not remain in the alley, but where else could they go? To whom could she turn? She was a stranger here, with no idea if any of Dur's comrades were still alive. Justan should be with the coach, but she and the others had climbed out before he had parked it. Before she could try to find him, she needed to find a safe place for her friend. Moving her would require a purchase and some assistance, she decided. She still had some money, so she returned to the square.

The kindly old woman selling carpets gave her a fair price and even enlisted her husband to take Marm and the rug she had purchased to the passageway. When they arrived, Marm hopped from the wagon saying, "Please wait here while I wrap my things. I have some personal items I would prefer a gentleman did not see."

He agreed and she left him peering after her. Marm did not know whether he would accept her story at face value, or if he would recognize the contents of a rolled carpet for what it was, but with so little time to prepare her story, this was the best solution she could contrive. She dragged her purchase into the passage and was relieved to find Dur where she had left her. She unrolled the rug and hurried to conceal her friend before the old man's eyes became accustomed to the gloom. If she didn't act quickly, he might soon realize what she was doing. As she began to roll the outlaw into the rug, she was startled to find Dur staring up at her.

"Oh, my! Pithien. Are you alright?"

Dur smiled weakly and said, "Do not worry. He will not suspect what you are doing." She closed her eyes. "I have fixed it."

It took Marm a second to understand what she meant, amazed how her friend, even in such a state, took care of things.

"I am ready," Marm called when she had finished.

The old man approached, backlit by sunlight.

"Wouldn't a chest have served you better?" he inquired.

"Once I settle in," Marm replied, "I will need a carpet more."

"So, you're thinking of making Bad Adur your home, are you?"

Too many questions would lead her into a tangle she could not easily escape. To distract him, she gestured at the carpet.

"Please, sir."

"Oh, alright. I hope it's not too heavy."

"I think we can manage," she encouraged. "It is such a short distance."

Each gripped an end and lifted.

"I'm glad for that," the old man said, already breathing heavily. "What exactly do you have in here? I swear this weighs as much as my wife."

Marm winced and replied, "The fabric has a dense weave, as you should know. That's how your wife persuaded me to buy it. Even without my possessions, it weighs nearly twice what I expected." Concerned, lest he drop it, Marm suggested, "Let me know if you think you might let go. It contains some things that might break. We should set it down first."

He did not reply, but nodded, conveniently forgetting he should know the carpet's properties. Fortunately, Marm's fears were for naught. Although he acted as if he might fail at any moment, they got their burden to the cart. With no small effort, they managed to place one end upon its bed. While Marm supported the other, the old man struggled onto the platform and dragged the bundle aboard.

Once they were seated, the old man, dripping with perspiration, turned to her. Panting fiercely he asked, "Alright. Where are we going?"

Marm hesitated. She was reluctant to request anything else, but knew it would be ridiculous to have worked this hard for nothing. After this much exertion, she did not expect he would do another favor out of kindness alone, so she fumbled through her purse and produced a silver coin.

"I'm afraid I don't know this town. Do you know of any accommodations on the east side?"

Justan had deposited them on the east side, so she presumed he would be waiting there.

"The east side. Hmm." He paused to consider. "I believe I do," he said, regarding her dusty clothes. "You won't have to be a person of means, either." He extended his hand, but instead of taking the offering, he closed his fingers around hers. "I won't require this," he said.

"It will be alright, though? I mean, for a lady. Will the lodging be alright? I can pay."

"Oh, yes. I imagine. I mean I've never stayed there myself. Never needed to. I live here. But I know Ohaz, and I'm told he runs a decent enough place. I believe you'll be safe."

If she hadn't put him through so much already, she would have pressed him for more information. "Very well. To Mister Ohaz' establishment it is."

"*Mister* Ohaz!" he snickered. "Right you are, Madam." With that, he cracked his whip and they were off.

Marm was glad, because they had traveled only a short distance when a man turned and stared as they passed, craning his neck to study their faces, leaning to see what the cart was carrying. She hoped the queasy chill she felt was imaginary, but the old man shivered and the horse spooked and would have bolted, save for a firm hand on the reins and its master's voice.

"Easy, girl. Easy!" he soothed. "That's odd. She never startles like that. I wonder what got into her."

"I'm afraid I couldn't say," said Marm. She drew her shawl closer around her shoulders, afraid to look back. "I'm not really familiar with such animals."

# 25

Marm opened her eyes. It took a minute to recall this was a hotel. She had slept poorly and she hurt. She sat up and stretched, then swung her feet to the floor and considered her surroundings: what the old man termed a decent place. Bad Adur boasted street lamps, unlike many frontier towns, and their light revealed a sparsely furnished room. Aside from the sofa on which she had attempted to sleep—torture device was more like it—there was an old table, marred by misuse, supporting a covered light globe. Against the opposing wall stood a bed whose mattress sagged badly under the weight of its occupant. The walls bore nothing by way of decoration and the bare wood floor had seen neither mop nor broom for a long, long time. The windows were draped with the remnants of curtains, much faded and coming apart at the seams. Marm arose carefully, allowing her muscles to adjust, then walked to a window and peered outside. She had no idea what time it might be, but since the street noise had died and the traffic had disappeared, it was either quite late at night or very early in the morning.

Across the room, the sleeper moaned and the covers shifted as she tossed beneath them.

"Marm," she gasped.

Marm hastened to the bedside and leaned over her friend.

"Here I am. How are you?"

"They're dead," Dur sobbed. "They're all dead."

"Who's dead? What do you mean?"

"All of them: Loral, Roman and Bedya."

Abruptly, Dur sat upright and drew Marm down beside her. She clung to her, crying so hard her body shook.

"That can't be," said Marm. "How could…?"

"Dalthin, Marm. The Dalthin got them. I couldn't help," she said, stifling her tears.

"What about Justan?"

"I'm not sure. He wasn't among them. He's…," she paused as if listening. "He's alright. He is still with the coach. We should go to him. He's not safe."

Marm grasped Dur's shoulders to prevent her from rising. "Please don't get up. None of us is safe, but you need to rest."

Dur would have none of it. "Let go," she insisted. She grasped Marm's wrists, removed her hands, then looked helplessly at her. "I couldn't stop them. All I could do was watch. One minute they were men. The next, they were things. One creature's belly opened and devoured Loral. I went for my sword, but my arms wouldn't move. It was like a nightmare. I couldn't stop them. I couldn't fight them. When they came after me, there was nothing I could do but try to run. I couldn't do that either. It was as though my legs were caught in something thick. I've never felt so helpless. All I could think was that I needed to hide, and then it was as if they couldn't see me. They looked around as though they were searching. I struggled to keep out of their way and somehow I managed. I don't know what happened next. I must have passed out."

"You did," said Marm. "I found you unconscious in an alley."

"An alley? We were in the market."

"Perhaps you crawled away."

"I don't remember." She looked at Marm and asked, "How did you find me?"

"You called me."

"I called?"

"With your thoughts. You called and I came."

"I don't remember that either," she said, shaking her head. "Thank you for coming."

"How do you know Roman and Bedya are dead? Were you and Loral able to find them?"

"No. We couldn't. But Loral saw them take Bedya and I no longer sense Roman. Justan is the only one I detect."

"What do you suggest we do?"

"I'm not sure. I had intended to use this town as a base of operations. Now, I don't think it's such a good idea."

"You can't go anywhere until you are stronger," Marm insisted.

"We have to leave. I can recover in the coach. Staying is too risky. In Ydron I could sense them. Now, I cannot."

"How will you decide where to go?"

"You told me these creatures were waiting to be joined by others, so it follows they are few in number. They have situated themselves in

Ydron, a population and political center, as well as here in Bad Adur, a trading hub. I chose this place because of its strategic location. It is likely they situate themselves similarly—in strategic locations. We need to find someplace less attractive. They can't be everywhere." She wobbled to her feet. "Let's find Justan."

"Before we go, I need to share what I know about the palace."

"We'll have time for that later," Dur replied.

"No. Something may happen. We may get separated. Any one of a hundred things can transpire in the hours ahead that would prevent me from sharing what I know. Please, take a few minutes. We are alone and may not have another opportunity."

The outlaw paused to consider. "You may be right."

"Come sit beside me," said Marm. "I have much to share."

As Marm began to relate what she knew, Dur said, "Don't tell me. I will forget your words. Open your mind. Show me. I remember pictures much better."

Uncertain where to begin, Marm hesitated. Then, bit by bit she began to imagine, first the palace grounds, then the palace's interior as most knew it, then each little tunnel and passageway the children had taught her. All the while Dur nodded encouragingly.

# 26

Crossing the Expanse had been difficult. Save for an occasional rivulet of fresh water and one small animal Loral had snared, Reg's party had fared poorly. They had lost their provisions on the cliff face ascent and were fortunate only in that no one had fallen. Further, in contrast to the vast, smooth plain of Nagath–réal, No'eth's undulating topography hindered swift travel, so it was many days before the group reached Losan, the monastery of the Katan.

Several residents descended the butte to help the new arrivals climb the trail to the summit, where it became evident why the monks had chosen this site for their refuge. Situated upon a towering monolith, Losan commanded an enormous view. The West Wind cleared the air, and while No-eth's rugged terrain might conceal travelers from one another, from this vantage any strangers would be visible long before they could approach. Since there was no expeditious route, none made the trek without real business to conduct.

Once Reg's company were within the walls, the monks insured each was bathed, dressed and fed before leading them to their chambers. After they had rested two full days, each was summoned before the high priest to present his version of the events that had brought them.

The high priest sat on a cushion at one end of a great chamber floored with hardwood and walled with marble. Behind him stood an altar upon which rested, open upon a stand, a sizeable book: the Katan. The only other decorations were an alabaster statue of its author, Mog'an, and a large bouquet of flowers at its base. Glassed windows from floor to ceiling opened two entire walls to the outside world and filled the room with sunlight. Reg's escort indicated he was to sit on a cushion before the high priest. By now, all his friends had been interviewed and he would be the last. Once Reg was seated, the monk who brought him bowed and departed, leaving the two alone. Reg bowed as instructed and the high priest returned the gesture, though less profoundly.

"Has your stay been a comfortable one?" the high priest inquired.

"Yes, indeed. Thank you, Revered One," Reg said, using the title as he had been instructed.

"What is the purpose of your visit? What do you seek?" the high priest asked. "I have been informed you are your company's leader."

"So they have honored me, Revered One. My requests are simple. The land we come from is in turmoil, so for my friends I seek safe haven. For myself, I hope for an opportunity to determine the full extent of my new abilities, as well as guidance on how to use them."

"We gladly grant you refuge for as long as you require. In exchange, we ask you and your friends to assist us in our daily work, for everyone works in a monastery."

"Of course, Revered One."

"But I am puzzled. What guidance can we give for these skills you profess to have? Although your companions attest to their existence, I remain skeptical."

Reg smiled. "This place was a beacon during my darkest hour. Not only because of the philosophy you profess, but also because, despite the closed nature of the monastery, you reach out with your minds."

The high priest cocked his head.

"In your efforts to be one with the world, when you meditate your thoughts extend outward. I found them focused and very coherent."

"We are not telepaths. We do not communicate with thought," the high priest countered.

"No, you do not."

"Then, I do not understand."

"While you do not possess my abilities, your thoughts are clearer, more focused and better controlled than any I have encountered. Although they were not intentionally directed at me, they were strong, coherent and I heard them. If I am to bring my abilities to their fullest, I require the same degree of control you possess."

"You must forgive me if I remain unconvinced. I believe you are sincere, that you believe you have unusual powers, and I believe you have convinced your friends as well. But I have no way to determine whether there is any truth to what you profess. Please understand, I mean no offense."

Reg persisted. "Would you be willing to allow me to touch your mind with my own? It is important you believe me."

"What do you mean?"

"I would like to make you aware, in a very tangible way, that we can communicate with thought, the same as we are doing with words."

"And you believe I will know when this has occurred?"

"Just as you know what I am saying when your ears hear these words."

The high priest looked intently into Reg's eyes for a long moment before responding.

"Very well, young man. You have piqued my curiosity. Please proceed."

With care not to startle him, Regilius reached out.

# 27

Lord Emeil considered it ironic the place to which he had fled was the site of the longest siege in Ydron's history. Still, it was a superb place from which to organize and offered unparalleled safety with no possibility of ambush. The menRathan plateau was a long day's ride from danYdron. Removed from Duile's grasp, it was nonetheless near enough to allow for a quick return once they were ready. Commanding an uninterrupted view sweeping from the agricultural fields of western Meden to the arid plains of eastern Ydron, it backed onto a ragged finger of the Tairenth mountains. This ridgeback, too steep and forbidding for any forces to ascend or traverse without the greatest difficulty, was unapproachable from the rear. The surrounding plains and the steep walls of its three remaining faces, as well as the one useable road by which they had arrived, provided no concealment for would-be assailants. That, coupled with menRathan's superior vantage point, left attacking forces exposed to assault from above.

As for those encamped upon it, the available resources greatly facilitated lengthy stays. Artesian springs merged to form a stream that coursed across the plateau. With some work, it could be diverted for irrigation so that, as provisions ran out, livestock could be raised, crops could be grown, and as happened when the historic siege extended beyond its initial year, a large force could be fed with careful rationing. In fact, siege was the only way to vanquish those taking refuge here, but it was a costly strategy requiring long and sustained supply lines. Half in jest, Emeil hoped circumstances would not force his men to remain long enough to test their agricultural skills.

It was the second day since their departure and they had begun to set up camp. Because they had left with scant provisions, he sent parties into every town and village they passed to scavenge for supplies. That had added a full day to their journey. He had even sent one group westward to the sail makers of Sandoval to gather canvas for tents, not only for shelter, but for a mess hall, a field hospital and a command center. He had sent yet another party to Nagath-réal, where provisions could be obtained in quantity. Those should arrive tomorrow.

"General Meiad, how long until camp is ready?" Emeil asked.

"We have nearly finished, my Lord. All should be in order before the evening meal. The night promises to be mild, so the men will manage with ground cloths and bed rolls, as will my officers and I. They can begin setting up their tents when the canvas arrives. I have a small group working with the materials we have to erect a shelter for Your Lordship."

"Tell them not to bother. Until all my men are sheltered, I will sleep in the open beside them."

"My Lord, it will be no great trouble."

"I appreciate your effort, General, but when the battle begins, it is important they believe we are one, so I will not enjoy one bit more comfort than they do."

Meiad smiled. "Very well, my Lord."

"How long do you think it will be before your messengers arrive at their destinations?" Emeil asked.

En route to menRathan, the two had counted allegiances, and as best they could determine, while all of the southern provinces had thrown in with the queen, only Miast in the north had done so. None in the west nor the east had taken her side and it was from these Emeil hoped to draw support.

"Assuming our messengers are granted immediate audience, we should hear from the eastern provinces within a few days, although Borrst and Yeset have probably not maintained forces of any real strength. I suspect Duile has ignored them for this reason. They will probably be neither friends nor foes to be reckoned with. It is more likely we will receive better aid from Nagath-réal and Meden. The trek north will be harder. I've ordered our messengers to keep to the foot of the mountains so, when they reach the river Em they will have an easy crossing. No'eth has never maintained an army and I am uncertain of the response we will receive from Monhedeth, but I suspect they will support us. Still, they may require some time to assemble their forces before coming to your aide. It is Lord Bogen of Limast, however, whom I believe will offer the strongest support. I hope to hear from him before the week is out."

Lord Emeil had been keeping count. "Well, General, at best we have the support of but five of the sixteen provinces."

"Six, my Lord. We must include your own province of Sandoval.

Further, although they will likely be of no real help, No'eth, Borrst and Yeset bring the count to nine lands that the queen cannot count on. While it is unlikely they will assist you, they will not help the queen either. Of the remaining seven supposedly on her side, I do not believe she can count on Lord Mon of Deth. He has grown old and has no appetite for a fight. Further, she has made an enemy of Asch, so Pytheral may not help either. All in all, the lines are drawn somewhat in our favor. I believe that we have every chance of turning the tide to our advantage."

"If help arrives in time," corrected Emeil. "We have no way of knowing how long it will be before Duile can contain us. Time is our enemy. The longer it takes us to obtain assistance, the more time the queen and her advisors have to organize our defeat. Late help is no help."

"You are right, my Lord," said the general in tight-lipped agreement. "I believe you will find the response you seek. Let us pray it arrives in time."

# 28

"And did no one think it peculiar Emeil needed all of his troops to round up an outlaw and a little girl? Could you retain no one, Lydon?

Duile's knuckles were white as she gripped her chair.

"Ma'am, I… They left their encampment intact, so we naturally assumed they would return."

"Even a horse's groom, had one remained, would have provided more of an inducement for Emeil's return than—what have we?—tents, cots and cookware?"

Jomal Ethalan, the Minister of Trade attempted a reply, but Duile cut him off. "Gentlemen, it is now one month since we seized power. According to our original plans, we should be secure and ready to expand our hold. Instead, Emeil has gone, taking his troops with him. Did any of you think to come to me before releasing them?" She rose from her chair as she gave each a long, hard look. "Of course, not. That would have been too easy."

"Ma'am," Lydon ventured, "His messenger seemed most credible."

A new speaker answered for the queen. "I'm sure he believed what he told you. He had no reason to doubt his superiors, but that leant no truth to the offering. Does any messenger you dispatch know the merit of the message he carries?"

All turned to face the speaker. Shrouded in shadow beyond the glow of the light globes, Husted Yar had been reticent until now.

"Had you asked him, he would have replied they headed east and that would have ended matters. The queen's daughter resides to our south, her son in the north. This simple truth would have been enough to unravel the lie."

"And that," the queen turned to Lydon, "is why you are no longer Chief Advisor."

Lydon, who still entertained hopes he might regain his former stature, said, "For one who has only recently ingratiated himself to Your Majesty, he makes easy claims without evidence. It would be simple for me or my peers to say, 'Your Majesty, we have proof your children can be found in Dethen,' or 'They are hiding in Monhedeth.' How it would soothe you, and for the time being, put us in your favor. Do we do so? No, we do not. And why do we refrain? Because we do not have any such knowledge and do not wish to insult your intelligence." He gave Yar a long hard look.

"Husted Yar and I have a long history together," Duile replied, ignoring her advisors' bewildered faces. "He has *not* recently ingratiated himself to me," she continued in a hoarse whisper resembling some animal utterance more than speech. "It is only because of your long years of faithful service and your demonstrated loyalty that I do not have your head separated from your shoulders, Lydon. I shall not tell you why, nor is it important you know, but my new Chief Advisor has given me sufficient evidence this is no deception."

Of course, the Dalthin had done no such thing. Rather, it had merely planted appropriate suggestions she accepted as fact.

Lydon had taken all he could of her humiliation. Before Yar had assumed his present position, Duile and these ministers had functioned as one. Now, it seemed only Yar had her ear. He knew the others felt the same, but they had to speak carefully. They had learned of the queen's promise to Badar Endreth, the late Minister of Foreign Affairs. He had failed in his mission to locate her children and six days ago he had ceased to be. No one saw his execution and the queen never mentioned it, but a fortnight after her threat, he disappeared.

"Your Majesty."

"Yes, Ethalan," the queen replied testily.

"We may have allowed Emeil to slip from our grasp, but for now at least, he is alone in the world. Ydron is as secure as originally planned. We should hasten to occupy Meden, then Limast, before they organize against us. If we do not, we shall never take the northern lands. Lords Hau and Ened have indicated they are ready to act on our behalf. They fear if we allow too much time to pass, we may lose our opportunity to seize barakMeden."

"Finally, you make sense," she said.

"What is more," he said, "if we move quickly, Emeil will be even more isolated. We can sever his legs from under him. We will reveal his treachery and you will no longer require his credibility, for all shall consider him a traitor."

Duile managed a smile.

Lydon joined in. "You know we have rarely erred. Let us turn this setback to our advantage. If we act quickly, we can demonstrate how turncoats like Emeil die for their treason. After isolating Bogen and Miasoth, we can crush him before he can retaliate. I suggest we mobilize Hau and Ened's forces now, while Emeil is waiting for a response from his friends."

"And what of Kareth and Danai's forces, now that their leaders have fallen?" she asked.

"Both Hau and Ened have generals to spare. It would be a fitting reward to place these forces under their commands."

"What do you think of this plan, my dear Husted?"

"Certainly, Your Majesty. It seems a good strategy. I am in complete agreement."

"Very well, Ethalan. Contact the Lords from Liad-Nur and Miast and notify them I have seen the wisdom of their concerns. Do we know where Emeil has gone, Lydon?"

"Yes, Your Majesty. He has made for the plateau of menRathan."

"menRathan?" Duile froze. Had she chosen the spot herself, she could have picked no better refuge. "Are you telling me you are not concerned he has fled to menRathan?" she demanded. "He may as well have fled to Diamath! How do you propose to defeat him there?"

"Your Majesty, do not fear. We will either defeat him or he will be forever isolated and removed as a threat. Either way, he is done for."

"For your sake, Lydon," she paused to survey the room, "For all your sakes, you had better be right or this will be the last time you are ever wrong." Their eyes told her she had made her point.

"Now hunt him down."

# 29

Dur and Marm left the inn while Bad Adur slumbered.

"Do you still sense Justan?" Marm asked, as they poked their heads from the hotel's doorway.

"He is sleeping in the coach," Dur replied. She probed the street in both directions. "Everything seems fine but, by Siemas, I wish I could be certain."

She stood, poised to move, obviously frustrated and reluctant to take the first step. Another minute passed. Perhaps realizing they could not afford to linger, she took a breath and said, "Let's go."

As one, they abandoned the doorway.

"Are you sure where he is?" asked Marm.

"I may not be able to detect the Dalthin, but Justan is this way." She pointed.

As they went, they peered into doorways, down side streets and alleys for anything suspicious. Gradually they gained confidence and quickened their step. Soon the pavement improved and they broke into a run. The neighborhood improved too, and Marm had begun to relax, then remembered it wasn't thieves she needed to fear. Roman, Bedya and Loral had been no match for the Dalthin and neither would she.

"Not much farther," Dur whispered. "We turn right at the next street, then two streets more and we're there."

Marm nodded, breathing hard, unaccustomed to the pace.

At the next corner, Dur signaled a halt. She examined the cross street while Marm scanned ahead. When all seemed clear, Dur motioned to Marm and they turned onto the final leg of their quest, keeping to a walk.

In the wake of the previous day, the going felt suspiciously easy. They crossed to the street's opposite side, avoiding the mouth of an alley. Marm's heart was in her throat and the hairs of her neck were bristling. Her eyes were everywhere and she expected Dur was frightened too. As they passed beneath a street lamp, a glimpse of

Dur's eyes revealed them to be as wide as she suspected her own to be.

The street curved to the right, restricting their view. This was a commercial area with shops lining the narrow lane. An old man in robes was sweeping a storefront's entrance. As they crossed the street to avoid this early riser, Marm saw Dur slip her hand inside the flap of her tunic. She withdrew it and there was a brief glint as she returned her hand to her side. The knife startled Marm. Despite the dangers of the times, she was never one to carry a weapon. Such things were simply not part of her thinking. A hand on her back cut her preoccupation short.

"Run, Marm!"

Dur shoved and Marm ran without question. Only after she had covered some distance did she look back to find she was alone.

"Pithien!" she cried.

She tried to stop and nearly fell as her feet scrabbled on the cobblestones. She recovered and whirled about.

"Pithien!"

The outlaw stood in a half-crouch at the bend in the road, her back to Marm. Her stance was wide, her left arm was extended for balance and the knife pointed upwards in the other. Where the old man had been, a larger figure loomed and Marm could see its belly undulate in the lamplight. The creature advanced and Dur staggered as if struck by a blow. She shook her head and gathered herself. She reeled again, regained her balance and began to circle the thing.

"Pithien!" Marm called again and the Dalthin turned its attention on her.

Terror struck and Marm screamed, but could not run. Her knees buckled and she staggered forward. She grasped her belly as her stomach knotted and the shops around her whirled. Drenched in sweat, her clothing clinging, she fell to all fours in the middle of the street, emptying her stomach onto the pavement. Her body quaked, perspiration streamed down her face and she could not stop crying.

Something like a scream tore through her mind—a cry of agony. In her gut, she knew it wasn't Dur and she hoped it was the Dalthin. She raised her head, pushed her hair from her face and could not believe what she saw. Dur was grappling with the beast, her arms and legs wrapped around it, repeatedly driving her knife into its body. As Dur plunged the blade, the Dalthin tried to retreat, but the outlaw held on, refusing to let it escape. It batted and swiped at her, first with one appendage, then with another, sprouting new ones in succession.

Unable to retain her grasp, Dur leapt aside. She tried to resume her assault, then visibly reeled under the creature's psychic attack.

The Dalthin seemed to have trouble dividing its attention and Marm found her strength returning. She staggered to her feet, knowing she must do something.

Clearing her head, she approached the combatants, frantically looking for any kind of weapon. She stopped at a storefront and leaned against an old wooden table, the kind used to display chobollahs and deleth fruit. A board that prevented produce from rolling off moved under her hand. Surprised by her discovery, she gripped it with both hands, planted her feet and pulled. Once again, the board moved. Encouraged, she pulled again, harder this time and it visibly separated from the table. Determined to have it, she tugged repeatedly, each effort loosening it further. When she saw it was almost free, she gave a fierce yank. It came away and she stumbled backwards, holding her prize in her hands.

Equipped with a weapon of her own, her fear transformed to anger as she turned to face the object of her hatred—one of those who had destroyed her life, her world and her people—one who was trying to kill her friend. She would have no more of it. She would not run again. Timber in hand, she advanced on the creature, determined to do it harm.

It must have sensed her intent, for as she approached it turned on her, rising until it towered above her. No longer intimidated, Marm raised her weapon. The Dalthin assaulted her mind, but the sickening flurry of thought only fueled her anger and she rushed at the beast, striking with all her might. It did not matter that the edges of the board tore into her hands with each blow. She was beyond pain, focused only on what harm she could deliver. Again and again she struck.

It is unlikely she inflicted any deadly harm, but her attack served as a distraction. As Marm battered the thing, Dur struck with her knife. Caught between two assailants, the Dalthin lashed out at one, then the other. But as it focused on one attacker, the second one moved in, and soon the injuries began to mount up. The Dalthin gave up fighting and retreated.

"Come, Marm. It's dying. Let's go," gasped Dur, exhausted and out of breath.

Marm, however, was not about to let it die in peace. She was possessed beyond reason with only one goal. She followed as it backed away, taking pleasure and encouragement as it flinched under each blow. It continued to retreat and Marm was determined to have her way so long as she had strength in her arms. She was flailing away when, on one of the swings, the Dalthin batted the plank from her hands. Glancing from the Dalthin to the board, she tried to decide if she could reach it.

Anticipating the worst, Dur ran at the creature. She was mere steps away when the Dalthin extended a pseudopod and wrapped it around Marm. Before Dur could prevent it, the creature thrust Marm into its abdomen. As Dur watched and her friend stared back, the gash closed. As quickly as that, Marm was gone.

"No! Marm! No!" Pithien dropped to her knees and screamed. This could not be. But it was. And the Dalthin, though dying, cast yet another wave of contemptuous intent at its remaining foe.

Dur, who was not vicious by nature, ordinarily would have preferred to let it slink away and die. But this was not ordinarily. She arose and advanced, one unwavering step at a time. The creature tried to stop her, to hurt her, to cause her to flee in terror, but the outlaw would not be turned. Perhaps she was simply in shock, beyond feeling, for when the Dalthin struck, she did not react. The next time it swiped at her, Dur slashed at the menacing appendage and the Dalthin withdrew it and started to turn away. Then, in a final attempt to save itself, it grabbed her and would have succeeded in stuffing her into its gut as well had not Dur struck back.

Until this moment, her mind had never been more than a useful tool, but she must have undergone some change during this struggle or else had learned something on a subconscious level, because now she knew exactly how to react. With every fiber of her being she delivered the fullness of her hatred, directing it with all the force she could muster at the beast's very core. As suddenly as the Dalthin had grasped her, it released her and a shudder ran through it.

Dur sensed its surprise and its reaction determined her further. She hurt it repeatedly, each time finding new ways to increase the intensity of her attack. Terror began to fill the beast and Dur sensed others of its kind were watching. The creature retreated as far as it could, backing into a wall. Gradually, in the face of this onslaught, it curled and huddled into the smallest mass it could become. Over the next few minutes, the shudders that wracked it diminished until, finally, they subsided altogether. Motion ceased. Dur watched as it died. Then, she stood over it.

As color spread above the eastern horizon and the sky turned a soft shade of green, she probed the creature for any sign of life, the Dalthin's or Marm's deep within. The Dalthin was dead and there was no trace of Marm.

"No!"

She tried to cry, to show emotion, but she could not find her heart and tears would not come. She stood for the longest time, unable to move. Finally, as the weight of what had happened became too great, her legs gave way and she sat hard upon the cobbles. She put her head in her hands and remained unmoving, eyes fixed on the ground before her.

After a while—minutes or hours, she could not say—she became aware of the city stirring. She wondered what the citizens of Bad Adur would think when they stumbled upon this dead horror's corpse and decided she didn't much care.

Knowing she had to leave, she gathered herself and stood. She wanted to cut the thing open and bury Marm's body, but there was no time. At least one more of these things was infesting this town and she was sure it would want revenge. Nor would it be caught off guard and killed so easily as this one. Even now, it was probably coming for her and her one remaining companion. It was time to go. It was too late for Marm, but she hoped she had enough time remaining to save Justan.

# 30

Reg had been striving to master his thoughts since his arrival at Losan. His progress was slow and he was frustrated. He knew it would be years, if ever, before he acquired the concentration the monks had attained. Their practice required him to spend nearly all his waking hours either meditating or under the high priest, Hazis', instruction. Patience was a virtue he thought he possessed until he tried to meditate the twelve hours daily the Katan required. Still, he had learned a little and was eager to test his skills.

The bell indicating the end of morning meditation sounded and the monks rose from their cushions, filling the halls and courtyards with the susurrus of flowing robes and the tapping of sandaled feet. This morning, Reg forewent breakfast in the community dining hall for the chance to gather news from the outside world. He stopped by the kitchen for a cup of tea and a slice of bread to take to the garden, then made his way to a bench under an eshed tree and sat. As he sipped the fragrant beverage and munched the rich grainy bread, absorbed in the taste, aroma and texture, he made eating a meditation. When he finished, he closed his eyes and extended his mind outward.

At first, he simply listened. Nearby, of course, were the monastery's residents. Then, some distance removed, the inhabitants of… *Ah! Yes. Limast.* The direction was correct. Although he was worried about reaching as far as Ydron, there was more to gain by attempting it than there was to lose. Over the past several weeks he had learned to skim the tops of thoughts, acquiring the thinker's identity without disturbing the one generating them. Now, as he reached out toward home, he hoped to locate a specific kind of mind without revealing his presence.

Thus he sat for nearly an hour, looking for clues he was on the right track. Eventually, he located the outer city, moving from there to the citadel, suppressing his excitement. Here was real danger, were he discovered. Here also was much needed information.

After what may have been another hour, he located the object of his quest—an alien mind, yet not unfamiliar—a Dalthin's mind. He settled in among those thoughts, listening, refraining from thinking his own. He quieted his breathing and stilled his mind, exactly as Hazis had taught.

… … … … …

Unlike many who were stationed in pairs, Husted Yar was alone within the palace. Actually, alone is not a word one can apply to a Dalthin in other than a purely physical sense. Each individual is joined to every other by a network of thought so interconnected each is immediately aware of the experiences and thoughts of the others. They are very nearly a single organism. Were Ai'Lorc asked to provide an example of similar intertwinement, he would have offered a forest of damass trees far to the north as the largest single organism inhabiting this planet. Occupying dozens of square miles, the trees are completely interconnected by a common root system, making it impossible to determine where one tree begins and another ends. The roots are not merely intertwined but have grown into each other to the point there is no distinction between them. Except where each trunk emerges from the soil, giving the appearance of a separate entity, they are one, each indistinguishable from the rest below the surface. So it is with the Dalthin.

At this moment, in the midst of a gluttonous feast upon several unfortunates, Yar was ruminating over the problem Duile's children were posing. Never had the Dalthin encountered another species able to use their minds as the male child had demonstrated. And while the female sibling had only shown she possessed a voice, it was not unreasonable to project her talents eventually surpassing her brother's. It was the uncertain extent to which their abilities might still develop that caused the Dalthin concern.

Then, there was the third, the unrelated other. While this female, when cornered in Bad Adur, had not exhibited the raw power the male had evinced, her demonstrated ability to kill made her more than an oddity to be observed. The one Dalthin still remaining in that town would need to keep its distance while it tracked her, or risk the same fate as its cohort. They could no longer pit one lone Dalthin against any of them. After the loss to date of seven of their kind, they resolved to eliminate this trio before The Arrival.

… … … … …

Reg could scarcely contain himself. This was more than he had hoped for. He carefully extricated himself from the creature's mind, grateful it had been absorbed in its feast. He decided to contact the third telepath and learn in detail what had happened. Because of her abilities, he expected her mind would stand out, making her easy to detect. He also wanted to locate his sister.

One more intriguing tidbit had turned up, just before he separated himself from that mind, suggesting Lord Emeil had turned against Reg's mother. Had he really? That would open possibilities Reg had until now only wished for. Although he expected Emeil would be harder to locate than the outlaw, he had touched him once, so perhaps he would recognize him again. Reg had already considered what he would do should anyone be so bold as to challenge his mother. If he could establish Emeil had really done so, he would gather his friends and set those plans into motion.

# 31

The caravan's dust choked Dur's throat and stung her eyes despite the kerchief she had secured for protection. She and Justan had joined this caravan to Liad-Nur, seeking safety in numbers. Although Justan had suggested she ride inside the coach to save her from the clouds of dirt, she longed for companionship and insisted she sit beside him. It wasn't conversation she needed, but his presence, so she leaned against his shoulder as they jostled and bounced amid oxen, horses and wagons, sinking deeper into her thoughts with each passing hour.

She was confused, depressed beyond words. Unable to protect the woman she had befriended, she had also been unable to perceive the murderers of her life-long friends. She heaped recriminations on herself: she should have stayed with them; she should have anticipated the danger; she should have taken precautions; she should have been able to sense *something*. Instead, she had been as oblivious to the Dalthin as would a blind person. Once again, as in the hotel room, she broke down sobbing.

Justan regarded her tenderly and placed a hand on her arm. Then, with nothing else to do, he let her be and settled into the driving.

As evening fell, ending a day already grown far too long, a new resolve began to take root. She was unaccustomed to defeat and these losses cut to her core. It was as unthinkable her friends should die for nothing as it would be for her to sit idly in response. While she did not yet know how she would repay the Dalthin, she could insure Marm's plan did not die with her.

"Justan."

"Yes, Pithien?"

"We are returning to danYdron."

"Are we going to Benjin and Jenethra's?"

"You are. The city grows more dangerous by the day. Have them pack their things, then take them to Mikah's in Limast."

"That doesn't sound like you will be joining us."

"I won't. I have work to do at the palace."

"Pithien, they will be looking for you. I have never questioned you before, but that is the worst place you could be."

"Sometimes the best hiding place is in plain sight. Besides, I have grown tired of running." Justan began to object, but Pithien silenced him saying, "I am in no mood to argue."

The coach struck a pothole, startling them and ending the conversation. As Dur huddled in the seat, bundled against the evening chill, a familiar mind touched hers. She sat upright. Prince Regilius was inquiring about the Dalthin she had killed and it startled her he possessed such immediate knowledge. She asked if he knew about his nanny. When he admitted he did not, she told him about Marm and his sudden, overwhelming grief made her forget her own for a moment. They spoke a while longer as he warned of the Dalthin tracking her. After he was gone, she smiled, assured she was not as isolated as she felt.

# 32

"I understand," Ered said, barely louder than a whisper. "Yes, Reg. I will." With that, he sat up, rubbed the sleep from his eyes and looked around.

His cell accommodated a cot, a mat and a cushion should he choose to meditate. There was also a small wooden table with a ceramic basin to wash up in. After nearly a month and a half, he found the furnishings and food barely tolerable. While the monks were hospitable, he remained only because Regilius chose to stay. Were it not for his friend, he would have gathered his possessions and made for more familiar parts. He rose and splashed water on his face, then dried himself. Refreshed, he went to join his companions as Reg had requested.

Finding the garden was easy. The monastery enclosed it on all sides and numerous doors opened onto the large open space. The well-tended vegetable plot provided much of Losan's food. In each corner, beneath eshed trees planted for shade, were benches where the monks could contemplate and study. He spotted Reg sitting on the ground beneath one of them, accompanied by Danth and Leovar and he hurried to join them.

"Good morning," said Reg. "How did you sleep?"

"Well enough," Ered answered, looking around. "Isn't Ai'Lorc going to join us?"

"He is coming." Reg replied.

"He is alright then?"

"He is doing much better. In fact, he helped plan this morning's meal."

Ever since Reg had told the group about Marm's death, they had all been devastated. After all, she had been the only real mother the boys had known. Even Pedreth was struck hard by her passing. Ai'Lorc, however, seemed impacted the most. He had been inconsolable. They had scarcely seen him, and on those occasions such a pall of grief hung over him that none dared intrude. They began to suspect he had cared for her far more than he ever let on.

"I am glad," said Leovar. "I feel sorry enough for him as it is. He and Marm were alone here before that thing killed her. Now, he's completely isolated."

"He is separated from his people, but he is not alone and doesn't feel that way," Reg said. "Even in grief, he knows he is among friends. He has thrown in with us entirely out of choice. As his sorrow lessens, he will return to us."

"And my father? Where is he?" Ered asked.

"We sent him to the kitchen," replied Ai'Lorc, coming upon the group from behind.

"Ai'Lorc!" Leovar, Danth and Ered exclaimed in unison.

"Good morning." He greeted them in a quiet voice as he found a place between Danth and Reg. "Thank you for your concern. I feel better now. Pedreth and I thought we would break fast in the open for a change and he is helping the monks bring what they have prepared. On a morning like this, eating outdoors is a wonderful idea."

"Also, I suspect this discussion is not for the ears of the monks," offered Leovar.

"Actually, Hazis is privy to much of what I will tell you," corrected Reg.

Leovar looked alarmed. "Really, Reg? How much does he know?"

"Almost everything."

"Don't you think that's a bit much? We really don't know him."

"I do not," said Reg. "The more I refine my abilities and touch other minds, the more honest and open I am compelled to be. Openness is never the threat, but rather another's deceit and treachery. When one can clearly perceive a person's honesty, trust follows. Naturally, when one cannot perceive the other's thoughts, fear enters into the equation and caution is the only recourse. If all the world could see as I am beginning to, deceit would be impossible. And no, the monks will not reveal us to anyone else because, for one, we are too remotely situated, and second, it is not their nature. We can count on them absolutely."

Looking up, Reg smiled. "Ah! Breakfast has arrived."

At that, everyone turned and saw Pedreth approaching, arms laden with treasure.

"Father!" Ered shouted.

"Good morning all. The baker was at his best this morning." With a flourish, Pedreth removed the cloth from the basket and placed it on the ground. To the accompaniment of exclamations, he began handing out sweet rolls and pastries, the likes of which they had not seen since their arrival.

"How did you convince him to make something other than bread?" asked Leovar.

"I think master Regilius had something to do with this extraordinary demonstration of his talents," Pedreth replied with a smile, adding a wink in Reg's direction. "Am I not right?"

"I let him know this is a special occasion," said Reg.

"Special?" asked Ered. "How so?"

"Let us enjoy this fine repast first," suggested Reg. "Afterwards, I will discuss the matters at hand." Then, gesturing toward a group of monks who were approaching with a number of items clearly intended for this breakfast, he asked, "Still more, Pedreth?"

"I thought we would enjoy hot mure tea and some fruit," he said.

The monks placed an urn, some cups and a large bowl of chobollahs beside the pastry basket.

"Thank you, brothers, and pass our thanks to those in the kitchen," said Reg.

The friends dug into the meal, grateful to enjoy something beyond the usual fare.

"Reg," said Leovar, wiping crumbs from his mouth, "Why do you never mention Lith-An? Whenever you mention home, you speak of your parents, but never your sister. Do you know how she is?"

"Lith-An is fine, Leovar. I never mention her because I know she is unharmed."

"She is alive?"

"She is alive."

"But where is she?"

"For the moment, I am only prepared to say she is unharmed." He paused, then catching Leovar's next thought, "Of course, I trust you."

"I'm sorry."

"That's alright. She and I have been in touch for several days and she is in no immediate danger."

Leovar accepted the obscure reply with a nod.

In truth, Regilius did not want to think about his sister more than he needed to. He still controlled his thoughts less perfectly than he would like and did not wish to provide the Dalthin clues to her whereabouts. Fortunately, detecting a mind did not reveal its exact location, only its general direction, so he could not accidentally provide specific information.

When he first set out to find her, he had contacted her without much effort, although he was unsure he had touched the right mind. To his great surprise, hers was no longer a toddler's. She had undergone profound transformation, more radical than his own, and was still changing. She had much to share and the information she provided, as well as what he had gleaned from Husted Yar, helped shape his plan.

Eventually, he set aside the remainder of his breakfast and studied his companions.

"It is time you know why I have brought you together, " he said. "You see, I must send you all on another mission. We came here together because, at the time, there was no alternative. Ydron was unsafe, then as now. But while there is still much left for me to accomplish here, these walls hold nothing for you."

"Reg," Ered interrupted, "We can wait by your side until Jadon grows as large as Mahaz. We're not at all bored."

Reg smiled. "I am not feeling sorry for you, Ered. My comment does not stem from a desire to alleviate the tedium of monastic life, but from a growing awareness how much remains to be done if we are to turn the events that brought us here. For the moment, it is you who must tend to these matters. Clearly you cannot return home. Mother's guards are searching for all of us. I doubt any of us would survive, once found. Yet there is much each of you can do elsewhere.

"Emeil is trying to amass forces to mount an attack against my mother's army. It is imperative he succeed. But many who might join him fear to do so, perhaps because they are unaware of his real motives.

"Danth, Lord Bogen owes your family many favors and his troops number more than three thousand. You need to return to Limast to persuade him to aid Emeil. Lord Jath of Nagath-réal is also beholden to you. It is time to call in your favors. And Leovar, for generations the house of Hol has supported both the houses of Basham and Miasoth. You must seek their assistance. This journey requires you to cross the river Em and will be the more perilous of the two. I only wish I had the foresight to send you east when we first set off."

"Reg," replied Leovar. "There is a crossing a day east of here. The route I have in mind passes near Miasoth's mines in danBashad. I can see him first, on my way to Yeset, and travel undetected making good time for the bargain. If I can obtain a horse on the way, I can make better time still."

"I will do you one better," said Reg. "The Haroun, the tribe of the fabled hunter, Bedistai Alongquith, have offered two prized hunting endaths. While endaths cannot manage the load a horse can, they will cover more than twice the ground in a day, so you won't require nearly the provisions and you'll arrive days sooner."

"Why two?" Leovar asked.

"I am sending Ai'Lorc with you. The route is not easy, and it will be best if someone accompanies you."

Leovar turned to Reg's tutor. "Do you ride? I must make good time."

"It has been some time," Ai'Lorc said. "But I was once quite at home in the saddle. It is something one never forgets. I won't slow you." Turning to Reg, he added, "Aside from its speed, an endath's gait is purported to be most smooth. My poor soft behind won't be sore at the end of the day. I thank you."

"Not at all," Reg smiled. Then, turning to Pedreth he said, "I am sending you with Ered and Danth. You will need to take a seaward route to reach Limast. I am hoping Lord Bogen will honor his relationship with Danth's family and will suitably equip the three of you for safe travel to Nagath-réal."

Pedreth nodded, but Ered objected.

"No. I will stay here! I know you trust these monks, but you can never tell when you will need a real friend."

Before Reg could reply, Pedreth said, "That's an excellent idea. Danth and I will do quite well by ourselves."

"I am not sure I agree," Reg responded.

"Father clearly agrees with me," said Ered. "You will need me here."

"That's not why your father wants you to remain behind." Then to Pedreth, he said, "He will indeed be safer here."

"And two can make better time and are less likely to be spotted than three," Pedreth emphasized.

"Although Ered is more agile," countered Reg. "Perhaps it is you who should remain."

Pedreth was indignant. "Did I slow you down or appear the least winded on the way up the cliff after we landed? I may be older, but I am not old! There's not one gray hair on my head, so don't speak condescendingly. And while my son is a good boy and reliable, I am quicker of wit and this mission may require it."

Reg relented. "You are right. I am sorry."

Ered, however, was clearly hurt. "So I am a dullard, am I?"

"No, son. Not a dullard. But I think more quickly on my feet. Do you remember how I got you to admit you had stolen the skiff for practice last year?"

Ered lowered his eyes and nodded.

"This is no time for bravado," said Pedreth. "Lives are at stake. And I must say, I am confused. Are you arguing to go or to stay?"

"To stay, of course."

"Then drop this defensiveness. If your feelings are going to be hurt by the least little comment, then you certainly should stay. In the heat of the moment on the way to Limast your feelings are certain to be hurt more than once. We will have no time to be diplomatic."

Ered shrugged.

"So it is settled," said Pedreth. He turned to Danth, putting his hand on his shoulder. "So, Lord Kanagh, are you up to this?"

"Thanks to Reg," he said. "I won't let you down."

"You never have," Pedreth replied.

"We are agreed, then," Reg said. "It is Ai'Lorc and Leovar to Meden first, then on to Yeset. And Pedreth and Danth to Limast, then Nagath-réal. Good. We have a new purpose. Ered, it seems you will stay with me. I must say, in the end I will be glad to have your company when I can, though I will continue to be busy and you will not be seeing much of me." He turned to the rest. "Let us busy ourselves. We have much preparation to do."

# 33

The endaths' strides were as smooth as rumors suggested, and Ai'Lorc soon became accustomed. Even the saddles were smooth and soft and they conformed to the backs of the beasts, serving only as a place to attach stirrups. With their serpentine necks and tails, endaths resembled long-extinct creatures sprung from the dawn of time. Bearing moderate loads, they are capable of ranging great distances, rarely tiring. This in mind, the monks had provisioned them adequately. As well as Ai'Lorc could determine, nothing essential had been omitted—essential being the operative word—bringing with them a few days' bread, two water sacks and some dried meat and fruit. Leovar and Ai'Lorc were each given a knife and a large sandiath skin that would serve as a blanket and double in a storm as protection from wind and rain. Because Leovar professed to be an archer, he was also provided with a bow and arrows. The Haroun did not use crossbows, so Ai'Lorc remained unarmed. There was nothing with which to start a fire, because smoke would announce their presence. Consequently, there were no cooking utensils.

Ai'Lorc glanced skyward and noted that Jadon, now partially occluded, would soon slip behind Mahaz. The vagaries of a planet orbiting binary suns prevent seasons of the sort he had known on his home world. Still, there were warm cycles and cold cycles and now, as this hemisphere tilted away, they were moving into a cold cycle. The orange giant appeared more distant and lower in the sky than normal. With Jadon masked by its cooler companion, this cold cycle would be unusually severe. At least they were not at sea. Hoping Danth and Pedreth would fare well, he drew his coat closer.

"How long, do you think, before we reach Meden?" he asked.

"We should be nearing the river soon. Once we cross, we are there. The fortress is another day-and-a-half farther, at best."

Just then, they topped a rise and Ai'Lorc realized the inexplicable roar he had been hearing all day was the Em coursing between its banks. He had been expecting a meandering current slowly making its way to the sea—not the fierce wide torrent before them. They reined in their endaths to deliberate their strategy.

"I think our crossing lies another hour upstream," said Leovar.

"Surely you must be joking," said Ai'Lorc as he eyed the whitecaps.

Leovar shook his head. "Long ago I heard of a crossing midway between the river's mouth and its source. The Haroun know it well and have told me how to find it."

Ai'Lorc was still staring at the flood, so Leovar asked, "Why do you think the Haroun have never been conquered from the south? Few fortress walls are as secure. But, yes, there is a place where the river widens and the current is somewhat abated. I don't wish to die either."

They studied the terrain before continuing, deciding to ride the ridgeline to better recognize the crossing. They had been riding longer than they had expected, when Leovar ordered another halt. The Em had indeed widened and the white water had lessened. He motioned Ai'Lorc to follow, then headed his steed into the river gorge. As they approached the Em, the sky darkened and the wind began to escalate.

"I think the gods disfavor us," Leovar quipped. "Twice they have set a storm in our path."

"Perhaps we should find shelter and allow it to pass," Ai'Lorc suggested.

"We don't have the provisions. Either we go now, before the wind builds to its fullest, or we turn back. In that case, it may be several days before we return and we do not have the luxury of time."

When Ai'Lorc still appeared uncertain, Leovar said, "If you cannot continue, then turn back and I will go it alone."

"I didn't elect to remain on your world to let Duile have her way. Let's go." With that, Ai'Lorc spurred his endath toward the river bank.

"Wait," called Leovar, urging his own mount forward. When he caught up with the alien, he asked, "Have you ever done anything like this before?"

"No," Ai'Lorc conceded.

"Then follow closely in my endath's footsteps," he ordered. "The crossing is hazardous under the best of circumstances."

Ai'Lorc nodded and followed Leovar into the river.

Each beast reacted to the river's cold with a start, rearing onto its hind legs. Then, at their rider's urging, they made their way into the rushing water. Each step they took was deliberate. Swift and sure-footed on dry land, here they were uncertain. Their legs had to work hard against the current and they craned their necks to see where next to step. By the time they were nearing midstream, they began to calm and Leovar began to gain confidence.

"Not much farther now," he encouraged. But when he turned to see how Ai'Lorc was doing, he saw how his animal was slipping downstream. "Careful! You're drifting. Bring her up behind me," he shouted.

It was too late. Ai'Lorc's endath was struggling. Its tail thrashed the water as it tried to maintain its balance. In the next instant, it stepped into a hole sending Ai'Lorc into the river. As the current carried the creature away, Leovar reined in his own. Without regard for his own safety, he dove after his friend.

The cold stunned him and he knew they could not survive long. He surfaced and shook his head to clear his vision. He saw Ai'Lorc's head and stroked furiously to overtake him. Drawing nearer, he could see Ai'Lorc's arms windmilling.

*Good. He is conscious and swimming for it*, he thought and pulled even harder. "Ai'Lorc!" he called.

The wind and water drowned out his voice, so he waited until he had drawn alongside before trying again. The cold was robbing his strength and his limbs, nearly numb, were becoming like weights.

"Ai'Lorc!" he gasped, spitting water. The alien turned. "Can you make it?"

"I think so. You?"

"Think so."

Ai'Lorc pulled for the shore with Leovar beside him. As near as the opposite bank had appeared from the saddle, it seemed all the more distant now. As if to taunt them, the wind was increasing, blowing spray into their eyes and water into their mouths.

Leovar was fading. It was all he could do to bring his arms to the surface to begin each stroke. No longer able to kick, he began drifting downstream into rougher water. He was abandoning hope of reaching shore, seeking only to stay afloat. He prayed for rest or sleep or some kind of miracle as he struggled keep his mouth above the waves. When he started to slip beneath the surface, he thought it nice he could no longer feel the cold. Just as his arms stopped working, his tunic tightened around the chest.

… … … … …

Ai'Lorc gripped Leovar's tunic. He had seen him go under, grabbed and got lucky with a handful of cloth. Leovar was too heavy to pull to the surface, so holding tight, lest he lose his friend forever, he took three deep breaths and dove under. The murk obscured everything, so he maneuvered solely by touch. Once underneath him, Ai'Lorc wrapped his free arm around, kicked hard, and with the other hand stroked for the surface.

They broke the wave tops and Ai'Lorc gasped. He saw the shore, prayed it was the nearer one and swam on his side for all he was worth, cradling Leovar's head in the crook of his arm. He could not tell if his friend were dead or alive and right now it did not matter. His own strength was ebbing. If he couldn't pull Leovar to shore, they would die together. He would not abandon him.

Closing his mind to the distance, the cold and the difficulty, he dealt with his task one stroke at a time. His strength had nearly vanished when his feet struck bottom. He was struggling to sit, taking care to keep Leovar's face above the surface, when his left hip bumped something hard. Too cold to feel pain, he knew it would hurt later. He tried to stand, but it was more than he could manage, so he crawled from the river. Strength ebbing by the second, he dragged Leovar up the embankment, examined him quickly and saw no sign of life. He needed to rest, but was beginning to tremble. He knew if they did not get out of the wind, they would die on the shore, if Leovar were even alive.

Desperate for shelter, he spotted a hillock a short distance from the water. Its nearer side had been hollowed out, perhaps by previous floods. Dragging Leovar as he crawled, Ai'Lorc reached it the moment his strength evaporated. Cold beyond bearing and shivering uncontrollably, he spied something that made him gasp—an endath approaching them along the river bank. After what seemed an eternity, the animal arrived beside them. Ai'Lorc grasped the reins and pulled it to its knees. The last thing he knew before lapsing into unconsciousness was heat from the creature's body as it lay down beside them.

# 34

Leovar awoke to a warm bitter taste. He opened his eyes and tried to sit, but something prevented it.

"Easy, Leovar," said Ai'Lorc, his hand on Leovar's chest. "Lie still and drink."

"What is it?" Although disoriented, he managed to take the cup.

"I found some herbs and prepared a tea."

"Tea? But how?"

"Do you think you are the only one with medicinal knowledge?"

"I don't mean that," Leovar protested. "I mean, how could you prepare tea?"

"With water and a small fire," Ai'Lorc explained.

"How could you build a fire?"

"Oh! I see." Ai'Lorc looked amused. "The solution is not obvious.

"Well, my fine archer, I sacrificed one of your arrows for its tip. It made a fine shower of sparks when struck against the blade of my knife. It wasn't easy, but with patience I managed to get some dry grass smoldering and ignited a bit of kindling. Watch it, my friend, or I'll challenge your reputation as a woodsman. Now, drink up."

"But what did you prepare it in?" he asked, still unsatisfied.

"You're drinking from it."

Leovar examined the cup, unable to recognize it. "We packed no cup."

"No, but your quiver had a fine metal bottom—not very deep, nor with room for more than a dozen arrowheads. Since I preserved a rim of the leather above it, the cup has enough depth to hold your tea. I am afraid the quiver is useless."

Leovar examined the cup, admiring his friend's resourcefulness. He took several careful sips then asked, "Do you think a fire is wise?"

"I will have to extinguish it in a minute or two, but I needed it to tend to you, and myself as well, if the truth be told. Now drink."

When Leovar finished the brew he sat upright. "Thank you. I feel better."

"It is probably more from having some warmth in your belly than from the medicine. That will take somewhat longer, I imagine."

"One more thing. How did we get here?"

Rising, Ai'Lorc smiled and said, "I can't leave the fire too long. After I have prepared a cup for myself, I will bring some fruit and explain everything. Now, lie down." He turned and limped away.

The small container came quickly to a boil. Once he had downed the tea, he kicked dirt onto the fire, extinguishing it. Satisfied it was dead, he scattered the ashes until there was no discernable trace, then made his way back and climbed under the sandiath blanket beside his friend.

"Here," he said, handing Leovar a chobollah.

"Returning to my question," said Leovar, "How did you save me? I would have thought it would be the other way around."

"Because you are young?" Ai'Lorc asked.

"I suppose."

"First, I have always been a strong swimmer. Second, I suspect it is a difference in constitution. Engineered as I am to survive here, I have always dealt with cold much better than Regilius. Whatever the reason, I am certainly glad one of us could manage the swim." He bit into the fruit with a deliberate crunch.

"But, the dry clothes, the endaths… "

"Ah, yes! The endaths. Such remarkable creatures. The Haroun believe they are empathic, remarkably sensitive to their rider's needs. We needed warmth. They provided it. We needed our gear and the change of clothing. They remained close by."

"I see."

"Speaking of warmth, how are you doing?"

"A bit weak, but fine I suppose. You certainly seem alright."

"I am managing," Ai'Lorc replied. "Do you think you can ride?"

Leovar nodded and asked, "Why? Must we get underway so soon?"

"If you feel you cannot rest well enough on your endath's back, then we will remain. But if you can, we should go. Food and care are waiting in Meden."

"You are right. I was forgetting. I can ride well enough. We should go."

"I am tired too," said Ai'Lorc, arising. "We will rest as we need to, but it is best we do not jeopardize our mission, either by pushing too hard or by resting too long."

Ai'Lorc stumbled as he carried the blanket toward the endaths and Leovar realized he was hiding how severely yesterday's ordeal had affected him.

"I will help you break camp," he said.

# 35

"Another minute and you would have been late for the watch," the corporal chided.

"You worry too much," said the private, breathing hard after bounding up the parapet stairs. "I am always on time."

"Yes, but barely."

"Do you really think I am eager to face a court martial for something this trivial? Listen, if I want the sergeant all over my back, it won't be for something minor. Believe me. I'll think of something really good."

The corporal shook his head. "Just remember," he said. "I won't cover for you."

"You won't have to," the private countered. "Although I have to tell you, I think Lord Miasoth is making too much of what is happening in Ydron. Here we are, two, maybe three days to the east of Manhathus'—excuse me, since we were discussing my timeliness—the *late* Manhathus' palace," he chuckled. "There is not a banner to be seen nor a trumpet to be heard, yet security is heightened, watches are doubled and you and I are spending our days and nights freezing on the battlements so Miasoth can sleep."

Saying barakMeden's guard had been doubled was an understatement. Normally, these two would have been the only ones standing watch. For the last few weeks there were nearly a dozen on the ramparts, regardless of the hour.

"Word has it Meden will not be safe much longer. The queen says she will repay those who did not help her secure the throne," said the corporal.

"You mean *take* the throne. But, really, do you think Duile wishes to be queen of the wilderness? Dominatrix of the wild frontier?"

"You make us to be as remote as Monhedeth."

"We are but a marmath's leap from No'eth. The Expanse is our back yard. Were it not for the Em, the Haroun would be our neighbors and we would be hunters."

"And that is all the difference in the world," the corporal said. "These cultivated fields are what distinguish us… " He swept his arm in a grand gesture for emphasis, then halted as he spotted something moving across the fields. "What is that?" He strained to see. "I could be mistaken, but I think the Haroun are coming to join us."

"Nonsense," sneered the private. But as he turned to look in the direction his comrade was pointing, his mouth fell open. "Are those endaths?"

"I have never seen one, but they must be."

The farmlands of Meden were normally gold under a clear green sky—the sky's coloration the result of the orange giant, Mahaz—and dun colored endaths, well camouflaged in the wild, should have stood out against them. Perhaps because the overcast muted the landscape, they had arrived almost unnoticed. Although never in recent memory had they been seen in these parts, no other creature shared the long neck and tail of these fabled beasts.

"Send out an alarm."

Even as he spoke, bells rang out, scattering pigeons from their roosts.

… … … … …

"Halt at once! Announce yourself!" came the challenge from the battlements.

Leovar looked up from his saddle and attempted to identify the source. As he clung to the pommel, he grew dimly aware they had halted before the gate of Meden's fortress. It had been three days since they had crossed the Em and the previous two were a blur. He was fever-stricken, close to delirium, and it was a miracle they had managed to arrive here at all. Glancing to his left, he realized Ai'Lorc was in no better shape. The remedy he prepared had served its purpose for a while. But when they needed it next, neither had the strength to prepare another dose. Their journey had taken longer than it should have because of their clouded thinking, and they had forged on because there was no alternative. More than once they found themselves going the wrong direction and had to retrace their route. In part because they had eaten, in part because the endaths kept them warm at night, but most of all because they were determined not to fail, they had come this far. Now, however, all one could say was they were alive.

As Leovar sat weaving in the saddle, he dimly remembered he should seek an audience with Lord Miasoth. Unable to make out who addressed them or what was said, he assumed a guard was challenging them, and attempted to give an appropriate response. The words, "Leovar Hol," emerged as a croak, then he fell to the ground unconscious.

# 36

Water splashed against the dinghy's bow and the oars thudded and creaked in the oarlocks as Danth put his back into rowing. That morning, when he and Pedreth reached the coast, they realized how poorly they had planned. It had never occurred to either the denaJadiz might be reduced to wreckage. When they came upon her shattered remains they were dismayed, for it was impossible to traverse the mouth of the Em except by sea. It was then, as they were bemoaning their luck, they spied a small miracle—a tiny boat, replete with oars, perched on a sandbar next to the ketch. The storm had destroyed the larger vessel, but the skiff had survived. They were delighted she was seaworthy since they didn't have far to go, at least by water. While Danth rowed, Pedreth turned his gaze to shore.

"What do you see?" Danth asked.

Pedreth searched the shore intently, then replied, "I see falls."

Danth squinted. "I see mist."

"Same thing," said Pedreth. "A wall of mist a mile wide. When there's no offshore wind to blow it away, the falls put up a wall of spray as wide as the river."

"I'm glad we didn't try to cross it."

"We couldn't."

Danth nodded. After a moment he asked, "How do you think Ai'Lorc and Leovar have fared?"

Pedreth paused to consider. "They are up to anything they encounter. They didn't take an easy route, but if any of us could have managed it, I would wager on those two."

"Do we have the easier route?"

"Son, there are no easy routes these days.

"Tell me," he said, changing subjects, "how goes it with you? You used to be quite the scrapper, always up for a fight. These days you're quieter than I remember. Has the fight gone out of you?" He cocked an inquisitive eye at the youth.

"I have quieted quite a bit, haven't I? I certainly understand I am not invulnerable, but you are wondering if I have lost my nerve."

Pedreth nodded. "We may be in for more than a stroll, my boy."

"I told you before, I will not let you down."

"And you're cautious, as well?"

"What do you mean?"

"If you still have some fight in you, my next concern is whether you are still a bit reckless. I need bravery without the emotion."

"Just because I went through all that and came out alive at the other end doesn't mean I want to try it again. Of course, I'll be cautious."

"Good."

Danth smiled. "You know I enjoy your company, but why didn't you insist Ered come instead of me? I should have thought you would prefer to travel as father and son."

"Ered is where he belongs."

"Have you two had a falling out I am not aware of?"

"Nothing like that, but I see where you're going. Let me try to explain.

"As much as I love him, I also understand where his strengths and his weaknesses lie. You and I are in the midst of a very dangerous undertaking. Should matters take a bad turn and we need to fight for our lives, I want someone at my side who will remain clear-headed in a crisis."

"But in the storm he never showed a cowardly bone," Danth protested.

"Different animal. Fighting a storm isn't like fighting a person. It can't look you in the eye to intimidate you. And, you're right. He was as brave and trustworthy as I could ask for. I would face the worst seas with him in a heartbeat. But would I feel the same in a fight? Ask yourself when you last saw Ered fight with anyone. I don't think he ever did. You, on the other hand, were never one to back down. That's why I asked if you were still scrappy. I had a hunch what you would say. People rarely change overnight and I wasn't about to settle on a traveling companion by playing politics."

"You don't think you hurt his feelings?"

"Did he act like I did? No, and he didn't hurt mine. He wants to be with Reg, and that is how I left it."

"Well, you're right. I won't be backed down, though I hope it won't come to that. We're not exactly well-armed."

Only a sword had survived the climb when the ketch ran aground and the monks had nothing but staves and pikes with which to arm them—an offer they had declined. The hunting bows and knives the Haroun had provided would leave them a poor second in an armed confrontation, so it would not be their abilities that would keep them alive, but rather, stealth and cunning.

"My turn," said Pedreth and he moved to change positions.

Danth didn't argue. "I need a rest. I think I've grown soft."

"I think you lads are the only nobles trying to keep your hands callused." Pedreth laughed. He took over and began nosing the boat shoreward. "I want to get close enough to the cliffs to see the place the monks told us about," he explained.

As time went by, they grew silent, almost hypnotized by waves lapping against the hull and the rhythmic sound of the oars. Suddenly, the cries of a passing flock of brill broke Danth's reverie. He glanced upwards, then noticed something beyond. The swells weren't very high, but the horizon disappeared each time the dinghy descended into a trough. To make seeing harder, the glare of Mahaz on the water was almost blinding. Between the two he nearly missed it—a speck where sky and ocean met.

"We are not alone," he said.

Pedreth scanned the horizon. After a minute he replied, "You have good eyes, my boy. Good eyes."

"More than that," said Danth. "There is a Dalthin aboard."

Pedreth gave him a long look. "What makes you say that?"

"I can't say." He paused, considering the question. "But I can feel it. What should we do?"

"Not a lot we can do except continue toward shore and hope we are harder to see than they are. When we make land, we hide the boat if we can, and make ourselves scarce."

Danth nodded and offered, "Hand an oar. Together, we can make better time."

Pedreth agreed and moved over.

"I don't see anything but cliffs," the ship's captain said.

"Order your men to turn toward shore," Pudath countered. "And put up more sail."

"To what end?" The captain was irritated. Duile had put this other in charge for no good reason. "There is no ship out here but our own."

"Not a ship, Captain." The Dalthin gazed shoreward at something none but it could see. "A boat. A very tiny boat."

The captain strained to see what his guest was looking at. He was about to tell the man he was insane, when the crow's nest called down, "Boat, Captain, to starboard!"

"Are you sure?" the captain called.

"I can barely make her with the glass," the sailor called, "but she's off the starboard beam."

"Hard to starboard," the captain ordered. "Raise tops'ls."

In these light airs it would be impossible to make any real speed, but the extra canvas would help. Nonetheless, the skiff would likely make landfall before they could intercept her.

"Thank you, Captain," Pudath said.

The captain scowled. He did not like being ordered, especially by someone he did not want on board, and he didn't particularly like it that Pudath had been right. Still, the bounty he would receive for a successful mission, and the queen's displeasure if he failed, kept him silent.

# 37

"They're coming, Pedreth!"

Pedreth glanced back. The ship had dropped anchor and was lowering a longboat.

"Grab your things. No time to hide her," he said as they removed their supplies and weapons.

"Now," said Pedreth, looking around, "where do you suppose those steps might be?"

"The monks said they would not be immediately apparent."

"Well, I wish they were a bit more obvious," said Pedreth, scanning the cliffs.

The men in the longboat had cast off and were placing their oars in the water.

"Let's move along the beach," Danth suggested. "Perhaps we can see them from a different angle."

Pedreth broke into a trot with Danth behind him, searching for a way to ascend the wall. "I hope the monks were talking about this beach. I don't know what we are going to do if they were referring to another."

"You heard them right. Wait! I see them! They begin behind that boulder."

Danth was right. As the two moved past a massive rock, they spied a series of roughly hewn steps following a natural fissure.

"Let's not stand on formality," said Pedreth, running toward them.

"I'm right behind you."

They had climbed roughly halfway up the face by the time their pursuers beached their craft. Several of the landing party were gesturing toward them.

"It seems they didn't have nearly the trouble we did," Pedreth grumbled.

"I'm sure they watched us—either that or the Dalthin sensed us."

"I think if we keep moving we will be alright. Once at the top, we will have the superior position. If they're foolish enough to come after us, they will be coming single file and we can pick them off one-by-one."

Danth started to reply when a wave of nausea struck and his field of vision began to waver. Looking up, he saw Pedreth staring blankly and he knew what had happened. That touch, once experienced, was not easily forgotten. He turned to face the pursuers, and all but one were running toward the stairs. The Dalthin was standing motionless, staring up at them. As Danth regarded the thing, he was overcome by an urge to return to the beach. Simultaneously, crossbow darts began striking the rock around him. A cascade of stones clattered around his feet and he looked up to see Pedreth descending.

"Pedreth. Stop!" he ordered, but Pedreth was beyond hearing.

When he tried to shove past, Danth grabbed him with both hands and forced him to sit. Pedreth looked into his eyes, wordlessly pleading for help.

"It's alright," Danth assured him. "I won't let you go."

"I can't stop myself."

"That's alright. I will take care of it."

"What do you mean?"

Ignoring the question, Danth said, "When this is over, promise you won't come looking. There are more lives at stake than mine. You must promise me you will complete our mission."

"I don't understand."

Danth removed a ring from his finger and held it out for Pedreth to see.

"This is my signet." He tucked it into Pedreth's shirt pocket. "You will need it to convince Lords Bogen and Jath you come on my behalf. They are beholden to my family and should respond favorably to your requests. Should they challenge you, remind them that year before last on the feast of Samsted, each one's eldest son became ill while visiting my home. My father and I nursed them to health. No one knows this incident save myself, my father, each lord and their sons. Such information should give you as much currency as if I had written, signed and sealed a letter of recommendation. Will you do this?"

Pedreth nodded and said, "I will."

Another wave of nausea more powerful than the first struck him and Danth nearly passed out from its force. As he grasped the rock face, fighting to remain conscious, he almost let Pedreth rise to his feet. It was only by force of will he regained control.

"Listen to me!" Danth's voice had become a whisper and sweat beaded on his brow. "You cannot go down. You must carry on for both of us."

"I don't understand," Pedreth repeated.

"Everything will soon become clear. I apologize for what I must do, but it is the only way. If I don't do this now, the Dalthin may win." Before Pedreth could say another word, Danth looked heavenward saying, "Borlon help me. I've only managed this once in a fight, so I hope I do it right."

He struck Pedreth hard on the temple and Pedreth slumped onto the stairs unconscious.

"I'm sorry," Danth said, more to himself than to Pedreth. "If I don't go ahead with this, we are both dead. For everyone's sake, I hope I know what I am doing." He unstrapped his satchel and dropped it, then stood. Raising his hands in a sign of surrender, he descended to the beach.

… … … … …

It took Pedreth a moment to remember why he was on his back and why his head hurt. He rubbed his face and tried to clear his thoughts. Suddenly, the memory returned. He tried to sit, but only managed to rise onto his elbows. It occurred to him Danth might be in danger, but his thoughts were still muddled. Taking a deep breath, he forced himself upright, grunting at the effort. Then, finding more strength, he rose to his feet, staggering a bit. He almost tumbled but steadied himself with a hand, and after a few more deep breaths felt almost himself. He looked toward the beach and saw it was empty, then glanced up and down the strand to be sure. He turned his eyes seaward. Squinting into the sunset, shielding his eyes, he recognized the silhouette of the longboat returning.

*Mas'tad! How long has it been?* "Danth!" he cried.

It was too far to be heard. He scanned the beach and spotted the dinghy where they'd left her, but stopped short of racing down to it. Not even with his mightiest effort could he hope to catch them before they sailed away. The realization struck with such force, he slumped against the rock face.

"Danth," he whispered. "How could I have let this happen? Siemas forgive me. Oh, my boy…" His words trailed off. He began to sob, not knowing if Danth were dead or alive and at the mercy of the Dalthin. He sank into the blackest thoughts and fears.

Night fell.

# 38

A stabbing in his side jolted Pedreth awake. He had been sleeping on a stone, and when he rolled, it had jabbed him. There was also a ringing in his ears that would not go away. Slowly he sat, rubbed his ribs and tried to stretch. When he saw where he had been sleeping, however, he leapt to his feet. A sea of scythe grass extended to the horizon in all directions. The chiming of blade striking blade was the sound he heard. Some time during the night he had gathered the equipment and made his way up the stairs and had hiked until starlight revealed a tree in the midst of what appeared to be a vast meadow. Now, by light of day, he could see this empty patch beneath its boughs had been the one safe place to sleep. It was only because the air had been still that the blades had provided no warning. Lying in the grass would have meant his death once the wind arose. During the crossing, oreth hide leggings had kept him safe. Half asleep, he had been unaware of the soft tinkle of blades scraping against them.

Clearly, he could not remain where he was, but returning to the monastery would be pointless and going home far too dangerous. Uncertain what to do, he broke into his rations to ready himself for the trek through the grass. Once he had eaten, he secured his gear. It was then yesterday's events flooded back, filling him with grief and despair. As he stood there, lost and uncertain, absently fumbling at his pocket, he came across the round hard shape of Danth's signet ring. It reminded him he had a promise to keep and Pedreth always kept his promises.

He hefted his sack onto one shoulder, slung the bag of weapons over the other and tried to determine the direction he must take. He reasoned he should find Bogen in danOzmir, Limast's capitol, southeast of the mouth of the Em. Mahaz had just risen, so he used it as a reference and set off.

The breeze was strengthening and stirred the blades of grass into furious motion, tearing ineffectively at his leggings. Farther south, perhaps a half mile away, a small herd of oreth were grazing, their dark brown hides standing out against the brilliant yellow of the grass. It still astounded him these beasts not only moved freely through the blades, but made a meal of the deadly vegetation. Were it not for their hide, he would never risk this crossing.

It took two hours for the tree under which he had slept to disappear behind him. In four more, it was midday. Another four and at his strength and wit's end, he spotted a grove of damass trees upon a small knoll. Again, as on the previous night, he found a bare patch beneath them. Although nearly two hours remained until sunset, he could go no farther. He collapsed, fell into a deep sleep and did not wake until dawn the next day.

# 39

Week old bread is nothing to be relished, but to Pedreth's hungry palate, it made a satisfying breakfast. He even found dried meat among his provisions, so he added that to his meal. Water completed his repast and helped it go down.

The loss of Danth weighed heavily and his emotions were still raw. Coupled with Marm's recent death, it was nearly too much to bear. Still, his body was rested from the ordeal on the beach and he believed he could finish what he had started.

The grove under which he awakened was not large, but it obscured his view to the southeast. Leaving his things where they were, he stepped through the trees to see what lie beyond. Standing in their lee, he spied the knife-shaped peaks called Seneth Lagalen, the Assassin's Daggers. He smiled. He was where he wanted to be. He reckoned he could cross the remaining stretch of grass in an hour at most and reach the Daggers in two, attaining the city by evening.

He was turning to retrieve his belongings, when he spied a dust cloud snaking below the peaks' western face. Its size suggested, if it were not something stirred by wind—and he doubted it was—then it likely marked a convoy of some sort. He decided to observe how it moved.

Eventually, it became apparent something large was heading toward danOzmir. This particular approach was not a caravan route, nor was it advantageous for troops invading from the north or west. But since the procession was coming from the south, possibly from Ydron, he deduced it was likely a military van.

*Why would they come this way?* he wondered. Even from the south, the procession must skirt the grassy savannah dotted sparsely with damass and barrel-stave trees where concealment is impossible. After that, they must negotiate Seneth Lagalen, a rocky ridge fifty miles long, thrust up through the plain ages ago, the last obstacle before danOzmir. While not high as mountains and hills are measured, there is no easy or quick way over it. The rocky teeth are nearly vertical. Crossing it takes most of a day and soon splits any party numbering more than a dozen into several smaller groups, or else strings them into a winding, single file. Large equipment such as catapults must be abandoned. The only way one can navigate this hazard and travel with any speed is through Hassa's Pass, a narrow passage the width of three men at its greatest breadth. Invaders choosing this route can be picked off by archers atop the rocky minarets overlooking the gorge.

The Haroun had advised Pedreth and Danth to take this approach. When at last he reached its mouth, following on the heels of those he had observed, he slowed, watching and listening. Deciding they had gone, and seeing no indication of a watch on the ridgelines, he expected this last stretch to be a solitary one. Consequently, he was startled when he was greeted a short distance into the gorge.

"Hallo!"

Pedreth had rounded a bend and was pausing to lay down his burden. The voice made him jump. His weapons were packed and he was vulnerable.

"You! Hallo! Are you mad?" came the odd salutation. A shabby figure, walking staff in hand, stepped from behind a boulder.

Seeing nothing threatening in the man's posture, nor the manner in which he held the stick, Pedreth replied, "Why do you ask, friend?"

"You came through the grass, man. None crosses the grass save a madman."

"I could see no other way to danOzmir. What other choice had I?"

"Other choice? Well, not to come from the sea is one. Easier it would be to approach from the south or the east, as all else do."

Pedreth was struck by the man's accent and odd manner of speech. "You are not from these parts, are you?" he asked.

The man took a minute to reply, as he perused Pedreth's own appearance. "Nor you," he observed, still studying. "From your leggings would I reckon you for Haroun, but the rest of your dress and your countenance say the contrary. Whence come you?"

"From No'eth," Pedreth replied, choosing not to answer more than he was asked.

"But you are not Haroun. Yes?"

"Indeed."

"Why, then, come from the sea? 'Twould have been easier from the east."

"Too far," Pedreth replied cryptically.

"Why go you to danOzmir?"

"Why not, friend? Where else should I go?"

"Why call me friend?"

"And you are not?"

"Enough!" cried the stranger and threw down the staff. "I harm you not. Why do you hide from my questions?"

"I do not know you, friend. Do you reveal yourself to everyone you meet upon the road? If you but use your eyes, you might not ask so many questions nor be so frustrated by the response. Let me tell you what I perceive about you."

The man crossed his arms.

"You do not dress as a man of means, nor have you a steed or coach," Pedreth observed. "Your boots are severely worn. You dress lightly for these climes and your speech does not reflect these parts but rather, the far south. In fact, you look and sound like a man from Rian or Pytheral. You are not a merchant. If you were, your business surely must be failing. This I deduce from your shabby attire, so you must not have the means to conduct trade so far from home. Nor are you on the business of another, or they would have dressed you better in order to represent them. You are, then, either a thief or a wayfarer. I suspect the latter, or you would have tried to rob me. You might merely be seeking fortune as you find it, but if that were so, you would have made your way to Nagath-réal or Meden or even to Ydron where the pickings are better."

The stranger offered no contradiction.

Assured he was on the right track, Pedreth continued, "I suspect you are not traveling for pleasure or from any sense of adventure. I would wager you are fleeing something or someone, possibly Lord Asch or Lord Kareth."

The stranger cringed.

"Only three questions come to mind. Why do they seek one such as you? Why do you also approach the city from this direction? And how is it you managed to avoid the grass? In answer to the last question, had you approached from the south and hugged the west face of the mountains, avoiding the grass is easy." Pedreth looked him in the eye and the stranger squirmed, turning to avoid his gaze. "And my other questions?"

Growing visibly uncomfortable, the stranger finally replied, "I was told to come so."

"By whom?" Pedreth asked, but the man did not reply. "If I tell you I am no friend of either Lord, will that make you feel more at ease?"

"Perhaps," the man conceded.

"Can you answer me this?"

The stranger cocked his head with interest.

"Did you see the party that rode through earlier?"

When the man was slow to respond, Pedreth pressed.

"I see the tracks of many horses. They would have been hard to miss."

The man's face darkened. "What seek you from those men?" he asked.

"Until I know who they are, I cannot say," said Pedreth.

"So you know them not?"

"Haven't I said as much?" sighed Pedreth, growing weary of the exchange.

"And no friend of Asch are you?"

Clearly, Pedreth was not dealing with the brightest star in the heavens.

"Voreth's horns! Are you deaf?"

The stranger studied his face, then replied, "Men of Lord Asch they are, or so their banners say. I suspect they were looking for me."

"And what would they want with you?" Pedreth tried in vain to suppress a laugh. "I mean no offense, but you are no warrior, nor do you appear to be a threat."

"Only a threat to the queen is my thought," the stranger replied, looking worried.

Pedreth, amused by the statement, asked, "And why might this be?"

"I am uncertain," the man replied. "Telling truthfully, I think I may be going mad. But, you see—please laugh not unkindly—I was sent by a little girl."

"A girl?" Pedreth tried to stifle his amusement.

"With her mind does she speak. Yes, with her mind. Look not with incredulity. With thoughts this one explained that her brother, dwelling this hour with the revered of the Katan, would send friends to Limast, the city of danOzmir and the house of Bogen. To them I should deliver a message and a mission."

Pedreth was stunned. "Her name. Did she tell you her name?"

"Ria she is called, but her name, in truth, is other than this. I know not her true name. One of those whom I seek, said the girl, would know her, since for her father did he work."

# 40

"Borlon's eyes, man, where did you encounter this girl who, as you put it, speaks with her mind?"

Although Pedreth was unaware of Lith-An's new persona, the description the stranger provided left little doubt of whom he spoke.

"You think me mad," said the man.

"Not at all. I believe you completely."

Now it was the wayfarer's turn to be suspicious. "You have trusted nothing else I have told you. Why do you believe me in this?"

"This little girl was perhaps three years of age, was she not?"

Looking startled, the man bit back his reply. Nonetheless, his eyes told Pedreth what he needed to know.

"And did she tell you anything about this person you were to meet?"

"Aye," he allowed reluctantly. "His name she told me, his occupation and where he comes from."

"My name is Pedreth."

The stranger's mouth fell open.

"I come from Sandoval and I am her father's boatkeeper."

"No, sir, you are not! You said you come from No'eth."

"And so I have of late, but that is not my home, only where my travels have taken me. Tell me, in all but this one detail, have I not spoken the words you were waiting to hear?"

The man seemed on the verge of believing him, so Pedreth pressed.

"Of all you might meet, who else would know what to say without being prompted? I asked nothing about the girl nor any specifics of what she told you, but I knew didn't I?"

"By Siemas, must I confess. Yes, Pedreth. Indeed, you knew." He ran his hand through his hair. "I thought I must be a madman. But, you knew! You knew!" He was giddy with relief.

"Will you sit with me a moment?" Pedreth motioned toward a large rock by the side of the trail. "Perhaps you will tell me your tale and the name you go by."

"Yes, of course." Following Pedreth's lead, he took a seat. Then, still distrustful, said, "The girl said three of you there would be. Where are your companions?"

"My son, Ered, stayed behind and the third, a young man named Danth, was taken by Duile's men. I am alone now. Does that answer you?"

"In truth, it does. Those were the names as well," the stranger confessed. He grinned and visibly relaxed. "There is no telling how much the fool I felt while telling my tale. But when this girl entered my mind, I felt so compelled I could not deny her."

"I can imagine," said Pedreth, recalling the days aboard the denaJadiz and Reg's ministering. There was such an honesty to Reg's presence that, had he been a complete stranger, Pedreth would have questioned neither his intentions nor his thoughts. It must have been equally compelling and reassuring for… "And please, friend, by what name shall I call you?"

"I am called Samel, sir. And correct you are. From the province of Pytheral I come and the city of danMaz."

"My journey has been long and it is well past morning," said Pedreth. "I haven't much to offer save some dried meat and a chobollah we might divide, but it will help keep hunger away."

"Why, thank you. I will partake, and if you find it none too coarse, I have a crust of bread to fill in some more. It is good to get off one's feet and take repast, is it not?"

"Indeed, it is." Then, with a careful smile, Pedreth asked, "Is that where you encountered the girl? In danMaz?"

"Near its outskirts, if truth be told."

"Please tell me about it. How did you come to meet her?"

"In an encampment of nomads from Shash it was. Far to the east of Nagath-réal and the Salt Plain lies their land. They make their living telling fortunes and selling such goods as might they come upon."

*Such goods as they might steal*, thought Pedreth, but he kept the thought to himself.

"And because it had come my way I might help them sell certain items, I paid a visit.

"While in their camp, awaiting to be shown those goods, I

encountered a man—Ganeth by name, if memory serves—and the child called Ria standing near a campfire. It was for the reason of their color and features, so unlike the others, my eye was drawn. Indeed, their eyes fastened on me, so I believe, for just such a reason. For a moment we spoke, though their demeanor was circumspect, when I was called away to talk of business. I had crossed half the camp when the girl commenced to speak. Turning to look, and expecting her to be behind me just so," he indicated the ground beside him, "speaking softly as she was, I did receive a start. She was neither shouting nor calling out loud, though she remained beside the campfire. Facing me, gazing straight into my eyes, she continued to speak, though her mouth moved not at all.

"Hah! I was reminded of a traveling entertainer from Liad-Nur, as I recall, or Dethen was it? No mind." Samel continued glibly, seeming relieved to unburden himself. "He had placed a doll upon his lap and did pretend it spoke of its own accord. In truth, it was he who spoke, or tried to between clenched teeth and parted lips, but with words so muffled it was clear it was but a lifeless thing upon his lap. Nonetheless, out of courtesy the audience laughed and clapped and made him out to be a man of great talent.

"But this girl! I tell you, though so great was the distance between us and so loud the commotion within the encampment, while her mouth did not move, it was as if we were side-by-side, so clear was her voice."

Samel leaned forward and brought his face close to Pedreth's.

"These were not spoken words. Thoughts they were. And I could see things within her mind as well. She let me see them. Of that I am certain. This was no imagining."

Pedreth could see he needed reassurance. "I believe you," he said, looking Samel directly in the eyes. "You see, this has happened to me as well."

Samel's eyes opened wide.

"Her brother," said Pedreth, "who is residing in the monastery of the Katan, has spoken to me in just this manner."

"No, you say!"

"Yes, I say."

"Hah!" Samel was beside himself and slapped his knee. He looked around as though looking for someone else with whom to share this revelation.

"I find it amazing as well," assured Pedreth. "Can you recall what the girl wanted you to tell me?"

He hoped he wasn't pressing the man to divulge before he was ready to give up this information. Samel was obviously enjoying his story and storytellers often like to arrive at important points at moments of their own choosing. To Pedreth's relief, Samel was not bothered in the least, however his tone changed to one of intense urgency, as did his entire posture as he began to relate the message to the object of his quest.

"Odd is the message I am to relate. I assure you, nonetheless, it is true. The words are burned upon my mind but I make little sense of them. It is my hope what I bring is of import."

Pedreth nodded, wondering what could have brought this man so far to intercept him.

Samel paused—either for effect or to make sure his memory was correct—then said somberly and not at all in his customary syntax, "'Fear the banners of Kareth and Danai, Ened and Hau, the harbingers of mother's holocaust. Seek refuge in ashes purple where friends lie. If Bogen will come to maiden's rescue while lightening fills the sky, the tide may turn.' Her words these are and sorry I am they make no sense."

"These do not sound like the words of a three year old girl," observed Pedreth.

"Hers were not the eyes of a child," Samel countered. "Never such eyes have I seen, let alone upon a young girl. Pierced me to my soul they did and her thoughts burned me to the core."

Pedreth searched the man's face for signs of humor or deceit. Finding neither, he decided he had no choice but to accept his story as fact, including the message. The two sat in silence while Pedreth replayed the words, looking for meaning.

"I think I understand the first part," he said, at last. "But I cannot say what is meant by purple ashes or the maiden. And does she mean that friends will not tell the truth? Or, instead, that they are to be found in the ashes? I am perturbed."

"I am sorry," said Samel. "I am certain I have the words right. Now you see why my sanity is suspect, for the message is the reason for my journey. My heart says the words are of import, but to my mind they are nonsense."

"If I did not know this girl and certain circumstances surrounding her, I would dismiss what you tell me and bid you farewell. But there are events I cannot relate, preceding our encounter, that will not allow me to dismiss you so easily. Far stranger things have happened of late."

Samel nodded.

"I will consider your message and perhaps in time it will make more sense." Pedreth stood and gathered his possessions. "Let us make our way to danOzmir."

# 41

Pebbles showered from above. Samel craned his head, shielding his face with a hand. "Do you see anything?"

"No, but I suspect we are being observed."

"What do you think they might do?"

"They will either let us pass or take us into custody. Both will serve our purpose."

"Not kill us?"

Pedreth surveyed the gorge's walls then set off, motioning Samel to follow. "It is hard to say, but I think not. We don't present a force of any consequence. I suspect they have orders to either observe or intercept strangers. They should have encountered Asch's party, and I don't see any sign of conflict. If they allowed them to pass, assuming there were sufficient numbers to engage them, they will likely grant us passage as well."

"Do you think we might turn back and return home instead?"

"Go, if you choose." said Pedreth. "I have a mission to fulfill."

Samel, however, elected to remain with Pedreth and by late afternoon both men had grown weary. They were passing the time discussing the prospects of dining on local fare, salivating at the mention of each new dish, when they turned a bend and ran into a party of soldiers.

"Halt!" the one in charge ordered. "Throw down your gear and raise your hands!"

Caught off guard, Pedreth was slow to obey. By the time he comprehended what the man had said, it was too late. The officer strode up and struck Pedreth across the face.

"I said raise your hands."

Straightening, Pedreth extended both hands skyward.

"That's better. Now give me one reason we shouldn't kill you both."

"Because Lord Bogen is expecting us," Pedreth bluffed.

Samel glanced at him in disbelief, but failed to contradict him.

"Hah! That's a good one," the officer scoffed. "I think I will slit your belly."

"If you wish to answer to the Lord of the Land, then do so. But we bear a message from the house of Kanagh and a pigeon is coursing toward the citadel to announce our approach, even as we speak. The message it carries alerts your lord to the route we are taking. Should we fail to appear, he will certainly question you as to our whereabouts."

"Why haven't we been alerted to your arrival?"

"Ask Lord Bogen. Perhaps the pigeon has just arrived. Perhaps it has yet to do so."

"And perhaps because it never will and this is a foolish attempt to save your skin." Then, drawing a dagger from its sheath and fingering its edge, he said, "I think I'll just do you in."

"Can you afford to take the chance?"

The soldier put the tip of his blade to Samel's throat. He pressed, and a trickle of blood ran down Samel's neck. "Maybe I'll do in one of you and let the other bring the message."

"Now it's my turn to laugh," replied Pedreth. "Each of us knows only half. It is of such importance Lord Kanagh could not trust its entirety to either of us."

The guard appeared uncertain, so Pedreth continued. "Perhaps you are unaware of the turmoil spreading from Ydron. Perhaps you merely wish to risk your career. I certainly don't wish to die and neither does my comrade, but if you intend to jeopardize your years of service for a little sport, there is nothing we can do to stop you."

Still suspicious, the soldier pressed. "What proof have you, other than your word?"

"I have been ordered to present a sign to the watch at the palace gate."

"I think you'll show it to me."

"I will do as I have been ordered. Examine it at that time if you choose."

Samel could hold his tongue no longer. Half in tears, he begged, "Pedreth. By all that's sacred, show it to him."

"No, Samel," said Pedreth. Then, returning to his inquisitor. "As you can see, my comrade knows what I carry. He is too terrified to bluff. And while I will only show it to the palace guard, I am not bluffing either. Besides…" Realizing any sign of weakness would place them in greater jeopardy at the hands of this bully, Pedreth kept his voice strong and added, "If I am found to be a liar, I am sure the watch will let you have your way with us. And you, my friend, can take credit for bringing us in."

The soldier, obviously uncertain, glanced from Pedreth to his men. He bit his lip and returned to his comrades to confer.

While they deliberated, Samel whispered to Pedreth, "I thought you said they would let us pass."

Seeing the soldier waiver, Pedreth replied, "They will. They don't dare take the risk."

"And if wrong you are… ?"

"Then we are dead. Do you have a better plan?"

Samel shook his head.

A heated conference ensued. Either no one had the authority to decide or no one wanted to accept the consequence of a poor decision. Eventually, the one in charge returned to confront his prisoners.

"If you are lying to me, I will see you die painfully," he threatened.

When they arrived at the gate, their captor approached one of the guards. After a brief discussion, the guard approached Pedreth with the soldier from the pass a step or two behind.

"What business do you have with my Lord?" asked the guard.

"My business is of a private nature," replied Pedreth. "I am on an urgent mission on behalf of my friend, Lord Kanagh."

"Your friend, you say," said the guard, grinning broadly. He circled Pedreth, inspecting his plain attire while Pedreth's captor smirked.

"My son was a childhood companion of Lord Danth Kanagh," Pedreth explained, "as well as of Lord Leovar Hol and Prince Regilius Tonopath. They all spent much time in my home and I regard them all as my friends."

"And I regard Lord Bogen as my drinking companion," the guard laughed, drawing a guffaw from the officer.

Pedreth reached into his pocket, and before the guard could draw his sword, he produced Danth's ring. Holding it so it was clearly visible, he said, "Tell your drinking companion I hold a signet bearing Lord Kanagh's crest."

The guard came close and studied the item. He tried to take it, but Pedreth returned it to his pocket.

"Tell me why I shouldn't turn you away here and now, and if asked, claim I never saw you. I know my friend never did," he said. The other guard smiled and nodded.

Unruffled, Pedreth replied, "I can see you are willing to jeopardize your career to impress your friend."

The guard's sarcasm turned to anger. "How do you figure that, old man?"

Pedreth ran a hand through his hair and smiled. "Old man? My hair must be starting to gray." He fixed the guard with his eyes and said, "Palace guard. Not a bad job, guarding the gate—until the weather gets bad, that is. After all, you could be guarding Hassa's Pass. I can understand why you wouldn't choose to be inside the palace when the weather gets cold and wet. That's too comfortable for the likes of you. Of course, if you really wanted to move up in your lord's esteem, drinking companion that he is, you'd get messages to him from those bearing the crest of nobility and let him decide if they have merit."

The guard studied Pedreth a moment, then turning to his counterpart said, "Watch him for me." He headed toward the gate, then paused and turned back. "But just you. Not your friend."

"My companion travels with me. Should he not be allowed to join me, it will go against you. Be a smart lad," he cautioned. "When you see how eager Lord Bogen is to grant me audience, you will think twice before throwing your weight around."

"We shall see," the guard repeated and Pedreth smiled.

Samel leaned toward him and whispered, "How can you be so cheerful?"

"There are times when getting the last word in goes against one. At such times, it helps to appear confident."

When told of Danth's signet, Lord Bogen had granted them audience. However, as they waited in the anteroom, Pedreth grew less optimistic. Would Bogen listen to his request and come to Emeil's aid? Or, now that Danth might be dead and his father was Emeil's ally, would it be easier for him to forget past obligations?

Samel was clearly uncomfortable. Like most of common birth, he had never been within any grand edifice and so, from the marble floors to the polished granite walls, everything was beyond his experience.

"Pedreth," he whispered, "Will you tell me my half of the message?"

"Nothing, Samel. That was a ploy to keep you alive. Now that our friend has left us, I don't have to invent anything for you to say."

"Could you have done as much?"

"I don't know. We would have found out." He winked.

"Pedreth, why did you insist I come?" Samel whispered. "I have no business here."

"Had we become separated, you might have disappeared. Although

Lord Bogen should be our friend, we have no guarantees—you least of all. Keeping you close is my way of insuring we leave together."

Samel nodded, just as their names were announced.

"Follow me," Pedreth instructed. "Remain a little behind, so you can observe me. Do as I do, bow when I bow, and remain silent unless the Lord speaks directly to you. Even then, only respond to what is asked. Offer nothing more." Seeing the terror in Samel's eyes, Pedreth smiled and said, "Besides, I do not think he will have much to say to you."

Despite the reassurance, Samel's face was a mask of fear.

Lord Bogen's Great Room was nothing compared to the grand chamber in which Manhathus had held audience. Yet, while the wealth of Ydron was unimaginable and Bogen's was within the bounds of comprehension, clearly this lord was no pauper. The room could hold two hundred comfortably. Tapestries depicting grand events in Limast's history covered its walls and an abundance of light globes illuminated the space as were seldom seen elsewhere. Samel's jaw hung agape as, out of his depth, he followed close on Pedreth's heels.

"Step forward and be heard," called the guard at the foot of the dais. When the two arrived at the bottom step, he leaned forward and began to instruct them. He was surprised, however, when Pedreth, then his companion, dropped to one knee, bowed deeply and held the posture as if they had done this before.

"Rise and approach," came a voice from above.

Pedreth, no stranger to royal protocol, rose, as did Samel, and ascended to the first landing, several steps below the topmost level. Once there, Pedreth knelt and bowed as before and Samel, a quick student, followed suit.

"State your names and your business," Bogen's aide commanded.

"Pedreth of Sandoval, boatkeeper to His Late Majesty, Manhathus Tonopath," Pedreth stated. "I bring a message and a request to Lord Bogen from Lord Danth Kanagh, son of Harven Kanagh."

"S-s-s-samel," Samel ventured, his voice cracking. "Of Pytheral, H-h-h-highness."

When he offered nothing more, the aide snapped, "State your business to my Lord."

Pedreth answered for him. "He is my traveling companion, if you please, my Lord. He is only here at my request."

There was a moment of silence, then Lord Bogen instructed, "You may stand."

The two arose and Pedreth, glancing quickly, saw Samel drenched in perspiration.

"I have been told you bear Lord Kanagh's signet ring, Pedreth of Sandoval. May I see it?"

Pedreth drew it from his pocket and held it aloft. The aide snatched it and carried it to the summit. After a perfunctory homage, he relinquished it, then returned to Pedreth's side. Bogen examined the ring, inspecting the stone and the inscriptions it bore.

"How do I know you have not stolen this?" he inquired.

"Lord Kanagh, concerned you believe he gave it to me, instructed me to remind you that Samsted before last your eldest son, Garth, as well as Lord Jath's eldest, Hon, became ill while visiting the Kanagh household. He told me that aside from his family, none but Your Lordship, Lord Jath and your sons know of this matter. By this special knowledge Your Lordship should understand the authenticity of my mission."

There was silence while Lord Bogen stroked his beard and thought.

"Why did he not come to me in person?"

Pedreth was afraid of this question and decided to be circumspect. "As Your Lordship will understand, since the unfortunate loss of her husband, Her Majesty Duile Tonopath has found it necessary to resort to unusual measures. So it was, while we were on our way to visit Your Lordship, she sent a party to intercept Lord Kanagh and took him from me. Her men did not state their purpose."

"I see. When you next see the young lord, give him my regards and tell him I am pleased to receive his emissary and his emissary's companion."

"I will, Your Lordship."

"You say you bear a message and a request, boatkeeper. Tell me, what is your message?"

Pedreth paused, then began carefully, so as not to offend his host. "Subsequent to the recent events at barakYdron…"

"You mean the assassination," Bogen interrupted. "You should know I do not look kindly on it, nor on friends of the queen."

"That is good, Your Lordship, for Lord Kanagh, his household and friends feel the same." Bogen's expression softened, so Pedreth began anew. "Following the assassination, certain events have required Lord Emeil, a friend of Lord Kanagh, to flee with his troops from Her Majesty's immediate grasp to menRathan."

"Hah!" Bogen interrupted. "Good for him! Is he organizing a

campaign against her?"

"You anticipate me, Your Lordship. That is exactly what he is doing. But if he is to succeed, he must find allies."

"I have received a message from Emeil of late and have been deliberating how to respond." Bogen placed his elbows on his knees and smiled. "She would deserve a good trouncing. How did he escape?"

"I'm afraid I do not know, Your Lordship."

"Well, never mind. So, boatkeeper, you have relayed your message and I must say it is well received. Now, what is your request?"

"Your Lordship must be aware of the queen's vast resources and that many provinces are poised to come to her side to share the power and wealth she will dispense. Lord Emeil hopes to thwart these alliances and remove her from power by direct conflict if necessary. Unfortunately, he has not yet amassed sufficient forces to do so. If he is to avoid being crushed, he will need help. Lord Kanagh hopes you will join him."

"Should he be successful in this attempt, who would replace her? Does Emeil aspire to the throne?"

"I cannot say, Your Lordship. Many would assert he would make a good and just ruler, but I cannot say this is his plan."

"I think I might make a good and just ruler, boatkeeper. What do you say to that?"

"You may, indeed, Your Lordship. This is not for me to say. You should also know Lord Emeil is a friend of the rightful heir to the throne, Prince Regilius."

"But is it not true his whereabouts are unknown?"

"It is true they are unknown to the queen, Your Lordship."

Bogen sat upright, eyes keen. "Are you saying you know his whereabouts."

"If I did and said as much, I would not be his friend, would I?"

Bogen paused to consider. "No, indeed. You would not. Are you his friend, boatkeeper?"

"Yes I am, Your Lordship."

"And Lord Kanagh hopes I would be willing to risk all to vanquish the queen?"

"He does, Your Lordship."

Bogen drummed his fingers upon his knees and Pedreth was growing concerned at his silence. All at once, Bogen sat still.

"It is a winding road the young lord asks me to go down," he said, "and not one to turn back upon. There is much to be lost. It would serve the scheming viper of a queen right, but I am not sure I am willing to risk everything to satisfy my sense of justice. While my forces would certainly add to his numbers, there still would not be nearly enough to succeed. Whom else might you approach?"

Pedreth replied, "My Lord has requested I go next to Nagath-réal to prevail upon Lord Jath. Further, Lord Leovar Hol has gone to Meden to gain audience with Lord Dural Miasoth. He plans to go next to Yeset to see Lord Basham. I am certain Lord Emeil has sent out his own emissaries, as well."

"These would be likely alliances. Perhaps if they choose to help him, I would consider joining his cause."

Pedreth was upset by Bogen's reluctance. "My Lord, the fate of all lies in the outcome of Emeil's plan."

"Are you lecturing me?"

"I am sorry, my Lord. I meant no disrespect."

"I will ignore your last remark while I consider your request. After I have deliberated further, I may allow you to continue on your journey. In the meantime, you and your companion will remain as my guests."

Bogen returned the ring and an aide showed the pair to their quarters. Pedreth, aware their visit could have ended far worse, was nevertheless dismayed. The delay did not bode well.

# 42

Something moist crossed his face and Leovar sat up with a start.

"Fear not. All is well," a woman's voice assured.

He turned, startled by her proximity. The hand she extended held something he could not identify and he recoiled.

"All is well," she repeated. "Please," she persisted. Her hand was still outstretched and he saw she was holding a cloth. "You have a fever," she explained. "Let me cool your brow."

"I am fine," he said, moving away.

"Your forehead is quite warm. The fever clouds your thinking, else you would not fear one such as I."

Leovar regarded her dark brown hair, deep blue eyes and delicate mouth and considered the young woman attractive. About his own age, she was sitting on the edge of his bed. She wore a pale blue kerchief around her head in the manner of some peasant girls, but she was not dressed in the coarse fabric of the poor. In fact, her clothes were fine and in her lap was a finely-crafted ceramic bowl. She returned the cloth to the vessel, then withdrew it and wrung the excess water from it.

"If you will, sir, please lie down and let me attend to you."

His head was spinning, so he complied, settling against the pillows as she returned to her task. As she worked, he considered the room. From the walls of finely cut and fitted marble, as well as the tapestries that adorned them, he deduced he was within the palace.

"Who are you?" he asked, as she dabbed his brow.

"I belong to the Miasoth household. My Lord requested I watch over you, Lord Hol, until you have regained your strength."

The manner in which she introduced herself told him she was a servant. The quality of her attire suggested she was a familial who worked and lived within the family quarters, as had Marm.

"How do you know my name?" he asked.

"Your friend, Ai'Lorc, told us who you are," she answered.

"He is alright?"

"He is in good health and is resting nearby."

"Can you tell me how long I have been here?"

"Three days, sir," she replied.

He was about to ask something more when the chamber door swung open.

"Leovar? Leovar Hol? Is that you?"

The girl arose, placed the cloth in the bowl and the bowl upon the stool. Then, turning to face the speaker, she bowed her head and curtsied. The speaker ignored her as she held her pose.

"I cannot believe it is you, Leovar! So many years have passed since I saw you last. My, how you have grown. I have been told you were ill. Are you recovering?"

Leovar looked beyond the servant to see the large bearded man who had entered. He was massively built and a full head taller than the guard stationed by the door. His golden mane, shot through with silver, cascaded past his shoulders. Two streaks of white originating near each corner of his mouth ran through his meticulously trimmed golden beard. Despite the intervening years, Leovar had no trouble recognizing Dural Miasoth, ruler of Meden, a giant among men.

"I am fine, sir. You have left me in good hands," Leovar replied, inclining his head toward the girl.

"What?" For the first time Dural noticed her. "Oh, yes. I have indeed." Then, to the still-curtsying servant he said, "Rise up, girl. Rise up. Gather your things and leave us."

She took the bowl into one arm, picked up the stool with her free hand, and curtsying once more as best she could, backed out of the room.

"When last I laid eyes on you, you were a lad of ten… twelve perhaps. But now look at you! You have become a man. I would never have recognized you on my own. Tell me, what brings you to Meden? Did you arrive at the gates by chance, or is there purpose to your visit?"

"Please excuse me," said Leovar. He struggled to sit before answering, moving slowly lest he become dizzy again. "I am here on a mission of some urgency. I apologize you had to come to me. I would have preferred to seek a proper audience with you in another day or two, once my strength returns, and present my request as custom requires."

"Nonsense, my boy. Your father and I were close friends when we were younger. I should like to think we still are. Please tell me your purpose."

Leovar nodded. "You must certainly be aware of the recent happenings in Ydron."

"How could one not be?"

"So you must also be aware of Duile's treachery."

"What of it? Such things have happened over and again in this land and elsewhere. If one is not strong enough to hold on to power, then one deserves to lose it to whomever can wrest it away."

Dural's attitude caught Leovar off guard. "You approve what she has done?"

"I neither approve nor disapprove. It has happened. Were I so weak and careless as Manhathus had become, I would deserve the same."

"Have you heard the recent news about Emeil? That he is taking a stand against her?"

"Of course," Dural said, and his face took on a sneer.

"Well," said Leovar, "I believe unless you and those lords who still remain sovereign do not join with him against her, you will all, one by one, suffer the same fate as Manhathus. Duile will not rest until she controls everything."

Dural shook his head. "As much as I love Emeil, he acted like a fool. Duile has superior forces. It is best to let her settle in and not rile her. Once she feels secure, she will calm down, rein in her troops and things will be quiet again. As long as she feels threatened, she will continue as she is doing."

"Then my father must be a fool as well, since he has joined Emeil."

"If that is the case, perhaps you should take him aside and convince him otherwise."

"I cannot believe what I am hearing," said Leovar. "One minute you say Manhathus got what he deserved because he was complacent. The next, you justify your own complacency. Do you think Duile will pass you by simply because you have not challenged her? Watch out, Dural, or you will be paying a price, if she doesn't remove you from power altogether."

"How dare you speak to me like that within my own walls? Is this how you repay my hospitality?"

"Sir, I would be paying you the greatest disrespect were I not to tell you what I sincerely believe. With all my heart, I am warning you because of my family's love for you."

"Then consider it is only because of my love for your father I do not put you in prison, or worse."

"You imply I am not already imprisoned. I have the distinct impression your guard will not let me leave this room."

"You presume correctly," Dural replied and turned to leave.

"I don't understand. You say you love my father, but I can see you placed a guard at my door before you even knew my reason for coming."

"These are uncertain times and call for precautions."

"You should fear the queen, then."

"Once again, lad, I warn you to mind your tongue."

"What about my friend?" Leovar pressed.

"He is taken care of."

"Meaning we are both under house arrest?"

"Take it as you will." Dural headed for the door and the guard saluted crisply.

"My father spoke too highly of you," Leovar called out. "He said you were a man of honor without fear."

Dural halted abruptly, but did not turn to face him.

"It is apparent he misjudged you," said Leovar. "You fear both me and the message I bring. As for Duile, you hope if you do not rouse her anger, she will leave you alone. You are pathetic and will soon see the truth in what I am saying. I only hope when you do, there will be time enough for you to act."

Dural remained in the doorway for a moment more. Then, either unwilling or unable to reply, he rounded the corner into the hallway and left. The guard closed the door and returned to his post. Leovar sank into the pillows. The effort had exhausted what little energy he had regained and he was utterly dismayed at his host's unwillingness to face up to the queen. This was not the man he remembered, nor of whom his father had spoken. If this were the sort of man upon whom Emeil depended, it was only a matter of time before Duile did control everything. Perhaps this was what she was counting on. She certainly knew her peers better than he and his comrades did. Could they really presume to halt such a well-planned and well-armed endeavor? Certainly, so long as Leovar were confined to this chamber, his own part would be thwarted. He tried to imagine his next course of action, but fatigue and fever overcame him and he slipped into unconsciousness.

# 43

"Goodness, man! Can't you see? If the enemy isn't already at your gates, they soon will be. What do I need to do to open your eyes?"

Frustrated, Ai'Lorc ran his hands through his hair as he paced. He had been trying to penetrate a wall of bureaucratic indifference for nearly an hour. The object of his irritation was Dural's pudgy agent who had introduced himself as Ghanfor. Ai'Lorc had arrived at his wit's end trying to fathom why Ghanfor, and therefore Dural, would be so oblivious to the impending danger. Ghanfor had made it clear while they would not assist the queen, they had no argument with her. They had so despised Manhathus, Ai'Lorc could not convince him they should unite with Emeil. An unimaginative bureaucrat, Ghanfor could not see beyond his comfort.

"You seem to believe, if you grant Duile her way, she will pass you by without so much as a backward glance."

"Sir, please lower your voice."

"My voice?" Ai'Lorc was at a loss. In the face impending danger, what troubled this man was a breach of manners.

"Her Majesty is not interested in our small city," Ghanfor said.

"I will wager she has more than a little interest in your mines."

"We have been neighbors, albeit distant ones, for years and she has always shown us the greatest friendship."

"She has never controlled the might to do otherwise."

"Her late husband controlled… "

"That's exactly it. Her late husband, Manhathus, received tribute enough that he was content. Duile, on the other hand, believes whoever is not with her is against her. I'll wager she will want more than token tribute from a province that has failed to assist her."

"If you insist on trampling all over my words, I will end our discussion here and now."

Ghanfor tilted his nose upward and Ai'Lorc bit back the impulse to throttle him. If he hoped to speak with Dural, he would have to go through this man. Any small victory he might take here would cost him in the long run. He knew his emotions were too apparent, so he swallowed his pride and apologized.

"I am sorry," he said, mustering all the patience he could.

"See that your actions reflect it."

"I shall. I promise."

This seemed to satisfy Ghanfor and Ai'Lorc was about to give matters one last try when trumpets sounded outside.

"By Siemas! What can that be?" Ghanfor moved toward the window.

"Perhaps it is the queen's army," Ai'Lorc suggested, half in jest.

"Don't be silly," said Ghanfor.

Their circuitous conversation, like as not, would have resumed had not a page burst in.

"Ghanfor," he gasped, "You must come at once!"

"Can you not see I am busy?" Ghanfor drew himself to his full height and placed his hands upon his hips.

"You are summoned by Lord Miasoth. He requires an emissary."

"An emissary?" Ghanfor raised his brows. "By all above us, why?"

"Please come. I will explain outside."

"You can tell me here." The pudgy man clearly did not like to be told what to do.

"Please step outside."

"Now! Tell me here and now!"

Catching his breath, the page explained, "Duile's troops have been encircling the fortress for the last half hour and her emissary is waiting outside the gate. We shall soon be surrounded."

Ghanfor looked at Ai'Lorc, who gave him a wink.

# 44

Clouds were gathering in the heavens almost at the rate troops were amassing outside barakMeden's walls, with no apparent end to either. Moments earlier, Dural had surveyed their positions from above the main gate before retreating to the parapet walk. There he consulted with General Mo'ed.

"How many do you believe there are?" Dural asked.

"They are double our number and growing, my Lord."

"But we will be secure, will we not?"

"If the gates hold. We have it from a rider, who managed to evade the approaching forces, they are bringing a ramming device. It should be here by nightfall." The general saw the look of alarm on Dural's face. "Nonetheless, they will have difficulty deploying it. They will sustain heavy losses if they attempt to bring it near the walls and the gate is massive enough to hold for quite some time."

"Quite some time?" Dural repeated. "How long might that be?"

General Mo'ed hesitated. "It depends on the size of the device and how many troops the queen brings. We can withstand the present number, but our scouts indicate another five hundred to one thousand are on the way, and there is no telling how many more may be following. At some point the balance will tip in their favor. I am not sure when that will happen. These walls have not seen battle for more than two and a half centuries."

"Are we sure these are Duile's forces?" asked Dural, gesturing toward the troops outside the gate.

"They carry banners from Liad-nur and Miast, but we believe they are allied with Ydron. Should Duile add her own to their numbers, they will certainly have enough to defeat us."

"I think it more likely she will send her own against that arrogant renegade, Emeil."

"I doubt it, my Lord," said Mo'ed. "Until she has defeated us, she will only use enough force to keep Emeil pinned down. Her army is sufficiently large she can split it into three or four divisions without presenting a weak front. She will use one to hold Emeil and the remaining divisions against opposing provinces until her own position is secure."

"But we still do not know for certain the ones we are facing are in league with Ydron," said Dural hopefully.

"My Lord, the queen's own emissary accompanied them. That leaves little doubt, but it will not take long to establish their intent, once we have parlayed."

"No. It shouldn't. Let us see where we stand." Then, looking around for his chief aide, he asked, "Where is Ghanfor?"

Ghanfor, in all his corpulence, was seated astride a horse as Dural had commanded. Although clad in armor, he was clearly neither a soldier nor an accomplished rider.

"With all due respect, my Lord," said Mo'ed. "I'm afraid if you send him out, he will soil his pants."

As Dural circled the horse, it became evident this was not the face he wanted to present. Ghanfor's station made it appropriate he act as emissary, but the Lord of Meden soon realized he should consider an alternative. "Is there someone we might send in Ghanfor's place?"

"I have a major under my command whose appearance as emissary would not provide an insult," said Mo'ed.

"How quickly can he be made ready?"

"My Lord!" Ghanfor began to object as he realized he was about to be replaced.

"With all due respect," said Mo'ed, "I was certain your wisdom would lead you to the obvious. He is ready as we speak."

He gestured toward a rider a short distance away. On Mo'ed's cue, the formidable looking soldier in armor put his spurs to his mount and rode up beside them.

"Can he speak?" Dural asked.

"He can clearly express your desires."

"Brief him at once, General, and help this other one down."

Ghanfor was indignant, but in no position to contradict his master.

"At once, my Lord," said Mo'ed.

The gates slid open on massive rollers. Even before they were they fully parted, the major urged his horse forward. Only a standard bearer accompanied him, a boy hardly old enough to serve.

"I would have sent out the lad with more than a flag," observed Dural.

"I doubt they will kill the boy," replied Mo'ed. "And the major will surely be allowed to live, else how will they get their message to you? On the other hand, they might consider an armed escort a threat to the one they have dispatched."

The riders cleared the walls and the major, with the standard bearer close beside, rode toward the center of the expanse separating the forces. He kept his steed to a deliberate trot as he surveyed the enemy. Their archers and foot soldiers were maintaining their positions, and the cavalry endeavored to remain as motionless as the stirrings of their steeds would allow. As the two from Meden neared their arbitrary destination, two riders from the other side peeled away from the assembled forces and rode out to meet them. Matching the protocol Dural had set, Duile's emissary and a standard bearer galloped forth. They reached the center of the field the same time as the major and the boy. When they were facing each other, the major spoke.

"You have entered the province of Meden uninvited. What quarrel do Miast and Liad-nur bring to this land?"

"We come in peace, as allies of Her Majesty, Duile Morged Tonopath, Queen of Ydron."

"In peace, you say? How do you make such a claim when you arrive as an army?"

Duile's emissary replied, "Her Majesty wishes to know your position. Does your lord swear his allegiance and will he pay her the tribute she requires? She sends such forces because she has no patience for those who will not so swear."

"My Lord has always been a friend and has already paid what was required of him this year."

"These days put a toll upon the queen's coffers. For many, such as your lord, the tribute may be increased, although less for friends than for foes."

"What is the price of agreeing to her demands?"

"For the time being, Lord Miasoth will be allowed to keep his title and his lands, but Her Majesty requires another half of your Lord's customary taxation in immediate payment. Whatever else she may require will be determined at a later date."

"It does not sound as though there are any guarantees in this offer."

"Your lord's retention of his lands and title will depend upon how faithfully and consistently he proves his loyalty."

"This tastes more of extortion than friendship."

"Take it as you will," grinned the opposing messenger. "We outnumber you and our force is growing. If your lord wishes to remain in power, he would be wise not to offend Her Majesty. How say you?"

"My Lord does not take kindly to threats, but I am not here to speak for him, only to carry your words to his ear. He will reply in short order. Tell your commanders they will not have long to wait." With that, the major wheeled his horse and ordered his standard bearer, "Ride!"

As the youth turned his horse and raced toward the fortress, he spurred his own to a gallop, hearing first one, then several arrows hiss past his ears. He glanced at the boy who was riding hard before him. Clearly no stranger to the saddle, the youngster had risen onto his stirrups on the balls of his feet. Hunched forward like a jockey, he was carrying the flag like a lance.

*Thank Siemas he can ride*, the major thought as they galloped back to safety.

# 45

Dargath finished its meal, luxuriating in the pleasure of satiation. It was full, but not stuffed. While the body of the second monk looked tempting, the Dalthin decided it could best complete its mission if it did not add to an already a generous repast.

It considered the monks, who in their own way were as odd as the queen's children. They had not screamed, as had others before them. In fact, they had been stoic about the pain it inflicted. And though Dargath had managed to elicit hints to the male child's whereabouts, they refused to be specific. Even when blood ran in streams from the apertures of their faces, the monks had remained defiant. Even when it tore off their limbs, they had demonstrated remarkable control and it could see they had disassociated their minds from their bodies.

Dargath had hoped they could hold out a bit longer, but the game came to an end. No matter. The structure situated upon the butte dominating this region housed the only cluster of minds in the vicinity and it believed the precocious male would be among them. With its goal in sight, it wanted to end matters quickly. Ignoring the fate of its kin in Bad Adur—never mind that two of its kind were hastening to assist—it roused itself and changed its size and coloration to resemble one of the corpses.

… … … … …

Lightening arced across the sky, illuminating the plain below. Here and there, a giant falo'an tree stood out against No'eth's scrub covered hillocks. The bolt was followed closely by a volley of thunder, indicating the strike's proximity. Twice more, electric flashes eradicated the darkness and twice the heavens rumbled in response. The wind was already at gale force and the monk on the watch did his best to make himself heard above the fury.

"Brother Osman, open the gate! Brother Jez'ir has returned."

Amid the cacophony, it was more likely Osman had responded to Bort's gestures than to his words. With his robes whipping about, Osman threw himself against the winch, and gradually the massive door opened. Only when their fellow monk was safely within and the gate securing the haven was closed, did the two clerics hasten to join him.

"Hail, Brother Jez'ir! How was your journey?" cried Osman.

"Yes, Brother," puffed Bort. "Tell us all about it."

"There is nothing to tell," replied Dargath with an expressionless face.

Osman and Bort exchanged glances. Jez'ir was probably the cheeriest, most loquacious member of the community. Ordinarily, he would have been laughing heartily, regaling them well past dinner and late into the night with the various turnings of his voyage. This was not like him.

"Where is Brother Mordat?" Osman asked.

"He is following a few days behind. He was detained."

"You are so quiet. Are you not well?" Suspecting fever, Osman placed the back of his hand on Jez'ir's forehead, then withdrew it. "By Mog'an! You are like ice!"

Bort also noticed something strange. "Where is your baggage? You have brought nothing. Were you robbed?"

Dargath, realizing it had blundered, attempted to alter their memories, but halted abruptly. Their minds were surprisingly controlled, nearly as much as the other two. It exerted more effort, but found the task impossible. Bort grasped his head under the Dalthin's assault, not understanding why he hurt or why Osman was holding his own. Then, as they watched in disbelief, Jez'ir began to transform. His body became larger, changed color and quickly outgrew his robes. The waist cord snapped, the clothing tore and fell to the ground as Dargath rose to its full height. Towering above them, nearly twice their stature, it advanced on Osman. It was intending to torture him until he divulged the prince's whereabouts, when suddenly there was no need. The spawn called Regilius revealed himself. He was in a nearby structure. Dargath's quest was at an end.

Several monks were seated upon cushions strewn across the floor of the meditation hall. The erstwhile prince sat near the altar, unperturbed by the tempest's din. He was absorbed in meditation when he sensed the Dalthin's presence and expanded his awareness to include the alien mind. Just as surely, he felt Dargath turn its attention on him. There was nothing furtive about this contact. Reg knew why it was here and that danger was immanent, yet he kept his mind quiet, studying the creature until he could decide what to do. Then, because he had been sitting for several hours, he rose carefully, allowing his muscles time to respond. With a bow to the altar and the memory of Mog'an, he took his leave and made his way out to meet the thing.

A novice scrubbing the floor of the anteroom was oblivious to Dargath's approach until the Dalthin was almost upon him. When at last he noticed it, he scrambled to his feet. Gathering his robes, he dropped the brush and knocked over the bucket as he backed away. Dargath was blocking the exit to the courtyard, so the young man tried retreating into the meditation hall. Were he not so terrified, a glance over his shoulder would have told him he was about to collide with a wall. *This way*, a voice in his head directed and suddenly he knew which way to retreat. *You will be alright*, the voice assured, *but go quickly*. The novice turned on his heel and ran into the hall without looking back. Had he done so, he would have seen the prince stepping past to confront the creature.

*You have hidden well, Regilius Tonopath*, Dargath observed. *That is not an easy thing. You have learned a great deal in a very short time.*

*I have learned a bit*, Reg replied without emotion.

Closing in on his quarry, the Dalthin continued. *It is all for naught. I will kill you, then explain to your mother the sad circumstances surrounding your death.*

*I think not, Dargath*, Reg replied. *For either you will leave peacefully, or I will kill you.*

*You know my name. That is even more impressive. Nonetheless, you need to know I am among the most accomplished of my kind. You should simply surrender, since none of your talents will avail you.*

*I am among the most accomplished of mine*, Reg replied. *I will not submit.*

In response, Dargath launched a mental assault. With an ease that startled the creature, Regilius set the barrage aside. Regilius, in turn, launched a counterattack and Dargath neutralized his effort with ease. Dargath struck again and Reg resisted effortlessly. So it went for several minutes until it appeared this stalemate would continue indefinitely. Suddenly, the Dalthin shimmered to assume a new form. Unsure what the metamorphosis would produce, Reg struck psychically before the change could complete. The alien wailed, recoiled and the transformation halted. More strikes and Dargath retreated, neither

Dalthin nor other, writhing and shimmering as it tried to coalesce.

"Master! Are you alright?" someone in the corridor called.

It was Ered, standing beyond the creature, holding a broom like a weapon.

"Get out of here!" warned Reg.

The interruption provided the relief Dargath needed to become a samanal—a large fierce lizard with a barbed tail, sharp claws and pointed teeth. It swiped at Ered with the barb. The tail dissected the air, Ered dropped to the floor, and the wall behind him exploded in a shower of splinters. When the samanal turned its attention on the prince, Reg directed another volley of thought and the samanal leapt at him, hissing and swiping with its talons. Reg dove aside and the lizard landed where the prince had been standing. It whirled, nostrils flaring, and Reg climbed to his feet, only to back into a corner as the lizard approached. It was scant feet away and Reg had nowhere to go.

Turning sideways and brandishing the barbs—each spike half the length of Reg's arm—Dargath raised its tail to strike. As well as Dargath had withstood Reg's strikes, the prince began to wonder if he really could kill it. It had not responded to the sort of strikes Dur had used in Bad Adur. Would such a one as he had used on the denaJadiz be effective? As much as he wanted to try, if it failed, the sheer force required to launch it would drain all his energy and leave him exposed.

He was afraid he was about to die when the lizard cried out. Ered was jabbing its ribs with the broom handle. It was only a distraction, but provided Reg the opportunity for another strike. Dargath shuddered, but threw a kick at Ered, sending him sprawling, then turned toward Reg.

*Yield and I will spare your life*, it commanded.

*Yield to me, and I will spare yours.*

Before Reg could react, Dargath sprang forward. Still cornered, Reg had nowhere to go. He ducked and the samanal tore open his shoulder with a claw. As he fell to his knees clasping the wound, the Dalthin resumed its natural shape. As it opened its belly to devour him, Ered ran toward it crying, "Get away! Leave him alone."

He had broken the broomstick across his knee and its end was now a sharp wedge. He ran at the creature screaming, holding the weapon with both hands. He lunged, putting the full weight of his body into the thrust and imbedded its end in the Dalthin's back.

Dargath turned to strike, but a new voice commanded, "Leave this place at once!"

Reg looked up to see Osman and Bort flanked by a dozen monks, each one holding a weapon. Some carried staves, but to Reg's surprise, most were armed with pikes.

Osman advanced and once again ordered, "Leave this place or depart not at all."

*If I leave, it will be with the one for whom I came*, the Dalthin replied.

"No one is taken from this place against his will," shouted Osman.

With that, the monks advanced. Dargath attempted to hold them off, but Reg hurled another volley of intent. Dargath was whirling to confront him when a pair of monks rushed it from opposite sides, spearing it in unison. The Dalthin produced pseudopods to remove the pikes, but others beat it with staves and Dargath was forced to retreat. As it attempted to flee, the monks surrounded it, attacking from all sides. It tried to metamorphose, but Reg hurled more thought its way and again it was caught mid-effort again, neither Dalthin nor transmutation, unable to defend itself with mind or with body. As the creature shimmered, failing to assume a shape, the monks descended and attacked it mercilessly.

When at last it was dead, they stepped back and surveyed the bizarre corpse lying at their feet. They were wondering among themselves what it might be and how to dispose of it when Ered noticed Reg. He had collapsed onto the floor and was lying in a pool of blood. Ered gathered his friend into his arms and saw he was bleeding profusely. Unable to staunch the flow, he cried, "Osman! Help me!"

The monk turned, and seeing the blood, summoned the others. Something had to be done quickly, but when the monks could not decide on a course of action, Ered took command, crying, "Take him to the infirmary!"

As they rushed Regilius from the hall, Ered ran alongside, determined his lifelong friend would not die.

# PART THREE

## Reckoning

# 46

*They found you, Brother.*

*One did, but it is dead now.*

*More will arrive in three or four days.*

*Then I must leave.*

*That would be wise.*

*Lith-An, what has happened to you? You have changed so much I hardly recognize you.*

*And I am still changing, even as we speak.*

*But why has it been so… dramatic?*

*We will discuss it another time.*

*Are you alright? You seem so distant, as if we are strangers.*

*I am fine, Regilius, but you must understand I no longer know you. My memories of you are those of a toddler. I am no longer that little girl. And though I love the brother I remember, I know that is not really who you are. In time, if all unfolds as I suspect, we will become reacquainted.*

*Where are you?*

*I am with some traders. They have taken me in.*

*And Ganeth?*

*I am taking care of him.*

*You mean he is taking care of you.*

*We are past that.*

Reg paused to consider, then asked, *When will I see you again?*

*When the time is right.*

*When will that be?*

*Soon, but now you should be preparing to leave.*

*I have more questions.*

*In time. Go now.*

*Alright. I love you, Lith-An.*

*And I you.*

Reg replayed the conversation in his mind. Lith-An was now his only family. This no-longer-little girl was right about what he should be doing and so, putting sentiment aside, he prepared to depart.

… … … … …

“Wake up, Ered,” he said as he shook his friend.

Ered turned on his cot, stretched and sat upright. He had grown so accustomed to the safety of the monastery, the hand on his shoulder didn’t startle him. Opening his eyes, he said, “Good morning, Reg. What time is it?”

“Not yet dawn—a good time to leave.”

“Are you leaving?” he asked, struggling to clear his head.

“We are going home. Get dressed. Everything is packed and ready.”

“But should you be traveling with that shoulder?" Ered pointed at the bandage.

“The monks have some tricks up their sleeve that would teach even Leovar a thing or two. The poultice they applied last night has completely stopped the bleeding and the tincture of kethna they’ve given me has taken away most of the pain. Some herb, whose name I cannot pronounce, has given me the energy I need and I can sleep in the saddle while we ride. Now get ready. A Haroun guide is waiting at the gate with some endaths.”

… … … … …

“Revered One,” Reg had said to Hazis the night before. “I would like to leave.” In fact, the monks had barely finished treating his wound when Reg broached the subject. “Have you supplies enough for a small expedition?”

“What kind of expedition, Regilius?”

“It is time Ered and I return to Ydron, Revered One.”

“And why is that?” Hazis inquired. “You and your friend may remain here as long as you wish.”

“I understand, but the Dalthin have discovered Losan and my presence puts all your lives in danger.”

“We are unafraid. We will stand beside you no matter the risk.”

“I thank you for that, but please understand, even had not last night transpired as it did, I would still have elected to leave. There is much remaining for me to do at home, and after much thought on the matter, I have decided now is the time to act.”

"Then of course we will equip you, but you will not travel alone. I will send two brothers with you."

Reg shook his head. "That would place them in harm's way."

"No one is safe from the dangers of the time."

"Osman and I will go," declared Bort as he put away the unused bandages.

Hazis nodded. "I think the two of you would make suitable companions. You are certainly far enough along the path you may set aside your studies for a while. Osman, are you of a similar mind?"

"Yes, Revered One."

"Very well. Regilius, have you any objection to this choice?"

"I question the wisdom of endangering these two."

Hazis shook his head. "I would have thought your judgment sounder than that. Anything that assures your safe return will spare more lives than it risks."

Reg nodded at Hazis' observation.

"You should also know we have other guests within these walls who may be of assistance. Yesterday a company of Haroun returning from the coast arrived at our gate. On their return to No'eth from Monhedeth they discovered the remains of your vessel. Although the ship lies wrecked near the mouth of the Em, they were able to board her and salvage a few things. By chance they brought those items here in hopes we might use them. They were surprised, and not a little pleased, to learn the ship's owner resides within these walls. I will let you examine what they brought, but I will also ask these travelers for whatever additional assistance they might provide."

Ered rose from his cot and dressed. This was news he had been waiting for. He gathered his possessions and followed Regilius to the courtyard.

As Reg had suggested, this was a good time to depart. During this break between storms, the stars would provide sufficient light to discern the trail eastward, yet it was dark enough for them to depart unobserved. Reg reached out with his mind for signs of danger, but told Ered he found nothing immediate. Bort signaled the gatekeeper and the massive door swung open. Beyond were the endaths and a Haroun named Bakka Oduweh. Ered had never seen one of these people and the sight startled him. He knew they were hunters and shunned civilization, but he did not expect to see their guide clad entirely in skins and pelts. Moreover, he marveled at the endaths, whose long necks and tails made them appear prehistoric. Rarely seen outside No'eth, almost mythical, he found it difficult to imagine he would be riding one.

Bakka secured their belongings behind the saddles and ordered Reg and the others to mount up. When Ered approached the endath designated as his, he circled it, looking for a way aboard, since the creature's long legs put the stirrup too high for his foot.

"How do I mount it?" he asked.

Bakka smiled. "Let me help," he replied. Lacing his fingers together so his hands formed a step, he said, "Place your foot upon them."

Ered obeyed, and as he stretched his arms upwards, Bakka gave a boost. Once in the saddle, he felt ashamed of his inability until he saw the monks and his injured friend also needed assistance. Reg grasped his shoulder and grimaced once he was securely seated, but gave no other sign he could not ride. Once the four were mounted, Bakka approached his own steed, and with three quick steps and a leap, landed atop the creature's back.

"Voreth's horns!" Ered exclaimed.

When they were underway, Reg fell silent and Ered eyed him carefully. As weary and sore as he was, he knew Reg hurt even more. He could feel the storm approaching, so he drew his mount beside his friend's. Ered tied him to the saddle and wrapped a sandiath skin around him, hoping the creature's gait would allow him to sleep. He prayed they were not leaving too soon. A long road lie ahead and much remained to be done.

# 47

In those moments when Duile was alone and Husted Yar was not molding her thoughts or soothing her fears, doubts would creep in. The tidy scenario she had envisioned had unraveled and events had taken unexpected turns. As a girl she had studied the chaos preceding The Joining. Now, she feared matters would spiral out of control as they had then, leaving her with a fragmented kingdom and much less than she now possessed.

*If only I had my children*, she thought, *all would be well.*

This was not a maternal thought. Duile was only ever a mother in the purely biological sense. No, this was an element in the process of exerting control. It was an over-simplification, but as her world fell into greater disarray, she took comfort in any plan that might lead to order. Interestingly, if someone could have assured her both children would vanish forever, she would have been troubled far less than had they surfaced safely beyond her grasp but within reach of her enemies.

Yar continued to offer vague assurances he had located the two, but while one search party after another returned empty-handed, each ensuing week left her more convinced they were lost forever. Consequently, when one group returned with Danth Kanagh, she was overjoyed. Now that he was secure within the castle keep, hope rekindled. She hastened to the dungeon and her heart leapt at the thought he could reveal where Regilius was hiding. She would have run, but her sense of dignity precluded any show of weakness, so she moved as fast as she deemed seemly. When she had descended into the bowels of the fortress and arrived at the prison, the jailor and ship's captain lead her to the young man's cell. They threw open the door and she recoiled. Aboard ship they had left him lying in his filth and the stench was overwhelming.

"Couldn't you have cleaned him before bringing him here?" she demanded.

"I'm sorry, Your Majesty. I was following Pudath's orders," the captain explained.

As much as excuses annoyed her, the prospect of interrogating Danth overrode all other concerns. She peered into the darkness until her eyes adjusted. After a moment, she could discern a shape on the floor. In another, she recognized the young lord shackled supine, arms and legs splayed outward. The cell barely accommodated him.

She smiled. "You have stolen my son, young Kanagh and I hear you have been most uncooperative since you were apprehended."

"Your men have been less than cordial, Majesty. I thought I should respond in kind." He smiled weakly.

"You might find I could be quite hospitable were you to tell me where my son is," she said, mimicking his feigned civility.

"Somehow, I don't think that would be in his best interest."

She acted wounded. "Do you think I would harm my own son?"

"I wouldn't have thought you would murder your husband, but you did."

"You have no understanding of what transpired," she hissed.

"I understand you have left a trail of bodies and more will follow."

"Will you be one of them?" Her patience was running thin and she trembled with anger. Husted would have been able to calm her, she thought, but "he" was not here. "Do you not think I can cause you a great deal of pain?"

"Oh, I have no doubt of that. Your henchmen have managed to cause me some already."

"Is this something you relish, boy? Because if it is, you shall have no shortage of it."

"I believe you. Unfortunately, I cannot help you."

"Are you saying you cannot or you will not?"

"Interpret it as you will."

"Under most circumstances, loyalty is an admirable trait and my son may count himself fortunate he has such a friend, but by the time I have finished with you, I do not believe you will feel the same."

"I shall always feel privileged to call him my friend. Nothing that happens here is his doing. The only things that puzzle me are how he was sired by that bumbler, Manhathus, and how such a good and kindly soul ever sprang from your loins."

"It is only because you are his friend that I will begin gently," she said through clenched teeth. "You will have only water for three days. Hopefully by then you will have found your tongue. If you cooperate you will have food, drink and suitable accommodations. Your family may even see how generous I can be to friends of the crown. Otherwise, we will reevaluate."

She turned to go, then decided she wanted to be clear. "Trust me. I will have the truth out of you if I have to whip, burn, crush and cut every syllable from your stubborn hide. And if you fail me, your dear mother will also feel my wrath. How fares she these days?"

"Are you sure you are not becoming too soft-hearted?" said Danth. "We wouldn't want anyone to think too kindly of you, would we?"

Duile clenched her fists but restrained herself. "See he doesn't smell like a sewer when I next pay a call," she admonished the jailor.

"Yes, Your Majesty," he replied, bowing low. When she was gone, he spat on his prisoner. "Let us bet she won't be back for a couple of days, eh?" he said. "Don't count on your bath any time soon." He closed and locked the door, plunging the cell into darkness.

... ... ... ... ...

Danth took a breath and tried to contain his fears. The floor hurt his back and head and the shackles cut into his wrists and ankles. These were minor discomforts, however, in the face of what the future would hold. He was terrified by what Duile might be planning and was unsure he could take any more beatings. He also hoped she would not bring his mother into this. And though he didn't know what he would do under that circumstance, he believed he would do what was right and she would understand. He prayed he would live long enough to see Reg crowned and Duile given the punishment she deserved.

# 48

Lightening flared and thunder boomed.

"Voreth's horns!" cried Pedreth.

He sat up in bed and smacked the covers. The thought that had been nagging at him had crystallized. Ever since he heard Samel's message, he had been troubled. It made no sense and it came to him in his sleep he had interpreted it incorrectly. In part, it was due to Samel's accent, but now Pedreth believed he had it right. Lith-An had not said purple ashes nor had she said ashes purple. She had said Asch's purple. That was his color and the banners the troops flew as they entered Limast were purple. Nor did she refer to any maiden. This certainly was Samel's pronunciation of Meden. The message he bore then was, "Fear the banners of Kareth and Danai, Ened and Hau, the harbingers of mother's holocaust. Seek refuge in Asch's purple where friends lie. If Bogen will come to Meden's rescue while lightening fills the sky, the tide may turn." She was referring to a storm—this storm—and Lord Asch must be here within these walls. As crazy as it sounded, Pedreth needed to find him.

He tossed aside the covers, uncovered the light globe and put his feet on the floor. He had no idea what the hour might be, but it was dark. Even if he located Asch he would not be able to see him until day had dawned. Still, he couldn't just sit here, so he rose, went to the basin and splashed water on his face. He dressed and checked his pockets to be sure he still had the signet. Carrying his boots to better tread softly, he stepped into the corridor debating whether to wake Samel. He decided against it. As endearing as Samel could be, he was a chatterbox and Pedreth needed none of that.

"Now," he said to himself, "which way?"

Success might depend upon the cooperation of a palace servant and the problem at this hour was where to find one. He decided the kitchen would be a good place to begin. If anyone, the palace bakers would already be plying their craft. Trusting his instincts, he set off in the direction from which he had been brought.

The interior of barakOzmir, Bogen's palace, was vast to say the least. After numerous wrong turns, Pedreth was beginning to grow frustrated. Then, as he leaned against a wall, trying to sort out the corridors, he thought he heard voices. They were almost inaudible, so he held his breath to better hear, but the pulse in his ears masked them. Still, he followed what he heard, and after a while the voices grew louder. He began to discern several speakers, and minute by minute, each voice grew more distinct. Shortly they were accompanied by metallic clashes and he grew confident they were the sounds of pots and pans. Spirits buoyed, he stopped long enough to pull on his boots, then hastened toward the commotion.

… … … … …

"You there! Are you trying to ruin everything? Keep the oven door closed or I swear I'll have your hide!"

"Yes, Orim. I'm sorry," replied a young man.

"Sorry isn't half of what you'll be," Orim countered.

Orim had spent most of his life preparing for the position of head baker. Having attained it, he led a comfortable life. No careless apprentice was going to spoil another perfect batch of bread if he could help it. Content he had prevailed, he turned his eye to the sous-chefs and assistants hurrying to be ready at first light. Racks of loaves and rolls were cooling, every crust a golden brown. It was then he spotted the face peering in.

"You!" he cried, pointing. "Who are you and what are you doing? You have no business here. Go away!"

As all heads turned as Pedreth stepped into plain sight.

"So sorry to intrude," he said. "I only wanted to see how this kitchen compares with the one at home."

Orim was caught off guard. "And where might that be?"

"barakYdron," Pedreth replied.

Orim had never traveled beyond Limast. For that matter, he had rarely been outside of barakOzmir. To his provincial mind, he associated anything bearing the name Ydron with images of grandeur. To be visited by one claiming to be from the fabled palace on such a routine morning at once disarmed and impressed him. Without being able to say why, he felt honored by Pedreth's presence.

"Do you work in the palace kitchen?" he asked.

"No, I do not," Pedreth confessed. "I am but the royal boatkeeper, but my friend Satsah is the chief baker and on occasion has allowed me to watch."

Orim's curiosity was piqued. "Why would a boatkeeper wish to see a kitchen?"

Pedreth, who simply enjoyed eating good food, felt offering the complete truth might not suffice, so he lied. "I have always wished it had been my lot to cook, so from time to time he shows me a thing or two. I must say," he said, changing the conversation's tack, "This kitchen seems every bit as well-run as his."

Of anything Pedreth could have invented, this fabrication appealed to Orim's ego and made Pedreth an instant friend. Beaming and standing taller, the baker asked, "May I show you around?"

"Of course," said Pedreth. "In all this land, there is nothing I would rather see."

As Orim gave him a tour, showing off the gleaming pots and trays, letting him taste a little of this and a little of that, Pedreth realized he could not have set upon a better plan. If anything were to be brought to Lord Asch this morning—*early* this morning—it would be food. He was as good as in. If he kept stroking Orim's ego without being obvious, he could be among the ones bringing the lord his breakfast. In this windowless kitchen, Pedreth had no idea what time it might be, but as his host regaled him with culinary accomplishments, other workers began to filter in and set to work. Eventually, he noticed prepared food being put on trays.

"Breakfast time already?" he inquired. "At home, the queen usually eats much later."

"Lord Bogen is no early riser, either," Orim confided, "But this morning we have visitors and they have expressed a desire to eat early."

"I suppose you prepare for visitors quite often."

"In fact, we do, although they typically break fast with lord of the castle."

"Your guests must be quite important to command such special service."

"Indeed," Orim replied. Thrusting out his chest he boasted, "This day I have the honor of preparing the first meal of the day for the Lord of Pytheral and his officers."

Pedreth feigned surprise. "Lord Asch?"

"Indeed. After today, I will be able to say I have served every Lord in Ydron," Orim boasted.

"Quite an accomplishment. I have heard he is quite fearsome."

"Not in the least. Despite his reputation, he is really quite decent."

"I never would have thought it."

"You should see how well he treats the serving staff. It would change your opinion of him forever."

Pedreth saw his opportunity. "Do you suppose I might?"

"Might, what?"

"See how he treats the servers."

"And how do you propose to do that?"

Pedreth took a deep breath. It was now or never. "Ordinarily I would never impose upon one in your position for such a favor, but I shall never have this opportunity again. If you would but let me carry a tray, so I might glimpse Lord Asch for a moment, I promise I will comport myself far better than any apprentice."

Orim appeared uncertain, so Pedreth sweetened the pot.

"And should you ever come to Ydron, I will prevail upon Satsah to let you visit his kitchen so you can see with your own eyes how yours compares with his."

Orim could not believe his ears. He had often dreamt about visiting Ydron, but now his was a dream with a purpose: to see if his kitchen compared in any way with the finest in the world! It was too much to hope for.

"I shall find you suitable attire," he said, "But we must hurry. It is already approaching the seventh hour and we cannot be late."

"Let us make haste then. I promise I will not embarrass you."

... ... ... ... ...

Breakfast was ready and the kitchen staff carried the meal to a dining room where Lord Asch had gathered his officers. After motioning to his staff to remain at the entrance, Orim approached the table where the lord and his entourage were seated. He bowed deeply and Asch acknowledged the gesture, indicating Orim and his party could bring the meal. Silently and with practiced deference, the kitchen staff began serving the food. Things went smoothly until Pedreth placed his tray on the table. Then, before anyone could react, he moved to Lord Asch's side, dropped to one knee, and extending his hand to display the signet, said, "Pardon, Lord, but I bring a request from the house of Kanagh."

Lord Asch turned in his seat. With raised brows he regarded the genuflecting server, then plucked the ring from Pedreth's fingers and examined it carefully. Returning his eyes to Pedreth, he asked, "How did you come by this token?"

"My good friend, Lord Danth Kanagh, gave it to me and sent me on an errand, Lord."

"A cook from Limast is a friend with a Lord of Ydron? How did this come to be?"

Pedreth replied, "No, Lord. I am Pedreth, boatkeeper for the late Manhathus Tonopath. I am afraid I deceived Orim, the chief baker, into letting me dress so."

"So you are accustomed to deceit."

"No, Lord. I am not. But I could think of no other way to gain your audience and the message I bring is most urgent."

"And I should believe a liar."

"Pardon me, Lord." Pedreth's heart was pounding in his chest. "It was a mistake born of desperation. I am so afraid things will go wrong for Lord Emeil, should I fail in my mission, I took a chance. I am afraid I have botched everything."

"Emeil? You bandy about the names of the powerful. What has Emeil to do with this? Else is it Lord Kanagh? You have me so confused," said Asch as he pocketed the ring.

"The young lord and I were sent on a mission to find help for Lord Emeil. Along the way, Lord Kanagh was captured by a party of the queen's men. Before they took him, he gave me the ring so I might be believed."

His patience running thin, Lord Asch pressed further, "And who would suggest I might be a friend to Emeil of Sandoval?"

Pedreth could not bring himself to say Lith-An. Things were going badly enough. Instead he answered, "The true heir to the House of Tonopath, Prince Regilius."

Asch's eyes widened.

Pedreth continued, "My Prince told us Lord Emeil has fled from Queen Duile and has taken his troops to menRathan. Lord Kanagh was sent to find allies who would rally to Lord Emeil's side and I was sent to help him in his quest." Sweat was running down his face in rivulets and he forced himself to look up so Asch might see the truth in his eyes.

If Asch were prepared to hear a tall tale, this news disarmed him. It was several seconds before he could speak. "And I alone might be the one to turn the tide? What folly!"

"Pardon me, Lord. Though I am but a boatkeeper, I can see certain things and—no, my Lord—you alone could not turn the tide. You bring with you, how many, perhaps two or three hundred? But you have more troops elsewhere, and of more immediate assistance, you are in the house of Lord Bogen who has an entire army. If both of you were to rescue Lord Miasoth, who is under attack as we speak, together the three of you could begin to make a real difference. Further, in addition to Lord Kanagh and I, Lord Leovar Hol and the Prince's teacher, Ai'Lorc, were sent to obtain the assistance of certain others: we to inquire of Lords Bogen and Jath; Lord Hol and Ai'Lorc to solicit Lords Miasoth and Basham. If I may say so, the five of you will pose a formidable opposition."

At that moment a page entered the room and went to Asch's side where he knelt on the side opposite Pedreth.

"Rise," Asch commanded, "What news do you bring?"

The page rose, moved closer and whispered.

"From Miasoth? A pigeon?" Asch asked.

The page nodded and whispered some more.

Asch turned to Pedreth. "Besieged is Meden, as you said, boatkeeper. If aid is to come to Emeil, Lord Miasoth must indeed be rescued. Perhaps I can convince Bogen to join me." Asch retrieved Danth's signet from his pocket and tossed it to Pedreth, adding, "You have done well." He rose, and followed by his officers, departed.

Pedreth was as delighted as he was relieved. Slowly, he arose. When he turned, Orim was standing before him. His hands were on his hips and he was scowling.

# 49

"More arrows and bolts to the battlements," came the cry and soldiers ran to the armory.

"They're bringing a ram!" shouted another.

General Mo'ed climbed barakMeden's parapet stairs to survey the surrounding forces. Duile would not allow Dural to reject her extortion without penalty, so her troops had continued to amass. Their number had grown from hundreds to thousands, and they attacked without pause. By the torchlight illuminating the plain, Mo'ed could discern a distant phalanx approaching. In an instant, multiple lightening flashes illuminated the plain, revealing the battering ram. His heart sank. If it breached the gates, the fortress would fall.

Despite earlier misgivings, Dural had allowed the general to prepare for an attack. Even though the ensuing events justified his efforts, Mo'ed could derive no satisfaction. Dural's hesitation had forfeited any advantage he might otherwise have obtained and limited his options. Had Mo'ed been permitted to establish a defense outside the fortress, he might have been able to cut off the enemies' supply lines and even reduce their number through attacks on their rear. Confined, however, within these walls, there was nowhere to go and nothing to do but try to buy time. He could only hope the arrows, food and water held out until some miracle occurred.

"Mo'ed!" called Dural.

The general turned to see his Lord stepping onto the parapet. Dural scanned the battlefield, then turned to face him.

"They must think we are ready to roll over," Dural sneered.

"I think they sense we cannot last," Mo'ed replied.

"Can we not?"

"If they succeed in breaching the gate, it is a matter of hours until we are finished. Without assistance we are doomed."

"Has there been no response to the messenger pigeons?"

"Only Bogen has answered and his reply was not promising. In diplomatic terms, he says he will not jeopardize his relationship with Ydron."

"The kethna-sipping sot! I hope he calls upon us when she turns her troops on him. As it is, we will fight to the end, help or none. If we go down, we will do so valiantly."

Mo'ed was not about to remind his master that, a short while ago, his response to Bogen would have been similar. His men would fight to the end because there was no other choice, but the outcome would be dismal. Duile's army took no prisoners.

"General! What do you suppose those men are up to?"

Mo'ed looked where Dural was pointing and saw a party of eight running toward the fortress. They were carrying a mat of woven reeds like a canopy. A group of archers running beside them were sporadically firing arrows. Despite casualties, the group reached the gate and tossed the mat aside. Arrows rained down, but those who did not fall set frantically to work. The mat had concealed something large, round, and from the glint of torches on its surface, something metallic. While another group stacked bundles of logs against the gate, the first group emptied the contents of the spherical object onto the bundles. Torches were thrown and fire roared to life. The flames soon revealed the object in question to be a pot that had contained a quantity of oil. The assault on the gate had begun.

There were cries atop the walls—"Fire! They're burning the gate! Water! For the love of Siemas, bring water!"—as the soldiers who had set the blaze ran back to safety. With all eyes on the growing fire, none on the battlements thought to cut them down.

As Mo'ed turned to mobilize his men, he could not miss the look of incredulity and dismay on Dural's face.

... ... ... ... ...

"Wake up, Lord Hol. Open your eyes."

Leovar awoke and uncovered the light globe by his bed. "Who is it?" he asked.

"I am the one who has tended you these past days," said the young woman.

"I remember," Leovar replied. "What do you want?"

"The fortress is ablaze. You must dress and depart."

Leovar, clad in a night gown, swung his feet to the floor and stood.

"Where are my clothes?" he asked.

"I've placed them on that chair," she said, gesturing. "I will step outside while you dress."

"First, tell me, has the enemy breeched the walls?"

"No, my Lord. I do not think so."

"And my guard?"

"He has gone to join the fight."

"Have you awakened Ai'Lorc?"

"I was going to inform him next."

"Once you have done so, please bring him here."

The girl nodded and hurried out. Leovar began dressing. They were probably surrounded, so could not leave the fortress, but at least they would not die trapped in their rooms. Still, he and Ai'Lorc needed to devise a strategy to survive, not only within these walls, but outside as well if they managed to escape.

A minute later, Ai'Lorc appeared in the doorway.

"How are you doing?" asked Leovar.

"Actually, I am quite rested," Ai'Lorc replied. "And you? All else aside, you look recovered."

"Thanks to this lady."

Ai'Lorc nodded. "We should leave."

"Any idea where we should go?"

"I don't think we will be leaving these walls any time soon," Ai'Lorc replied, "but we have to assess our options and we can't do that here."

"You're right," said Leovar. Then to the girl, "Will you come with us?"

"No, my Lord. I've risked enough. I can suggest where you might hide for a while, but it would not be to my advantage if we were found together." Then, averting her eyes downwards, she apologized. "I hope I have not offended you."

"Not at all," said Leovar.

She told them about a room where foodstuffs were stored, an unlikely place for anyone to look while the attack was underway.

"I'm sorry I can't assist you further," she said. "It was an honor to serve you."

She curtsied, gave one last smile, then turned and hurried down the corridor.

"We would be wise to follow her example," offered Ai'Lorc. "Someone is bound to remember to check in on us."

As they departed, distant drums began to beat.

Mo'ed peered over the wall and saw the battering ram had arrived. Its column, once the trunk of some large tree, was metal-capped and banded at the striking end to concentrate its force and insure it did not split. From above the colossal device, amid volleys of arrows, Mo'ed's soldiers were attempting to douse the fire, now grown to such intensity it was impossible to extinguish.

"It won't be long now," observed Mo'ed. "The gate weakens by the minute."

For the first time, Dural grasped the gravity of the situation. "I am sorry I didn't listen."

"No matter. I doubt we could have prevailed against such numbers. The provinces have become so isolated, it is only a matter of time until Duile conquers us all."

The battering ram's strike halted conversation.

"Captain!" Mo'ed called to an officer. "Where are your archers?"

The officer, unaccustomed to the stress of battle, had frozen. At the reprimand, he came to his senses and rallied his archers against those positioning the ram for a second strike. Many fell and it was several minutes before replacements arrived. By that time, those on the ram had devised a new strategy.

Soldiers manning the device were paired with soldiers holding shields overhead. Together, they hurled the ram at the gate a second time. That was followed by a third strike and a fourth, upon which the gate shuddered. Duile's troops sent up a cheer in anticipation of their impending triumph. The device backed into place yet again, pausing as if for effect, then struck. It wouldn't be long before the gate yielded. Flames reached half way up its face and commanders on the walls began issuing orders to reinforce it. War drums began beating. Mo'ed, however, had turned his attention from the immediate assault to something in the distance.

"Captain!" he called. "Have you a glass?" The officer gestured he couldn't hear, so Mo'ed pantomimed a telescope. "A glass!" he snapped.

The captain nodded comprehension. He looked around, then, seeing one, retrieved it from a cranny and held it aloft.

"Bring it," Mo'ed shouted, motioning with a sweep of his arm.

The officer tucked it under his arm and ran to his commander. Mo'ed tore it from his grasp, put it to his eye and aimed it toward the horizon. He adjusted it repeatedly, unable to discern anything through the darkness. Then, as if in answer to the unasked question, lightening illuminated the battlefield. Abruptly, he lowered the instrument and turned to Dural.

"There is hope," he said.

# 50

The Grand Causeway had not been used since The Joining. It had been built during the Great Conflict to facilitate the movement of troops and supplies from Limast against its greatest adversary, the land of Meden. Now it served a similar function, but this time the legions of soldiers coming from Limast were aiding a friend.

Over the centuries, the highway's surface had become buried under soil and overgrown with scrub, but if one took time to clear some brush and dig through the dirt, one would find a flat, almost uncompromised road of hexagonal stones. The way was still easy to ascertain because the nearly unbroken surface prevented the growth of significant cover. Occasionally a sapling managed to spring up between the crevices, and in those instances, the growing tree forced up the underlying stones so that they jutted and stood akimbo around the intrusion. By and large, however, the path of that ancient route was relatively clear and the troops traversed it quickly.

Bogen turned in the saddle to survey the trailing column. His kingdom was neither large, nor in comparison with his neighbors, extremely populous. Still, of his army numbering three thousand, he had elected to leave only one sixth to guard danOzmir, hoping if he succeeded in bringing victory, the queen would have to turn her attention toward menRathan and Emeil. It was a gamble, but it would take a substantial force to even the odds, so he brought as many as he dared.

"You know, my friend," Bogen conceded, "you put up a very convincing argument."

"Can you see how she has betrayed every ally?" said Asch. "She will sever your own legs from under you, given the chance."

Bogen had to agree. He, like Miasoth, had deceived himself into believing if he posed no threat she would leave him alone, but Asch had explained how Emeil had been forced to flee. Emeil's character was such that none, including Bogen, could believe him a traitor, so it became obvious Duile had murdered Kareth and Danai. It amazed Bogen she would do this to two of her most loyal allies—one of them her uncle—in order to frame Emeil. Asch, whom she had also framed, had seen through this ploy, realizing it was only a matter of time before his own head would roll and she confiscated his lands. Unable to convince Hau and Ened to join him, Asch had fled with his immediate guard and a small number of soldiers to Limast, leaving the greatest part of his army to guard Pytheral. Until he knew for certain who his friends were, he was not prepared to take the same gamble as Bogen.

He had fled to Limast due to the long-standing friendship between their families. Bogen had taken him in like a long lost brother, so he took his host aside at every opportunity to educate him on what had transpired since the coup. Eventually, he convinced him to mobilize his army. Unfortunately, because Bogen had already released the only pigeon that homed to Meden with an unpromising message, he could not alert Dural to the coming support.

To make up for his tardiness, Limast's lord consulted with Pedreth. Both agreed it was too late for the boatkeeper to complete his mission, so Bogen dispatched pigeons to Borrst and Yeset—albeit with no time to learn whether they arrived, nor how the Lords of those provinces would respond.

Glancing skyward, he regarded the clouds. They were dark and the wind drove them with a fury presaging a coming storm.

"This is not a time I would have chosen to go into battle," he observed.

"Then can you imagine a more perfect time to do so?" Asch countered. "We will arrive after dark and Duile's generals will not expect us. We could not have planned more advantageously."

Bogen nodded. Never had he dreamt he would go to war, but if he must, he would rather have surprise on his side. Better to be on the offensive than to sit at home, as Dural had done, and let the fight come to him on the enemy's terms.

It was the nineteenth hour when they arrived on this plateau overlooking barakMeden. Although night had fallen, it had not been difficult to locate the fortress. The battlefield was ablaze with torches and their glow was visible over the crest of the surrounding hills. As Bogen, Asch and their generals looked out upon the battlefield, they observed how Duile's troops were spread, apparently placed to intercept anyone escaping the fortress, not to repel outside forces.

"I don't consider their number much greater than ours," said

Bogen. "If we can liberate the castle and add Dural's to our own, we will outnumber them."

His general nodded. "The queen is smug, my Lords, and considers herself without peer. If we attack with the bulk of our force, placing a few hundred on either side of the western passage through which her forces arrived, we can drive them back and cut them down as they flee through the gap. Dural's generals will relish the opportunity to join us."

"How much time will it take to position an ambush?"

"Half an hour should suffice," the general said.

"I have enough men to guard the passage," Lord Asch volunteered.

"I agree," said Bogen's general.

"How will we know you are ready so we can signal you?" asked Bogen.

"Count on us to be ready. As for a signal, the movement of two thousand five hundred soldiers will more than suffice." Asch grinned, then wheeled his horse around and rode off.

Despite the size of his army, Lord Bogen was understandably nervous. "How do you think we will fare, General?"

"Had they time to prepare, my Lord, the battle would be nearly even and the outcome unforeseeable. But because they are dispersed, we can cut the bulk of them down without much resistance. It will give us not only physical, but psychological advantage as well."

Lord Bogen sat back in the saddle, more at ease.

… … … … …

"Ready the ram," came the order.

"Ready, sir!"

"Prepare to roll on my command!"

"Aye, sir!"

"To barakMeden! Forward!"

"Forward the ram!"

At that command, two dozen bodies hunched forward over bars projecting from either side of the cylinder, straining to overcome inertia. The ground upon which the giant machine rested was soft, so it was an effort to set it into motion. Gradually, however, the device began to move. Once rolling, it gained momentum quickly. Its large wheels easily traversed the bumpy field and the field marshal's concern it might be too heavy turned to optimism.

Forward of the ram, troops parted to make way for its assault. As the behemoth followed, cheers went up in anticipation of victory. Across the plain, captains began issuing orders, readying their units for the moment the gates would be breached. When the gate was set ablaze, another cheer went up. War drums began beating, and as their cadence quickened, excitement mounted. The battering ram dealt blow after blow, and when the gate began to yield, word spread that the end was near. The commander of a company heading to the front flashed a congratulatory smile and saluted the field marshal who returned the salute before turning to observe the rear units' advance. His smile faded, however, as the once orderly procession began to turn chaotic at the rear. He wished for silence so he could understand what was happening, but the cheers drowned out everything else. Still, he strained to see what the problem might be. Then, one unit after another began looking back, and as they did, their cheers turned to cries of dismay as they realized they were under attack.

Now, it was the defenders' turn to cheer. Banners of allies appeared in the distance. Archers on the walls rained arrows upon the attackers, no longer conserving bolts and shafts in the face of a prolonged siege. The gate swung wide and mounted soldiers surged through. Behind the cavalry ran the infantry, brandishing swords, pikes and axes. In the face of this assault, the drums quieted and panic began to set it.

At first, there was no ordered retreat and those who turned to flee were easily overtaken or cut down by Asch's forces. By the time the order was given, Duile's forces were caught between Dural's and Bogen's armies. Outnumbered and outmaneuvered, they tried to fight back, but their opponents were merciless. Had this been another time and circumstance, Bogen and Asch might have taken prisoners, but this was the beginning of their campaign and they did not have soldiers enough to guard them, so they spared no one.

When morning arrived bringing rain, the plain outside barakMeden had grown quiet and peace had returned. Dural left his walls and rode through the downpour to join his rescuers. From atop a ridge, as they surveyed the land and the bodies of the fallen, he was still struggling with the queen's duplicity.

"I never imagined she would do this to me. I was loyal and would have defended her cause," he lamented.

Bogen, seeing himself in Dural, said, "We have all grown naïve and complacent. She took advantage of us and we allowed it."

# 51

Even after the rains had extinguished the fire, the massive gate continued to smolder, sending smoke across the plain. Those soldiers who were not chasing down Duile's troops were tending the wounded or gathering up the dead. With too many to bury, once the rains abated, they would build pyres. Amid this activity sat Ai'Lorc and Leovar.

"We cannot stay," said Ai'Lorc, sitting on the helmet of one of the fallen. "Someone is certain to recognize us. The question is where do we go? It is dangerous abroad. "

Leovar, surveying the corpses littering the plain, agreed. "It is dangerous everywhere."

"What, then?"

"We should continue to work toward ending Duile's reign."

"But how? We only number two, and I am certainly no soldier," protested Ai'Lorc.

"Neither am I, although we may still have to fight before this is over."

"What do you suggest?"

"I have an idea. Even though we are small in the scheme of things, by multiplying our number and adding chaos to the mix, we can make life harder for Duile."

"I don't follow," said Ai'Lorc.

"Who in this land are most dissatisfied and least in control of their fate?"

Ai'Lorc thought a moment, then offered, "The slaves?"

"Yes, and they would love to cause her grief if they were but free to do so."

Ai'Lorc smiled. "Are you proposing we try to effect their release?"

"I am. The quarries and mines are poorly guarded, since no one has ever attempted it. Still, we might be arrested approaching the pits unless we appear as friends of the crown. If we decide to try, we will need to find disguises."

"That shouldn't be difficult. There are disguises aplenty all around us. The battlefield is rife with uniforms, albeit many in worse shape than others."

Leovar paused to consider. "But dressed as soldiers of Ened or Hau, Miasoth's troops would cut us down before we could reach the pass."

"That is why we will only gather what we need and find a way to conceal them. Before we cross into Ydron, we can change."

Finding useable uniforms proved harder than expected. Most were bloody and damaged. Still, after an hour, they had found a complete uniform Leovar could wear, as well as a soldier's backpack, a pair of boots and a second helmet for Ai'Lorc. Naturally, they had recovered swords and daggers, but were otherwise unsuccessful. They were tiring and becoming dejected when Ai'Lorc cried out.

"I have found an officer! I think he died much as yours did. His head is bashed in. His size appears right, as well."

"Wonderful! We may need his authority before we are done."

They examined the uniform closely. A damaged or bloody one would lead to questions. Deciding this one was satisfactory, they folded it so it did not look too rumpled when they needed it. They would not be able to clean or to hang it, so it would not look as crisp as it should, but it was unmarked.

"I only wish we could locate our endaths. We can't walk all the way to Ydron," said Ai'Lorc.

Leovar pointed. "It seems the gods are smiling today. I see two unattended horses."

Two of Miasoth's soldiers had dismounted and were attending to the injured some distance away. Their mounts had drifted off and were grazing.

"After providing such abysmal accommodations," Leovar said, "Dural owes us this much."

"We had better hurry, before their riders notice."

They hoisted their satchels over their shoulders and ran for all they were worth.

"Which way from here?" puffed Leovar as they ran. "Through the pass?"

"Too perilous," said Ai'Lorc. "That will put us north of menRathan, sending us through the heart of the battle. I once came through Meden before you were born and I dimly recall a way to the south or southwest." He scanned the distance. "There! Do you see the notch in those hills? That's a pass that will take us from here to barTimesh and the quarries of Ead."

"You lead. I will follow."

# 52

"Boudra, take the stew off the fire. It should be ready."

"Don't bother," said Ganeth. "I will do it."

"Don't spill it," Sa'ar cautioned.

"I am a big boy, Sa'ar. I can manage," he replied with a smile.

When the nomads had carried Ria and Ganeth to their encampment, Boudra and Sa'ar had taken them in. It was not because these wanderers from Shash were kind and generous. They often captured children to use or sell as slaves. But Sa'ar and Boudra had trafficked in slaves enough to recognize Ria was exceptional, so they decided to keep her for their own. Since she was more cooperative with Ganeth around, they found a use for him as well. Over time, however, the two grew to feel an almost parental fondness for the girl. Because Ganeth had such an easy way about him, they grew to regard him as a as one of their own.

During the ensuing months, Ganeth also came to realize Ria was exceptional. As the days passed, her vocabulary grew at an astonishing rate and soon she was speaking as an adult, not the three-year-old she really was. He did not know what to make of it, but as much as her precocity left him in awe, he was even more amazed when she first addressed him in thoughts.

One afternoon, he set out to gather firewood. He was lost in thought as he foraged through the underbrush when, suddenly, Ria's voice filled his head.

*Ganeth! Stop what you are doing and return to camp.*

Caught off guard, unaware the words were not spoken, he stood erect and looked around. He could not imagine she had traveled so far from camp.

*Ganeth. You cannot remain where you are. Danger is imminent. A camarr is moving in your direction. It does not sense you at the moment, but it soon will.*

He had only heard of this great cat in tales, but the very name made his heart stop. Stories had it a camarr was capable of killing an entire hunting party and Ganeth was alone and unarmed. Until now, it had not occurred to him such creatures might be real, but the girl's words carried an urgency he could not ignore. Still, he saw nothing, so he resumed his task.

*Ganeth. Return to camp at once! Believe me or doubt me, but come home. This is not the time to be right or wrong. Please hurry!*

"Ria!" he called, looking around.

*Ganeth. Be quiet! I think it heard you.* Then, as he continued to search, her thoughts returned. *Ganeth. I am not where you are. I am still in the camp. Please hurry! There is not much time.*

As incredible as those words sounded, Ganeth had no time to question. A distant cluster of bushes shook and he decided he did not want to see what had caused the disturbance. He began to walk, but when the creature growled, he dropped his bundle and ran.

Arriving at the campsite, bent and out of breath, he searched for her. He was wondering if he might be going mad when he spotted her and called out. "Ria! Did you… ?"

Before he could finish, she looked at him and said, "You listened. Good," she said, then walked away.

Astonished and speechless, he heard himself say, "I listened," to no one in particular. Dumbfounded, he went off to find a quiet place where he could reflect on what had occurred. As he walked, Ria's thoughts found him again.

*No, dear man, you are not crazy.*

If he did not think he was slipping before, he now took it for fact and vacillated between accepting what had happened and questioning his sanity. Over the ensuing weeks, however, he and the rest in the camp began to acknowledge her ability.

… … … … …

"The stew smells wonderful, Sa'ar," said Ganeth, as he brought it to the table. "What is in it?"

"Boudra got lucky this morning," she said. "He managed to trade for some fresh umpall. I had to use the last of the vegetables, but it should provide us with two or three days' meals."

"That is good," said Boudra. "This lousy weather has put an end to trading. I was thinking we would move on to Rian, but now I think we should return home. With enough food to take us to Nagath-réal, we can stock up in Bad Adur."

Ganeth's eyes widened and he began to panic. This was bad news indeed. So long as these nomads remained in Ydron, he was content to follow. But should they return to Shash, beyond the eastern rim of the Great Salt Plain, he did not know what he would do. How could he ever return Ria to Marm?

"Ganeth."

"Yes, Sa'ar." The interruption returned him to the real world.

"I really wish you would listen. Will you fetch Ria and tell her dinner is ready?"

"Of course," he said.

He found her in their tent, examining some of her possessions.

"Please join us for dinner."

"Of course," she said and rose to join him.

"Aren't you going to bring your raggedy doll?"

She turned and glanced at the toy. "I am past playing with dolls. Sa'ar and Boudra can take it home and another child will enjoy it."

"What makes you think they are going home?"

"Weren't you listening to Boudra?"

Chagrinned, Ganeth hesitated, then said, "You sound as if you don't plan to come along."

"I don't. I am returning home."

"They won't let us, Ria. As nice as they seem, we belong to them."

"I am going home tonight, and while you cannot come with me, the camp will be filled with confusion. If you keep your head and gather your belongings, there may yet be an opportunity for you to escape."

"Don't be silly. You are too small to travel alone."

Lith-An did not reply, but accompanied Ganeth to dinner.

"Are you sure we should leave?" Sa'ar asked as they ate.

Boudra looked up from his meal. "The only reason to stay was the chance to trade for more light globes. They would have fetched a handsome price."

"I should have let you buy them when you asked."

"It's alright, love. I thought you were right at the time."

Just then, a robed stranger entered the tent and Boudra noticed two others in similar garb waiting in the darkness beyond. He hated being surprised, but addressed the newcomer with a wise trader's courtesy.

"Can we help you, friend?" he inquired.

"We have come for the girl," the stranger stated flatly.

"You've done no such thing!" said Sa'ar. "How dare you come into our home so rudely? Get out!" She shooed him with her hand.

"I don't know who you are or what put such an idea into your head," said Boudra, rising for emphasis, "but we'll have none of it. Unless you have legitimate business, you can leave."

He tried to shove the intruder out, but the robed figure shimmered and grew until it stretched the tent's ceiling, revealing its true form. The Dalthin generated a limb and hurled him across the tent.

Although terrified, Sa'ar shouted, "Get out! Leave us. You'll not have the child!" She picked up the stew pot, preparing to throw it, and Ganeth rose as well.

*Stop! Ganeth, Sa'ar, Boudra. Stop!* The force of Lith-An's thoughts halted them. Even the Dalthin stood still. Then, softly, she added, *I will go with them.*

"Child!" gasped Sa'ar. "What are you saying?"

"You can't go with… with… What is this thing?" demanded Boudra, pointing a finger.

*It is a creature of great power,* Lith-An replied. *I have been awaiting its arrival, as well as its companions.*

"Waiting for them?" Ganeth demanded. "Darmaht protect me, Ria. What do you mean?"

"Dear Ganeth," she answered, switching from thought to speech. "You have taken such care of me. I do not expect you will understand, but this creature will not harm me."

Ganeth would not listen. "That's crazy. Look at that… Voreth's horns… What is that thing?"

"It is a Dalthin," she answered.

"Well, the Dalthin will not take you. I promised Marm I would keep you safe, and I will." Then, turning toward the alien, he rose taller than he ever had, insisting, "You cannot take her."

Before anyone could react, he grabbed a knife and ran at it. The Dalthin knocked the weapon aside, then, with its belly opening to accommodate, it lifted Ganeth, inserted him and the gash closed upon him.

"No!" screamed Lith-An. Although her mind had developed to such an extent, her few years had not prepared her for this. "Release him!" she ordered, but the Dalthin was unmoved. She struck out with her mind, but while the beast reeled under the force, it refused to obey. Instead, it created a mouth with which to speak and addressed her audibly.

"Come with us now, or we will kill your friends."

"Release Ganeth," she cried, "or I will hurt you."

"I cannot. There is no point. I have drained almost all his life force. Were I to do as you ask, he would not survive. Come with us. If you refuse, we will devour this man and this woman and bring great harm to this encampment."

Lith-An glanced from the Dalthin to her foster parents, then back. As much as it pained her, she was in no position to refuse. She tried to sense Ganeth, but the Dalthin was right; he was dead or nearly so. She wanted to hurt these creatures, but did not wish to bring harm to Sa'ar or Boudra. Furthermore, she needed these invaders to take her home. Too small to make the journey on her own, she swallowed her anger and said, "I will come with you, but you will not harm one more person."

The Dalthin agreed. "We will hurt no one if you come at once."

She turned to the couple and tried to explain. "You cannot prevent this and though I cannot expect you to understand, do not attempt to stop us. Believe me when I tell you everything is as it should be."

"Ria, I cannot stand by and watch this thing take you," said Boudra.

"The two waiting outside are the same," she said. "Ganeth could not stop them. I cannot and neither can you. Take your wife and return to Shash. I will be alright. I cannot explain why, but these creatures need to keep me alive."

"Please don't go," begged Sa'ar and turned to her husband. "Can we do nothing?"

"You would die just as Ganeth did," said Lith-An. *Return home,* she continued in thought. *There is more in play than you can understand. Trust me. Go home and be happy. All will be well.*

While Boudra and Sa'ar watched helplessly, Lith-An donned her cape and walked into the night with the three who had come for her.

# 53

Dur was angry. She was angry at the Dalthin, angry with Duile, but most of all, she was angry with herself. She had never been a coward, nor allowed herself to wallow in self-pity. Although she had stopped blaming herself for the deaths of Bedya, Roman, Loral or—bless the sweet woman—Marm, she could not condone the funk into which she had descended afterwards. Now, as she crouched in the rain and darkness below the palace checkpoint, waiting for an opportunity to cross the road, she vowed to end it.

The plan Marm had outlined centered around entering the palace and opening the gates to Emeil's forces, thereby reversing the coup. As Marm saw it, Regilius would then be able to assume the throne and determine his mother's fate. Unfortunately, Emeil was still perched atop menRathan and Dur was not about to wait for events to turn in his favor. While she sensed Reg was returning, there was no telling when he might arrive. Consequently, the most effective thing she could do was to find and kill the queen on her own. Nothing less would do. Further—and she found this fact particularly enticing—there was a Dalthin inside the walls. If she never came across another, she was going to make this one pay for what the others had done.

Ordinarily, the road entering the palace was not so heavily trafficked. But the security measures Duile had established were so stringent each check took several minutes. The line of persons and vehicles had grown so long, it was becoming apparent she could be stuck here until morning. As she drew her cloak tighter, wondering how to break this impasse, she remembered Marm's instructions. She had avoided revisiting their last encounter, so the key to entering the castle undetected lay forgotten within the recesses of her mind. Now, while the rain drummed upon her hood and cape, she began to review the "memories" Marm had imparted. *Mas'tad! They are so extensive.*

Marm had known the fortress intimately and the information she had passed on was intended to assist Dur through any eventuality.

Unlike real memories, however, these were not yet sorted, so could not easily be called up, nor would they be until Dur perused every one and studied how each related to the others. She chuckled. Thanks to the traffic she had been cursing a moment earlier, she had time to do what she would not be able to later, when it mattered.

Gradually, the palace's layout, the grounds and the area outside the walls assembled into an orderly understanding. Little by little, the manner in which one passage lead to others became clearer until she became confident all those images had coalesced into something she could sort out.

She looked around and realized a drainage culvert with a loose grate could be found a short distance to her left. It would take her under the road and through the wall. She arose and paralleled the roadway above, relying on darkness for cover.

"Halt!" someone shouted. When she did not respond, he repeated, "You! Down there! Halt at once."

She paused, wondering how the speaker could see her. She was some distance from the checkpoint, and aside from the tiny light globes the guards carried, the night was pitch black.

"Approach the checkpoint," the speaker cried.

Dur hesitated, reached out with her mind and discovered a Dalthin. So! It was not only Duile's guards who were inspecting the vehicles.

The Dalthin was insistent. "Approach!"

She was not about to hand herself over. Assessing the distance to the culvert, she bolted. With pounding heart, she ran, tripping and falling over the wet ground in the dark, hoping her pursuers would have as much difficulty following.

Nearing the ditch, she splashed into a stream she hoped flowed from it. Dropping to her knees as her pursuers' voices grew louder, she felt with her hands for the drain's mouth. She glanced back and saw light globes approaching. She could not remain where she was, so finding nothing, she rose and moved upstream, nearer the road under which the culvert passed. Her foot caught and she fell, striking her face against something hard. Dazed, trying to rise and seeking purchase, she extended her hands and grasped vertical, metal bars. It was the grate. She pulled herself to her knees, feeling it shift under her weight. She tugged and it shifted. The voices sounded almost behind her, so mustering all her strength, she pulled harder and felt it begin to tilt. Another effort and it almost fell onto her. Pushing the grate upright and using it for support, she climbed to her feet. She held it steady and stepped beside it as she felt for the opening. She smiled as her palm fell on the drain's curving lip.

"She's close," the Dalthin ordered. "Spread out."

Without further ado, she maneuvered around the disk, stepped into the tunnel and replaced the cover. Some of the voices were coming closer, so she reached out blindly and her fingers grazed a wall. Guided by touch, she retreated into the tunnel, putting the opening behind her.

… … … … …

Dalthin experience neither joy nor any other emotion, but Husted Yar was as close to feeling satisfaction and contentment as it ever would. Its efforts were bearing fruit. Although the queen's male offspring had eluded capture, he was nonetheless returning of his own volition. He would arrive in a matter of days and his sibling was also returning under escort. Now, for reasons beyond its understanding, the female who had eluded capture in Bad Adur was entering the fortress. Once the queen was placated and all three were within her grasp, she would no longer require so much attention and Yar could rest. Soon the Dalthin ship would arrive and Yar, as well as its companions, would be rewarded with a life of ease. Within days, all its problems would be over.

… … … … …

Rain water thundered down the tunnel, making for a hard uphill slog. Dur feared reaching behind with her mind, lest the pursuing Dalthin detect her. Nonetheless, the culvert's stream would wash away any traces of her passing, while the rain should eradicate any sign that she had entered.

Some distance in, she encountered the first tributary to the route she was following. Until now, she had no idea how far she had traveled, but this landmark indicated she was half way to the outer wall. The next of such feeders would put her just inside. A short distance beyond, she would encounter a maintenance ladder leading to the first way out. If she took it, she would emerge in the middle of a courtyard. Were the fortress not so closely guarded, she might have chosen that exit, but the opening was too exposed. Instead, she would seek the next maintenance ladder, where she would emerge behind the servants' housing.

Having obtained her bearings, she continued onward. Once or twice she paused to listen, but the tube amplified the water and the exercise proved fruitless. Deciding these pauses only allowed her pursuers to gain ground, she pushed on through the darkness tracing the wall with her hand.

She had traveled farther than she had expected and was worrying she had missed the second way up, when she noticed dim light above. Gazing skyward, her eyes gradually focused and she thought she could discern stars through the bars of a grate. She reached overhead, patting one side of the shaft, then the other, until her hand fell upon a ladder's rung. It was none too soon. Behind her appeared first one light globe, then a second and a third.

The lowest rung was above the top of her head and Dur grasped it with both hands. She pulled herself up as far as she could, and placed the soles of her boots against the tunnel wall, using the additional purchase to boost herself higher. As her chest drew level with her hands, she pushed with her feet. They slipped, but not before she had grasped the second rung. Now she had sufficient leverage to pull herself higher and grasp another. By the time she had managed to reach the fourth, she found the lowest rung with her foot. The climb was no longer a struggle and she scrambled up as the light globes neared. Reaching the grate, she thanked the gods the globes could not throw light this great a distance. She pushed against the barrier, hoping to shove it aside, but the thing wouldn't budge. She tried again and failed. Nothing Marm had related indicated these grates were fastened, so hoping her "memory" was correct and the cover was merely stuck, she climbed as far up the ladder as she could. Lowering her head and putting both shoulders against the lid, she gripped the bars with her hands and pushed hard with both feet. Still no luck. The voices were almost beneath her. At any minute they might see her. Taking several deep breaths, then suppressing a groan, she gave a mighty shove and the cover yielded.

Unstuck, it was not very heavy at all. She stood fully upright and was rewarded with breeze-driven moisture across her face. Lest she fall, she tossed the lid aside and placed her forearms on the ground to either side of the opening. As best she could tell, there was no one above, so she pulled herself through. Replacing the cover, she drew away from the hatch to avoid being spotted.

The hairs on her neck stood as voices passed below. She could not distinguish their words, but was relieved when, as quickly as they had come, they continued down the tunnel and faded. Breathing hard, as much from the effort as from the excitement, she rolled onto her back. She opened her mouth to the rain and delighted in its freshness.

After a few moments, when the tension had passed, she climbed to her feet. All around her, lighted windows and light globes on posts revealed the shapes of this place she had heretofore only imagined. She grinned. The fortress was hers!

# 54

"Welcome, Pithien Dur. We have been waiting for you."

She whirled to confront a short, squat figure in courtier's attire. "Who are you?" she asked. She could not imagine who in the palace would know her.

"In this place, I call myself Husted Yar."

A veil lifted and she understood this was a Dalthin. A shiver knifed through her, a mixture of anger and revulsion. Until this moment, it had concealed its identity. Now, however, she saw it for what it was.

Concealment was a tool the Dalthin had only recently acquired. When Prince Regilius first erected barriers against their thoughts, they saw in it a new application. Building walls around themselves could conceal them from others. Now, the Dalthin dropped the shield and presented itself.

"We have long awaited your company. You have been quite an adversary—although to your misfortune, not capable enough—and your arrival marks the first of three milestones. In a while, I will present you to the queen. Tomorrow I will present her daughter. The day after, her son arrives. Shortly thereafter, we will dispose of you all and our work here will become measurably easier. Now you will come with me and my escort."

As if on cue, half a dozen of the queen's guard stepped into the open. As the soldiers surrounded her, Yar cautioned, "Don't try to resist. As clever as you are, I am far more powerful. Your safety—and for the time being, your survival—depend entirely upon your cooperation. I am keeping you alive only because the queen wishes it, but I have little patience for resistance. Now, come. The queen awaits."

For the first time in her life, she was a prisoner and without a plan. Vastly outnumbered and mentally outmaneuvered, she had no choice but to follow.

After half an hour's march, they arrived at their destination and it struck Dur that these soldiers must have been on their way to intercept her even while she was crouching below the checkpoint. By the time they entered the palace proper, she was drenched, miserable and on the brink of despair. With Yar in the lead, they took Dur through a narrow, dimly-lit passage and down a series of stairwells and corridors she recognized as one of the routes to the dungeons. Eventually they arrived, and she was bound then seated on a simple wooden chair in the middle of an otherwise barren room. Once the guards had secured her to it, they stepped outside, leaving her alone with the Dalthin.

A door flew open.

"My dear Husted!" the queen exclaimed, half out of breath and not concealing her delight. "Have you captured the outlaw? Where is he?" she asked, glancing about.

"She sits before you," Yar replied, gesturing toward the chair.

Duile eyed Dur and Dur stared back.

"This?" She pointed. "This soaked marmath? Husted, this is a woman. Are you trying to tell me this is the nefarious scourge of Ydron? This tiny, pathetic thing? Please tell me I am mistaken."

"No, Your Majesty. I assure you. This is indeed the criminal you have been looking for."

"I don't believe it." She gave Dur a long hard look, then began circling the chair, digesting every wet inch of her. "No. This cannot be the fearsome warrior who defeated my soldiers." She stopped for a moment, looked up at Yar, then back at Dur, and resumed her walk. "How could this be the person who kidnapped princess Vintyara? Could this little rodent feed the rabble? I don't think so." Stopping again, "Though I love you, dear Husted, I am afraid you are mistaken. Did she tell you that was her name?"

"No, Your Majesty. I am not mistaken. I have followed this one's activities for a long time. I am certain, beyond any doubt, this is indeed the one you seek. Do you see why she was so difficult to find? When all the land is pursuing a man, what could have been a more perfect disguise?"

"Well, we shall certainly find out if you are right. We will make sure she dares speak naught but the truth."

"Oh, I promise you he's right," offered Dur.

"The rodent has a voice!" exclaimed Duile. Then, putting her face to her captive's, she growled, "Who gave you permission to speak?"

"I'm sorry, Majesty. I thought that was the purpose of an interrogation room, but what do I know? This is my first time."

"I promise it will also be your last." Peering into Dur's eyes, she asked, "How much pain can you endure? I'll wager not a lot. I will quickly learn who you are. If you really are Pithien Dur, I know exactly what to do with you. And if you are not, you will regret ever having entered my fortress."

Dur returned her stare and mustered a smile.

"Take her to a cell," blurted Duile. "Other business demands my attention, but I will return when I have finished. I want to be here for every minute of her interrogation. Don't dare begin without me."

"Yes, Majesty," replied the jailor.

"Dear Husted," Duile crooned. "Will you join me, please? There is a diplomat from Deth awaiting my audience. I expect he has come to pay tribute."

The Dalthin considered whether it would be wise to leave the prisoner in the hands of the head jailor and decided it would be alright. She was vastly outnumbered and would be in their hands until her death.

"Of course, Majesty," Yar replied. "It will be my pleasure.'

Almost as soon as they had departed, the jailor began tormenting his charge.

"Hah, pretty one. I think I will get you primed. What will you have, a hot poker or a sharp edge?"

Dur wasn't having any of this. "The queen wants to be here for every minute of your ministering. Do you think she will be pleased if she learns you have disobeyed her?"

"And who is going to tell her?" he snapped.

"Why, I will, of course."

"Do you think this will make me go easier on you?"

"Were you planning to go easy?"

He looked puzzled.

"I didn't think so. Now, if you don't mind, I would like to be taken to my cell as the queen commanded." Finishing with a hard look, she said, "If you please."

"Oh, little missy! I am going to have such a time with you."

At his gesture, the guards stepped forward to assist him. But while he loosened her bonds so she could rise, other thoughts intruded.

*Pithien Dur?* sounded a voice in her head.

She gasped and her head snapped up. Her jailor misinterpreted her reaction.

"Oh, we didn't hurt you, did we?"

Dur shook her head.

"Answer when I address you," he bellowed.

"No," she said, "I am quite comfortable, thank you."

He struck her with the back of his hand and shouted, "None of your insolence!"

"Whatever your pleasure," she replied as a trickle of blood ran from the corner of her mouth.

By the time the query repeated, the guards had brought her to her cell.

*Pithien Dur?*

*Who are you?* she asked, a bit annoyed.

*I am Regilius Tonopath.*

*And to what do I owe this great honor?* Then, thinking better of her tone, said, *I am sorry. Please forgive the sarcasm. Old habit.*

*My sister asked me to contact you for help.*

*Your sister?*

*She knew you were here.*

*Who but the Dalthin would know where I am?* Too late, she tried to suppress the thought.

*My sister possesses remarkable abilities and is no friend of those creatures. I must say, I was surprised when I called your name your mind responded, even before you did on a conscious level.*

*Minds do that automatically. Now, please, I haven't much time.*

The jailor had produced a ring and was fingering the keys.

*What do you want, Prince of Ydron?*

*I have a friend in the dungeon. I was hoping, if you can locate him, you might set him free.*

*That is a lot to ask. Why don't you free him yourself?*

*I am still two days away and I fear harm will befall him before I arrive.*

*Well, Your Highness, I need to secure my own freedom first, whether I help him or not. But tell me, assuming I choose to help, who is he?*

*His name is Danth Kanagh.*

*Of the noble house? Yes, of course. Whom else would you know?*

*My friendship includes many, not just the nobility. Please. I will repay you when I can. You must know the dangers there and I am afraid he will not survive. If it is possible, please, free Danth Kanagh.*

*Danger? Are you referring to your mother or her Dalthin advisor?*

*There are two Dalthin within those walls.*

That stunned her. She had not sensed the presence of the second. That information alone was of great value. Was the second the one at the check point, or did he mean there was still another inside? In any case, she would be more alert. She considered the request, then said, *I will free him if I can.*

*Thank you*, he said, and was gone.

The conversation gave her pause. She had never encountered a mind like his, let alone conversed with one. It was such a clear unambiguous experience she had trouble returning to the present. Return she did, though, as her jailor opened her cell. If she were not to spend one minute within its confines, she needed to alter the jailors' perceptions. That part was routine. She had done it many times before. She would allow them to see her the moment they loosened her bonds, so her hands would be free. Then, she would make the jailor and the guard "see" themselves locking her in, while in reality she hid.

When, to their minds, she was secure and the cell was locked, they joked about having captured her, even pausing to taunt her. Then, they departed. She watched the jailor replace the keys, and when they were gone, she retrieved the ring, hoping she held the keys to the entire dungeon, not to just this part. She would find out soon enough.

# 55

Bakka Oduweh turned the skewers and sniffed the meat. He had reluctantly deferred to Regilius and Ered's insistence the food would be cooked. He had found a good campsite. A rock formation enclosed it on three sides, obscuring most of the fire's glow, and a pocket in one of its faces made a fine oven for baking small unleavened loaves.

Brothers Osman and Bort, who preferred vegetarian fare, were returning from a quest for herbs, roots and whatever else they could find. Ered had found firewood and water. As for Reg, he was standing a short way off, using the time to learn what lie ahead. With his hood raised against the wind, he quieted his mind and reached out to Lith-An. He was startled when she responded almost immediately.

*Greetings, brother.*

*Lith-An! I thought it would take much longer to locate you.*

*Your thoughts are clear and crisp, Regilius. You called and I responded. What is wrong?*

*I need to sort out many things.* He paused to consider his question. *You have changed so much in such a short time. Your mind is no longer a little girl's. How did this happen?*

*I was much younger than you when the Change occurred. Young minds are more facile than older ones. They learn with greater ease and absorb new concepts readily. Children learn languages without struggling to absorb or comprehend. Learning to communicate with thoughts is like learning a language. Probably because living in isolation is unnatural, communication is one of the mind's early abilities.*

*As for my maturity,* she said, *I have visited dozens of adult minds since the Change began. I have shared their thinking, their emotions, and more importantly, their experiences, learning from them so I can never again think as a child.*

*So sad. You have lost your childhood.*

*I have the childhoods of all whom I have touched. I am therefore blessed. Do not be sad for me.*

Reg turned to a different matter. *I departed Losan as you suggested and am returning to Ydron.*

*As am I. A group of Dalthin are bringing me and we will arrive there tomorrow.*

*Dalthin! Voreth's horns, Lith-An, they are dangerous.*

*They can be managed. I grow stronger every day. Yesterday I was nearly helpless against them. Today I manage. You have already experienced a little of that yourself. In time, as you require, I will teach you more.*

*I am still troubled. How many are with you?*

*There are three, although two more occupy the palace.*

*That will bring the total to five,* said Reg. *Their power multiplies as their numbers increase. You may be able to handle three, but I am not at all sure you can manage five. I am afraid they will kill you.*

*If I have grown more than able enough to handle three, then we two will be safe in the presence of five. What is more, I believe they intend to keep me alive until after you arrive. They seem eager to bring us both to mother.*

*Is this their idea or mother's? In other words, are we doing the right thing by coming home?*

*Your decision to return is correct. You and I need to be close and we need to confront her. There is a sickness in the land we need to heal.*

*Then I will see you tomorrow.*

*Regilius?*

*Yes, Lith-An.*

*I have visited mother's mind and I have learned a few things. There is work for you to do before you arrive. She has imprisoned Danth Kanagh and I fear she wishes to harm him.*

The revelation startled him.

*However,* she continued, *there is another within the dungeon who might help secure his release. Have you heard of one called Pithien Dur?*

*I have. In fact, I have spoken with her once already.*

*So you know she possesses a mind quite like ours. Reach out to her again. Ask her to free your friend. I will assist her when I arrive. The three of us will help each other.*

*I will.*

*Good-bye for now, dear brother.*

Reg could hear Ered summoning him to eat. Before he returned, however, he paused to locate Dur. Finding her was not as quick as locating his sister, but her thoughts still stood out. He was delighted when her mind responded. Once he had made his request and had warned her about the Dalthin, he drew his cloak around himself and rose. He would eat what Bakka had prepared, but only because his body required food. He had no appetite. The danger to his sister and his inability to help her tore at him. His mother's treachery distressed him even more. How could he make the mental leap from knowing her as the one who gave him life to accepting it was she who had murdered his father? Even after all this time, his mind would not wrap around it.

Then there was the problem of restoring his land. Not so long ago, everything seemed so simple. Return home, confront Mother, somehow assert his claim to the throne, then right the wrongs within the kingdom. Regilius laughed at his naïveté. He may have been born heir to it all, but wresting it away from her would not be easy. It was preposterous to expect his mother would see the error of her ways, come around to his point of view and renounce her claims and aspirations. Further, much of his plan hinged on Emeil's victory, if that could be brought about at all. He tried to set his worries aside. Things were as they were, he told himself. Still, Father was dead and Mother would kill both him and Lith-An if she could. His sister, though he still loved her, was all but unrecognizable. His few loyal friends were dispersed across the land. He felt so alone as he returned to camp through the descending darkness.

Well, that wasn't entirely true, he decided. Ered was here, and amid all this misfortune this small truth held a blessing. He trusted Ered completely. Perhaps it was time to rely on his lifelong friend and ally. No one else was more perfectly on his side. With that realization, things did not seem so bleak. He picked up his stride and realized he was developing an appetite.

Approaching the campfire, he became aware of a new danger. It would be best to deal with it later, he decided, somewhere between here and Ydron when the correct moment presented itself. Now he would put all else aside and dine with his friends. They were already eating and he was glad they had not waited for him.

"Thank you for this meal, Bakka," he said as he sat between Ered and the Haroun. "Thank you all. I am sorry I was no help in its preparation."

"You have been doing things we could not," Ered said. "Can you tell us what you have learned?"

"Nothing we didn't already know. There is danger ahead and I am questioning the wisdom of inviting you all to finish this journey."

He turned to the hunter.

"Bakka, you have brought us this far, but the battle I am undertaking is not yours and has no bearing on your people. The

Haroun have always been apart from the politics of this land and I cannot ask you to risk your life for our folly. It will be better if you return home. You have my gratitude for bringing us this far."

"It has been my privilege, Prince Regilius."

"As for the two of you," Reg said to the monks, "Given the choice of sending you back, or of bringing you with me… "

Bort interrupted. "We will come along."

"Brother Bort speaks for me," Osman chimed in. "We will accompany you to the city gates, even into the bosom of your home. We will not abandon you here."

"As I said in Losan, I am not convinced of your decision's soundness."

"Master Regilius, returning to the monastery will not make us any safer. There is danger all along the way. We are fortunate to have come this far without incident."

Although Reg was uneasy, he relented. "Very well," he said and the monks seemed pleased they had prevailed. "As for you, Ered… "

At the mention of his name, Ered looked up. "No, Reg! No! I am coming with you. I belong at your side."

Reg smiled. "That is what I was hoping you would say."

Ered's mouth was agape, but he offered nothing more.

"I need you," said Reg. "The battle for Ydron is as much yours as it is mine. I need someone I can trust to watch my back. There is no one I trust more than you and you have proven your ability to handle yourself in a fight."

"Thank you, Reg. I will not let you down."

"There is no question of it. We will protect each other."

He would talk to Ered at greater length later, when they could find a minute alone.

Turning again to Bakka, he said, "I have a favor to ask."

"What might that be?" asked the hunter.

"May we keep our endaths until our journey is over? They will greatly shorten the final leg."

"Regilius," said Bakka. "You may keep them as a gift. If I may not see you through to the end of your quest, I could not forgive myself if I failed to provide at least this much assistance."

"Good," said Reg. "It is settled. If it is alright with you all, when we finish our meal we will depart at once. We have far to go and cannot afford the luxury of spending the night."

"I've finished my meal," said Ered. "You eat and I will pack. We can leave within the hour."

"Is that alright with you, Brothers?" Reg asked.

The monks nodded.

Although the danger Reg sensed worried him, the storm that was building threatened to delay his return home. He would consider how to deal with the impending trouble after they were under way.

# 56

The fortress dungeons were foul places indeed, their stench an accumulation of years of intolerable living conditions. The passageways were dark, lit only by sufficient light globes to allow one to navigate, and the cells were unlit, so there was no way for prisoners to mark the passage of time. Consequently, any confinement seemed interminable. A hole in the floor was the only amenity provided, if one could find it in the dark. Nor was there a cot to sleep on. There were no trials for the accused. All were deemed guilty with only the whims of the jailor and queen to determine their fate. Despair and pain filled every soul and the jailors delighted in making the place a living nightmare. That the queen would visit this place at all spoke volumes about her.

As Pithien Dur made her way through its corridors, she wondered at the many sounds she heard: some from prisoners, some from small unseen creatures, many from unrecognizable sources. She stifled her fears and pressed on. When at last she felt she had come far enough, she set about locating Danth. Risking discovery by the Dalthin, she reached out from cell to cell.

Marm did not know this place, so Dur was forced to explore one sector at a time. She wanted to free all whom she encountered, but she could not. Eventually, if everything turned out as planned they would all be free, but for now she would keep her promise, then leave. So, cell by cell, mind by mind, she searched. She used a technique she had stumbled upon many years ago. As she had hinted to Regilius, if one merely inquired—wondered is more like it—as to the identity of the mind she had touched, the soul at the core of that being would give up its identity involuntarily. So it was, as she inquired of yet another prisoner, the mind spoke the name she was seeking.

"Danth Kanagh," she called through the door.

Danth came awake. "Who is it? Who is there?"

"I am a friend. I am going to try to open the door."

He did not reply and she realized in this place one would naturally be suspicious. Without further ado, she began trying each key. She sighed with relief when, after only a few attempts, the latch yielded and the door swung open.

"Darmaht!" she gasped. The stench made her gag. "What have they done to you?"

"I'm sorry." Danth faltered and could not meet her eye. "They were supposed to let me bathe."

"Well, at least that means there is a place where you can. We can't leave while you're in this condition. Let's clean you up and find some clothes for you to wear."

When she had unfastened his shackles, he struggled to rise. "I'm sorry," he repeated when he was standing and covered himself with his hands. He looked at her with inquiring eyes and asked, "Who are you?"

"I am Pithien Dur. Prince Regilius, asked me to help you," she explained.

"Is Reg here?"

"He is coming, but he is still some distance away." He opened his mouth to respond, but she held up her hand saying, "Let's not worry about anything else right now. Until you bathe, we can't go anywhere. A blind man could find you. Do you know where they were going to take you?"

He shook his head.

"You have no idea where to wash off that filth?"

"No. I was taken directly to my cell."

"Mas'tad!" she swore. "Now what are we going to do?"

"Pssst!"

Someone was trying to get her attention. She looked around, but saw no one.

"Pssst! Here, in the next cell."

"What do you want?" she asked.

"Let me out and I will take you to the bath."

"I don't have time," she replied testily, not knowing how long they could remain undetected.

"If you don't want to spend all day searching for it, release me"

She was annoyed, but the prisoner was right. Marm did not know the dungeons, so without someone to show the way, they were not going anywhere.

"Alright," she relented. "I will release you, but I will go hard on you if you are lying."

"I just want out," the voice replied. "I'm not lying."

Dur went to his door, and on a hunch tried the same key. The door opened and a man stepped out wearing a dingy, rumpled uniform.

"You're a soldier," she said. "One of Duile's own, if I read the colors correctly. How did you come to be here?"

"Long story," he replied. "Let us just say I did not show enough respect." He performed an exaggerated bow and said, "I am in your debt."

"You can repay the favor by showing us the bath."

The soldier looked at Danth. He held his nose and started to laugh. "My, but he does need one, doesn't he?"

"The bath," she hissed, "or back you go."

"I'm sorry. Follow me."

He hurried down one corridor, apparently familiar with the place. After a few turns, they found themselves in a small, bare room with a metal tub in its center. Nearby was a pump and a bucket. Against one wall stood a stove and a pile of wood.

"One of you, grab the bucket," ordered the soldier. "The other, man the pump. I don't think you want to take time to build a fire." He stepped aside and leaned against a wall.

"Since I am freeing you," Dur replied, "you will man the pump. And when the tub is full, you will find soap, something with which he can dry himself and clothing—at least a pair of pants."

The soldier began to back away. "If they find me here, they will kill me. I have already done what I promised."

She grabbed his tunic, drew her knife and put it to his throat. "If you don't do what I ask, if you anger me more than you have already, I will kill you."

The soldier swallowed hard. "Alright," he said, then angrily to Danth, "Grab the bucket. We don't have all day."

They set to work, and Dur decided to use the time to explore. A half hour later, she returned and admired the young lord's transformation from filthy beast to a fine looking man.

"It appears your mother might even recognize you, Danth Kanagh. Now, I have to decide what to do with you. I need to deposit you somewhere, so I can complete my mission."

Danth's head came up and his eyes widened. He went to a door and peered out. "A Dalthin is coming. It is not here yet, but we need to leave."

"You know them?" Dur was startled.

Danth nodded.

"How do you know one is coming?" she asked Danth.

"They attacked me once, and for some reason I can now sense their presence."

Dur searched the corridors with her mind. He was right. Perhaps confident after capturing her, unaware she was free, Yar was no longer concealing itself. "You are right," she said.

"We need to vanish," said Danth. "Do you have any magic up your sleeve?"

"No magic," she replied, "But if our soldier friend can show us a way out, I may be able to lose the thing once we've reached the palace proper. Do you know the way?" she asked.

"Come with me," the soldier said.

They followed a corridor leading upward, communicating with gestures, speaking only when necessary. Several minutes later, Dur recognized where they had arrived.

"I know this place," she said. She had at last returned to one of the places known to Marm. "For the moment we are safe, but the queen's guard are everywhere. I can't take you with me, so I must find somewhere for you to hide. The problem is where."

The soldier said, "There is a storage room within the guards' quarters. It is used to house banners and such for major celebrations and processions. I doubt anyone will be looking in there for some time to come. It would make a perfect hiding place."

"The guards quarters? Were you one of the guard?" asked Dur.

"I was, until the queen thought I did not salute smartly enough. It's a sign of disrespect, you know. She was right. After she demoted me, she didn't like me as a soldier either. Can't say I liked her."

"Well, that says a lot," Dur observed. "But tell me, once you are in the storage room, what will you eat or drink?"

Once again, he smiled. "I still have a friend or two in the guard. They salute nicely, but don't regard the queen any better than I do. We will be fine."

"Let's go," she said, and they were off again.

# 57

"Riders, m' Lord! Riders approaching!" came the cry.

Two riders were driving their horses up the muddy face of menRathan amid a hail of arrows. One steed slipped and fell, throwing its rider to the ground. The man lay motionless as his companion continued to the summit. As soon as Emeil saw the mishap, he called to a soldier near by.

"Sergeant! Send a party to retrieve him. Don't leave that man lying there."

"My men are on their way as we speak, my Lord," the sergeant replied, pointing to a group running to the place where he lay.

Six archers among them took up positions and began returning fire. The remaining four secured their shields to their backs for protection, stooped, gathered up the injured rider and carried him back to the encampment. By this time the second rider had reached Emeil's banners. He dismounted, ran to Emeil and dropped to one knee.

"Arise and speak," Emeil commanded.

"I bring good news, my Lord. Lord Aman of Monhedeth has pledged full support. His army is already following close behind."

"That's wonderful news," exclaimed General Meiad.

"Further," the rider continued, "Lord Aman was informed by pigeon that Dar will also come. Lord Yued's forces will follow Lord Aman's by one or two days."

"That is unexpected. It is beginning to look as though we may have some chance after all, General," Emeil said to his chief of staff.

"It does, indeed, my Lord," Meiad smiled.

Emeil turned to the sergeant. "Make sure this man has food, drink, a place to rest and medical care, should he require it. Then, locate his companion. When you have insured he is also being attended to, report back to me with his condition."

"Right away, my Lord," the sergeant replied and hurried off.

"My Lord, I do not believe any more riders will get through," said

Meiad. "We will have no further news until help actually arrives."

"Let us hope it arrives soon, General. Look below."

The forces who had been merely containing Emeil's army, were repositioning themselves as new weapons were moved to the front—catapults.

"I don't believe they are going to wait until our reinforcements arrive," Meiad observed.

"Nor should we. Move your men back from the plateau's edge. I believe the assault has finally begun."

"Back, my Lord?"

"We have no defense against catapults except distance. We need to assess their capability."

"Immediately, my Lord."

As Emeil watched the queen's forces maneuver, he could see she did not intend for him to escape again. He also knew she did not intend for him to become a farmer raising crops. His own troops, augmented by recent arrivals from Sandoval, were still outnumbered two- or perhaps three-to-one. And while it was encouraging two more armies were now on their way, he did not believe their numbers would be sufficient to tip the balance in his favor. He needed Limast and Meden, if not Nagath-réal, to attain real superiority. Furthermore, even if all were to come, they would have to arrive soon. Catapults were a part of the equation to which he could not respond. They had not been invented at the time of the siege that gave this place its page in history, and he doubted those atop this rampart would have lasted had such weapons existed then. Surely these would be slow to cause damage, but there was no shortage of ammunition. The plain was littered with boulders. On the other hand, the uneven weight and size of those stones would make hitting any target a guessing game. While initially they would be mostly ineffective, serving merely as psychological weapons, the rocks that did strike would cause great harm. The longer the assault, the greater the damage.

As if on cue, a boulder smashed a nearby tent, killing three soldiers and an officer. It would be hard to keep his troops calm while they waited for reinforcements. Arrows were nothing in the face of such weapons. Emeil ordered the tents broken down and reassembled farther back. Tonight there would be more than water raining.

… … … … …

The following morning, Emeil arose early, wondering how long he must remain corralled. Forgoing breakfast, he walked to the plateau's edge and surveyed the plain.

"Mas'tad!" he swore and tore the lens from his eye. The downpour was rendering it almost useless. Today, as on every other, he scanned the valley for any encouragement. While Duile's troops could not climb to the summit without being cut down, his own forces were so outnumbered descending into the valley would be folly of the worst kind.

"No luck, my Lord?"

"I cannot tell, General. Everything is a blur. Does anyone have a dry cloth?"

General Meiad instructed one of his men to fetch what Emeil needed. The soldier saluted, then ran off, returning shortly with the requested item. Emeil thanked him and dried the lens as best he could, then tucked the cloth into his tunic. Once more he raised the glass, trying to see before the drops obscured his view. He could discern nothing new and was beginning to put it away when he paused. Had he seen something? Unsure the image his mind retained was real, he wiped the telescope's objective. Clinging to hope, he returned the glass to his eye and scanned the horizon—first left, then right—and stopped when it fell upon what he was looking for.

"General!" he exclaimed. "I believe I see banners. If I am not mistaken, Limast and Meden have arrived."

"Really, my Lord?"

"Indeed. Wait! They are accompanied by the purple of Pytheral. Asch is an ally of the queen. Have they come to fight with us, or against us?"

"My Lord, Bogen and Miasoth would never side against us. Of that, I am certain. As for Lord Asch, Duile betrayed him when she betrayed you. I suspect he has seen her for who she is."

"Well, we cannot continue to remain idle. Sound the alarm. If help has arrived, I want to be ready to join them at the first sign they have engaged the enemy."

Meiad beamed. This was the order he and every man had been waiting for.

"Yes, my Lord!"

Trumpets sounded and the entire encampment galvanized into action. Weapons were gathered, horses were saddled and voices raised as excitement spread and the army began to mobilize.

"General Meiad!" Emeil called when they were all in formation.

"Yes, my Lord."

"Are the men ready?"

The general grinned. "Indeed they are, my Lord. They await your order."

"Wonderful! Bogen and Miasoth have moved into flanking positions and are coming toward us down either side of the valley floor. Asch's troops appear to be much smaller in number, but as best I can tell, they are attempting to cut a path straight through the center. That is the course we shall take. If they are not to be devoured by the surrounding forces, they will need us to intercept them. Inform your officers of our strategy, then sound the charge. Speed will be our ally."

Meiad wheeled his steed and spurred it toward the group of officers waiting nearby. No sooner had they conferred than they, in turn, rode to the head of each column. As fast as orders could be issued, cheers went up, horns sounded, banners were raised and the army of Sandoval, finally free to fight, charged at full gallop from menRathan into battle.

# 58

Once Dur had deposited Danth and the erstwhile guard, she tested the door of a nearby weapons cache, hoping to arm herself. It was locked. Fortunately, every palace guard carried something. She merely needed to disarm one in order to complete her mission. She paused a moment to probe the palace and learned the queen was still occupied. While the Grand Hall was too public and well-guarded a place for an assassination, she was confident she could intercept and dispatch the monarch when she returned to the dungeon to begin her interrogation.

Dur was well on her way to intercept the queen when horns sounded up and down the corridors. Startled, she wondered why, then realized Yar must have returned to the dungeon and found her missing. It wouldn't be long before more guards would appear than she could manage. Probing with her mind, she discovered one nearby room was empty. She tested the door, and to her relief the latch yielded.

The chamber was appointed with fine fabrics and furniture beyond what most servants could expect. But since this part of the castle was servants' quarters, she deduced it belonged to either an overseer or a highly placed familial. As with Marm's apartment, there was no back door. Were she found, Dur would be trapped. Shouts told her it would be only moments before searchers arrived. She peered inside a wardrobe with room enough to hide. She stepped inside, and with some difficulty, owing to the lack of an inside handle, she closed the door and hid behind the rack of clothes and coats, trying to quiet her breath.

Almost immediately, the door to the room opened. Fearing the second Dalthin might be among them, she closed her mind. The footsteps and voices indicated several men were in the room. They sounded hurried and she hoped they would not linger. She held her breath as one of them approached. The wardrobe opened, then closed almost immediately.

"Nothing," he assured his companions.

She let out a gasp when the chamber door closed, then listened as the tromps of boots faded. She wished to depart, but remained hiding until sounds of the search disappeared altogether. When all was quiet, she emerged. Stepping out, she glanced around, but the room was empty. She took a deep breath and smiled. The room's door flew open. Her heart stopped. Her hand flew to her chest and she gasped, then relaxed. It was a servant girl, carrying folded laundry.

Dur exhaled. Feigning nonchalance she quipped, "Lots of commotion about the palace today, isn't there?"

The girl stopped abruptly and her eyes widened. "What are you doing here?" she demanded. "You have no business in this room. Who are you?"

"I'm sorry." Forgetting where she was, she tried to improvise. "I was looking for Lord… " she mumbled a fictitious name, "and walked in here by accident."

"There are no nobility in this part of the castle," the girl said. "You are lying." Then, as the circumstances of the search and Dur's presence coalesced, she realized, "You are the one they are looking for! Guards! Guards!" She dropped her load, opened the door and shouted, "Guards! She is here! I've found her! Guards!"

Dur considered silencing her, but thought better of it. The girl was only doing what she believed to be right. Shoving the servant aside, she stepped into the corridor as thoughts converged from all directions. She chose the way where they seemed most remote and set off.

She paused where the passage split into three and listened. Several minds were coming down one branch, but one of the remaining two seemed empty. As luck would have it, in taking it she could still intercept Duile, who by now had concluded her audience. In her haste, Dur nearly missed the second Dalthin. Although it was near, she could not locate it precisely. She weighed the danger against her best chance to complete her task. *Darmaht protect me*, she prayed. She knew what could happen, but steeled herself against the possibility. Now more than ever, she needed a weapon. Failing to find one would mean killing Duile barehanded. She sighed, knowing she would do what she must. This was no longer an exercise in cunning and stealth, but rather one of speed and daring. Abandoning all caution, she turned down a passage intersecting the corridor Duile was taking and was bounding down a short flight of stairs when, almost too late, she detected a party of guards around the next corner. Probing their minds, reassured they were yet unaware, she counted heads. There were five. It was a stretch, but she believed she could manage.

"Hello, boys," she called.

She hoped to render them oblivious to her presence, then run up, snatch a sword or a dagger and disappear. She was starting to do just that when the Dalthin's mind touched hers. She reached out toward the soldiers, but it was neither among them nor anywhere ahead. Had it outmaneuvered her? At that thought, the hairs on her neck rose and her scalp prickled. Cautiously, she turned and nearly screamed. It was hovering over her, almost touching her face. The tentacles writhed and dripped fluid onto her.

*I will enjoy digesting you,* it told her.

She became nauseous and weak as it bombarded her with thoughts. Her knees began to buckle and Pudath extended a pseudopod.

"Voreth's horns!" came a voice from behind her. "What is that thing?"

The outlaw glanced up to see the group of guardsmen gaping. As they drew their swords, Pudath retracted the newly manufactured limb and turned its attention upon them. Almost immediately, they began to cower at the manufactured nightmares. Two began to weep. Taking advantage of the distraction, Dur ran to the nearest, took his sword and faced Pudath.

*Come, if you have the courage,* she told it. *Are you hungry, you horror? I'll give you something to eat.*

It advanced and began to morph.

Hoping to reach it before the transformation was complete, Dur charged, her sword poised for the kill. Pudath, however, completed its change, dodged her attack and the camarr swiped at her with a claw.

Dur halted. She glanced at her right arm to see what damage it had inflicted. Four, bloodless tears on her sleeve showed how close it had come. Appraising her foe, she began to circle, forcing it to continually adjust its stance. She thought she was gaining an advantage when the Dalthin dealt a fiercer blow with its mind than she had ever experienced. She dropped to her knees, awash with nausea. Then, realizing she could use her collapse to her advantage, she feigned incapacity and doubled over, holding her stomach. The camarr studied her a second, then pounced. Just as quickly, Dur pointed the blade's tip at the airborne creature's belly and impaled it as it fell upon her. The blade pierced to its hilt. She clasped the handle with both hands, driving it deeper, insuring it remained imbedded. She knew she must have struck something vital because the Dalthin shuddered once, then again, then stopped moving altogether, lying motionless upon her.

Victory, however, took an unexpected turn. Although the Dalthin had adopted the cat's smaller form, its weight remained unchanged and the carcass pinned her to the floor. Breathing was becoming difficult. Dur struggled frantically to free herself as Pudath began to enlarge, assuming its real shape in death. She pushed and kicked and tried to roll it away to no avail. When the corpse attained its true size, it covered her completely. Unable to move, she tried to cry out, but its flesh pressed against her face, smothering her.

As her strength faded and her body screamed for air, the irony of her situation drove itself home. Was this what her scheme amounted to? Did it all come down to an epitaph? *Here lies Pithien Dur, the scourge of Ydron.* In killing the creature, had she inadvertently murdered herself?

# 59

The West Wind churned Lake Atkal, sending white caps scudding. The endaths struggled against the gale and the going slowed. Earlier, Reg had halted the party for two hours to avoid a division of his mother's troops. Fortunately, visibility was so poor they couldn't have been seen unless the column stumbled directly onto them and Reg had made certain that would not happen. Now, however, he worried they might not reach home for another day. Adding to the delay, the monks were falling ever farther behind and their mounts appeared to be struggling.

"Reg?" said Ered.

"Yes?"

"Something is wrong with Osman and Bort's endaths."

"I know. That is because their riders are not Osman and Bort."

"Of course they are. Who else would they be?"

"Osman and Bort were murdered last night while they were foraging for herbs."

Ered gasped. "What do you mean?"

"Those are Dalthin, and the endaths are struggling under their weight. I don't expect they will last much longer."

Ered adjusted his hood so he could better see his friend. "Why didn't you say something? How could you let such a thing happen? For that matter, how could you let these *things* accompany us?" He turned in the saddle to see them better.

"The monks were killed while they were away from camp. I sensed it when I sat down to dinner. None of us could have prevented it. Anything I might have said or done afterwards would have endangered Bakka. That would have been poor thanks for all he did for us. Besides, as lightly armed as we are, it is possible we too would have died, despite my abilities."

"But we could have tried. We might have died, but they would have been avenged."

"You are probably right, and Bort and Osman would still be dead."

"I don't understand," Ered said, scowling at Reg. "I used to think you were brave."

"That kind of bravery might appease one's anger, but it accomplishes nothing. We have important work ahead and inadvertently these creatures want to assist me. Many lives will benefit if we are successful and these Dalthin may yet pay for what they have done."

"We may not get to Ydron. They can kill us at any time."

"I don't believe they will. They intend to bring me home. Like the three escorting Lith-An, they want to deliver us to mother."

Still facing rearward, Ered gave the Dalthin a long, hard look.

"I need your advice," said Reg. When Ered looked back, he explained. "Every time I consider how to wrest control from mother, each solution I arrive at seems wrong. They all involve violence, and perhaps because she is my mother, I refuse to consider them. I cannot see a way to succeed Father."

"I understand," said Ered. "But tell me, do you have to be the one?"

"What do you mean?"

"I have been thinking about it, myself, and I keep returning to that question. Do you have to be the one who rules Ydron? In all our years together, you have never once referred to yourself as king. I would have thought, had you ever seen yourself in that role, you would have said something reflecting it. But you never did. Not one word. Even aboard the denaJadiz you said it might not be your destiny. So I am wondering, do you have to be the one?"

Reg considered this odd proposition as Ered continued.

"For centuries," said Ered, "everyone in Ydron has followed his parent's footsteps. I certainly have never seen myself in any role other than boatkeeper. But now we seem to have arrived at a crossroads. Things are no longer as they were or may ever be again. I don't know what advice to give you. I have no answer to any of this. But I somehow suspect—and for the first time in my life, I might add—life can take a different turning."

Reg smiled. Of all the things he might have wished for, this simple honesty was what he needed most.

"Thank you. I am glad you have said this. I have had somewhat the same feeling myself, but haven't been able to express it. I suspect you may be right. I will give the matter some thought."

Suddenly, Reg sat up in the saddle and his face paled. "Ered! Something terrible has happened in barakYdron."

"What is it?"

"Something has happened to Pithien Dur."

"The outlaw?" Ered said.

Focused upon that distant event, Reg did not appear to have heard him. Ered eyed his friend for a moment, but when Reg's attention remained elsewhere, he turned towards the Dalthin. Despite Reg's assurances, he could not bear to keep his back to them. He wished he could penetrate their thoughts or see them better through the rain. Although they had fallen so far behind and the downpour obscured them, he imagined one was returning his stare.

Eventually, Reg shifted in the saddle and Ered could see he had returned.

"Is everything alright?" he asked.

"I am not certain," Reg answered looking troubled. "I have set certain events into motion, but I am not sure what will transpire."

Ered wanted to press for more information, but something was happening with their escort. "Reg, look! One of the endaths has fallen."

The prince turned in time to see it collapse, too weak to rise. "Osman" begin to change shape, began to shimmer, then transform into…

"What else?" exclaimed Regilius.

… an endath.

"So that is how it expects to keep up," Reg mused.

"It certainly isn't coy about our seeing it," said Ered.

"They already realize we know. I am surprised they maintained the charade this long."

As if on cue, "Bort" dismounted, mimicking its companion while its more fortunate mount moved to the fallen one's side.

"Lets see how they manage beside real endaths, Ered."

"What do you mean?"

"If I am to keep my promise to Lith-An and arrive at the palace tomorrow, we must sleep in the saddle. Endaths do not sleep as we do, and our mounts will be able to keep on indefinitely." Reg smiled. "I don't know if a Dalthin can do the same."

"But the other endaths could not keep on indefinitely."

"They should recover soon. There is a difference between carrying a horrendous load and the more customary burden our mounts have."

"Then on to Ydron it is," said Ered.

The two friends drew down their hoods and tied themselves into their saddles, preparing for the long night ahead.

# 60

"Really, Husted? Do you mean it?"

"Yes, Majesty. She is here."

Just as Emeil's troops had been under siege at menRathan, Duile believed she was under attack. The seizing of Ydron had gone awry. Provinces were revolting. Her armies were suffering defeats. Her advisors were unimaginable incompetents and the constant reminder her children were missing discredited each search party's expressed optimism. Adding insult, a would-be assassin had entered the palace. Consequently, Yar's report that Lith-An was finally within the palace walls seemed too much to believe.

"When can I see her?" She was frantic and sounded it, but did not care she had broken decorum.

"Soon, Your Majesty. Do you want her brought to this place?" Yar gestured expansively to emphasize they were in the dungeon, "Or would you rather she see you in nicer quarters?"

"You are right, my dear Husted. You are always right. I am so eager to see her, I wasn't thinking. Could you bring her to my chambers? Oh, and perhaps you might have my servants insure she is fed and bathed and wearing one of her dresses? I cannot imagine what she has been through, but I am sure she must be a sight."

"Of course. That will take, I imagine, somewhat more than an hour and should give you ample time to complete what you have begun here."

"Yes," she almost hissed, glaring at the prostrate form before her. "I am sure I will be in a much better mood to meet my daughter once I have finished with you. I guarantee you will not escape again."

Her prisoner seemed not the least intimidated. "Don't be so certain, Dearie. I haven't finished with you, either."

Duile regarded the outlaw and sneered. "Do you really believe you can unfasten these shackles? Can you imagine what the dolt who permitted your escape is suffering, even as we speak? Can you hear him?"

Guttural screams from the adjoining chamber described the price of the jailor's incompetence. Duile was right. There was no breaking these bonds and Yar was in firm control of the new dungeon master.

Still groggy from her near-death encounter, Dur tried to remember how she had arrived at this place. She recalled having sent out a desperate thought to anyone who might hear, before she blacked out, and dimly recalled Prince Regilius answering. Perhaps it was the guards in the corridor who had come to her rescue. She tugged at her restraints and did not know whether to be grateful or upset.

"I guess we are going to become acquainted," Dur managed.

"That is an understatement, my little marmath," the queen hissed. "I intend to learn things about you even you don't know."

Duile seemed eager to begin and Dur tried not to anticipate what might come next.

"Unfortunately," said the queen, "we will have to wait until the new jailor is finished with his predecessor. He doesn't like to interrupt what he has begun—an admirable trait, don't you think? So long as he has the strength to do a proper job with you, I am content to wait."

"And are you going from here to a nice, homey visit with your daughter?" asked Dur. "I certainly understand how important it is to have the right frame of mind for such a delicate get-together."

Duile struck Dur with the back of her hand and the outlaw smiled.

"Oh, look, Your Majesty. Blood. You've soiled your hand. Well, that should help bring out your maternal instincts. Is that why your little girl left home?"

The monarch raised her hand once more, but before she could strike, a page interrupted.

"Your Majesty," he gasped. Out of breath, he dropped to one knee. "Thank Siemas I found you! I bring urgent news."

"Voreth's horns! This had better be of consequence or I'll have the jailor show you what happens to someone who interrupts his queen for nothing."

"Yes, Majesty," he said, bowing low. "I understand."

"What is it? I haven't all day."

"Your Majesty," he panted. "The slaves… " He paused, trying to catch his breath.

"Yes, boy?" She had no patience. "Which slaves? What about the slaves? Do I have to drag this out of you?"

"No, Your Majesty," he replied and managed, "A pigeon has

arrived from the quarry at Ead. Someone has freed the slaves and they are revolting. They have slain their guards and fled."

"But they have no weapons!" she protested.

"Your Majesty, with all due respect, it is a quarry."

"I know it's a quarry."

"They have rocks."

Duile was outraged, not only at the news, but also at the page's insolence. "What do you think I am?"

This time, he knew better than reply.

The queen hesitated, looking first at Dur, then at the page. She did not enjoy being interrupted, but could not ignore the news. Slaves represented a substantial portion of her wealth. The outlaw could wait. The escapees had to be rounded up at once. She was shaking with rage.

"I will deal with you when I return," she said and stormed out.

# 61

Fewer than three months had passed since Marm had carried her out, away from the murders and carnage. But now, upon her return to the palace, much differed from her recollections. Lith-An surmised it was she, more than her home, that had changed.

The servants' faces reflected a mixture of emotions. On one hand, they were overjoyed to see her and smiled broadly, even laughed or giggled when they addressed her. Yet, when they spoke among themselves, their voices and expressions reflected the turmoil that had shaken the kingdom. A toddler would have been oblivious to any such undertones, and though the staff tried to conceal it from the princess, their distress was evident so that home was no longer the warm, nurturing place it once had seemed.

Then too, she missed her nanny who, in many ways, had been her real mother. The maturity she had acquired over these past months did nothing to lessen the impact of that loss. Marm had been a large part of her short life and the void caused by her absence was almost beyond bearing. Until today, she had been able to shove Marm's death to the back of her mind and dwell, instead, upon the daily activities of the camp. Here, however, where Marm had been almost everything, the loss was inescapable and her memory filled each room and every act.

Lith-An wiped a tear from her eye and pretended to be excited by the dress the servants produced and by the pastry that waited on the nightstand. On another occasion, she might have enjoyed these things intended to delight a little girl.

"Please be still, Your Highness," a servant implored, "so I can place these ribbons in your hair. You should look as happy as your mother will be when she sees you.

"You were such a sight when you arrived," the servant went on. "How did you ever get to be such a mess? A princess should always look her best," she said as she remade Lith-An into the image of a young royal, instead of a child dwelling among nomads. "Now, please hold still."

"Yes. You are right. I have not been at all cooperative. I apologize and will endeavor not to fidget," Lith-An conceded.

The servant girl halted and looked up from adjusting the hem, appraising the toddler. Except for the manner in which the child spoke, she found nothing unusual and resumed her work.

Out of one eye, Lith-An noticed a page peering through the doorway. When a servant approached him, he whispered into her ear and the girl stood upright. She glanced around the room, then ran to each worker who, in turn, became agitated. The atmosphere transformed from leisurely and gregarious to urgent. One girl ran to the servant dressing the princess, whispered, then darted away.

"Your mother is on her way," the servant explained. "She will be here in a minute."

"I understand," Lith-An replied. "Do what you must to ready me. I won't be discomfited if you are inadvertently a bit rough."

The servant looked askance at the princess. Although the response was inappropriate for one so young, the servant would never dare mention it. "Right," she said and resumed her work. "Well, you are nearly ready. If you will just hold still another second… " She inserted a pin and examined her work. "There! That does it. You look beautiful."

"Thank you very much. I am sure you have done an admirable job."

Another incredulous look. "Thank you, Your Highness."

The servant stood, curtsied and backed away to join the others. They hurried to straighten the room, gathering their implements and arranging themselves. When everything was as it should be, they stood at attention and awaited Duile's entrance.

… … … … …

Suddenly, with neither announcement nor escort, Duile Morged Tonopath, Queen of Ydron swept into the room.

"By Ydron's walls! It is you, Lith-An."

All of the waiting came down to this moment and Duile felt her knees quiver. She ignored the staff's curtsies. They would hold their postures until she released them.

"You are alright, aren't you?"

"Yes, Mother. I am fine. Thank you for asking."

"And these girls have taken good care of you, have they not?"

"Yes, Mother. The care I have received has been exemplary."

"The care you've received has… ," she repeated, then trailed off. Her daughter's response, or rather its quality, began to register. "Lith-An?"

"Yes, Mother?"

"You are not my little girl." Duile looked her up and down. "Who are you?"

"Well, I am certainly your daughter in the physical sense, but I am equally certain I have not taken after you in any other regard."

Duile looked closely at Lith-An and could see no difference between the girl before her and the daughter she remembered. Coincidentally, she noticed all of the servant girls holding their pose. She found their presence annoying and wanted them gone.

"Get out!" she shouted.

The girls, startled by her outburst, began to straighten, although not quickly enough for their mistress.

"Did you hear me?" Duile demanded. When they began to back slowly from the room, their faces full of uncertainty, the queen shouted, "I said get out!"

That was enough. They gathered up their skirts, turned and disappeared through the door.

"Now," said Duile, taking a deep breath. "Where was I?"

"You were expressing incredulity," Lith-An replied.

"You will call me Your Majesty when you address me," said Duile, confident the one before her was a fraud.

"That's quite odd, Mother. You never required that of me before."

"Before? What do you mean before?"

"I mean before you murdered my father and I was forced to flee or risk losing my own life."

Duile could not correlate this small person and her adult way of speaking with the child whose memory was still so fresh.

"Why do you insist on calling me Mother?" demanded the queen.

"I have been wondering about that myself. Probably out of habit, I would guess."

"If you don't tell me who you are, I will have you imprisoned."

"Well, that is certainly better than the fate I have been expecting."

Then, turning the tables, Lith-An circled Duile.

"I fully expected, upon my return, you would have had me executed. After all, my brother and I are your only obstacles to the throne. Are we not?" Duile started to object, but Lith-An continued. "I understand you are having trouble accepting who I am. I have changed substantially during my absence and I realize you cannot comprehend the transformation. Perhaps it will help if I remind how you instructed Marm to sing the lullaby Quiet Child, Sleepy Child when she put me to sleep, and that I preferred Satsah bake me pastries filled with deleth fruit. Or that I had a jeweled mobile of the suns, moon and stars suspended above my crib. Not many would know those things, don't you agree?"

"How do you?" Duile demanded.

"Certainly my appearance has not changed these last few months. You recognized me at once when you entered. I admit my speech has changed—shall we say, matured? So you have missed my childhood. You would have, in any case. What a shame. Instead of a lengthy explanation, shall we just say I am a prodigy? The result is the same. Whether you believe me or not, I am Lith-An."

"I still cannot believe it."

"Then you have lost a daughter."

Duile regarded Lith-An up for a long minute. She could not deny this girl appeared to be her own. It was, she conceded, the speech she could not accept. But, yes, this prodigy resembled her daughter, so she had no choice. "Alright, Lith-An, what would you like to do, now that you have returned?"

"I was seeking a reunion with my mother, hoping she was someone other than what her actions made her appear. Since that isn't going to happen, I will wait to be reunited with my brother."

"And when do you expect that will occur?"

"He is returning as we speak. He will arrive in the morning."

"Then Husted was right," Duile exclaimed, clasping her hands. "That is wonderful."

"Yes, Mother," Lith-An agreed. "Things will be much better once he is here."

The queen was lost in her imaginings for the moment.

"One small favor," her daughter asked.

"Yes, Lith-An?" Duile asked.

"You have a prisoner. A woman."

"What of it?"

"Promise me you will not harm her."

"I cannot promise that. The jailor has his instructions."

"Then promise me you will not harm her until after Regilius has returned and we have been reunited. Is that too much to ask?"

Duile paused to consider the request. She decided since both children were returning, she could afford to be magnanimous.

"Alright, child. If the jailor has not yet started, I will send word he is to wait."

"Thank you, Mother. You have no idea how much that matters."

"I am curious, though. How do you know about the prisoner and why is she of any concern?"

"Everything will be plain once Regilius has arrived. I promise. Have patience and everything will become clear."

# 62

Dawn had broken and the storm had passed. The battlements of barakYdron, bathed in the morning glow of Mahaz and the sliver of Jadon peeking from behind, shone surreally above the city. The crisp, morning air was so fresh and invigorating it was hard to imagine the fierceness of the day, either the battle raging at menRathan or the bloodshed at Ead.

Reg brought his endath to a halt and Ered's drew alongside. They had come full circle. Although every fiber told him returning was the thing to do, he still did not know how he would undo the damage. Could the lands be reunited in the face of so much mistrust? Was he the one to do it? More to the point, could he even survive if he tried?

He coaxed his endath closer to its companion, leaned from his saddle and gently shook Ered.

"Wake up, dear friend. It is morning and we are home."

Ered looked up. He took a deep breath and smiled.

"Home, are we?"

"Nearly."

Ered regarded the battlements and soaring towers. "I had forgotten it was so beautiful."

"The same thought came to me. We take these things for granted and nothing is granted, not even the next breath."

"How do you plan to get us inside?"

"I don't think that's going to be a problem. If anything, riding out will be the poser." Reg laughed.

"What's so funny?"

"I am talking about coming home and feeling as if I'm going to my funeral. It is all so perverse."

Ered nodded. "We have a tough day ahead. Do you feel like eating? I have some of the food Bakka prepared, as well as some water. We will think more clearly with food in our bellies."

"I suspect you are right," Reg agreed, turning to look over his shoulder. "It will give our escort a chance to catch up."

"I really don't care about them, one way or another."

"I agree," said Reg, rising in his stirrups. "Let's dismount. I am weary of the saddle."

They alit and led their endaths to a nearby knoll.

"I have a sandiath cloth to sit upon," offered Ered. "The ground's a bit soggy."

Reg nodded. "Let us be comfortable and enjoy ourselves. This is a beautiful morning and it might be our last."

"Don't even think it, Reg. We have much to accomplish and we haven't come this far for nothing." Ered unfolded and spread the cloth, laid out their provisions, then raised the water sack in a toast. "Death to wrongdoers. May we make a difference."

"I am tired of the killing," said Reg. "But, yes, may we make a difference."

When they had eaten, Reg and Ered rode to the palace's main gate with trepidation. While they hoped to be simply admitted, they did not believe it would be quite so simple. The number of guards had been increased, and instead of the customary uniforms, they wore light armor as if expecting combat.

A short distance ahead, a scuffle arose. A man was taken aside, searched, then carried off to the castle. As it became their turn, they approached the guard and were greeted with the challenge, "Halt and identify yourselves."

"I am Regilius Tonopath, Prince of Ydron and rightful heir to its throne."

The guard motioned his counterpart to join him. "Do you have any proof?" he asked.

"No, I'm sorry. I had to leave unexpectedly and didn't have time to pack." Reg realized the dig was unnecessary, but he was tired. "Are you new to this post? Most of my guard know me on sight. I know I haven't seen you before."

"Yes, sir. I haven't been guarding for long." Then, apparently deciding he was being too chatty, he said, "Sir, I will need some identification."

"First, soldier, the appropriate salutation is Your Highness, not Sir. Second, my mother will be more than willing to identify me. Please summon her or one of her advisors."

"Your mother?"

"Hasn't anyone instructed you that Duile Morged Tonopath is

queen of Ydron?" demanded Reg, losing patience.

The guard was reaching for his sword when his counterpart grabbed his hand and whispered something.

"We will summon someone to identify you." The guard sheathed his weapon. "Can you vouch for your companions?" he said, gesturing toward Ered and the others. The Dalthin had caught up and had resumed the appearance of the two monks.

"Once I am identified, you will pass us all. My presence alone vouches for my company."

Ered leaned toward him. "Reg, do you have to go so hard on him?"

"I am sorry. You are probably right, but I have come a long way and I am not used to being questioned at my own gate."

The first guard stood by while the second ran off. Reg and Ered didn't have long to wait. Within minutes, they were surrounded by dozens of armed guards whose swords were drawn and whose obvious intent was to arrest them.

"Guard!" shouted Reg. "What do you think you are doing?"

"Exactly what your mother instructed them to do," someone replied.

Reg turned to see a courtier. "Who are you? I don't know you," Reg said.

"That is true, Prince Regilius. But I know you and that is all that matters. I am Husted Yar, your mother's advisor."

Without further warning, the guards dragged Reg and Ered from their saddles, bound their wrists and carried them into the castle.

# 63

It was not the Grand Hall into which her children were ushered. While the queen intended to keep this reunion to a formal note, she required none of the ostentation of that room. The place she had chosen was a smaller chamber in which she sometimes granted audience to visiting dignitaries and was well-enough appointed to remind her offspring whose hands held the reins. After all, this get-together was not to reunite mother and children, but rather to inform the two what must follow. She intended to put all the uncertainty that had plagued her, all the anxiety of these past months behind her forever. She was certain the meeting's outcome would not meet any of Reg or Lith-An's expectations, but that was inconsequential. After today, she would never have to worry about either one seizing the throne.

"Good morning, Regilius. Good morning, Lith-An. How good it is to see you." She managed a smile of genuine delight. "I have been trying to locate you both for quite some time. I cannot begin tell you how pleased I am you returned of your own volition."

"My sister and I thought it important to return. We have many things to discuss and many questions to ask."

"Such as… ?" Duile prompted.

"Why did you kill our father?"

"My!" Duile said. "You jump in with both feet. Where are the niceties I taught you?"

"You act as if I were pointing out your petticoat is showing. I find it incredible you are concerned with trivialities while seeming oblivious to the magnitude of your act. You murdered our father, the man who gave us life. You didn't throw out the wash water."

"I rid the land of incompetent garbage. Everyone is better for it."

"No, Mother. None have it better than before. The people certainly fare no better. The rulers of the surrounding lands, for the most part, are worse off as well."

"They will all adjust to the new reality," asserted the queen.

Reg struggled to remain calm. "Even your allies are questioning upon which side they have landed. Do you think they are unaware who murdered Kareth and Danai? They are not stupid. Your treachery is too blatant. Fear will not hold their allegiance for long. Your greed certainly will not. This is not how greatest grandfather Obah united this land. You will be lucky to hold the throne until the Warm Months return."

Lith-An stepped in. "Even as we speak, the tide is turning at menRathan. Emeil and his allies are winning. By tomorrow, or the next day at the latest, he will emerge as victor. Where will you be then? With whom will your allies side?"

A hint of worry flickered across Duile's face, then disappeared. "How do you know these things? You have been away for months. With whom have you been speaking?"

Lith-An replied, "We have changed, Mother. You noticed my transformation earlier. My brother's, while less obvious, has been no less profound. With those changes comes a new awareness."

"You are certainly not the little girl I remember. I still don't understand what has gone wrong. And you, Regilius, what has happened to the nice, dutiful son I knew?"

"That would require some explanation and I am not sure you would believe a word."

"Nonetheless," said Lith-An, "You will have your evidence soon enough."

"Children—and realize that is what you are, children—my ascent to power was not an accident. It was carefully planned and orchestrated. I am quite secure, I assure you."

"Do you really believe you can stay in power?" Lith-An asked. "I cannot believe you are so oblivious to all that has gone wrong."

"Well, you shall certainly not have it, little girl. I will see to that," Duile countered.

"What makes you so sure either of us want it?" asked Lith-An.

"I have no desire to be king," said Reg. "The fact I was next in line doesn't mean I am suited to govern."

Lith-An picked up the thread. "Ydron and her people would have been better served had Manhathus and Berin each arrived at that conclusion."

"Hereditary rule has held this land together for generations," snapped the queen.

"Why, then, did you choose to interrupt it?" demanded Reg. "Such hypocrisy! Mother, your sole motivation is greed. The wealth of Ydron was fabulous beyond measure when Father ruled. Half that treasure would have been more than anyone could put to use and still it was not enough for you. How much is enough, Mother?"

Duile smiled, but did not reply.

"If you possessed all sixteen provinces, you would still find their treasure lacking. How sad."

Lith-An jumped in. "And that is what makes you dangerous. Fortunately, many can see this. When enough people arrive at this conclusion, you will fall. I only hope you will live through what must follow."

Duile's eyes widened. "I thought so! You are planning my death."

"Not at all," Reg replied, "We are not like you. We have no interest in another coup. Even had we desired it, we would not need to act. It will be your allies… "

"It may even be the people themselves…," Lith-An interjected.

"Or the slaves, who are already in revolt…," continued Reg.

"Who will bring about your fall from power," concluded Lith-An. "You have nothing to fear from either of us."

"Have I not? You come together against me, even now."

"We will see justice done," said Reg, "but we will not be the agents of its making. We have no interest in causing your downfall."

Shaking her head, Lith-An said, "Sadly, that would be redundant. You have already insured the end of your brief but deplorable reign. So sad. Father certainly needed to be removed from power, and possibly, you might have done so legitimately. Much was wrong in the land. The very admiration some had for you, the qualities that drew your allies to you… "

"Aside from greed," said Reg.

"… would have garnered enough support to allow you to lead Ydron from the abyss into which she had fallen."

"That may have allowed you to retain power."

"And Father would still be alive," Lith-An concluded.

"And that is why I disbelieve your forgiveness," Duile countered. "I did, indeed, murder your father, my—I choke upon the word—husband. And although you are the issue of my loins, I never wanted to be your mother. I had you out of duty. I hold no love for you. I am therefore amazed when you say, with all the wisdom you purport to have acquired, you do not wish my death."

"We are not murderers, Mother," said Reg. "Oh, we have had our thoughts. We certainly wish we had been born of another and we are certainly not saints. Even though vicious thoughts may have sprung from our anger—and we are very angry—the difference between us is that we will not act upon those thoughts."

"Your end is coming," said Lith-An. "It will come at the hands of the many whose lives you have made intolerable."

"We won't deprive them of their satisfaction," Reg added. "The thousands of unfortunates have a right to exact a price for the evil you have done."

"Well, for two children with a lot of questions," Duile sneered, "You certainly have a lot of answers. What font of wisdom, may I ask, has provided you with such profound insights? Dolls? Games? How many years' experience have you?" Turning to Reg. "Twenty-one?" Then to Lith-An. "Three?"

"I bring with me the depth and experience of dozens much older than I," Lith-An replied.

"What rubbish!" replied the queen. "I grow tired of your lecture. You are no longer my son, Regilius. And as for you, Lith-An, my daughter has completely vanished."

"I am glad she has," Lith-An replied. "Were I still the child you remember, I would have been oblivious to your evil, had you allowed me to live. Even now, as I look into your heart, I realize you do not intend for either of us survive the day. Do you never tire of the blood-letting?"

"No, my child. I do not. Although, all the time I awaited your return, I did envision a different sort of reunion—nothing too sweet, but with a bit of pleasant conversation."

"Right up to the point you ordered our execution, I suppose." Reg made no attempt to conceal his disgust.

Duile ignored him. "Since it appears we will not have the pleasure of that little luxury, I wish to move on to other matters."

She strode to the captain of the guard and said something under her breath. He, in turn, walked to one of the chamber's doors, opened it and spoke in a hushed voice to someone unseen, then stepped aside to admit Husted Yar.

"Dearest Husted," gushed the queen. "You have performed as you promised."

Yar bowed.

"You have returned my children and I can continue my plans

without distraction. I have one, last favor… one last request, if you will."

"Your Majesty?"

"Will you take them to the dungeon and rid me of them, NOW?"

"Certainly, Your Majesty. It will be my pleasure."

"Thank you."

She calmed noticeably, then turned and without so much as a backward glance left the room. Reg observed that she seemed to skip once as she departed. Then, he and Lith-An were taken away, never to return to the splendor.

# 64

The distance between the royal chambers and the dungeon was considerable and the captain of the guard was using this unprecedented opportunity to amuse himself.

"You have certainly managed to displease your mother," he chided, "so today will not be a pleasant one. I hope you enjoy your new accommodations," he snickered. "As brief as your remaining time among us may be." He laughed aloud, as did a few of his company.

After the visit with his mother, Reg had been sent into a deep funk, destroying any hope for some remnant of family. Nonetheless, he responded with restraint. "Captain, you have always served my family well and I know, even now, you believe you are acting in my mother's interest. You believe your own situation to be secure, but realize this: the land is in turmoil and fortunes are shifting. Tomorrow will be different, so you should act with prudence, even in this."

Again, the captain laughed. "Tomorrow will certainly be different. You won't be here!"

"Perhaps," admitted Lith-An. "But you may find you will have to reckon with Lord Emeil."

"And who will tell him? Certainly not you, little one."

"No, not I," she said. "But you are surrounded by witnesses. Who knows what they will admit to at a trial or inquest?"

"I will take my chances," he snapped. It wasn't clear whether he was reacting to the truth in her statement or the fun she was spoiling, but he raised his hand, threatening to strike. "Now, shut your mouth or… "

"Or what?" Reg interrupted. "You will shut the little girl's mouth for her? My! My! My! How brave and bold. I bet your men are impressed. I certainly am."

The captain glanced from face to face. If they disapproved, their faces remained impassive. He hesitated a moment, then lowered his hand, probably suspecting that striking a child would endear him to no one.

"Quiet, both of you!" he snapped.

The cloud raised by the siblings' remarks hung heavily and they continued in silence.

Reg was struggling with somehow freeing his sister when her thoughts reached him.

*Please do not attempt anything foolish on my behalf. There are too many. Please wait. If I am correct, there may yet be a chance.*

Reg sighed. *It is so hard doing nothing.*

*Doing nothing is sometimes the best thing.*

When they arrived at the dungeon, they were led through the room where Ered and Dur were strapped to tables.

"Ered," called the prince. "Are you alright?"

"I am fine, Reg. Don't give them any satisfaction."

A man Reg assumed to be the jailor strode over to Ered and backhanded him across the face.

"Who gave you permission to speak?" he said.

*Don't worry, Ered,* Reg communicated. *They'll not get a sound from me.*

*Nor from me,* Ered replied.

Dur's thoughts interrupted. *Prince Regilius?*

*I am. Thank you for freeing Danth. I have not had time to locate him. Do you know if he is alright?*

Dur paused a moment, then replied, *He is still safe, although I cannot say how much longer.*

*He will be alright,* Lith-An assured. *Now that we three are together, everything will be alright.*

*My!* remarked Dur. *Your mind is so clear. Your thoughts are so crisp. I would like to believe you, but…*

*Now that we three are together, everything will be right,* Lith-An insisted. *Everything.* She was emphatic. *I can feel it begin.*

*Feel what?* asked Dur.

Reg answered. *My sister seems to understand things beyond my comprehension, but I am learning to trust her. Believe her when she says all will be fine, no matter what happens here.*

The guards led Reg to one of the tables the dungeon master used for torture and Lith-An to another. Four of the guards, one to each limb, lifted Regilius and placed him supine upon it, holding him in place as they secured him.

"Alright, boys. I have him now," the jailor said, and the guards stepped away. "Would you be good enough to leave me to my work?"

The captain of the guard ordered his company to stand against one wall, but the jailor objected. "Her Majesty wants this to be—how should I say," he grinned, "an intimate affair. She asked me to have you all leave once the prisoners were secured."

"I don't think that is advisable," said the captain.

"Captain, do you see any way for these," he emphasized the next word, "*children* to escape? I don't think so. Shall I tell Her Majesty, you countermanded her orders?"

The captain was clearly displeased, but caught between his own judgment and the queen's wrath, he chose discretion. The guard filed out, but Yar and the Dalthin remained. Yar had not been certain if two, or even three of its kind would be sufficient to control the trio, so it had summoned all the others in the city.

"We will stay until Her Majesty releases us," said Yar.

"Very well." The jailor relented grudgingly, knowing Yar was special to the queen. "In that case, please stand aside."

They stationed themselves along one wall and the jailor, irritated by the lack of cooperation and respect, tugged hard on one of Reg's straps.

"Mas'tad! What do you think you're doing?" Reg cried.

"Making sure you're secure. I expect to have a very enjoyable afternoon. I've never done a royal before. Your mother has been very good to me today. In fact, she has kept me and my late boss very busy since she took over." The jailor chuckled. "There have been days when I thought my arms would fall off from all I've had to do but, you know, I've always managed to find that last bit of strength to finish the job. And I do mean finish, if you catch my drift." He winked, then doubled over with laughter. When he straightened, his eyes were tearing. "I only wish you were going to enjoy this afternoon as much as I will. So much the pity. No one appreciates the work I do, except her. Even my old boss didn't much like it when he got to sample my talents. Ah, me. What's one to do?

"Now, before she comes down and orders me to begin—I think she's going to want to watch. She does that sometimes—I need to decide where to begin and with what. What do you think?"

He gestured at a wall full of instruments. There were varieties of whips and cudgels, as well as numerous other items that looked as though they were best suited for a livery where repairs were made to carriages. Reg didn't want to imagine how they might be used here, though he suspected he wouldn't need an imagination today. He shook his head, more in silent discourse with himself than in reply to the jailor, but the jailor slapped him hard across the face.

"I asked you a question! Don't ever—I said EVER—wag your head at me when I ask a question. I don't give a horse's turd who you are. When I speak, you will reply civilly. Do I make myself clear?"

"I am sorry," Reg replied with a deliberate hint of sarcasm. "I thought I would rely on your expertise."

The jailor smiled and gently wiped the drop of blood that seeped from Reg's lip. He placed both hands on the edge of the table, brought his face close, then said in a low voice, "Oh, I have a great deal of expertise, Highness."

The stench of his breath nearly made Reg turn away, but he thought he could anticipate how the jailor would react, so he returned the man's stare without flinching.

"You are going to learn how much of an expert I am. I enjoy my job. Do you know that? Most folk don't have the stomach for what I do, but I relish it. I'm very fortunate to have found work that suits me. Most simply endure their jobs, but I rise every morning, eager to find what the new day holds. I am lucky indeed and I suspect today will be the high point of my career."

"Jailor!"

His head snapped around and he stood at attention. "Yes, Your Majesty."

"You haven't begun without me, have you?"

"No, Your Majesty. I would never without your instruction."

"I appreciate that," said Duile. She smiled. "Leave me with my son for a minute, if you will. I'd like some words with him before you begin."

"Yes, Your Majesty."

"Hello, Mother," said Reg, straining his neck to see her. "I must say, I never really imagined what you had in store for me."

"No, Regilius?" She moved around the table to a place where they could see each other. "Actually, I had also imagined a different scenario with a more abrupt ending. But Husted Yar, dear soul, suggested that after our earlier tense meeting, we could undo some of my anger and frustration by beginning this way. Frankly, after a little thought, the idea appealed to me."

"In light of the last few months, that doesn't surprise me. Although, after the way you disposed of Father, I expected you would have done with me already."

"Well, you know, dear, you have caused me a great deal of grief and anguish these last months. I detest living like that and I thought you should have a taste of what I have been enduring."

"You hide your scars well."

Duile's face darkened. "I should have the jailor begin with you now."

"Do, if you are so inclined. Whatever you have in store for me will be over in a while. For you, though, this is only the beginning. You may have thought our return would secure the throne. I promise, this will not do it. You will not sit easily nor long."

"The power I possess is so exhilarating, perhaps I should offer you some."

"It is not yours to give. And after you have killed me, there is Lith-An to contend with. You haven't had a taste of what she can do."

"She will follow you this day, I promise."

"Really? You would torture and kill a little girl? You are incredible."

Her face darkened. "I've had enough. Jailor!" she called. Then, returning her attention to Reg, said, "He is never far away. We will begin so I can return to more important matters."

He turned away, refusing to look at her any longer.

"Jailor!" she called with increased urgency.

"Yes, Your Majesty," he panted as he hurried into the room. "I came back as fast as I could. What is your pleasure?"

Without attempting to conceal her anger, she replied, "I want my son's punishment to begin at once. I want him dead this afternoon, but I want every minute he is on your table to seem like an eternity. Can you manage that?"

"I will certainly do my best. Would you be good enough to stand away from the table? I wouldn't want any of your fine fabrics stained with either my sweat or his blood." He bowed slightly.

"Certainly. Where would you like me to stand?" she asked, looking about eagerly, like a child anxious to receive a reward.

He finished the bow with a sweeping gesture toward the corner farthest from the table. "I think you will be safe enough over there, Your Majesty. You will be able to see everything while, at the same time, remaining out of the way of our comings and goings. I may have my assistant help from time to time," he explained. "May I have him bring you a chair? I expect this will take a while."

"No, thank you. I want to see everything," she replied as she took her position. "It will be better if I stand."

"Very well. I will begin slowly." The jailor walked to the wall holding the tools of his trade and fingered half a dozen whips before settling on one. "Ah, yes. I think we will begin with this. It's the least in my collection, but it will allow me a great deal of latitude in deciding how I will escalate matters. We wouldn't want him to pass out too soon, but I think it will still deliver the right message to his delicate skin." He removed it from its hanger and examined it carefully as he approached the table. He circled the prince, looking from the whip to the prostrate body and back again.

"Shouldn't you remove his shirt first?" Duile inquired.

The jailor's voice sounded distant when he answered. "Oh, it will come off of its own accord. Don't you worry."

Without warning, he struck Regilius across the chest with a backhand stroke, arching his back and rising onto his toes, looking like a dancer as he completed the move. Reg's body arched in response and his teeth clenched, but he managed to keep silent. The jailor continued to circle and Duile watched with rapt attention, leaning forward to take in every detail. When the jailor reached the opposite side of the table, he lashed out again. Still, the prince made no sound. His body shuddered, however, making apparent how effective was the strike. Sweat beaded on Reg's brow and his eyes were closed.

The jailor halted, placed the whip on the edge of the table and walked to the wall where his instruments were. He removed his shirt and hung it carefully where the lash he was using had been. Then, as if suddenly self conscious, he apologized to the queen.

"Pardon my lack of modesty, Your Majesty. This work can make a body hot, such as this place is, no ventilation and all."

Duile did not respond, but returned her gaze to her son. The look in her eyes showed how eagerly she awaited whatever might come next. The jailor paid her no further notice as he retrieved the quirt and returned to his work. He paused for a moment, then, with every bit of force he could muster, he delivered half a dozen lashings across Regilius' torso in rapid succession.

# 65

"Mas'tad!" Dur swore as something crawled across her face.

She strained to bat it away, but was shackled so tightly she only managed to chafe her wrists. She was as angry at being fettered as she was at failing her mission. Now it appeared Duile would to have her way, not only with her and the prince's friend, Ered, but also with Reg and Lith-An. If Dur had despised her before, what she planned for her children amplified Dur's hatred even more. Manhathus had robbed Pithien of her childhood when his soldiers abducted her father, forcing her and her mother to go into hiding. That had plunged her into an existence deprived of normalcy, most especially of family and motherhood. Perhaps this is why she dreamt of children. That Duile could contemplate, let alone enact anything so reprehensible as the torture and murder of her own, determined the outlaw to eradicate her, even were it to be her final act.

"Hello, pretty!"

Her head snapped up at the jailor's voice.

"We're not too uncomfortable, are we?"

"So nice of you to ask. I was admiring how well you've handled the décor."

"In a sarcastic mood, are we?"

He lifted a hand, apparently to strike, but altered the gesture, and with a smile that showed he was boss, stroked her cheek instead. She shuddered, but concealed her revulsion. Relaxed, he would be easier to manipulate than he would be were she to anger him.

"I have the perfect solution for sarcasm, little Missy. You will have to wait until I've taken care of the two ahead of you, but don't you worry; I got plenty of sleep last night anticipating today. When your turn comes, I will have strength enough and more.

"You know," he continued, "today is a historic one. I will have to mark it on my calendar so I don't forget to celebrate its anniversary. Imagine: I have the pleasure of administering a lifetime of carefully acquired skills to Prince Regilius, Princess Lith-An and the fabled Pithien Dur, all in one day. Gracious me! How did I ever become so fortunate? I shall have to retire immediately after. There is no way I can ever equal, let alone exceed such a day, don't you think?"

"You are right," she said. "Today will be historically unique, although not in the way you imagine."

"Oh? How is that?"

Dur smiled. "Allow me to demonstrate."

Without another word, she entered his mind. She checked the adjacent chamber to insure the Dalthins' attention was elsewhere and none would interrupt. Then, satisfied all was well, she altered the jailor's perceptions. He believed himself to be tightening her bonds when, in reality, he was doing exactly the opposite. When he had loosened them, she sat up and climbed from the table onto the floor, although he still saw her lying upon it. She had timed it perfectly. At just that moment, Duile summoned him and Dur permitted him to hear. As he turned to go, he assured himself she was securely bound, and she insured he perceived exactly that.

After the jailor had gone, Ered, who had been watching this bizarre scenario, asked, "What just happened?"

"No time to explain," she replied.

She started to leave, then halted. She had intended to go to the adjoining chamber to release Duile's children, but even as she contemplated it, she fell into a deep rapture. A process, perhaps the one Lith-An had referred to, was underway and she was a part of it. Her mind was becoming entwined with Reg's and Lith-An's as though the three were becoming one. The intimacy was intoxicating. She "heard" Lith-An assure her brother the torture would soon stop, and though Pithien did not understand how that might happen, she felt confident it would of its own accord. Although it was tempting to pause and enjoy this mingling of minds, it was distracting her from her mission. She put a finger to her lips, indicating the conversation had ended.

"I have work to do. I need a knife and I need to think," she said.

In fact, there were knives aplenty in the room where the children were. Conveniently, the queen was there too. Problematically, so were the Dalthin. If only she could get them to leave, she could do as she wished with Duile. The how of it stumped her. She was pacing to the cadence of the jailor's whip, momentarily flummoxed, when an idea surfaced. Could she alter the Dalthin's perceptions, as she had the jailor's? Could she make them see, hear or react to some phantasm? She knew she could not influence all seven, when the greatest number of people she could manage was four or five, but perhaps she could manage one. If it were the right one, the rest might follow. The strategy was risky, but there was no safe alternative. She reached into the next room and the minds of the Dalthin were at the forefront. Did they sense her, she wondered? No. Their thoughts were on the siblings. With the greatest care, she inquired of each its identity until one mind replied *Husted Yar*. Ever so delicately, lest she arouse it, she explored the structure of its mind. As she probed, she grew increasingly confident she could do as she intended. Although the minds of the others were interwoven with Yar's, she found by treading between their thoughts as it were, she could turn Yar's attention upon her, then make it perceive what she wished. All she needed was to disturb it just so…

She gasped! As soon as she shook it, as one rouses a sleeper, Yar became aware of her. She had to act quickly. She showed herself rising from the table and preparing to flee. Her hunch proved correct. If anything would capture this one's attention, this was it. Yar had labored too hard to capture her and was not about to allow her escape. Galvanized into action as few of its species ever were, Yar did not question the authenticity of this perception. The other Dalthin, immediately aware of what Yar was seeing, turned as it turned and together they set off in pursuit. They filed through the chamber past Ered and her. While the young man remained strapped to the table, Dur was hiding—apparently vanished—so they continued into the corridor down which they believed she had fled. Dur waited until they had gone, then went to Ered's table and unstrapped him.

"Stay out of sight. It will be a while before you are safe," she cautioned.

"Thank you," said Ered, rubbing his wrists. "What about you?"

"I have pressing business with the queen," she replied.

Ered raised an eyebrow.

"When I have finished, you should look to Regilius and his sister."

She hurried toward the next room. As she peered through the doorway, the jailor was losing his enthusiasm, looking befuddled. Duile appeared confused as well, and Dur realized they, too, were caught up in the process of mental entwinement.

Deciding her opportunity had arrived, Pithien faced a new problem. How could she murder the queen in front of her children? It was inconceivable. Instead, she would confront Duile in hopes she would flee. Then, after a brief pursuit, she would overtake and dispatch her. The children would be aware, of course, but wouldn't witness the assassination directly. It left her with a bad taste in her mouth, but better alternatives were in short supply.

"Your Majesty," said Dur in a cheery voice, as she stepped through the doorway. "Are we amusing ourselves? I would have thought an ordinary spanking would have been sufficient for these naughty children. Oh, me. I guess parenting techniques have changed since I was little."

Duile rubbed her face, trying to clear her head, then glanced around in a panic. "Guards!" she cried. "Guards!"

"I'm afraid they have gone, Dearie. You sent them away. Remember? It's just us now." The outlaw winked. She strolled to a nearby table and chose one of several knives lying upon it.

"Jailor," Duile called. "Help me."

The jailor looked from the lash in his hand to the knife in Dur's.

"Please, jailor," said Dur, stroking the blade with her finger. "Help her. I truly would love you to come to her defense."

"I'll find one of your guards, Your Majesty," he said and edged toward the doorway.

"Are you abandoning me?" Duile shrieked.

"No, Ma'am. I will return shortly," he lied, then disappeared.

The queen stared after him, her mouth agape.

"Seems it's just us two, sweetie. Shall we play?"

Duile took one last look around the room, then hoisted her skirts and fled. Pithien glanced back through the doorway from which she had emerged.

"Ered," she called, "Come help Reg and Lith-An." Then, she ran through the door in pursuit.

# 66

The initial strike came as a surprise and it was all Reg could do to contain himself. He refused to give either the jailor or his mother the satisfaction of hearing him cry out. He was better prepared when the second blow landed and managed to hang onto his composure. During the flurry that followed, he was on the verge of screaming as the jailor fell into a cadence. All he could do was close his eyes. After a few minutes more, he could not tell if he were indeed screaming or imagining it. Inexplicably, his sister's thoughts intruded and he was no longer inside his body.

*Hello, brother.*

*Lith-An? Am I dead?*

*No, you are not.*

*What is happening? Everything seems distant, yet you feel so close.*

*And you to me.*

*I don't mean physically.*

*I understand. The nearness you refer to is different, more profound.*

Remembering his sister would soon suffer the same fate, Reg panicked. *You must leave this place, Lith-An.*

*That will not be necessary. The jailor will stop soon. Everything wrong in this place will stop soon. Do you feel it? You are no longer simply sensing my thoughts. We have become intertwined, and not just you and I. Pithien Dur is part of us now. Because of this, an extraordinary thing is happening. When two minds come together, they are far stronger than one mind plus another. The addition of a third multiplies that effect even more, as with the Dalthin. Because our minds are so different from theirs, however, something happened during the Change that intensified that uniqueness. Even Pithien was transformed.*

*Dur was not a part of the Change*, said Reg.

*Everyone was a part of it. Everyone was touched by it. Marm was caught up in the visions while she tended me by the playing field where you fell. Everyone, everywhere was caught up in the transformation, whether they understood what was happening or not.*

*But they did not change as we did.*

*You and I were engineered to be special. I don't expect those who worked on us understood everything their work would accomplish or how we would respond, but we were chosen because our nervous systems resembled the Dalthins'. When their ship had drawn near enough, and the number and proximity of all these minds—on the ship and here in Ydron—gained critical mass, we responded and were transformed.*

*You said the three of us are causing something extraordinary,* said Reg.

*I did. Just as the number of attuned minds achieved critical mass when the Change occurred, today, here, now, in this place, the close proximity of you, Pithien and I has achieved a different kind of critical mass. Something even greater has been set into motion.*

*But Dur wasn't engineered,* Reg objected.

*No. She is very special. She had evolved on her own into something similar to what we became, but long before the Change occurred. What is happening to her, however, is not surprising. Marm's people recognized our own special nature. We were able to become what we did, not by how they engineered us so much as because of what we already were. The work they performed accelerated what we would have become, given enough time, enough generations. Everyone on this world inherently possesses these capabilities, some more than others. Even Dur has noticed how certain minds respond to her thoughts to varying degrees.*

*Today, however, something special is happening. For the first time since the Change, you, Pithien and I have come together in the same physical location. While I suspected it was important for you and I to do so—that something good might result—the coming together of us three seems to have catalyzed a process I did not anticipate. My intuition told me this convening was necessary and I felt the rightness of it, but I did not understand why. Already, a global transformation is occurring that, with just us two as factors, might have taken years to set into motion, if it could have happened at all. But now, only hours after your arrival, those in our immediate vicinity are undergoing a new change. Notice that the jailor has stopped beating you.*

Reg laughed aloud. His mind was so removed from his body he realized he might not have been aware of his own demise had the beating continued, though in returning to the physical world he became aware of his body's pain.

*He has,* Reg agreed, although his laughter turned to tears.

*He is changing as we speak,* said Lith-An. *Even mother is affected. And the change is spreading all the while. Soon it will spread beyond these walls. I suspect it will spread throughout the entire land and beyond.*

*The Dalthin seem unaffected by this process. I don't understand.*

*We are similar, but not identical.*

At this moment, Dur entered the room and Regilius knew what she intended. Even though he had considered his mother's demise, when actually confronted with the possibility, he recoiled. Despite all Duile had done, despite what she had inflicted, she was still his mother.

*Pithien, is this necessary?*

*Yes, Your Highness, it is.*

*But Lith-An and I were going to leave justice to the people.*

*And so you have, Your Highness. I am the people.*

In truth, if anyone could be their agent, it was she. Reg knew it. He also understood, were he suddenly freed, he could not stop her, nor could anyone. Lith-An was far too small, the jailor was a coward, and Duile, whose pleas for assistance were being ignored, was certainly no fighter. Even as Reg and Dur were speaking, his mother hoisted her skirts and fled from the room.

Reg studied Dur and knew she could taste Duile's panic. Dur smiled. Revenge for all the years spent hiding, for all the crimes inflicted on her family, her friends and the citizens who regarded her as their hero, was literally just around the corner. She turned to Lith-An.

*Look to your brother. Summon a physician.*

She called out to Ered, "Come, help Reg and Lith-An," and set off to fulfill her mission.

# 67

"Guards!" cried Duile.

Of course they would not answer. They never ignored her orders and she had ordered them to leave. In retrospect, that command seemed to have been the most foolish thing she had ever done, but at the time it made perfect sense. Her children represented two of many distasteful acts she had been required to perform in order to acquire power and to satisfy Manhathus' appetite. When the opportunity came to undo those acts and make her children pay for every painful thing she had endured bringing them into the world, she wanted to relish their passing in private. As for that rodent of an outlaw, many fiercer, larger, stronger men had been kept quite securely in the dungeons and without incident. So how could she have foreseen her present predicament? How she wished the guards had disobeyed her. They would have been fools for doing so. Still, she wished this once they had been fools. She would have forgiven this lapse, forgiven anything if they would respond to her now—but they were gone. No one was here but her prisoners and the assassin who stalked her. There was no mistaking her.

*Run, Your Majesty. Run and hide. I am coming. It won't be long. I will find you.*

Duile thought she might be going mad, but the outlaw's imprint on those thoughts was unmistakable. Although unspoken, they carried her voice. Duile wished they were products of her imagination, but she could tell they were not and it frightened her. She was running as she had not since she was a child and her legs were trembling, rebelling beneath her.

"Guards!"

Her cry had become little more than a croak as fear gripped her throat. Her temples throbbed, her arms and legs tingled and her chest grew tight so that breaths came in short, shallow gasps. As she ran, pleading for help, the dungeon's population came alive at her distress.

This was no ordinary visit and her fear was audible. As if in chorus, they joined Dur's harangue and their calls followed her down the corridors.

"What's the matter, Your Majesty? Something wrong?"

"Are we afraid, Your Majesty?"

"Need help, Your Majesty?"

"Let me out. I'll help you. Ha! Ha! Ha!"

Duile glanced over her shoulder and stumbled. She fell hard against the stone, banging her knees and scraping her palms. She tried to rise but her foot caught on her petticoats and she fell face first, striking her mouth. She feared her pursuer must be almost upon her and again she glanced back but saw no one. This time, before rising, she sorted out her dress's folds, then staggered to her feet. Her mouth hurt and felt wet. She put her hand to her lips and cried out when it came away bloody.

*Are we afraid? Run, Your Majesty. Be very afraid.*

She looked back in the direction from which she had come, but the passage behind remained empty. She cast about, unsure where to flee. She was standing where several corridors intersected. Although she knew the dungeons well, she did not recognize this place. One passage inclined slightly, so she followed it, knowing the way out was upwards. One last look to see if the outlaw had found her, and still she saw no one. That should have reassured her, but it did not.

*Don't worry, Majesty. I will find you.*

She released a terrified sob, gathered her skirts with both hands and ran.

... ... ... ... ...

Husted Yar brought its company to a halt as they were about to depart the dungeon, realizing they had been the victims of a ruse. Yar was still unaware the outlaw had been responsible, but its suspicions were aroused. It sniffed down the corridors through which they had come and saw that the queen's offspring were free. Had they created the deception? It searched for the queen and found she was running and her emotional state was agitated. That was decidedly odd. It had expected her to be calm after her children's return. Probing deeper, it could sense this unrest was the emotional state called fear. Why was she afraid? From what was she running? When Yar realized the captured female had escaped, it understood she was the reason.

It then perceived a curious process underway. Yar had always taken the entwining of minds, its species' most significant trait, for granted. It had given them dominance over all others. While lesser races were made up of isolated individuals, Dalthin interconnectedness provided greater awareness and the ability to collaborate with ease. Now, however, a non-Dalthin network was forming. For the moment it was only seminal, but it was growing. Were it allowed to continue, it could unite the lives on this planet into an entity the Dalthin could not subjugate. Yar deduced that the triad—the queen's spawn and this other—were the phenomenon's nexus. This, in turn, lead it to conclude were the three destroyed before this process gained momentum, the new network might dwindle and die before it could attain completion. It decided it must eliminate all three, and quickly.

It sent the other six to intercept the son and his increasingly dangerous sister. The queen and her pursuer were coming toward Yar. Logically then, it would intercept them on its own.

... ... ... ... ...

Duile was caught between rage and tears. She was the Queen of Ydron! When this was over, she would repay them all doubly, no, trebly for this indignity. She had never endured such abuse. Was there no end? She clasped her hands over her ears, but it did little to shut out the clamor. As if to add insult, her legs failed and she could go no farther. She needed somewhere to hide.

She peered through a doorway on one side of the corridor. It opened into a large, nearly empty room that housed a pump, buckets and related items. It lacked a door, so she ruled it out. Across from this room were other doors without the characteristic peephole apertures of cells. Perhaps one of these would serve.

Her hands struggled with the first latch, but it was locked. And though she tugged with all her might, the next two also refused to yield. Then, just as she was despairing, the fourth door flew open when she pulled. She peered inside. The air was stale, the room was dark and full of—what?—boxes, perhaps. It would have to do. She closed the door and fumbled in the darkness. She knocked her knees against what felt like a small container, low enough to sit upon. Her hands trembled as she located its edges, then assured herself its top was clear. Taking the smallest of steps, she maneuvered so it was just behind her, then placed her palms upon it and sat, waiting for she-knew-not-what.

*This is all wrong*, she told herself. *This should not be happening*. The

Queen of Ydron was sitting in a closet, in the dark. Alone. Her plan had unraveled and she could not see how to fix it. She would never have admitted to anyone her children were right. It was but a matter of time until it was over. She thought she was going to be ill. She sobbed once, loudly, and then her whole body quaked as sobs poured forth. She was lost and would never escape this hole.

She remained like this for several minutes, listening through the door for the fate that must surely find her, when the door opened and light poured in.

"Majesty," someone said.

The door closed again and the corridor's torchlight was replaced by the soft blue of a light globe. Duile gasped, then let out a rasping sigh when she recognized the voice of her trusted friend.

"Oh, Husted! How did you find me? I have been so afraid."

Husted Yar placed the light globe on one of the crates.

"It is over," it said.

"I am so glad you are here. Have you brought my guard?" she asked, drawing hope from its comment.

The Dalthin did not reply. It came closer, and as she watched, bewildered at first, then horrified, it transformed from courtier into its true form and towered above her, tendrils writhing, belly opening and closing.

"Darmaht protect me!" she gasped. "What are you?"

Yar did not answer. Duile tried to scream but could not. She tried to rise, but her legs buckled and she sat down hard. The Dalthin produced a pseudopod, grasped her arm and Duile screamed. In all the nightmares she had ever dreamt, she had never conjured such a thing. Her strength vanished. She could neither move nor cry out. She felt the power of its grasp and knew, even if she tried to escape, she could not.

"Why?" was all she could say.

Unmoved, it pulled her close, thrust her into its gut, and as the aperture sealed, the Queen of Ydron ceased to be.

The door flew open with a bang.

"Mas'tad!" a new voice shouted.

*Ah. The female.*

The Dalthin turned to face her and Pithien realized she was too late. Her dagger hand dropped to her side.

"You beat me to her," she cried. Looking up at its eyes she said, "I am so tired of your kind. I am so tired of you."

The Dalthin regarded this female briefly, then reached for its second meal.

"Oh, ho!" said Dur. "Is that what you think?"

She was no longer afraid and unsure as she had been in Bad Adur. Buoyed instead by what she had learned in that place, as well as by the infusion of strength from the forming network, she stood her ground.

"I have a present for you," she said, and sheathed her dagger.

Yar's pseudopod encircled her, but she was oblivious to its touch. She gathered her anger, forming it into a mass, ignoring the threat, turning her hatred into something useful. As the Dalthin lifted her from the floor, she concentrated on shaping the energy, filling it with clear, certain intent. Even as the creature's abdomen opened to accept her, she remained focused, unhurried in her task. It was only when Yar had enclosed her in its abdomen and shut the light of the world from her eyes, only when its digestive juices began to burn her skin, was she satisfied she had it right.

She released her creation.

… … … … …

In that instant, Yar realized several terrible truths. When it had elected to eliminate the queen first, instead of finding and destroying this female, it had made a critical mistake. As a result, the network of minds had grown beyond the point where it might be dismantled. More important, it remembered too late Dur could kill with thought, and now, all who were part of the newly formed entity also shared this knowledge. Their number was growing exponentially, so days hence, when the ship finally arrived, its occupants would number too few. For the first time in its race's history, the Dalthin had failed.

… … … … …

Pithien came to her senses the instant the Dalthin began digesting her. Marm had died after only a few moments, so she knew she did not have much time. She fumbled for her knife and nearly dropped it. Her entire body was on fire, but she didn't dare falter. Ignoring the pain, she grasped its hilt and drove the blade into the Dalthin's abdominal wall. Hoping, but not knowing whether it had penetrated far enough, she held tightly with both hands and forced the cutting edge downwards in a sawing motion. She shut her eyes and mouth against the acrid fluids but could not protect her nasal passages. The pain nearly halted her. Throwing her entire weight into the effort, she leaned on her tool, encouraged only by the sensation the blade was moving. She was burning. She screamed, but would not stop.

Just when she thought she could do no more, the resistance against the blade vanished and her body pitched forward. She fell from the belly onto the floor, but her agony continued as the juices digested her.

She picked herself up and ran to the hallway, searching frantically, trying to decide what to do, where to go. Recognition struck. Across the hall was the bath, the glorious bath. She ran to the tub, but it was empty. She spied the pump, and bending low put her shoulder against the basin and pushed, coaxing it until she had positioned its lip beneath the spout. She climbed into the tub and pulled hard on the pump handle. Blessed water spewed forth. She put her head, then each arm under the stream continuing to work it, contorting her body, struggling to put every part under the cold, healing flow. As she pumped, the tub gradually filled. She was mindless now, not stopping to wonder how she found the strength. Perhaps it was merely the will to survive, but she pumped and pumped and pumped until the basin was nearly full. Exhausted and hurt, she collapsed and sank into the cool, blessed liquid. Only then did the balm of unconsciousness envelope her.

# 68

The soft sweet fragrance of morrasa blossoms filled her nose, as well as something herbal, something medicinal. Her entire body stung.

"Ah, at last! She is opening her eyes," someone said. "Good morning, Pithien. How are you?"

Dur struggled to see against the glare of sunlight, tried to focus and the two blurs before her slowly resolved into faces.

"I am alive," she said to Regilius and Lith-An. She tried to sit but sagged against the pillow. "Let's leave it at that. How about you?" she asked Regilius. "I'm surprised to see you up and about."

"I came when I sensed you were waking. I will return to bed soon."

"Borlon's eyes!" Her face darkened. She turned away and covered it with her hands. "I am so ashamed. Forgive me. I tried to murder your mother. What do I say to you? I am so sorry."

Lith-An took Dur's hands into hers.

"But you didn't, Pithien. You didn't kill her."

"I would have if I reached her in time. It is only because the Dalthin found her first… "

Reg interrupted. "Many would have done the same. It is hard for me to say this. Even now I am trying to come to terms with how evil she was. You were not the only one who wished her dead. In fact, I am ashamed to admit even my sister and I had such thoughts."

"But not many would have actually killed her," the outlaw argued.

"Few, if any, could have gotten close enough," said Reg. "Given enough time, Emeil might have done the same.

Pithien shook her head. "No. Emeil would have tried and imprisoned her. He would not have taken her life."

"Still, we hold no animosity," Lith-An insisted.

"We forgive you," said Reg. "Whatever you intended, it was not you who killed her. Intent is not the deed. If it were, we should all be imprisoned for our thoughts. That you did not rush to kill her, that you slowed as you pursued her, demonstrates something inside was holding you back."

"I was adding to her suffering, protracting her fear."

"Perhaps for a part of you, feeling her terror was enough," suggested Reg.

Lith-An added, "So you waited for another possibility. Fortunately, it presented itself. The fact remains it was not you who killed her."

"Even then," said Reg, "I think we would have forgiven you."

"Yes," Lith-An agreed. "Even then."

"Thank you, Your Highnesses." She looked at each, in turn. "Thank you both," she said.

As tears began to form she tried to smile, but her face hurt. Its skin was stiff and she found the act impossible. She touched her face and her fingertips came away covered with goo.

"What is this?"

"It is a salve," Reg explained. "A number of physicians from Rian to Monhedeth collaborated on its composition. Another from the hospital compounded it. In their opinion, you will experience only limited scarring. It was your actions immediately after you climbed from the Dalthin's belly, that saved you. And please, Pithien, we would like to dispense with titles once and for all. I will never again live as a prince, nor Lith-An as a princess. Please call us by our names."

"No? You will not assume the throne?"

She struggled to sit upright and Lith-An hopped onto the bed to adjust the pillows.

"I have renounced all claim to it," Reg replied as his sister hopped down. "Things have changed… are changing even as we speak. It is as unlikely we will return to the palace, as it is that you will continue to live outside the law.

"Reach out with your mind. You will find you can touch others as far away as the outer provinces, though it will be noisy inside your head until you learn to shut them out."

He waited while she followed his suggestion. Her eyes opened in amazement, as she touched and was touched by so many others. Her expression changed to one of discomfort, however, as she struggled to silence them. After a few minutes, she succeeded.

"It gets easier," Lith-An reassured. "Although there are times when the voices still overwhelm me."

"It feels so different," Dur said. "Before, the voices were muddled and indistinct. Now, so many are clear and focused."

"Everything is different," said Lith-An "When the first Change occurred—the one that transformed Reg and I—only we two were noticeably affected. There were many around us who experienced something palpable, such as visions. If they were changed at all, it was only a preparatory alteration. Danth demonstrates that best. Although he never achieved the ability to initiate psychic communication, after the Dalthin had touched him, he grew sensitive to their presence. Those more distant from the original site demonstrated none of this.

"This time, however, the transformation was far more powerful and every mind has awakened. Those who were not immediately affected by the three of us have since been altered by the ever-increasing number of transformed minds around them. By now it has spread throughout the land and I sense it has begun to affect those in more distant places. As the number of transformed minds continues to grow, the change gains impetus. Soon the entire world will awaken. Every mind will come alive. It is very exciting."

"Tell me," said Dur, "if you won't be returning to the palace, who will rule?"

Reg laughed. "I suspect it will be the people themselves. I cannot say what form the new government will take or how it will be implemented, but with each mind touching every other, it will be impossible for any one individual to seize power the way Mother did, or abuse it like Father. Perhaps some sort of central body will form. Something of the sort will be necessary."

"Until that happens," Lith-An observed, "we are fortunate anarchy has not set in. There is still order, although many governmental functions have been suspended."

"Like the gathering of slaves," Reg sneered. "Further, the war seems to be coming to an end. The armies at menRathan have laid down their arms. It is pointless to fight another when your opponent can anticipate your every move, and you his. We will have to find other ways to resolve conflicts."

"With the increasing levels of empathy," said Lith-An, "I am certain we will."

Dur was losing strength. Her body began to sag and her eyes grew heavy.

"There will be time enough to discuss this in the coming days," said Lith-An. "Why don't you rest?"

"Yes," Reg agreed. "Lie back down. You are going to need plenty of sleep if you are to heal."

"I suspect you are right," Pithien replied, her voice reflecting the effort she had made.

They helped her settle onto the mattress, adjusted her bedding and drew the window's curtains shut. When Regilius and Lith-An had finished, they departed hand in hand. Peace was returning to Ydron. As the people awakened and the land began to heal, it was time for this brother and sister to heal their own wounds and become reacquainted.

# About the Author

Raymond Bolton divides his time between Santa Fe, New Mexico and Portland, Oregon. Prior to being published, he won several awards for his work. Most recently, under its working title, Renunciation, *Awakening* was a finalist in the Pacific Northwest Writers Association's 2013 literary competition from among hundreds of entries from the US, the UK, Canada, Europe and Australia. It also won writerstype.com's June 2013 First Chapter competition. From April 2011, until it was disbanded in December 2012, Raymond was an invited, featured contributor for the writers' blog, Black Ink, White Paper.

# DEAR READER

I hope you've enjoyed reading *Awakening*. If you're hoping for more stories to follow this one, I won't disappoint you. As I write this page, I am working hard to finish *Thought Gazer*, the first volume of a prequel trilogy, due out between Summer and Autumn 2014, and I've already begun *Foreteller*, the second volume of the set.

If you'd like to be among the first to learn when they're about to be published, as well as how they're coming along, please visit my website, **http://www.raymondbolton.com** and sign up for my newsletter. I also hope you will like my Facebook author page **https://www.facebook.com/RaymondBoltonAuthor**, and follow me on Twitter, @RaymondBolton.

Oh, yes. If you would be so kind, please return to Amazon, **http://amzn.to/1eu75Rj,** or Goodreads, **http://bit.ly/1kxMRJs**, to let others know what you thought about your experience by supplying a review.

Thanks for purchasing *Awakening*. I look forward to joining you as we delve into the Ydron Saga together.

20845544R00210

Made in the USA
San Bernardino, CA
26 April 2015